There were at least a h___ ___ ___ ___ reasons she shouldn't be in a cemetery in the dead of night. And the longer Spencer stood in the darkness, the longer the list became and the more foolish her vigil seemed to be.

It was just that…she had to do something.

Someone had to do something. She'd tried very hard to let the police do their work. She'd even understood when they'd grilled her, relentlessly, apologetically, relentlessly again, about her husband's murder. She applauded their efforts— at least *then* it had seemed as if they were investigating every possible avenue.

And she even believed—no, she *knew*—that David Delgado would have stopped at nothing to catch Danny's killer. After all, they'd been best friends.

It was just that they weren't doing enough.

A cloud rolled over the moon. It was very dark. A breeze suddenly stirred the humidity and heat of the night, and Spencer was startled to feel a creeping sensation of cold sweep over her.

HEATHER GRAHAM POZZESSERE

SLOW BURN

MIRA BOOKS

ISBN 1-55166-000-8

SLOW BURN

Copyright © 1994 by Heather Graham Pozzessere.

All rights reserved. Except for use in any review, the reproduction or
utilization of this work in whole or in part in any form by any electronic,
mechanical or other means, now known or hereafter invented, including
xerography, photocopying and recording, or in any information storage or
retrieval system, is forbidden without the written permission of the publisher,
Mira Books, 225 Duncan Mill Road, Don Mills, Ontario, Canada M3B 3K9.

All characters in this book have no existence outside the imagination of the
author and have no relation whatsoever to anyone bearing the same name
or names. They are not even distantly inspired by any individual known or
unknown to the author, and all incidents are pure invention.

MIRA and the star colophon are trademarks of Mira Books.

Printed in U.S.A.

This book is dedicated to the memory of
Officer William Craig,
City of Miami.
Truly one of the finest.

And with love to his children, Sandy and David,
and to Debbie, the best of friends no matter
where we are in time or place.

1

"**W**ait!"

Danny Huntington paused at the foot of the stairway, looking back.

Spencer was standing on the marble landing, both hands gripping the mahogany banister. She was wearing a cobalt silk nightshirt, and her hair was sleep tousled and wild and spilling all around her face. She had an exotic look about her, as if she belonged in one of her own promo pieces, beauty against a backdrop of elegance. Behind her in the hallway was the Victorian love seat, above it the handsomely carved mirror. A maroon runner, picking up the shades in the brocade tapestry on the love seat, ran beneath Spencer's bare feet and manicured toenails. It drew attention to the length of her legs. In the old Mediterranean house Spencer had salvaged and brought back to glory, Spencer herself looked like a million bucks. Sometimes Danny thought that she'd been born perfect. She had crystal blue eyes, corn blond hair and classical, delicate, stunning features. He'd known her most of his life and been in love with her for half of it. It probably hadn't been much of a surprise to others when she married him, but it had been a shock to Danny. And not only had she married him, but she'd understood him, his need to be something other than what was expected of him, to join the police force instead of the family business. And when the chips were down—or at least scattered all over—she had come to the fore with a smile and a laugh, and done everything in the world to make sure that he didn't feel the least bit badly about anything. Sometimes, when he thought of all Spencer had been willing to go through for him, he felt a sweat break out on his palms and he shook a little bit inside just to think about how much he loved her, and how good she had made his life.

"Danny, I'm blue!" she said the words with tremendous excitement.

"What?" He arched a brow, looking at her with confusion.

"The test, Danny, the little line on the ovulation predictor test turned blue!" she said, smiling at his confusion.

"Oh. *Blue!*" he repeated.

Then he stared at her blankly for a moment. He was due at David Delgado's house. They were going to jog together before combining their information on the Vichy case. But if Spencer was *blue*...

He was the one who wanted children so badly. He and Spencer had been only children themselves, both born to wealthy parents, what they called old money families, though, frankly, some of the money on his side wasn't all that old. But enough years had passed for the world to forget that it had originally been made in heavy-duty bootlegging. They'd both grown up in Miami, as well, down in Coconut Grove, where what there was of old-time Southern gentility and Northern snowbird affluence sat side by side with poverty and the ghetto. He'd always had the best of everything, and gone to the best schools. What he'd lacked was people to love, and as he'd watched friends with their sisters and brothers, he'd realized from a very early age that happiness wasn't something that could be purchased from a store. He'd promised himself then that his own children would never be lonely—he would have a dozen if he could. He'd gotten over the concept of having a dozen, but he still wanted a family, two to four children, whatever Spencer thought best.

They'd started out the marriage trying, but after two years, when they still hadn't become parents, Spencer had suggested they start testing. She had quietly gone about getting every test possible, and she hadn't cared that a few were painful and humiliating. He'd sat in a little cubicle himself, chagrined to discover that the setting made his penis as limp as overcooked fettucini, but he'd needed to be tested, so he'd endured whatever procedures the doctor ordered. The only good thing about it all was that, in the end, he had been told they were both normal—the doctor's suggestion had been that they were just too busy, too tense. Since her grandfather, Sly had semiretired, Spencer was all but running Montgomery Enterprises herself; and *his* schedule was worse than *hers*. They just might be missing the right time to try for children, and that could well be all there was to it.

"Can you take the day off?" he asked her.

"You bet," she told him. "What about you?" She hesitated just a moment. "I thought you had set up a meeting with David Delgado?"

"I had," Danny told her. "I'll get out of it."

"Can you?"

Danny grinned at her good-naturedly. "I'll just tell him the truth. That you and I are trying to be fruitful and multiply."

"Danny—"

"Spencer, I'm kidding. I'll find a way to reschedule. Don't worry about it." He wished she hadn't turned quite so dark a shade of crimson, but, in truth, he was more amused than anything else. Once upon a time his wife and his best friend had been one of the hottest things going—but hell, that had been all the way back in high school, for Christ's sake! Spencer wouldn't talk about it on pain of death, and David Delgado was just as much of a clam about the whole thing. Until recently, David and Danny had been partners on the force as well as longtime best friends. But then David had quit being a cop because he had saved up enough money to open his own security business, and so far, with his experience, he had done very well. They still saw each other frequently on a professional basis, though, because David sometimes did work for the city, and then they needed each other's files—and opinions.

Spencer and David were always polite when they met. He knew they both worried about his feelings regarding the past, so they avoided each other as much as they could. And when they did meet, they were civil and cool, and managed to make him feel like hell over their damned determination to be honorable.

They *were* honorable; he knew that. And he loved them both all the more for it. But every once in a while, when they had no choice but to meet, the tension in the air was as hot and heavy as the August humidity in this searing place they all called home, and he had to admit that he was afraid—just in a little tiny corner of his heart—that if the two of them weren't so damned moral, they would be naked, in the heat and crawling all over one another, and it wouldn't matter one bit that they didn't have a thing to say to each other anymore, that they'd broken up explosively all those years ago, and that even back then they'd been as different as night and day, Spencer so fair, David so dark, Spencer the height of society, with ancestors who had all but stepped off the Mayflower, and David the child of an immigrant and a refugee. But if twelfth-grade rumor had been true...

He'd been in twelfth grade with them, known them both all his life. And now Spencer was his wife, David was still his best friend, and one day he would manage to turn the two of them back into good friends, too. Maybe if he and Spencer could actually get this parenthood thing going...

He was already in his jogging shorts, T-shirt and sneakers. He'd been eager to get all the help he could from David on the Vichy case, but nothing in the world was more important that sharing this morning with Spencer. "I'm supposed to meet David right out on Main Street. We were going to jog over to his place and then go through the files over breakfast. I'll meet him on the street like we planned and give him some excuse. It won't matter what—he won't press me. I'll be gone about twenty-five minutes, then I'll be home. How about it?"

"I'll be waiting," Spencer promised solemnly.

He grinned, gave her a thumbs-up sign, then started walking to the door. He was jogging before he reached it.

Twenty-five minutes! Spencer pushed herself away from the staircase and tore into their bedroom. In seconds flat she arranged the covers and pillows invitingly on the bed. Then she spun around and headed into the shower. This was going to be Danny's day, and she was going to make it the best one he had ever lived.

Work! She raced for the phone.

She told her secretary she had a touch of flu, but would be in the next morning. She felt a blush touch her cheeks as her secretary sympathized and told her that she hoped Spencer would feel better. How strange! She was married—not to mention the president of Montgomery Enterprises—and Audrey was a good friend, but she still couldn't quite manage the truth. *You see, we're trying to procreate here, but our schedules are so screwed up that Danny's at work on the nights that count, and I'm usually in another city when it matters most. I'm staying home just to spend the entire day screwing around.*

"Do you need anything, Spencer? Can I bring you something?" Audrey asked with concern.

"No, no, Danny will be back after he's done jogging. I'll be fine, thanks," she said firmly, a touch of guilt stirring within her again. She was the boss! she reminded herself. She worked long, hard hours, and she deserved a day off with her husband.

"Stay in bed now," Audrey warned her.

"I, ah—yes, I will," Spencer said, stared at the receiver, then set it down.

So what *was* Danny telling David?

A hot flush crept over her body; she didn't want to think about it. She didn't want to think about *David*. She tried so damned hard not to think about David most of the time.

She turned on the water full blast.

"I love Danny Huntington!" she said fiercely out loud. And it was true. She did. Very much. There just seemed to be so many levels of love. Sly had told her that once. And it was true.

"I love Danny!"

She loved him; their life was good. They laughed together; they talked together. Danny was kind, concerned, wonderful, gentle. She was lucky, so lucky. She stepped into the shower. Danny wanted a baby. This time they were going to do it the right way—and at the right time!—to have one.

The water rushed down on her.

Danny left his house behind and inhaled the clear morning air. The day was going to be a scorcher, but it wasn't dead hot yet. He loved the early morning and the late night, when the sun hadn't gotten its grip on the city yet. He loved to run when even the early birds weren't out, when dew still touched the grass and the leaves of the gnarled trees that lined the road.

He smiled. Just what the hell was he going to tell David? The truth would be best, but he had told Spencer he would think of something else. How the hell was he going to manage when he was grinning from ear to ear, anticipating the day? They hadn't had a chance to do anything like this since their honeymoon. Since that day in Paris when they had watched the sun rise over the gargoyles, gilding the City of Lights. He quickened his pace, anxious to get back home.

He came out of his private road and rounded the corner. To his amazement, he saw a familiar figure jogging toward him. Curious. Talk about someone he'd never expected to see here . . .

David Delgado ran in place by the street sign, then looped around a few times on the jogging trail that ran alongside the road. Six foot two, black-haired, and with eyes so dark a blue that they appeared black at times, he was an arresting figure. But then, in Coconut Grove runners came in all kinds, the squat and the lean, the muscled and the nearly anorectic. But even amidst the healthy, muscled, tanned and sometimes very young and almost bare bodies that jogged through this old but still-trendy section of Miami, David was a striking man. The best of a strange mixture of genes had combined to make him as tall and broad shouldered as the Highlanders of his mother's Scottish kin, while his raven dark hair and clean-lined, classical features had come from his father's side, Spain by way of Cuba. Thanks to his Hispanic heritage, he was a natural in the sun, bronzing quickly, and since he had spent most of his life in that sun, he didn't notice the heat too badly while he jogged around in another circle, glanced at his watch and considered heading to the house and giving Danny a call. It wasn't like him to be late. Especially when he didn't have far to come to meet David. David's house didn't compare to the old Twenties manor Spencer and Danny had bought and fixed up. Though he was doing well at his new business—so well, in fact, that it almost scared him at times—he didn't have the kind of income to purchase such a place, not to mention keeping it up. He had to hand it to the pair of them, though. There was nothing ostentatious about their home. It was in a quietly affluent neighborhood, and it had lots more character than it did dazzle. It was a warm house to walk into, with a good feeling about it, it just felt a little bit too much like Spencer Anne Montgomery—Spencer Anne Huntington, he reminded himself. But there hadn't been anything between him and Spencer in well over a decade, and Danny was one of his best friends. It was still amazing to him that someone who had been born with a silver spoon—hell, a silver knife and fork, as well—in his mouth could have grown up to become such a decent human being. But Danny had always been good, ever since they had first met, and Spencer was as cold as ice to him now. Hell, it was ancient history. They were long past whatever feelings they'd shared, and they'd both built their own lives. It was something they could all laugh about. Except that they never did. Maybe, David thought, it was because there had been something vulnerable about all of them way back then. As kids, they had all learned each other's weaknesses, and maybe some of those weaknesses hadn't gone away. He and Spencer were still, after all these years, wary of one another, though they both tried, for Danny's sake, to be civil.

Just as he tried like hell not to let his best friend know how much he remembered about Spencer Anne Montgomery.

Spencer Anne *Huntington*.

He jogged around the loop again, looking down the street. Things hadn't changed much here since he'd been a kid. The foliage still grew right up to the edge of the winding road, and the old houses still stood almost on top of it, except where long drives led to mansions unseen by the general public. From the time he'd come here as a kid not quite four years old, he'd loved the Grove, even if life there hadn't always been easy. Back then, in the early sixties, it had been a laid-back place, not at all ready for the boom that was about to seize Miami and erase its small-southern-town status forever, turning it into a huge metropolis with an international flavor. Back then, they'd had lots of snowbirds, Northerners down just for the winter. They still came, but now they mostly went over to Naples, up to Palm Beach, down to the Keys, or to the dead center of the state, to Disney. But Miami still thrived, and the Grove had grown right along with it. In the late sixties and early seventies, the Grove had gone right along with the hippie movement. The shops had sold Nehru jackets and incense and black lights. Artists had thrived, smoking pot in back rooms, and psychedelic music had filled the air. But then things had moved upscale; the yuppies had moved in, and now the trendy shops sold high-priced jewelry and expensive collectibles, while the restaurants offered the height of nouvelle cuisine. He thought rather affectionately of his home as a very bright whore—Coconut Grove twisted whichever way the money came and the wind blew, doing whatever it needed to do to survive. It was one of the oldest sections of Miami, right on the bay, and there were still a few old-timers around to tell him what it had been like in the early days. Spencer's grandfather, Sly, could talk about the old days with the ability of a born storyteller, and there were still times when David missed the hours he had spent with the old man almost as much as he missed Spencer.

He swore at himself. He didn't miss Spencer. How could you miss someone who had been out of your life for most of it? He just missed the feelings he remembered. She was part of all the other nostalgia about growing up, certain music, the sight of bougainvillea, the salt scent of the sea on a balmy day. It was just his bad luck that they'd all been friends forever.

David jogged farther and found himself looking down the street where he'd first lived when he'd come here. God, what an awful year that had been. Spanish had been his first language, and the only thing he could remember being called for years had been "refugee." Not boy, just refugee. He'd had it better than most, though. His father had been in the Cuban prison where he was destined to die, his mother had passed away soon after Reva's birth, but his mother's father, old Michael MacCloud, had managed to swoop down right in the middle of the crisis days to help them. He had taught David and his sister, Reva, English. At least then David had been able to understand the Americanos who looked

down their noses at him, though what English he did
speak he spoke with the old Scotsman's accent. His folks
gone, thrown into a world that didn't want the upheaval
coming its way, he'd started off fighting. That was when
he'd met Danny Huntington. Danny had left his pristine
public school to walk over to the yacht club to meet his
folks, but he'd been stopped by a group of toughs. David had seen it from the small park where he'd been
playing, and there had just been something about Danny
that had gotten to him. He'd been a skinny kid, and he'd
obviously known he was about to take a beating, but he'd
stood his ground. Then David had moved in. He'd taken
a black eye himself, but he'd still managed to come out
on top. The fight had been one of those "you should see
the other fellow" occasions, and when it was over, Danny
had just stared at him as if he was some kind of hero.

"Hey, thanks, man!"

David had shrugged, determined that no one was going to see that he was hurting like hell himself. "You're
just a skinny little rich kid. I could see you needed help."

"Jeez, that's some shiner!" Danny had told him, taking no offense at his comments. "You'd better come with
me and get it taken care of."

That had been the first time David had entered Danny's world, and it had been a strange time for him.
Bloodied, ragged, he had been drawn into the club with
its spotless windows looking out on the bay, its rows and
rows of sleek, beautiful boats. Everyone had stared at
him. The ladies in their pristine white, the gentlemen in
their leisure suits. He hadn't been able to look at the
people, the men and the women talking about how the
riffraff and the refugees were bringing down the neighborhood. He'd looked out at the boats, instead, and decided he wanted a boat right then and there—more, even,

than he wanted a life where he could eat all the mouth-watering food being served around him, play tennis on the perfect courts or dive into the pool. Just a boat, that would have made him happy.

He hadn't been too fond of Danny's parents, but he'd met Sly that day, and though he'd had a few opinions about the rest of the lot at the club, he'd known right off that he liked Sly, just as he'd known that one day he would buy a boat.

Sly knew something about politics. He'd heard of David's father and even knew his grandfather. He'd bought David a meal, and when he'd seen the boy's eyes, huge and a little overawed, he'd told him, "America, boy. This is America. Trust me. You reach out and get what you want here. The only difference between you and these folks is that their folks got here and did it for them!" And then he'd winked.

When David left that day, he'd thought he would never see Danny or Sly again. But two weeks later out of the blue, he'd gotten a scholarship to Danny's prestigious grade school, and Michael MacCloud had insisted he take it. When he'd been on the outs, an object of fun for some of the rich kids, Danny had been there, stuck to him like glue, his best friend. Luckily he'd been a damned good athlete, and it was amazing what that could do for a poor boy. A refugee. Soon after David's strange scholarship had come through, David's younger sister, Reva, had received one, as well. And Danny had been just as great to Reva.

Spencer had come . . . later.

He glanced at his watch again and thought about jogging to Danny's, then decided to jog home, instead. He would call Danny rather than appear. It would be easier to talk to Spencer on the phone. But maybe Danny would answer himself—still there for some reason—or the housekeeper would be in.

It was a strange situation. Danny, the kid born into a world of wealth, was a cop. A homicide detective. That was where they had met up again, after years of going their separate ways after high school. Danny wanted to be D.A. someday. Actually, he wanted to go much higher, but he wanted to take the long route into politics. He wanted to know how the working stiff on the street managed; then he wanted to buck the system all the way, not just catching the criminals, but managing to put them away. Spencer had been upset at first about Danny going into homicide, but Danny had been quick to tell her that it was all right. "The cases I'm called to are really safe. Spence. What are the victims going to do to me? They're already dead!"

Spencer had reminded him that they had gotten that way through the ill will of others, but it seemed that Spencer really did love and support her man, because Danny was still working homicide. And sometimes the thought that she was there for someone else, not for him, brought a little twist of bitterness to David's heart. Maybe he hadn't been quite fair to Spencer Anne Montgomery all those years ago. Or maybe Spencer had changed; he didn't know. Anyway, it didn't matter anymore. She was Danny's wife, and theirs was a good marriage. She and Danny had come from the same world. They knew how to live in it, and also how to fight it. Everyone had probably expected the two of them to wind up together, just as they had shaken their heads at the thought of Spencer Anne Montgomery winding up with David Delgado.

It was the past. Ancient history. David had his own life. He lived it. But sometimes it seemed that no matter how fast he ran from times gone by, they still caught up with him in the end.

Hell, where was Danny? The sun was beating down mercilessly on his head. He gave a final look around and started jogging to his own house.

A good house. Modern, three bedrooms, on the water, his boat docked in the back. He pushed open the front door and strode to the phone.

"What's going on? What the hell are you doing here?" Danny demanded.

The answer came quickly in the form of three hastily fired bullets. One burned by his ear. The other two sank into his middle.

The figure raced on as Danny Huntington opened his mouth to protest. No sound came. He fell to the ground.

He didn't lose consciousness. Not then. He started to crawl. Blood trailed from his wounds, over the dark earth, over tree roots, fallen leaves. Over dirt and pavement.

He kept crawling. David's house was straight ahead. The door was open. Sweet Jesus, but he was in pain. Oh, God, oh, God, oh, God, how could one person lose so much blood? His life, oh, no, not yet, he couldn't die yet....

Spencer...

"Danny!"

David dropped the receiver he'd just lifted and raced to the doorway. Danny was there, crawling toward him, covered in blood. David started to pick up his best friend, registering almost blankly that Danny had been shot. Years of training sprang into his mind, and he ran for his phone again, dialing the police dispatcher.

"Three-fifteen!" It was the code for *Emergency! Officer needs assistance.* "It's Danny Huntington, and he's been shot." He gave his address, then added, "Hurry, damn it!" He'd already said enough, he knew they would hurry for any officer, but this was Danny. In his heart he kept pleading. Christ-oh-God-please-get-here-it's-really-bad.

He raced to Danny and cradled his friend in his arms, trying to discern just where the injuries were. Shot, oh, hell, Danny had been shot twice, and he'd lost a lot of blood, but he still had a pulse, his heart was beating, and his lungs were still laboring. If the trauma unit could just get here and get him over to Jackson, they worked miracles there.

Staunch the blood, you asshole, staunch the blood. You've got to keep him alive, David told himself.

But the bleeding wouldn't stop, no matter what he did.

Suddenly Danny's eyes opened. He reached out a bloody hand, circling it around David's neck. He tried to form words.

"Easy, Danny, easy. Help is almost here. You know the cops, you know how fast they come for one of their own."

"Spen ... cer," Danny croaked.

"Yes, yes, I'll get Spencer. Danny, listen to me, you've got to help us. Come on, buddy! Danny, who did this? Who—"

"Spencer!" Danny managed again. Blood oozed past his lips. He tried to form words again. "Spencer!" Danny mouthed. His eyes were glazing.

"Hold on, Danny, hold on. Don't you die on me. I love you, you skinny little rich kid! Danny!"

He could hear the sirens. He could even hear the chopper blades. He'd said he needed the trauma unit, and they'd believed him. Help would be there in a matter of seconds.

The med techs arrived, already ripping open packages of bandages, starting an IV. There were hands on David's shoulders.

"David!"

He turned.

Lieutenant Oppenheim, Danny's superior, once his own, stood behind him. "David, let them do their work. If anyone can save Danny, it's these guys. What happened? Who did this?"

Oppenheim was an old-timer on the force, white-haired, tall, solid as a barrel.

"I don't know—he was supposed to meet me on the street. He was late. I came back to call and turned around—"

He looked at Danny. His friend was on a stretcher. Someone was radioing to the helicopter, and they were choosing a place for it to land.

"David, what the hell happened. Do you know? Did Danny say?"

David shook his head, staring at Danny as if he could keep him alive by watching him. "He was supposed to meet me. He was late. I came in to call his house and he was at my door. Just like that."

"Did he say anything?"

David shook his head. "Just Spencer. His wife's name."

Ten minutes to go! Spencer switched off the water and stepped from the shower, toweling herself strenuously, a slight smile curving her lips. She dropped the towel and picked up her brush and hair dryer, fluffing up the heavy blond mass on her head as best she could in the time she had left. It was going to be perfect, she determined. Just perfect. And she knew just what she was going to do.

Seconds later she was slipping into a black garter belt with sheer black stockings and a pair of black heels. She found Danny's black silk tie in the closet and tied in loosely around her neck. She stared at her reflection in the mirror. Basic black. Danny had told her once that he liked her in black, and that he would like her best in a black tie and nothing more. Well, that was what he was getting today, because this was going to be special.

She turned quickly from the mirror and hurried down the stairs, pausing only to make certain that the drapes were drawn.

They were.

She rushed into the kitchen, dragged out and filled the ice bucket and grabbed a special bottle of Dom Perignon, then ran to the living room. She threw a lace cover over the Victorian coffee table, plopped the ice bucket on it with the champagne, and raced to the kitchen to fix two crystal bowls of grapes, one bunch green, the other purple. She glanced at her watch. Five minutes. He should be back within five minutes.

She arranged herself on the coffee table, sitting between the two bowls of grapes, the champagne behind her and just to the left. She jumped up, glanced at her watch again and hurried to the front door. It had to be open. She would ruin the whole effect if she had to open the door for Danny, which she would, since he didn't carry a key in his jogging shorts.

She raced to the coffee table and sat down again, legs crossed Indian fashion. She waited, her heart ticking furiously. Did she look sexy? Or foolish? She smiled and decided that it didn't matter; they would laugh one way or the other. And if they managed the desired result, then anything was worth it! Danny wanted kids so damned badly. He'd been a lonely little boy, which so few people understood. And she felt uncomfortably as if she had failed him in so many ways, and yet she wanted what he wanted more than anything in the world.

She stared at the door a bit uneasily. What if the mailman opened the door? No, the mailman never came until past noon. Never. UPS? No, they rang the doorbell, they didn't just walk in.

A bum? A psychopathic murderer?

Spencer! she chastised herself. It would be just minutes until Danny came back. Maybe he was having coffee with David. Maybe, being Danny, he'd felt guilty about canceling an appointment. Maybe—despite what he'd said to her—he was even telling David the truth. They were best friends. Always best friends. Nothing had come between them. Not even her.

She'd never wanted to ruin anyone's friendship; it was just that she had been so certain that David Delgado was out of her life. That the hurt was gone, that the tempest was over. She'd been so young when she'd fallen for David. She'd never imagined that anything could be as wild as it had been with David, as passionate, as hateful, as...

"Stop!" she charged herself out loud, closing her eyes tightly. She was sitting all but stark naked on a coffee table waiting for her husband to come home so that they could make a baby together. A baby they both wanted. A husband who was one of the best men in the entire world.

She was waiting for Danny, but if she didn't get a grip on herself, she would be remembering the first time she'd ever made love. With his best friend.

David Delgado.

"If it's a girl, I think I like the name Kyra," she said out loud. "I wonder what Danny thinks of it? He'll never tell me, I know. He'll be so happy we're going to have a baby that he won't give a damn about a name at all."

It had been at Sly's house. She'd been sixteen years old at the time, and he hadn't been much older. And, like everything that had happened between them, she'd forced the issue. He never wanted to touch her; she was Sly's granddaughter, and he'd loved Sly ever since he'd met him. But Terry-Sue was after him big time, and Spencer just hadn't been able to bear it. She had known what she wanted all the time she was forcing the fight and pushing him into a corner. She had known what she wanted....

She just hadn't been prepared for what she had gotten. Or what would follow...

"If it's a boy, it will be Daniel, of course," she said loudly.

Then she heard the tapping at the door. She smiled. Danny was home, and she really did love him. Together they always dispelled all the demons of the past. Almost made them go away for good.

"It's open, come right in!" she called.

The door swung inward, and she saw a tall silhouette framed there against the rising sun. He took a step into the house, and even before she saw his features, she knew he was all wrong, too tall, too broad shouldered to be Danny, wire muscled, tense—and dark where Danny was blond. This man had ebony dark hair and bronzed, taut features.

"David!" she gasped. Her breathing seemed to cease, her heart to stop beating. She felt like an idiot, cross-legged, naked on the table—her black tie perfectly in place.

She leaped up and all but hurled herself across the room, tearing an afghan from the back of a sofa and wrapping herself in it, then staring at the man who was staring at her in return. She wished that she could crawl *beneath* the coffee table.

Then she started babbling. "I'm—ah, I was just waiting for Danny to get back. He was going to talk to you. Did you miss him? There's coffee in the kitchen. If you'll excuse me, I'll just go get dressed—"

"Spencer," he said. Just that, and nothing more. His tone was level, but it held a wealth of agony. He didn't tease her, didn't even make an offhand comment. He just stared at her, and suddenly she felt a gripping chill. And she knew. She knew from the raspy sound of his voice, from the look in his eyes.

"Danny?" she whispered. And then it all fell into place. There were red splashes on the Marlins tank top he wore, on the white trim of his black jogging shorts. And there were tears in David's eyes. Tears. The only time she'd ever seen David Delgado with tears in his eyes was the day they'd buried Michael MacCloud....

"Danny. Oh, my God. Danny!" she breathed. She'd never been so afraid in her whole life. She was going to be sick; the world was starting to spin; it was going black.

"Spencer, you've got to come with me. Quickly."

She heard the words, but just barely. She wanted to fight the encroaching darkness, to go with him. No good. Consciousness was slipping away from her. Black heels, stockings, tie and afghan, she sank to the floor, and everything went black, just as if someone had turned out a light....

She made it to the hospital in time. David had brought her to with a cool cloth and a few shakes, and she had immediately wished that she could plummet back into the darkness. Danny hadn't even been at work! He hadn't been in uniform, or even on plainsclothes duty.

"Spencer, he's alive. Come on, hurry."

That had brought her up short. She'd found some strength and some dignity and taken only minutes to dress. A police escort had brought them to Jackson Memorial in less than ten minutes.

Danny had already been taken into surgery. For hours she and David paced the hospital corridors, drinking bad coffee out of paper cups from a machine, waiting.

Danny lived. Amazingly, he survived the surgery. The list of things the bullets had done to his body was endless, ripped and torn pancreas, liver. Damaged lungs and intestines.

But he held on. For days he held on. Day by day, she held his hand as he lay in the trauma unit.

Then, three weeks to the day after the shooting, the doctors told her that he had gone into a coma. David was there with her, standing behind her along with Sly as they explained what had happened, what she hadn't wanted to understand. None of the injuries to his body had really mattered. Somehow an infection had gotten started and spread to his brain. And the brain was the one thing they absolutely couldn't bring back. So Danny was alive. But he was dead. They wanted her permission to take him off the machines.

She signed the papers. And she sat by him again in the hospital. She held his hand. His hand looked so good! So strong, so normal! Long, still bronzed fingers. Clipped nails. Those hands had touched her, loved her. She could still draw them to her face, feel his knuckles against her cheeks. It wasn't fair that he should still be the same....

Four weeks after the shooting, he drew his last breath. David was with her again, not speaking, just watching, waiting. He'd been there all along. There were always cops around, too—waiting, praying, guarding. David wasn't a cop anymore, but it didn't seem to matter. He'd let his business go straight to hell to sit with Danny. With her. He was silent most of the time. But he was there. And the past remained buried. A silent truce held between them. They both loved Danny, and for his sake, everything else was set aside. Her family came; her friends came. They offered words of comfort, words that, despite the very best of intentions, could do little. David's silent presence was the only thing that mattered. She heard him talking sometimes to the cops who came. They were completely baffled as to who had done this to Danny. It hadn't even really hit her yet that he was going to die, was already dead in the only way that mattered. She still thought that he would twist, turn, move, listen to her, awaken. They had said that he was brain-dead, but his heart was so strong. It kept beating. And David kept his quiet vigil behind her.

And after it was over, he was there to hold her when they came for the body, when she shrieked out, unable, after everything, to believe that Danny was really gone.

David was the one to give the eulogy when hundreds of people appeared at Danny's funeral. He talked about Danny the boy, and Danny the man, and what Danny had meant to those who loved him. He talked about how he'd been a good cop, too, always there, the most moral man David had ever met, the finest.

When he was done, he stepped away from the microphone while the dispatcher stepped up to it.

"Detective Daniel Huntington is now oh-six," she said softly.

Officer off duty, out of service. A twenty-one-gun salute exploded in the air.

And then it was over. Danny was, at last, at rest.

2

He'd been reading the file on his desk when she suddenly swept in, just like a relentless breeze. No, just like a damned hurricane, was more like it. She threw the morning paper down on his desk, and those beautiful, crystal blue and accusatory eyes stabbed into him like twin knives.

David looked up, arching a brow. "Spencer. How nice to see you," he said dryly. It *was* nice to see her. No matter that she looked like a lioness on the hunt—ready to go right for the jugular. No matter what, Spencer looked good. The last year had take its toll on her, her face was leaner, her cheeks a shade more hollow, but even tragedy looked good on Spencer Anne Montgomery. *Huntington,* he reminded himself, as he so often seemed forced to do.

He'd been avoiding her, and he knew it. She'd made it easy for him at first. Right after the funeral, she'd gone to one of her mother's family's estates in Newport; then she'd come back and worked in her own West Palm offices for a few months. But she'd been in Miami for nearly two months, and now she was standing in his office, staring at him with barely suppressed fury.

"I take the *Miami Herald,*" he told her.

"Taking it doesn't mean you read it," she said. She inched the paper closer to him with a long, slim, beautifully manicured finger, and he was convinced that if he didn't pick it up soon, she would press his nose right into it. He knew the article; he'd already read it—and ached over it.

All this time, in the year since Danny's murder, there hadn't been an arrest. There still wasn't even a solid suspect. The police had worked on the case continuously, and David had put all his energies into it, called in favors, prowled the streets. They still didn't even have a firm motive, though a number of them had been conceived and then dismissed. Hell, *he'd* even been questioned. So had Spencer. Wives were automatically number-one suspects, just as best friends were often number two—unless, of course, there were a number of ex-wives or mistresses running around in the background.

"Want to sit, Spencer?" he asked her, indicating the leather-upholstered chair in front of his desk. "Or do you want to keep standing there, glaring at me."

"I want you to do something!"

By that time Reva had come to the doorway. "Spencer's here, David," she informed him cheerfully. No one else could have gotten past his kid sister. Reva knew how to stop anyone in his or her tracks—except Spencer. He almost smiled. It had been like that even when they'd all been kids.

"Thanks, Reva. Why don't you suggest to Mrs. Huntington that she sit down?" David said.

"Spencer—"

"Reva, have you read this article?" Spencer demanded, swinging around. She and Reva were both of an age, and both striking women, David thought, watching the two of them, a bit distracted for the moment. He'd been feeling that way lately. Frustration did it, he thought. They looked a little like a pair of modern-day fairy-tale princesses, Rose White and Rose Red, Spencer with her sweeping golden hair and sky-colored eyes, Reva with a curling mass of nearly black hair, tanned to the hilt, and though her eyes were really a very deep blue, just like David's, they often looked as if they were black. They had always liked one another, but their relationships with him, he knew, had kept them from ever becoming close friends.

"I've read it, Spencer," Reva said. "But you've got to know that David has done everything in his power—"

"It's not enough!"

"But, Spencer—"

Spencer turned to face David again. "He was your best friend. How can you just forget him? Read the article! The reporter is claiming police incompetence, that no one seems to care anymore."

David stood. "Spencer, I did read the damned article. And in case you didn't notice, that reporter is also suggesting that you should have been more thoroughly investigated."

"And all the while the real murderer is walking around at large, laughing at everyone."

"Spencer," Reva said, beginning to grow protective, "David almost allowed his entire business to fall apart, he was so desperate to find Danny's killer. You've got—"

"Then I'll hire David and the entire damned agency, and that way no one will be worrying about anything falling apart."

David stood. He'd had it with Spencer carrying on, and he would be damned if he'd have his little sister fighting his battles for him, even against Spencer.

"I won't work for you, Spencer," he said flatly. "And for the moment, you can either sit down, in which case I'll go over everything I know, or you can get out."

"Damn you, David, I will *not* leave."

"You *will* leave, because I'll set you out bodily, then call the cops and tell them you're harrassing me and affecting my business," he told her, then sighed with exasperation as she continued to stare at him as if she were about to explode any second. "Spencer, please, sit!"

She sat. Reva caught his eye. "I'll get some coffee," she said.

"If it's for Spencer, make it decaf. She certainly doesn't need the caffeine!" David said.

Spencer let that pass. When David sat down behind his desk again, he felt a wave of guilt and sorrow sweep over him. She was so pale, and so damned thin. All her life, she had dressed beautifully but simply, and that hadn't changed. She was wearing a sleeveless dress that stopped just above the knee. But the cut was perfect, and David assumed it was some kind of designer original, although Spencer also made a point of buying things just because she liked them, not because there was a name attached to them. Spencer had never acted as if she came from money, but it was always there in the background, just the same. He had to admit, though, he wasn't sure just who had buckled to the family pressure, him or her.

Whatever, the dress, simple, perfect, looked wonderful on her. One minute she seemed like a tempest, and now she seemed all but ethereal. She needed more meat on her bones, more color in her face. Her eyes were haunted. Hell, his probably looked that way, too. It had been rough, learning to live with Danny gone.

And hunting for his killer.

"It's been a year, David," she said almost tonelessly.

"Spencer, have you been to the police—"

"Of course. Lots of times. They're always as nice as they can be—except, of course, when they start questioning me again."

"They have to do that, Spencer."

"How could I have killed him?" she asked bleakly.

He hesitated. "The way they see it, anything is possible. You might have run out, shot him, run home, then waited for someone to come and give you the news."

"But you know—"

"I'm telling you what the D.A.'s office could come up with in terms of motive. You were his wife. You inherited a sizable fortune on his death."

"But you found me—"

"Stark naked. What a great way to shed bloody clothing."

She was standing again, staring at him as if he were a cold-blooded killer. "You bastard! What about you? He died in your arms!"

"Spencer, sit down, or I'll *make* you sit down in about two seconds!"

She didn't sit. He swore, rising. She sat, teeth grating, staring at him. "Spencer, damn you, they questioned me, too, over and over. Guys I worked with for years. They had to explore all the possibilities."

Tears were hovering in her eyes. She was trying very hard not to shed them. "I loved Danny."

"I know that, Spencer." He clenched his teeth, feeling as if he'd been punched in the heart. He'd loved Danny, too. Just about everyone who ever met Danny Huntington cared about him. Except, of course, the killer. Or killers?

"Spencer, remember the case just a few years ago? Right on Bayshore Drive. Wife calls in, her husband's been shot. Says some men broke in and killed him. Turned out she hired the men who shot them, let them in and out, waited long enough for them to disappear, then called emergency. Remember, Spencer?''

"Yes, I remember," she said impatiently. "She was also much younger than he was and wanted his money. The two cases are nothing at all alike."

"Spencer, the police can't help it. Most murders are committed by people close to the victims. Wives rank right on top."

"Damn you, David, I didn't come here to listen to you explain why the cops questioned me. Danny has been dead for over a year. A cop, David, a cop murdered—and no suspect in sight! And you sit there justifying why they questioned me! I want to know what else they've got! And all anyone will ever tell me is that, oh, we've a few leads, we're following this one or that one! They humor me. They pat me on the back, but nothing happens!"

"Spencer, they're trying. It takes time—"

"I want to know what you've got."

"Spencer, go home. Reconstruct something," he told her. Was reconstruct the right word? He wasn't sure. Montgomery Enterprises wasn't really a construction company, nor was it a decorating firm. Sly had begun the business in the very early days of the city's existence. Back then he'd done detail work, cornices, moldings, mantels, working with the best architects and builders. He had liked to remember those old times, when the now bustling, international city had been nothing but a small southern settlement carved out of a swamp. Now they preserved the old, making it as good as new. They restored buildings, down to the small details, the tiles, moldings and cornices. David found it hard to imagine that there was enough here to keep them going, but it was remarkable to see sometimes, through Sly's eyes, just how much was considered to be of historical value. Especially in the last decade or so, with the Art Deco boom, the refurbishing of the beaches and certain other areas of Greater Miami, the old had become in. Montgomery Enterprises was doing extremely well.

"Go home, or go repair a quaint old bathroom or something," he told her, rubbing his temple.

Her eyes narrowed. "I went home, David. I went away for a year, and I left everything to the cops and to you, his best friend, the hometown boy who could find out anything! I went away, but damn it, it seems like I'm the only one who really cares! I have to stay on this if we're ever going to find Danny's killer. The eulogy was just great, the cops who turned out were wonderful, the twenty-one-gun salute was grand! But that buried him, and he's *stayed* buried. And the case has stayed buried with him. I want something done now. I want to know what you've got. He was a homicide cop. What was he on to? Why was he meeting you that morning?"

Reva cleared her throat from the doorway. "Coffee!" she said cheerfully.

David was glad for the interruption. It bought him a little time as his sister came into his office and set the tray on his desk. He was deterred from his thoughts by the tray, though. They kept mugs in the office. Good sturdy mugs. But there were china cups sitting on a silver tray, and the coffeepot was silver, as well, along with the creamer and sugar bowl.

He stared at Reva, who glanced at Spencer and shrugged. He smiled, shaking his head.

"Thanks, Reva," Spencer said, restlessly standing again, approaching the tray.

"Spencer, please, relax!" David said.

"I can't just sit still!" she exclaimed, reaching for the coffee server. She glanced at Reva. "I don't mean to be difficult—yes, I do, except not about the coffee—but do you still have those great mugs around here anywhere?"

"I—" Reva said blankly, then stared at David again. "Yes, sure, of course."

Reva went out. David leaned back in his chair, not knowing whether he wanted to grin or pick Spencer up bodily and remove her from the office altogether.

He leaned forward, fingers folded on his desk. "Spencer, if you believe that I cared about Danny, then you know that I'm doing what I can. Everyone in the world knows that cops will do anything they can to catch the killer of another cop—"

"Why was he meeting with you that morning?" Spencer interrupted determinedly.

"To go over the Vichy case."

"I want to know about the Vichy case."

Reva returned with the mugs. Spencer flashed her a smile of gratitude. "Thanks. I don't know why, but coffee always tastes better in a mug."

"A quick cup of coffee shouldn't matter much," David said.

"But it may not be quick," Spencer warned.

How the hell was he going to be able to get rid of her? He stood up. "I'll pour the coffee."

"None for me!" Reva said, casting David a quick glance and grinning. "My work is looking good at the moment." She made another quick departure.

"Spencer, damn it, if you're staying, sit down!" David said, his tone carrying the rough edge of aggravation. Spencer sat, and he poured coffee into two mugs. "Still black, one sugar?" he asked her.

"Yes, please."

Still black, one sugar. Exactly the way she'd been drinking coffee since high school.

Some things just didn't change. Like the way he had always felt about her.

He almost slammed her mug down in front of her before returning to the chair behind his desk. He opened a drawer and threw a mile-high pile of folders on top of his blotter. "This is what I've been doing all year, Spencer. There are over two hundred interviews in here, notes on people, places, stakeouts. Five of the files are completely closed—they concern homicides Danny was working on that have been solved and could in no way have anything to do with his death. The Vichy case remains open and may remain open forever."

"Why?"

"You know Eugene Vichy."

"I know him?"

"He belongs to your yacht club."

Spencer frowned. He realized that she probably hadn't been to the yacht club in a very long time.

"He's fifty-something, white-haired, good-looking, always looks like he just walked off a movie set. His wife, the late Mrs. Vichy, was sixty-something, and not quite so good-looking but very rich. She expired from a knock on the head. The house had been ripped up, some diamonds were missing. Vichy claimed to have come in and found the place in disarray and to have been brokenhearted at the loss of his beloved Vickie."

"Vickie? Vickie Vichy?" Spencer said.

"You know her?"

She shrugged. "The name sounds vaguely familiar—and absurd—but then, maybe Danny talked about the case. I don't remember. But why do you think the case will remain unsolved?"

"Because Vichy passed a lie detector test and he still holds to his story."

"Maybe he's innocent."

David shook his head. "I don't think so. Not for a minute. And neither did Danny."

Spencer sat forward, suddenly very intense. "So Danny was pressuring this man. And Vichy knew that Danny wouldn't quit. And he'd already proven himself adept at murder—"

"Spencer, the cops have to have some kind of evidence to make an arrest."

"Fine. Go on."

"Go on?"

"Who else is in the suspect lineup?"

"Spencer, you should go home—"

"I'm not going home until you tell me exactly where you are in this investigation."

"Spencer, I don't have to tell you anything. I'm not working for you."

"Then *start* working for me."

"No."

"David, financially I can compete with any other clients you have. I need—"

"Damn it, Spencer!" He'd been planning to remain calm. Understanding. They weren't kids anymore; too much of life had already cracked them over the head. But there was something about Spencer. He wanted to either hold her or shake her. Shaking her was a whole lot safer. "I can't be bought, Spencer. You know that."

"You shouldn't have to be bought!" she lashed back, trying to keep her anger in check. "He was your best friend. He—"

"Spencer, get out."

"I won't leave until you finish."

"Spencer, I'll pick you up and put you out!" he warned her.

Her eyes narrowed sharply. "I'll leave on my own accord. I just want to know what else you're doing, who else you're watching."

He groaned. "They threw you out of the police station, so you've come to torture me."

"David—"

"Yes, Vichy might have been tired of Danny's determination to prove him guilty," he snapped coldly, staring out the huge plate-glass window to the garden beyond. A slatted wood fence surrounded the garden, making it private and quiet. A mass of deep purple bougainvillea grew clinging along the fence. Wood chips filled in the space around deep green ferns and impatiens. It was a pleasant and peaceful view, but he felt anything but pleasant or peaceful now. "There are only two other people Danny was investigating who might have had the motive and method to kill him. The first is Ricky Garcia, who—"

Spencer gasped, interrupting him. "I've seen the name. In fact, I definitely remember Danny talking about him. He's a crime boss, the head of a Cuban Mafia-type ring. He controls drug rings and prostitution, gambling—"

"Exactly. He's as slippery as an eel, as well. He can snap his fingers and find a dozen hit men."

"Then it must be him," Spencer whispered, her eyes steady on his. "And there must be a way to trap him."

"If there is, Spencer, the police—or I—will find it. And there's no guarantee that Danny actually had anything on him, or that he had anything against Danny. In fact, he liked Danny."

"He liked Danny?"

"It's more common than you think for criminals to like the cops who are after them," he said with a shrug.

"But—"

"Then there's Trey Delia. You must know that name, as well."

She nodded, frowning. "He's the cult leader."

"He's not exactly a cult leader."

"He was the one accused of raiding graves for body parts!" Spencer exclaimed. "For his rituals."

"He was accused of grave robbing, but the police weren't so certain he was after body parts. They think he might have been trying to hide evidence. A number of his church members were dying inexplicably. He managed to get most of them cremated. Danny thought he was behind the vandalism in several cemeteries. He was digging up some of his own people and making sure nothing could be found if the police did decide to exhume a few bodies. Now, that's it, Spencer. I've given you every name I've got left on my list of possibilities. I haven't been sitting back idle, I'm doing everything I can. Now I want you to get up, go home and forget it."

She was up, hands on his desk, staring at him as he stared at her. "I can't forget—"

"You have to." He gritted his teeth, wishing again that he didn't feel the awful urge to either shake her or wrap his arms around her. The last would be one dreadful mistake. She would welcome him with all the warmth and comfort of a porcupine. Nothing would ever be right between them again; Danny's death had made that an even greater certainty. He needed to keep her away from him. He'd always needed to keep her away from him. Temptation was too great when she was near. And temptation with Spencer was pure torment. He'd learned the hard way that there was nothing in the world quite like wanting Spencer. And nothing in the world quite like the way a man could find his soul wrenched right from his being by the void she could leave in his life. She looked as if she belonged on a pedestal. A blond goddess with her perfect alabaster skin. An Anglo goddess with a perfect pedigree. Yeah, Danny had matched her just perfectly.

"Get out, Spencer."

"Damn you, David!"

"When I know something, I'll tell you. If you can do something, I'll tell you. Until then, leave me the hell alone so that I can keep working."

"David..."

She fell silent as he approached her with pure menace. He forced himself to close his hands around her arms with some control—but not a lot of it. He turned her bodily around and ushered her out of his office as quickly as he could, wishing even for those few seconds that he didn't have to touch her at all. He could smell her. He didn't know what the scent was, only that she had worn it as long as she had worn a bra, that it wasn't just cologne or perfume, it was soap and body lotion, as well. It was subtle, mixed with something that was just plain Spencer, and it was also intoxicating and sensual. Feelings of guilt instantly began to creep over him, like a crimson tide. He felt the attraction just as he had felt it when Danny was still alive, just as he had felt it when he and Spencer had both been young and a little bit wild and alive with the sheer power of their youth and growing sexuality. He wanted Spencer, he'd always wanted her, had never stopped wanting her, even when she had been married to his best friend. But he would never have touched her when she was Danny's wife, and as Danny's widow, somehow she seemed twice as taboo.

"David, damn you," she began again, as he escorted her past Reva's desk and through the reception area.

"Say goodbye to Spencer, Reva. She's got to go out and get on with her life now."

Reva looked up miserably from her desk. Furious, Spencer snatched her wrists away from David. "Thank you, Reva," Spencer told his sister; then her eyes, ice blue now, met his. "And thank *you*, of course. For your unconditional support and assistance!"

"Spencer, how many times can I say this? I swear, I'm doing everything I can!"

"It's not enough, David. It's just not enough."

But that was Spencer's final volley. She was out the front door of his office. He watched her heels click smartly on the pavement as she marched to the small parking area just off Main Street.

Maybe he should have put his office out on the beach, he thought. Up in Miami Springs, or over on Key Biscayne. Somewhere other than where Spencer had always lived. No, he had always lived here, too. And Spencer and he would be entangled now even if he'd moved his office to Never Never Land.

He turned around. Reva was staring at him. Something seemed to close around his heart. "What?" he snapped to his sister. "You think she's right? You think there's something else I can do that I haven't?"

Reva shook her head, watching him almost sadly. "I know that you've spent more than a year trying to trace Danny's killer," she told him flatly. "I just feel so sorry for her."

"Wonderful. She bursts in here like hell on wheels, and you feel bad for poor, poor Spencer."

Reva ignored that with a shrug. "None of us could believe what happened to Danny. It seemed that everyone in the world loved him. I mean, can you remember a time in our lives when Danny didn't come through for anyone? And Spencer was married to him. The rest of us may be able to accept that, as awful as it is, the killer will never be found. But Spencer...Spencer will never be able to rest until the case is closed.''

David swore softly, turned away from his sister and headed toward the door.

''Where are you going?'' Reva asked him.

''Somewhere quiet. To visit Danny.''

To visit Danny...

Well, at the very least, it really was quiet. After he'd stopped the car, at least. He drove an accelerated Mustang, not ostentatious, not a junk pile, and fast enough to follow just about anything on the road. And besides, Michael MacCloud had always believed in buying American.

The cemetery wasn't far. Just through Coconut Grove and north past downtown Coral Gables, then to the right where it became the City of Miami again. Danny's grave was almost at the center of the graveyard; he'd been laid to rest beneath a marble angel. David stood over the grave. The grass was all grown in, and a bouquet of fresh flowers sat in the brass vase just above the headstone that stated Danny's full name, his rank and ''best friend, beloved husband, always cherished within our hearts.''

Sometimes, he still couldn't believe that Danny was gone.

''Why couldn't you have talked to me, buddy?'' he said softly. ''You didn't tell me anything about the killer—you had to whisper her name! Well, I suppose I just might have done that, too. But it would have helped me a hell of a lot now if you'd just given me a clue.''

There was a slight motion behind him. He wore a gun beneath his jacket, but instinct told him that he wasn't in any real danger in this realm of the dead. He turned around slowly, expectantly.

Sly was there. Sly Montgomery. David wasn't sure just how old Sly was—but it was definitely *very*. He'd come south with some of the earliest pioneers, not too long after Julia Tuttle had sent Henry Flagler an orange blossom to convince Flagler to bring his railroad south. Sly was somewhere in his nineties—unless he'd hit a hundred—but age didn't seem to affect the man much. He was slim as a reed and straight as an arrow. He'd never lost his hair. It was snow-white, but there was a lot of it. And he had the most intense blue eyes David had ever seen anywhere—unless he compared them to Spencer's. Sly had made enough money to retire anywhere on earth, but this was his home, working with his hands was his craft. When David had been young, Sly had told him that he intended to die working. He'd meant those words.

A smile curved old Sly's lips. "David. How nice to see you."

David arched a brow. "We just happen to be out here at the same time?"

"Of course not."

"Then . . . ?"

"Reva told me where you were."

"Why were you looking for me?" he asked, then sighed, staring at the grave again and speaking once more before Sly could answer the question he'd been asked. "Spencer was by, and I've got to tell you the same thing I told her. You can't hire me to look for Danny's killer. I'm already doing everything I can. You've both got to believe that. He was my best friend. I don't need to be paid to put everything I've got into it."

"Oh, I believe that," Sly said. "And I didn't come to ask if I could hire you."

David turned to Sly, arching a brow. "Surely this isn't a social call, not in a cemetery, Sly." Sly grinned. They couldn't be his own teeth, David thought, but whether they were or not, they were perfect.

"I didn't come about Danny."

"Then . . ."

"I came about Spencer."

"What?"

"I want to hire you to look after Spencer."

"Why?"

"I think that someone is following her. No, that's not right. I'm *sure* that someone is following her, stalking her. In fact, David, I think that someone is trying to kill her."

Jerry Fried, Danny Huntington's last partner in homicide, drummed his fingers on the table, staring unhappily at the headlines on the front page of the *Miami Herald*.

More Than A Year After His Death,
Humanitarian Cop's Killer Remains At Large

The reporter had done one hell of a slam job, throwing suspicion on everyone, including the untouchable Mrs. Huntington, David Delgado, half the crooks in the city—and half the police force.

Jerry groaned and reached across his desk for the large bottle of cherry-flavored antacids he kept there. He took a huge handful as if they were candies.

It was Spencer being back in town that was causing all this brouhaha again. Why couldn't they just let Danny stay buried? Everyone knew that cops did everything they could when another cop went down. Just like everybody knew there were some crimes that were destined to go unsolved. Maybe everybody didn't know quite how many there were, but people had to know they existed, especially in a city as big as Miami.

A queasy pain swished in his stomach again; he chewed another handful of antacids. Damn Spencer. Why hadn't she just stayed in Rhode Island? It would have been better for all of them.

Gene Vichy read the headline at the breakfast table while enjoying the elegant view of water and yachts at his club. He smiled slightly, shaking his head. It was one self-righteous reporter who had done the job on this one! The police were, it seemed, a handful of incompetents. His smile deepened. The general public didn't always understand the law. Take the case of his poor murdered wife. The cops sure as hell thought he had done it, but they didn't have a shred of proof. The D.A.'s office could never prosecute him; they had nothing but their certainty that the motive had been money. Now, as to Danny...

The poor cops. They didn't even have an obvious motive. In the murder of a husband or wife, as he well knew, the cops instantly looked to the surviving spouse.

Spencer had inherited a fortune on her husband's death, but what did that matter to a woman who had several fortunes of her own already. Then there was jealousy. A lover, perhaps?

But, alas again for the poor cops! Spencer Huntington seemed purer than the driven snow. Where to go from there. To a best friend?

To all those crooks Danny Huntington had been after?

A friend, a foe—a snitch?

He laughed out loud softly. He could almost feel it in the air. Fur was going to fly again.

Ricky Garcia swore violently in his native Spanish and threw the paper on the floor.

¡Merde! The cops were going to be crawling all over him again. Coming down on his gambling, on his prostitutes.

All because the wife was back in town, stirring up trouble!

Jared Monteith hadn't read the paper at home that morning. He didn't see the headline until he sat down behind his desk. Even as he sat, his line rang. He winced before picking up the receiver, knowing full well that it was going to be his wife.

"Did you read the damned paper?" Cecily could screech extremely well when she wanted to.

"Yes, I'm looking at it right now."

"I told you Spencer was trouble."

"Cecily—the reporter is down on Spencer!"

Cecily sniffed. "As if Spencer is going to worry!"

"Sly's calling me," Jared said and sighed. "Cecily, no big deal, okay? Gotta go."

Trey Delia read the paper in his incense-filled room. He was sitting cross-legged and naked on his floor. The two young women who had recently come to fulfill his needs giggled softly from somewhere behind him as he sipped herbal tea laced with ox blood. Raw chicken hearts sat on a plate before him.

Something human would have been better.

The ancients understood. Consuming an enemy gave a man his enemy's strength. A heart offered courage and wisdom. Some organs gave strength. Bonemeal gave a man physical and mental powers.

Ah, and now this....

Everyone would be up in arms again.

The cops would be going crazy. It must be Danny's widow stirring up the dust. Spencer, the beautiful wife. Trey had seen her picture. Very blond, elegant. Tempting.

He popped a chicken heart into his mouth and drew a deep breath from the hashish pipe at his side. The girls were still giggling.

Spencer...

She was trouble. So pretty. So much trouble. So pale, slim, elegant.

He wondered how she would taste.

In his office, Sly read the headline and groaned.

Audrey was sipping her coffee and reading, as well. Poor Spencer. The wound Danny's death had left was being ripped open all over again. Of course, Spencer was doing it herself, but still, it was sad.

So many people would be upset! Dangerous people. But there would be no stopping Spencer. Audrey knew her well, and she didn't really blame her.

Audrey bit her lip and continued to scan the paper.

Jon Monteith, Jared's father, Spencer's uncle, lay his head wearily on his pillow.

If only they could let matters rest!

After all, it hadn't been a drive-by shooting, and any fool knew Spencer wasn't guilty. It hadn't been robbery.

So why kill a cop?

It was simple. The way he saw it, the cop had known too much.

A cop learned things on the streets. He was an investigator. He found things out, and sometimes he was careful about telling even his associates what he knew.

And pursuing what was going on could be dangerous. Danny had been bright. Danny had been on to so many things. And with Spencer raising a fuss and the newspapers going crazy, things were bound to happen.

Yes...

A veritable Pandora's box could fly right open.

He swore and groaned.

Spencer had come home, and she wouldn't let things rest. She just didn't know what was good for her.

Spencer was one royal pain in the ass.

He picked up the phone and waited for an answer. "Have you seen the headline?"

"Yes," came the reply. "I'm on it. I've *been* on it, damn it!"

"Make sure you stay on it. Make damned sure, because if you don't..."

He let the force of the husky threat fade, then replaced the receiver with a sharp click.

Accidents did happen. Oh, yes. Accidents did happen.

3

There were at least a hundred good reasons she shouldn't be in a cemetery in the dead of night, Spencer thought.

And the longer she stood in the darkness, the longer the list became and the more foolish her errand seemed to be.

It was just that...she had to do something. *Someone* had to do something. She had tried very hard to let the police do their work. She had even understood when they had grilled her, relentlessly, apologetically, relentlessly again. She applauded their efforts—at least it had seemed as if they were traveling along every possible avenue.

And she even believed—no, she *knew*—that David Delgado would have stopped at nothing to catch Danny's killer.

It was just that they weren't doing enough.

She'd gone away for a long time. She'd stopped working for a while, but idleness had been sheer misery. She knew that she couldn't bring Danny back. But she also knew that she would never be able to live the new life David was ordering her to until she had laid Danny's ghost to rest by seeing his killer caught.

But this...this was probably sheer stupidity. She might not find out anything, and she might well be mugged by some petty thief. Or worse. The casual crime in South

Florida was as scary as the acts committed with premeditated malice.

Sly was worried about her, she knew. It was because of the beam that had collapsed in the old house she'd been working on last week. But the place had practically been condemned, and she'd only agreed to work on it because her cousin Jared had set up a meeting with an ace architect and one of the best builders in the city. And it had been a gracious old place, designed by DeGarmo, with fantastic huge beams in the ceiling, the original tiles and stenciling—all crying out to be saved. The beam could have fallen on anyone, and it hadn't actually fallen *on* her. It had missed her by several inches. She wouldn't have thought anything of it, herself, but Sly had been with her. . . .

A cloud rolled over the moon. It was very dark. A breeze suddenly stirred against the humidity and heat of the night, and she was startled to feel a creeping sensation of cold sweep over her.

The paper today had carried a wealth of information. The grave robbers were at it again, and the police again suspected Trey Delia's offshoot of Santeria. Santeria was indeed a strange religion, from what Spencer knew of it. It was a form of Catholicism mixed with some very odd theologies from the islands. Its rituals often called for live sacrifices—chickens and goats, usually, although human body parts were also considered useful, especially by some offshoot groups. Grave robbers had absconded with fingers and toes and the like before.

Today in the office, Audrey had idly pointed out how the grave robbery had seemed to follow a pattern the first time, a pattern that circled the city, then came dead center back into it. And now it seemed that things were happening just the same way again.

Was that what had brought her here?

She had one contact left who no one knew about. Not the police, not anyone. His name was Willie Harper; he lived on the streets in downtown Miami, and though he didn't have a drug problem, he did like a good bottle of Scotch. Spencer had once been very unhappy about Willie, telling Danny that he was paying the man just to help him kill himself with his alcoholism. But it wasn't really that bad. Willie was a good sort. Danny paid him well, and before he drank any of it away, he bought food for all his friends, blankets, sometimes even a cheap hotel room for the night. But Willie liked living on the streets. He liked to make money, too. When he'd contacted Spencer, she'd promised to keep paying him for any information he could give her that might help find Danny's killer.

He'd called her that afternoon—with the same observation that Audrey had made.

She exhaled, leaning against the edge of the small family mausoleum that sheltered her from the view of anyone who might have been driving along the twisting roads that led through the cemetery. The stone felt very cold, and she felt like an absolute idiot for being here. It wasn't as if she was carrying a gun—or as if she would know how to use one if she did. She had pepper spray in the car—Danny had always insisted she carry it, and he had shown her how to use it. But she hadn't thought to bring it with her; she wasn't planning on accosting anyone. She had just come to see what was going on, to make sure that if any grave robbers did come, they wouldn't touch Danny's grave or desecrate his tomb in any way.

She started to shiver.

This was nuts. What did she think she was going to do, if someone *did* show up? Was she going to yell at some ghoul in the middle of a dark cemetery and tell him to stop?

Especially when he might be her husband's murderer?

It was an old cemetery, filled with trees and foliage. She tried to tell herself that her car was parked relatively close by at the doughnut shop just across Eighth Street, that even though it was very late, the main streets were teeming with people—even though the cemetery did seem unbelievably dark and still and silent, and far from civilization. In fact, there were probably a number of cops eating doughnuts right by her car. But then, that was at least half a mile away.

An owl let out a hoot, and a nearby tree rustled, and she nearly jumped into the mausoleum. She forced herself to remain still and stare toward the tree. Images of Dracula came to her mind. Creatures breaking out of their tombs. Maybe the human monsters from *Night of the Living Dead*. Werewolves, mummies...

But this wasn't Egypt, and there was no full moon. In fact, with the clouds, there was barely a moon at all. She felt like an idiot. And she deserved to. She shouldn't be here. A squirrel had rustled the tree—she could see it now, even in the shadows, leaping from the ground to a monument, and then to another tree. No creatures from beyond the grave were going to come after her. In fact, she'd gone through a period of mourning when she'd lain awake at night just praying that Danny could come back as a ghost, in voice, in spirit—in anything. But Danny hadn't come back. It was just as her father had once told her, the dead were the least threatening people in the world.

No, it wasn't the dead she had to fear. It was the living.

The cloud broke over the moon, and a silver light fell down on the cemetery. It was time to go home, she told herself. A very light fog was rising, and it was growing cool and damp and uncomfortable here. It was time to go crawling over the wall and go home. Nothing was going to happen. Unless she was arrested in her black jeans and black denim shirt and sneakers for breaking into the cemetery. No, the cops would never arrest her. They would just suggest to someone in her family that Danny's death had been her undoing, and that it was sad, but she really ought to be put away somewhere—fast.

She started to move, but then a chill swept over her again, and for some reason she couldn't fathom, she stood dead still. She tried not to give way to flights of imagination, but the fog had added a strange feeling to the graveyard. It was a ground fog, deepening, swirling around marble images of Christ and praying angels. She heard a rustling sound again, and this was different. Something much larger than a squirrel was coming around one of the old oaks just down the trail past the vault she was leaning against.

She breathed quickly, her heart hammering. She could hear footsteps; then a figure appeared. Then another figure, and another, all dressed in black. Carrying spades and picks. They emerged in silence from the fog, walking her way. Walking as if they were staring right at her.

They couldn't possibly see her; it was just coincidence that they were heading in her direction. Her fingers icy, her heart slamming so loudly that she was certain someone would hear it, she ducked very low against the mausoleum.

"Where?" someone demanded in whisper.

"There, in the center," someone whispered back.

Keeping low, Spencer swung around. She noticed what she hadn't seen before in the darkness—a new grave, the earth just packed over it. This was crazy, she thought. They were living in the twentieth century, and people weren't just dumped underground, they were well protected before being placed in their graves. But apparently these grave robbers knew what they were doing. They moved furtively and quickly, six of them, she counted, and every one of the six carrying a tool with which to dig—or to break open a coffin. She wasn't even sure just what all the tools they carried were, exactly.

She couldn't tell one man from another—if they *were* all men. They were dressed much like she was, in black, but they wore black caps, as well, and ski masks. They looked like bank robbers, she thought, and realized that hysteria was bubbling up inside her. The way they were moving, she had to inch around the mausoleum to keep from being seen. When she had rounded a corner, she sat on the earth, her back flat against the stone, staring into the night. She couldn't get up and run now; she would be seen. She could only sit where she was, barely daring to breathe, listening.

She heard the sound of spades hitting the earth. Somehow, just the sound made her flinch. She twisted to peer around the corner of the small mausoleum. As she did, her sneakered foot scraped against a rock.

It was a small noise. It shouldn't have been heard, not against the determined shoves of the spades digging into the earth. But somehow...

One of the diggers went very still, staring in her direction.

"What is it?" a husky voice asked.

"Don't know... something," was the muttered reply.

She flattened herself against the stone, afraid to exhale her pent-up breath. She had to look. She peered around again. One digger had remained standing perfectly still, staring in her direction. It was dark, she was in shadows... and she'd been seen.

She stared at the figure in black and felt the figure's stare in return. Felt the eyes, felt the danger...

She didn't think—there was no time to think. She stood and ran, tearing down the central path, aware that her best bet would be to head for the main street. She was fast, she'd always been fast. And she knew the layout of the cemetery well enough.

But figures were tearing after her at tremendous speed.

She veered off the main path, around the huge, central mausoleum. She tore along a pathway to a gate but found it locked.

She could hear footsteps coming closer. Furtive, but moving quickly, coming in her direction.

She burst away from the mausoleum, ducking low to run behind angels and Madonnas that rose high against the shadows and the fog. She ducked behind one and listened. Running footsteps passed her by. She remained where she was, thinking herself an absolute idiot for the thousandth time. There was enough danger in Dade County. She hadn't needed to go looking for it. And these people had come to rob a new grave for body parts. They seemed to like them fresh. The fresher the better.

Hers would be very, very fresh....

She leaped up, bordering on panic. She could see a figure farther along one of the trails. She turned to run the other way.

Fingers suddenly curled around her ankle.

A scream of sheer terror rose in her throat, but she never managed more than a strangled gasp. Even as she inhaled, she was falling to the earth, falling into a hole, into darkness, into what seemed like an incredible void.

She landed against flesh. Terror wound more tightly within her, but she couldn't catch her breath to scream. It was like a nightmare.

A hand clamped tightly over her mouth, and horrible visions of the living dead raced into her panicked mind. The scent of the fresh damp earth filled her lungs, and it seemed as if it was the smell of death.

She felt herself being lifted and righted. Then she heard a whisper, hushed, dictatorial. "Shush! Whatever the hell you do, don't scream. It's me. David."

She was shaking. She'd probably never been more frightened in her life. She registered slowly that it *was* David—she really had run into David in a freshly dug hole in the middle of the cemetery in the middle of the night. It seemed impossible.

"Get down!" he told her.

Easy to do—her knees were buckling beneath her. She could scarcely breathe, and she was willing herself not to pass out.

"What in God's name are you doing here?" she demanded in a whisper. It felt as if the blood had drained from her body. Her hair had probably turned completely white.

She clenched her fingers tightly. Wound them into white-knuckled fists.

"Damn it, David."

"Shut up, Spencer!" he repeated in an emphatic whisper.

She managed to make a few observations. Basic black was really in. David, too, was in black. Black jeans, black T-shirt, black cotton jacket. She had a feeling that he was wearing a shoulder holster beneath the jacket.

"What are you doing here?" she asked again, barely mouthing the words. Despite the darkness, she was sure he heard her.

"What are *you* doing here?" he demanded in return.

"Watching for the grave robbers," she admitted flatly.

"Well, they're watching for you now, Spencer, so please, can we talk later?"

She gritted her teeth, and leaned back. She came against a wall of dirt. Very damp dirt. She looked up at the night sky and realized that she was six feet under. It wasn't a comfortable feeling.

It was very dark. She could barely see David, but she could sense his movements, at least. He'd reached into his jacket. For his gun, she was certain. But then she heard him talking. Softly, barely a whisper.

Number sequences, the name of the cemetery, the address. "Southeast of the main mausoleum," he said at last.

He was on a very small cellular phone, she realized, and stared at him incredulously.

"A phone, no gun?" she said softly.

He replaced the phone and pulled his gun, arching a brow at her. "Six of them, one of me. I'm good, Spencer, but, hey, cut me a little slack here, huh?"

She started to answer then went still again as they both heard trees rustling nearby and felt the tremor of the earth near them. Loose particles fell around them. Spencer felt the blood draining from her face.

David motioned to her to get down. She shrank against the wall of the grave, hunching as low as she could. Someone came nearer and nearer, very near. So near that he was looking into the open grave...

Suddenly David pressed away from the opposite wall, catching the man's ankle as he had caught hers, causing him to plummet wildly into the grave. He landed with a hard whack, sending dirt flying into Spencer's face. In the darkness she barely saw him raise his head. A moonbeam caught the light of his eyes against their frame of knit ski mask, making them glitter. He opened his mouth, but before he could speak, Spencer heard a click as David cocked his gun.

"Rise slowly, quietly—and carefully," David warned.

The figure began to follow instructions. Even as he did, Spencer could hear the sound of sirens in the night. Closing in. But she was still standing in an open grave— empty other than the living, she prayed—with David and a grave robber. The space seemed to be way too small for the three of them.

She became aware of shouting, the grave robbers calling out in anger, warning one another, some cries in English, some in Spanish. Lights were flaring, and there were other calls now. "Halt, police! Stop, or we'll shoot!"

The cemetery suddenly seemed ablaze as the beams of flashlights cut across it.

"Can we get out of here?" Spencer asked David.

David shrugging, keeping an eye on the robber who was sharing their hole in the earth. "Since the police have just warned everyone that they'll shoot, we might be better off down here for a few minutes." He grinned. "Then we can let our friend crawl up first."

Was it seconds, minutes or eons longer? Eventually someone called out, "Delgado, where are you?"

"Here!" David cried.

In a few moments a uniformed officer was staring down at the three of them, perplexed. Spencer realized that she knew him. She had danced with him one year at the policemen's ball. His name was Tim Winfield. "Mrs. Huntington?" he inquired incredulously.

"Give the lady a hand up, Officer Winfield," David suggested.

"Oh, yeah, of course."

Tim Winfield was young but strongly muscled. He clutched Spencer's hands, lifting her easily out of the grave. He kept staring at her once she was standing by his side.

"Now you," David told his captive. He looked at the young cop. "Might want to give this fellow a hand, too, Winfield. But keep an eye on him while you do."

David hopped out of the grave even as Tim Winfield pulled the ski-masked culprit up to ground level. When they were all standing, a plainclothes man Spencer hadn't met before came forward. She might not know him, but David did.

"Lieutenant," David acknowledged.

"Mr. Delgado," the cop said, offering him a handshake and staring at Spencer. "We've been after these guys for a long time. Thanks for the call." He stared again at Spencer, taking in her black outfit, smiling.

"A new investigator on the payroll, David?" the lieutenant inquired, amused as he assessed Spencer. He was tall and lean, with thinning brown hair, but he had a decent enough smile.

Officer Winfield gasped, letting out a choking sound, then pretending to cough.

"No, Lieutenant Anderson, this is Mrs. Huntington. Mrs. Daniel Huntington."

"Oh!" the lieutenant said, looking at Spencer in a new light. He was, she knew, wondering what the hell she was doing dressed up like one of the grave robbers.

"Spencer likes to walk at night. In strange places," David offered.

"Dangerous places," Anderson said, looking Spencer over very seriously once again. "How did you know that something was going to go down here tonight?" he asked David suddenly.

"I didn't," David answered flatly, holstering his gun as a uniformed cop came to take the grave robber away. The cop instantly began to read the man his rights.

"Then—"

"It was Spencer," David said politely. "You see, I followed her here," he told Anderson, watching Spencer from the corner of his eye. "It seems that Mrs. Huntington doesn't believe that either I or Miami's finest are really doing our jobs to the best of our abilities."

"Mrs. Huntington," Anderson said, and now he sounded worried, "you can't take these things into your own hands, you know."

"I don't actually want them in my own hands—" she began, but Anderson interrupted.

"What were you doing here, then? Who tipped you off? What is going on?"

"I came here because..." She paused. She was never going to tell them about Willie. Never. And it didn't matter. Audrey had drawn the same conclusion. Anyone could have. "I came because I thought the grave diggers might show up here. I didn't want them digging Danny up."

"And how did you intend to stop them, Mrs. Huntington?"

Spencer opened her mouth, then shut it. They were both staring at her. David was delighted to see Anderson harassing her—he wouldn't have to do it himself.

"Yes, Spencer, just what *was* your intent?" David asked, his tone irritatingly polite.

She stared at Anderson. "I—"

"Withholding information from the police is against the law, Mrs. Huntington. You must know that."

"Withholding information?"

"Where did you get your tip?" Anderson asked impatiently.

Spencer inhaled deeply. "No tip-off, Lieutenant. My secretary happened to notice the way the last wave of grave robbings made a circle around the city. All she did was read the newspaper. Maybe the police should try taking that direction on occasion!"

"Mrs. Huntington, I'm afraid that we'll have to ask you to come down to the—"

"Anderson," David interrupted, "I really don't think that will be necessary. There's nothing more Spencer can tell you, and you've got at least one of these ghouls to grill. Maybe your men have come up with a few more. I'll take Mrs. Huntington home."

"You two know each other, huh?" Anderson said.

"Not that well—" Spencer began.

"For ages," David interrupted.

Anderson grinned. "Well, you sure do dress alike. I guess I don't need anything more for tonight. I know where to reach you, Delgado. And Mrs. Huntington—"

"I haven't moved, Lieutenant. I'm still at Danny's address, and you can reach me at the same number. And I've been down to the station plenty of times, so I'll know where to go if you decide you *do* want something from me."

"We just want you to let us do our jobs, Mrs. Huntington," he said, taking her hand. She thought for a moment that he was going to kiss it. She almost wrenched it away.

"Come on, Spencer, let's go home," David suggested.

They started walking. She resented his hand at the small of her back, but she resented Lieutenant Anderson more. Even as they started walking away, he called her back.

"Mrs. Huntington, it *is* illegal to trespass in graveyards at night, you know. Don't make a habit of it."

She swung around. "Ah, but I did catch a few crooks for you before they could chop up any more bodies, didn't I?" she inquired sweetly.

Anderson suddenly seemed to have run out of taunts. Spencer turned and started walking again, David close on her heels. He caught her arm as they neared the wall and the row of patrol cars parked next to it.

"Spencer..."

She shook off his arm. She felt as if she were on-screen, in front of all those headlights. "So I shouldn't have been here, David. At least something happened."

"Hell, yes, something happened. And we could have found pieces of you all over this place in the morning."

"It's over, David. I just want to go home. Will you please leave me alone and let me go?"

She wrenched free and started walking again. He remained right behind her. She came to the wall and realized that the gates hadn't been opened, all the cops had jumped in the same way she had. She reached for the wall and found herself being assisted. David's hands were on her hips, and then his palm was on her rump, pushing her up. He leaped up beside her, dropping to the sidewalk on the other side and helping her down before she could protest.

"My car is over there," she said, pointing.

"I'll follow you home."

"There's no need for—"

"Spencer, it's past two in the morning. There's every need."

"I'm sure I can get home safely. There aren't any more cemeteries between here and my house."

"Actually, there is one, that small one in the Grove," he said with a wave of his hand. "I'll follow you, Spencer."

"I'm telling you—"

"God damn it, Spencer, I was Danny's best friend! I am going to follow you home. Let's go!"

She stiffened her shoulders and started for the doughnut store. He followed. Cops were everywhere, calling out curious greetings to David, staring at her, the ones who knew her offering awkward hellos.

Well, she was glad of the cops. She remembered thinking that they were so far away.

And they might have been. But David had been there. And his car was parked right next to hers.

She ignored him, ignored his car. But as soon as she was driving, she knew that he was right behind her. And that he would stick to her like glue. Well, she was grateful. It was a big city; night could be dangerous.

In her driveway, she slammed out of her car and walked to the driver's side of his. He rolled down the window. "Get in the house, Spencer," he told her. "I'm not leaving until you do."

"Why were you following me tonight?" she demanded.

"Spencer, I'm not leaving—"

"Good. We'll just both stand here all night."

She jumped back, because he suddenly swung his car door open. "Give me the keys."

"David!"

He took them from her and walked up the tile path to her door, which he opened, then stepped into the house. He looked around the foyer and up the stairway. She thought she saw a small smile curving his lips, and she wondered if he was sniffing at Montgomery elegance, Montgomery money. The house wasn't ostentatious in any way, she thought resentfully. It was sleek, warm, inviting.

She held out a hand. "My keys, David."

He handed them over. "Don't forget to set the alarm when I leave," he told her.

"I've been managing on my own for over a year now," she informed him briskly.

He nodded and turned to walk out. She was appalled at herself when she suddenly slammed a fist against his back, causing him to turn with a look of surprise on his features.

She swallowed hard, determined not to back down. "What were you doing there?" she demanded.

"I told you. I was following you, Spencer."

"Why?" she exploded.

He shrugged. "Sly asked me to."

"You're—you're working for Sly?" she gasped.

He hesitated for a moment, then shrugged again. "Yeah, I'm working for Sly."

"As of when?"

"As of this afternoon."

"I don't want you following me."

"Take it up with Sly."

"Damn it, David—"

"Take it up with Sly, Spencer. He thinks you're in danger."

"But I'm not!"

"And as of tonight, I agree with him. Hell, Spencer, you're a damned danger to yourself, if nothing else. Don't forget the alarm," he said again.

"David, I'm telling you—"

"Don't tell *me,* Spencer. Tell Sly."

"Damn you—" she began, but he'd managed to exit, pulling the door shut behind him. She slammed the door, just as she had slammed his back, swearing.

"The alarm, Spencer!" he called back to her.

She told him what he should go do to himself.

"The alarm!"

She set the damned alarm, then turned away from the door, hurrying for the kitchen. She had good brandy somewhere, and she had never wanted a swallow of it more.

She downed half a snifter in a gulp, then stood there as it warmed her. Dear God, what a night. She knew what a stupid move she'd made. She'd been scared out of half of her hair pigment, but in the end they'd caught someone, and something might be solved because of that.

Might be. They hadn't been after Danny's grave, no one knew yet what had really been going on. But...

But something might come of it.

David was following her. Sly had hired David to follow her. Oh, God. Sly had paid David to watch her. The last thing she wanted in her life was David following her, watching her.

Oh, God. She poured more brandy and gulped that down, too. And then she had some more.

It might be nearly three o'clock in the morning, but brandy was the only way in hell she was ever going to get to sleep tonight.

4

Sometimes the past seemed forever away. And sometimes, especially in dreams, it felt as if it had never gone away.

It was almost as if she was there again, on that long-ago day by the rock pit where they all congregated after school. She had been sixteen, David and some of the others were almost eighteen then. The dream had texture and taste. She could feel the stinging warmth of the sun.

It probably wasn't such a great place for them to be. There certainly wasn't any kind of supervision. The water was very clear, so clear that you could swim down and see all the wrecked cars that had gone off or been dumped. The boys liked to tease the girls and tell them that there were still bodies in the trunks of the cars, that there were a few skeletons still sitting right in the front seats, as well. "But we all know that's not real," Cecily would inform them regally. "Boys just like to scare girls. It's easier to get into a girl's pants if she's scared. At least, that's what boys think," she assured them all.

"All" meant their group, one they had formed when they were around twelve and pretty much kept together ever since. Danny Huntington was the leader of the male pack, with Spencer's cousin Jared coming in a close second. Then there were Ansel Rhodes and George Manger, followers to the core. And then, paradoxically a part and yet not a part, there was David Delgado.

It wasn't that they didn't want him in their group—they did. It was funny. When they had been even younger and Danny had first dragged him in, they'd all stuck their noses up just a bit. David just didn't come from the same kind of family. He spoke Spanish as easily as he spoke English. He was dark; even his eyes were dark, though they were blue, not the black they often appeared. His clothes were mended and remended, and a lot of the time he couldn't do things because he had chores to take care of for his grandfather. But he didn't seem to resent not having a good time.

Then, suddenly, he was in school with them. He worked hard; Spencer saw him staying after school to study almost every day. It was a hard school; homework took about three hours a night. Unless, of course, you were Jared and skimmed by, paying other kids to do the work for you. But it wasn't academics that really got David Delgado noticed—it was sheer athletic ability. The small private school had never had great baseball or football teams. With David playing, they suddenly began to win a few games. By the time they got to the rock pit on that particular afternoon, David was probably the most popular kid in the school. He could accept the acclaim that came his way, but he never sought it. He still did chores for his grandfather. He came to things when he chose and backed away when he chose, too. He was never with them at the country club dances or some of the other social events their parents planned for them.

None of that mattered, or maybe it helped. To Spencer, just like the other girls in her circle—Cecily, Terry-Sue and Gina Davis—David Delgado was even more appealing because of that little touch of something different about him. He was the kind of boy their folks didn't quite approve of; he wasn't one of *them*. It didn't matter that he wasn't into drugs, didn't rob convenience stores and was a hell of a lot more moral than most of the kids in their circle. What mattered was that he didn't come from the old guard—that he was a refugee.

Spencer didn't give a damn. She thought it was wonderfully romantic—and *erotic*, a word she was beginning to find fascinating. Maybe there was something else a little bit deeper than those feelings, as well. She knew that Sly liked David. Really liked him. Not conditionally, the way her parents did. Sly just out and out liked David; it didn't matter one iota to him whether David had come from Cuba or the moon. And for all her life, Sly had been Spencer's favorite person. So if Sly approved of David...

Actually, that day, thinking hadn't really entered into it. It was summer, and the heat was piercing, and they'd packed picnic lunches. Spencer had gotten a brand new cherry red Jeep for her birthday, Jared had his mom's last-year's Volvo, Ansel Rhodes had a new Firebird, and David had a great '57 Chevy he had bought himself, earning the money at a photo lab where he worked Saturdays and some afternoons.

Spencer almost wished she hadn't gotten the damned car. She had driven that afternoon while Terry-Sue had all but crawled on top of David in the front seat of his car.

Reva was with them that day. She was in Spencer's class, but she'd become part of the gang because of her brother. She was in school due to the same strange magic that had gotten David in, the same "scholarship." Sly denied that he was paying their tuition, but Spencer knew in her heart that he denied it only because he didn't want

David's hardworking grandfather to think that he couldn't do the best for his grandchildren on his own. Sly was great about that. He never needed accolades for doing what he thought was right.

And Reva was sweet, so everyone enjoyed having her around. She had a disposition like gold; she laughed at everyone's jokes. She was also an incredibly pretty girl, and the guys certainly appreciated that—not that any of them would consider touching her, or even cracking any of their adolescent jokes about her. Maybe David was being raised by a strange old Scottish grandfather, but he showed no lack of Cuban machismo where his sister was concerned. He watched over her like a hawk. But there was really no need, anyway. They were all friends. Just friends. Nobody was actually with anybody else.

Except for Terry-Sue, who was still climbing all over David once the cars were parked, the blankets laid out and the food baskets set up.

In her crimson bikini, lathered in suntan oil, Spencer was stretched out on one of the blankets, half in the sun, half out of it. She could feel her flesh turning hot, sticky. She could feel the heat beating down on her, then the coolness of the breeze whenever a stray cloud wandered over the sun and the pines that ringed the rock pit began to bow and sway. She pretended to be oblivious to anything but her lazy sunning. Her head was down, her back exposed, and she had an arm stretched carelessly over her eyes.

Not really.

She was watching.

Watching—and seething.

Terry-Sue was having the time of her life.

She was a cute girl with a cap of rich dark auburn hair. She was short, petite—with a chest that didn't quit. In fact, Spencer thought, just a little bit maliciously, that Terry-Sue was just one gigantic set of boobs. It wasn't that her bikini was any more daring than anyone else's, but...

It was just that she spilled out of the damned thing. All over. And she had her chest just about shoved beneath David's nose every other second.

A giggle, shrill, very feminine, crossed the air and seemed to rip right along Spencer's spine. "David!" Terry-Sue called out in laughing protest. He'd lifted her up, her hands on his shoulders, and he was about to dunk her again. He was laughing good-humoredly. None of the guys looked as good as David. One day they might. One day. But David had matured first. His shoulders were broad, he was deeply tanned—he even had hair on his chest. His stomach was rippled, hard and flat. They were all very nearly adults, but physically, David Delgado was there, and his appeal was both sensual and sexual. Spencer had always liked him; she'd thought he'd always liked her. She'd even helped him a few times with English grammar, a subject that came to her naturally.

And since they all had to take Spanish in school, she'd sweetly asked for help back. And gotten it. If anyone was going to get any closer to David, it should be her. He didn't spend all his time with their group; he had dated other girls, she knew. She had even spent a few nights staring at the ceiling, wondering what he did with other girls—no, women. David would go after women. He was almost two years older than she was, but girls matured faster, or so she had always been told.

Like Terry-Sue. She was definitely mature. She was so damned mature it looked like she might just topple forward with maturity at any second.

"They're just fooling around, you know," Spencer heard someone say. She moved her arm, startled. No one should have been able to realize that she'd been watching the horseplay in the water, but someone had. Reva. Still a little shy around them, and just a shade too darn intuitive.

"I don't know what you're talking about," Spencer said flatly. She stretched and sat up, yawning. She wasn't about to admit to Reva that she had been watching her brother. "Hand me a Coke, will you, please, Reva?" she asked, determined to coolly dismiss the subject.

Reva, on her knees on the blanket, reached into the cooler for a Coke. She might be shy, but she wasn't about to be so easily dismissed. "He really likes you, Spencer. He always has."

"Sure, we're friends. We like each other," Spencer said. She stood up restlessly. "Never mind the Coke. I'll just cool off in the water."

She could swim well, and she knew it. She could dive like an expert, as well—she should be able to, her mother had insisted on enough lessons. Now she was determined to use a little of what she knew how to do. Through training—and instinct. There was a small overhang that jutted out high over the water. A dive from there was dangerous, because there were jagged outcrops of rock surrounding very deep water. Maybe it wasn't such a great idea, since there were so many wrecks in the water.

But it was the only place where she could get any height. She strode up to the overhang with a lazy, long-legged stride. She wasn't stupid, and not only did she not want to die, she didn't want to wind up maimed or in pain, either, so she took a very careful look at the water as she got her bearings.

"Spencer Montgomery, what the hell do you think you're doing?" came a shout.

She was so startled that she almost took a misstep. It was David. He was still in the water.

And Terry-Sue still had her arms around him, her "assets" crushed to his chest.

"Diving!" she called irritably.

And before he could stop her, she took the plunge.

The water, cool and fresh, enveloped her, and she knifed downward at a fantastic speed. She just missed the edge of a crashed Valiant, then managed to reverse her direction and move toward the surface. She was almost there when she felt hands on her shoulders, wrenching her up.

David.

Well, that had been the idea, hadn't it? To attract his attention? She had it now.

Except that she didn't want it this way.

He was glaring at her, hair wet and slicked back, features harsh. "What the hell did you think you were doing, you little fool?"

"I knew what I was doing. I can swim, I can dive!"

"And you were being a snot-nosed little show-off!" he assured her. "You could have gotten yourself killed!"

"And if I had," she returned, humiliated, infuriated, "it would have been none of your goddamned business." For a moment she thought incredulously that he was about to slap her across the cheek right then and there, while they were treading water.

"You're right, Miss Montgomery. It's none of my damned business. But Sly would have been upset if something had happened to you, and I happen to care a whole lot about Sly. So if you have to show off, try not to do it in front of me. We all know you're just about perfect, Spencer. You don't have to prove it to anyone.'"

He let go of her, leaving her shaking. At least, with the water to hide her, no one could tell. Everyone was watching them from the banks of the pit, but, she thought gratefully, David hadn't shouted. His words hadn't been heard.

He was getting out of the water, all six feet plus of him, asking someone to toss him a towel. Spencer got out, too, chin high, determined to keep her dignity intact.

Danny came toward her, offering her a towel, a grin and a thumbs-up sign. "I wasn't worried," he teased softly. Like Reva, he had a disposition like gold and an encouraging grin for everyone. He could be very serious, though. Danny wanted to change the world. He had always been the idealist in their crowd. "I guess I know you too well."

He made her smile as she accepted the towel. "I'm not feeling much like a picnic anymore. I'm going to sneak away," she told him.

"I'd sneak away, too, except I don't want to go home," he admitted. He wrinkled his nose. "Mom's there with her bridge club discussing the charity auction."

She grinned. "I'm not going home. I'm going to Sly's. He's down in Key West, looking at an old place some eccentric intends to save. I'll have the house all to myself."

She wanted to be alone. To lick a few wounds. Danny seemed to understand. Danny always seemed to understand everything. She never got an argument from him.

She slipped away quietly.

Sly didn't live in a rich neighborhood, certainly not like the one her parents had chosen. His house was like his business—old. It was a testament to all that he did.

It was on one of the city's oldest golf courses, with nice—but not outrageous—houses surrounding it. It was what they called "Old Spanish," with lots of arches, balconies and a courtyard entrance, and another courtyard to the side, surrounding the pool, which was a fairly new addition. Sly liked golf, but he liked his privacy more.

Despite the air conditioner in her brand-new Jeep, Spencer arrived at the house feeling hot and sticky and cranky. She left the car in the driveway, brought in her grandfather's mail and set it on the Victorian buffet in the entry. Sly lived quietly, without live-in help. And he believed strongly in the work ethic, though he had told Spencer he agreed with her parents and was glad she hadn't taken a job through high school, because keeping her grades high was just too important. "Money can be lost, young lady," he used to tell her. "I had friends who lost everything in the Great Depression, but you know what? Even then, some of them were left with something—and that was an education. They had the know-how to pick their fannies back up out of the dirt and get going again." But he didn't mind letting her work a bit for him, house-sitting when he needed it, keeping an eye on his mail and bills when he wasn't there. She fed Tiger, his fat alley cat. The arrangement worked well for her. She loved his old place; she'd learned a lot about building from him, and she appreciated the craftsmanship of the place.

She climbed the stairs to the guest room and found one of her sleeveless summer dresses in the closet, and underwear in a drawer, and ducked down the hall to the main bath, where Sly had installed a whirlpool to add to the value of the home. She turned the water to hot and the jets up as high as they would go, then stripped off her bikini and sank in, hoping the warm water would ease away some of humiliation of her encounter with David. She sank down beneath the water, letting it soak her hair.

The next thing she knew, there were hands on her shoulders. She nearly inhaled the water, she was so frightened, but he jerked her out of the water too quickly. To her amazement she found herself staring at David Delgado, still damp, still in swim trunks, but unarguably right there with her.

"What the hell do you think you're doing now?" he demanded.

She stared at him, incredulous. "I was about to wash my hair!" she responded furiously.

"What?" He sounded stunned.

"What did you think I was doing?"

He looked taken aback. Abashed. Even embarrassed. "Damn it, Spencer, I knocked about twenty times. And when I came in and found you, you were underwater and you weren't coming up!"

"You thought I was trying to drown myself. Over you? Oh, my God! And you're supposed to be so wonderfully humble!" she seethed.

He sat back, balancing on his ankles. His teeth were clenched, his eyes narrowed. "You really are a piece of work, aren't you, Spencer Anne Montgomery?"

She didn't want to look at him, didn't want to feel or hear his contempt. She stared straight ahead, belatedly realizing that she was naked and feeling terribly vulnerable. She hugged her knees to her chest. "Since you think so little of me, David Delgado, I'd appreciate it if you would let yourself back out of my grandfather's house and leave."

He stood. He was going to leave, she realized. Just like that. He was walking away. Of course, it was what she wanted him to do. Wasn't it?

She stood up, wrenching a huge white towel from a nearby rack and winding it around herself. He was already out in the hallway, and she followed him. "Rich doesn't mean evil, you know!" She felt as if she were choking. She didn't know whether she wanted to hit him or to...

He turned around, staring at her. "I came to see if you were okay. You left so quickly, I was afraid you might have hurt yourself, and I know you would have been too proud to let anyone know."

She waited a second, trying to decide whether he was insulting her or offering her a strange compliment.

"I really did know what I was doing."

"It was dangerous, Spencer."

She exhaled. "Maybe. But just a little."

They stood there in the hallway then, staring at one another. Though Spencer could feel her wet flesh growing cold in the air-conditioning, she felt hot and flushed at the same time.

"Are you going back to the rock pit?" she asked him finally.

He shrugged. "I guess not. The party's probably broken up by now. Did you want to go back?"

"I guess not. I imagine everyone's gone off to get something to eat by now."

He grinned. "We were having a picnic."

"Yeah, but you know that crowd. No ice-cream sundaes on a picnic. Too many bugs."

"No doubt," he agreed. He paused again. "You want to try to find them?"

She kept staring at him, wishing she knew what to say. She didn't really want to do anything. She wanted him, his attention. No distractions.

No Terry-Sue.

She shook her head. "No. Umm, Sly's fridge is always full."

David nodded. "He's got a great pool out there, too."

"Yeah, he does. You've been in it, haven't you?" She didn't quite know David's relationship with her grandfather, but she knew he'd been to the house.

"I've never been swimming here," David said simply.

"Well, there's always now." She tried to say the words lightly.

"Look, if you wanted to be alone..." he began.

She shook her head. "No, really. Sly is gone for the weekend, so the place is mine. Go on out the side door. I'll just put my suit on and join you."

He shrugged and headed for the stairs. Spencer dived into the bathroom and plucked her bikini from the floor. She donned it in two seconds flat and went flying after David.

He was already in the water, swimming cleanly from one end of the pool to the other. She dived in after him, recklessly going straight for him. She caught his ankle, dragging him under just after he surfaced for a breath.

She jackknifed as far from him as she could while he came to the surface, sputtering, deep blue eyes glittering with laughter as they touched on her. "You do like to live dangerously, don't you, Miss Montgomery?" he asked her.

"It's the only way!" she called back. He kicked off the bottom, coming after her. Spencer let out a little shriek and started down the length of the pool. She was good, but he was stronger and caught up with her just as she reached the deep end. He let her get a breath, then dragged her down.

She would gladly have given up breathing altogether. His arms were around her, her body crushed flush against his. She could feel the muscles in his arms, the bones in his hips, the shape of his sex beneath his swim trunks. It was intoxicating. She'd never in her life felt anything like what she was feeling now. A strange, almost unbearable excitement.

They came to the surface together. He could stand where they were; she couldn't. His arms remained around her, and he was looking at her. It was different from his angry look or his amused look. The water reflected a strange light in his eyes. "Spencer," he said huskily. "You should—"

He was going to push her away. She couldn't let it happen.

She smiled, pressing closer and parting her lips just slightly, almost whispering against his.

He groaned, and then his lips touched hers. They were incredibly hot, hungry. They brought a tidal wave of sensation. She had never felt so flushed, nor so very sure of what she wanted. She felt his tongue press into her mouth, then all but devour it. The world faded away as they kissed. It came back when she felt his hand covering her breast, holding it, feeling the weight and texture, his thumb rubbing over her nipple through the thin material of her bikini top. Something hot pulsed through her body, centering between her thighs. She had never felt so wonderful, nor could she remember ever wanting anything so badly, even though she wasn't exactly sure what it was she wanted. Him. More and more of him. Touching her. Making her feel this wonder.

He broke the kiss, still holding her. "Oh, God, Spencer, I can't..."

She didn't want to hear it. "David..."

He pushed her away, swimming hard for the edge of the pool, then jumping from the water to the deck. Spencer followed him, feeling a flood of brilliant red embarrassment rush to her face. Well, that was it. She had practically thrown herself at him, and he was walking away.

She leaped from the pool, completely humiliated again—and crushed. She almost turned away to run up the stairs and throw herself on the guest bed to cry herself into oblivion. But she didn't back away from things. And she was mad enough to have it out then and there.

"What is it, Delgado?" she demanded, keeping her voice as low and scornful as she could, her hands on her hips, her head tossed back. "I don't come with equipment big enough to rival Terry-Sue's?"

He'd been walking away, but that stopped him. He turned to her, dripping wet, his hands on his hips, the length of the pool between them. Then he started walking to her. "You know Spencer, I'm trying to remember that you're younger than I am. That you're just a naive little rich kid trying to get her own way."

"How dare you say such a thing to me? I've never acted like that!"

"The hell you haven't! You put your nose in the air every time your back is against a wall."

"I *fight* any time my back is against a wall."

"You're Sly's granddaughter!" he lashed up harshly.

"You're afraid of my grandfather!" she said incredulously.

He took two menacing steps toward her, but she held her ground. "I'm not afraid of anybody, Spencer. I like Sly. I like him a hell of a lot."

"He's a good man," she said coolly. "A kind one. Kind to refugees."

It was a low blow, but she wasn't able to stop herself.

And it had an effect on him. She could see his pulse beating furiously in his throat as he took the last few steps toward her. She was almost five foot eight, but David could stare down at her, and he did, so close that he was almost touching her, but not quite.

"What is it, Spencer? What do you want? *¿Que tu quieres?*" Then his hands were on her shoulders again, forcing her to back away. "You want something different from the other light-skinned *gringa* girls, don't you? You think I'll give you something hotter? Something better? Fine, let's go. There's the floor. Is that what you want?"

"Stop it!" she shouted at him, shaking, longing to shove him but suddenly afraid to. She wasn't quite sure what she had let loose. She hadn't known that he was aware that their folks talked about him sometimes, that they hadn't quite accepted the fact that Miami was becoming an international city. She'd never imagined that he might be sensitive about it, not David Delgado.

"Stop it! Damn you!" she snapped. "It's nothing to be ashamed—"

"Ashamed!" he almost roared at her. He swore. In Spanish. She wasn't sure exactly what he called her, but she got the general impression. "I'm not ashamed," he told her. "The only time I even feel the least bit embarrassed is when I stop myself from telling your high-and-mighty friends what bigoted asses they are! Tell me, Spencer, what kind of a game is this? Do you want to grow up and be able to whisper to your bridge club that you were intimate with a Hispanic once upon a time? What the hell do you want? Have all the rest of them *fucked* except for you?''

''I really don't know what anyone else has done,'' she told him. ''And I don't care. I care about you,'' she whispered flatly. ''I've always cared about you, and I wanted you—I wanted to make love with you—for that reason, and that reason alone.''

He stared at her, opened his mouth, then closed it. Then suddenly he was holding her again, crushing her in his arms. She had never felt so cherished.

''Oh, God, Spencer!'' he whispered. ''Oh, God, I feel like an idiot.''

''If you don't care about me . . .''

''Don't care about you? You fool. I've thought you were the most perfect thing in the world since I first set eyes on you.''

''Really?'' she breathed. She leaned against him and wound her arms around his neck, breathing in the scent of him. She was so giddy she was afraid she would fall. She leaned back instead, holding on to him as hard as she could. She raised herself on her toes and kissed his lips, moving even closer against him, if that was humanly possible. She teased his earlobe with a flick of her tongue, kissed his throat, his shoulder. She did things she'd only seen in the movies or heard whispered about by the other girls.

He let out a groan. ''Spencer, if you don't mean this, it's time to stop.''

''I mean it,'' she told him solemnly.

He stared at her, waiting, his pulse still throbbing at his throat. Then he picked her up, swept her from where she stood and into his arms. ''A bed?'' he queried.

"The guest room. Upstairs," she told him. She was a little bit embarrassed again. Afraid to breathe. Afraid to take her eyes away from his. She clung to him as he started up the stairs.

When they entered the guest room she thought the light was just right. It wasn't night, but the sun had fallen. He laid her down on the bed in a field of shadows. She heard the soft thud of his damp trunks as they hit the hardwood floor. She felt his hands on her again, tugging the string of the bikini top, easing the pants off her bottom. Then they were both naked. She felt herself shivering, though she wasn't cold. She wasn't even frightened, really. She was just afraid that she wouldn't please him, that she wouldn't prove to be everything he wanted.

His flesh was against hers. Warm, wonderful. He was touching her all over. It was so intimate it was almost unbearable, and so wonderful, because it was him. She could accutely register each and every different sensation, the rough hair of his legs against her own, the warmth of his breath touching her, the texture of the hair at his nape, where her fingers raked it. He'd been chewing gum; he tasted of spearmint. His weight was settled between her thighs, and she was so keenly aware of his sex that it was a form of anguish.

He went slowly. Kissing her lips. Making her feel the longing again, the excitement, the explosiveness.

"You've done this," she whispered.

He hesitated for a minute. "Yes."

She hoped it wasn't with Terry-Sue.

"Want to stop?" he asked.

"No!"

A minute later she almost wished she'd said yes. Sex had been made out to be such an incredible, ecstatic thing. She was supposed to be in paradise. She wanted to be shot.

"Spencer?"

She couldn't speak; she simply clung to him as things became bearable. Because it was David. When it was all over it was wonderful in a different way. Wonderful because he had become so impassioned, so excited, because she had felt him reach some incredible plateau. He was drenched; he had come into her like liquid fire, and then held her as if she were the most precious thing in the entire world. And they had lain there together while the night fell and the shadows deepened. She thought he'd fallen asleep, but she didn't dare. She had to be in her own house before eleven.

But he hadn't fallen asleep. He was suddenly leaning over her, a slight smile curving his lips. "Well?"

"Well what?"

"What was it like?" he asked.

"It was..."

"Awful?" he suggested.

"No!" She felt his amused stare; he knew.

"It was..." she tried again, but he laughed.

"Well, I don't suppose the first time has to actually be awful, but it's usually not great. Now the second time is supposed to be great," he said.

Just his voice, that husky tone, made excitement stir inside her once again. She felt breathless even before his lips touched hers, before his fingers played over her breasts, roamed downward, teased where both the fire and the pain had burned. He kissed her lips, then moved down her throat. He took the tip of her breast in his mouth, teasing it with his teeth and tongue. The excitement lapped higher and higher. He kissed her belly, her inner thigh. Higher. She almost screamed in protest, but then he was hovering over her. She didn't quite have the nerve to touch him *there* yet, but it didn't matter. He was lowering himself over her, into her. Kissing her mouth again, his tongue playing with hers while his body penetrated hers a second time. It was every incredible, sensual, erotic, forbidden wonder she had ever heard that it could be, the magic shared by those who knew. She climaxed with a surge of passion that amazed her, and even then she thought she'd never known such happiness. Such intimate, binding pleasure. She'd shared it with David, found it with him. And still she lay in his arms, bathed in a soft sheen of perspiration, feeling the crisp hair on his legs brush against the softness of her own, the sheets a tangle around them. . . .

She bolted awake, feeling as if she almost reached the ceiling above her head as the alarm let out a shattering screech. The sheets were in a tangle, as if she had tossed and turned through the night. Her pillow lay on the floor.

It was morning. Six o'clock. Time to get ready for another workday.

She stared across the bed, to where Danny should have been lying. Except that Danny had been dead for more than a year now. A long time.

Not nearly long enough for her to be dreaming about her first encounter with his best friend. Even if it *had* occurred long, long before her marriage.

She stood up, stripping off her nightgown, heading for the shower and swearing beneath her breath.

"Damn you, David Delgado. Damn you. And damn you, too, Sly, you old fox!"

The water was pouring down on her. She could dimly hear the phone ringing and decided to let the machine pick it up.

It did. She heard her own voice, then the voice that had plagued her sleep, her dreams, her nightmares. David.

"Trey Delia is in the county jail, being questioned. He asked to see me. If you promise to be a good girl, you can come with me. But, hell, if you're not there—"

She didn't bother with a towel. She simply came flying out of the shower, heedless of what she was doing to her hardwood floor and carpets. She wrenched the receiver from the cradle. "What time are you going?"

"I can be by for you at eight-thirty. If—"

"Yeah, yeah, I plan on being an angel."

She thought she heard a doubtful chuckle. "I mean it, Spencer. You have to keep quiet and let me do the talking."

"You really are a chauvinist."

"Call it chauvinism, Cuban machismo, anything you want. Just keep quiet. Got it?"

She hesitated for a second. Her "Got it!" was only a little bit stiff.

"And Spencer?"

"What?"

"Have some decent coffee ready, huh?"

"Coffee? Decent coffee?" she sputtered.

But he had already hung up. And she didn't know whether he had spoken in jest or out of his Cuban machismo, or maybe with just a little bit of both.

It didn't matter. He was gone. She had no recourse left but to slam the receiver down. It didn't do much good, but it did make her feel a little better.

Trey Delia. So last night *had* done something. A suspect was in jail, maybe not for Danny's death, but they still might be able to learn something.

She finished showering and got dressed, and she was humming with pleasure when she went downstairs. She was halfway through making morning coffee when she stopped suddenly, her tone stopping just as if the power had gone dry. She always made morning coffee.

But, she realized, she had made a full pot. Without even thinking about it. And she hadn't done that since...

In well over a year.

She plugged the pot in.

"And it's damned decent coffee at that!" she said aloud, then turned away.

The doorbell was already ringing.

5

Sly Montgomery read about the vandalism in the cemetery that morning.

He was in the courtyard by the pool, at a old tile table beneath the palms, sipping his coffee—decaf, these days—and looking at the front page.

Cult leader Trey Delia hadn't been among the grave robbers, but one of the men who'd been caught—an illegal alien from Port au Prince—became hysterical under interogation and implicated Delia in just about everything from robbery to murder to vampirism. The story about the man's capture was an unusual one. A private investigator had happened to be in the cemetery, along with an unknown female assistant.

Unknown, my royal rump! Sly thought, shaking his head.

He set the paper down and stared at the pool. He still loved to see the sun hovering over water. He liked it at the pool at his house, and he liked it by the bay, watching the deeper colors there, the cobalts, the greens, the deep, deep azures. Maybe that was partially what had kept him here all these years, when some said the city was going to trash. It was evolving, that was all. When you got to be over ninety, you knew a lot. You'd seen a lot. Too much, most of the time. He'd seen this place go from being just about nothing but swamp to a city capable of eclipsing many others the world over.

He looked at his hands. They were shaking. Well, they had a right to shake. They were ninety-something years old. Ninety-four this year, wasn't it? It seemed incredible the way he went on, and bless God, stayed healthy, his mind intact. But ninety-four years was a long time to live. He'd lost Lucy long ago. But before that they'd built their dreams together. Just like he'd helped build some of the great old houses here, right out of the swamp and coral and muck. He'd always wanted kids. He would have had ten if he could have, but there had just been Joe. Well, that was God's will. Then Joe had married his little posh prom queen out of Newport, and one baby had been more than Mary Louise Tierney Montgomery could handle.

But Spencer was worth a million grandkids. From the start, she had belonged more to him than she'd ever belonged to either Mary Louise or Joe. She loved the old, cherished it. She liked to work with her hands, to build. She liked history—young as it might be here—and when she was just five, she could rattle off the names of most of the major architects and builders who had put South Florida together. She was blessed with intelligence and a nature that was both sweet and aggressive. Usually, when she wanted something, she went for it with a smile on her face and both hands open. Danny Huntington had been a fine husband for her, too, though Sly hadn't imagined the two of them together when they'd been kids.

Sly had been watching them all for years now; other than his work, the kids had been his life. He'd watched them struggle to learn their values, struggle to grow. He'd seen them mature from stumbling adolescents into assured adults.

He'd seen Danny die, and it had been one hell of a tragedy, but that was the past.

Spencer was the present. And the future. She was all that really mattered in life to him, after all these years of learning just what counted and what didn't.

"And I wish you were still little enough to take a switch to, young lady!" he muttered aloud.

Well, that was the hell of it. Spencer was a grown-up. He couldn't take a switch to her. He couldn't insist that she move in with him for a while. He couldn't force sense into her, couldn't tell her that it would be better for her to live a full life rather than discover who had killed Danny if it meant dying herself.

He read the article again. He would talk to David Delgado later, but for the moment, he wanted to read between the lines again. He did. And decided maybe it wouldn't matter if he talked to David later or not. He could pretty much tell the story.

Spencer had somehow gotten wind that the grave-robbing ghouls might be coming to Danny's cemetery. She'd gone, and David had been on the job. Just like he'd promised, however grudgingly. He hadn't wanted to follow Spencer, and Sly was no fool; he knew why. Some things just didn't go away when you grew up. You could get old, you could think yourself past the hurts and the desires that had plagued you when you were young, but they were still there, lurking in the heart. No, you just didn't get past some things, no matter what.

Maybe that was bad. And maybe that was good. Maybe it meant that whether he liked it or not, David would stick to Spencer like glue.

The phone started ringing. Sly rose to answer it, certain that he knew who was calling.

* * *

Jerry Fried, Danny Huntington's last partner in the homicide division, sat down at his desk and stared at the memo in front of him. At fifty-five, he was getting too old for this shit. He ran his fingers through his cap of snow-white hair and hunched over, thinking he needed to exercise more. Walk, at least. He still cut a fairly decent figure in and out of uniform, but it seemed to get harder and harder. His paunch was threatening to protrude over his belt.

He hadn't been on duty last night; he hadn't heard a thing about the graveyard arrest until he'd come in this morning. Now everyone was talking about it. And there was this damned memo on his desk from the lieutenant.

So they had Delia in custody now. And Danny's widow had something to do with it. Tall, slim, elegant, Mrs. Huntington had managed to get herself into the right cemetery when the police hadn't been able to add up two and two and get four. Why couldn't she believe that the police always took care of their own? And why couldn't she just stay out of all this? Keep out of harm's way? If she kept messing where she shouldn't be, there was going to be trouble. Big trouble. And she was going to be in danger.

Danny Huntington... He'd been dead more than a year now, but he still seemed to haunt Jerry's every waking moment. Danny had been so damned popular. The rich boy, playing cop. Because he wanted to know the streets, real life. Everyone had liked Danny. Everyone. The politicians. The police brass. The guys on the force. The frigging crooks had even liked Danny. And Danny had known things he hadn't thought to share with his own partner!

Jerry groaned and put his head down on his desk, spilling his morning coffee as he did.

He sat up, swearing at Danny's widow once again. Danny Huntington just couldn't seem to stay buried.

Cecily Monteith lounged in the sitting room adjacent to her bedroom, sipping the coffee that Maria, her maid, had just set on the table along with her toast—done well, but not burned, just touched with margarine, not butter, the crusts carefully trimmed off—and read the paper with a growing sense of dread and unease.

Jared, in a tailored shirt, stood in the doorway, slipping a tie around his neck, struggling with the knot, then scowling and swearing profusely. "You'd think Sly Montgomery would come to terms with the modern world. It's hot enough to fry eggs on the sidewalk today. Everyone has gone casual, but that old man still dresses up for meetings as if he were going to a presidential dinner."

Cecily waved a hand in the air, dismissing his complaint. "You've got to read this."

Jared stepped forward, sweeping the paper from her lap. He arched a brow at her, scowling again as he read the headline.

"How long has your cousin been back in town? A few months?" Cecily said consideringly. "Let's see, in that time she's managed to completely turn the old man around to her way of seeing things, even though you were his number-one idea man all that time she was up in Newport. The second she walks in, you're second fiddle. And now this!" Cecily stood, snatching the paper out of his hands. "You didn't know what she was up to? Hanging on to David like a leech? She won't stop, Jared. She'll be into everything."

Jared snatched the paper back, staring at her. "You more worried about Spencer delving into things—or the fact that she's running around with David Delgado?"

"I don't know what you're talking about," Cecily said coolly.

Jared shrugged, looking her up and down, then smiled slowly, just the slightest hint of malice in his gaze. "Let's see, way back when, you and Terry-Sue and all the sweet young things just coming to life were all after David. Maybe he had balls of gold or something, I don't know, and I came in second fiddle. Then—thank the Lord!—he up and joined the army, then went to school in England. Not that I ever had anything personal against David. It just seemed that whenever he was around, the rest of us paled in comparison. We didn't have that forbidden allure, that color, something. Even Danny, Mr. Save-the-World Huntington. Well, Cecily, I know you've been to David's office several times since he left the force and opened up on his own. I know you've made damned sure his name was on every invitation list you've had a say in, and I watched you trying to console him—and begging to be consoled in turn—at Danny's funeral." He hesitated a second while she stared at him in shock. "Stupid idiot," he continued softly. "He'll never have an affair with you."

"Jared, how dare you imply that I'm trying to have an affair with him?" She pouted at him angrily.

Jared shrugged. Maybe she was right. They'd had their ups and downs. Sometimes they argued like kids, but then, they'd dated since they were kids and had really still been kids when they'd gotten married. Now they had two kids of their own. A boy and a girl. They had a great house in Cocoplum; he drove a Ferrari, and she carted the kids around in a brand new Mercedes-Benz. It was a good life. He liked living it.

He felt a trickle of sweat forming beneath his collar. Yeah, he liked living it. And he was scared. Spencer had a bee in her bonnet over Danny. And Spencer wouldn't stop until she got what she wanted.

"What makes you think David would never have an affair with me?" Cecily suddenly demanded, her eyes darting over his shoulder to the mirror behind him. No matter what else she was worried about, Cecily was always concerned about her appearance, as well. He grinned again. She was always worried about weight and wrinkles. She moaned constantly about the time she'd spent in the sun as a stupid kid. But her obsession did have its merits. Two kids and thirteen years of marriage, and Cecily still looked great. She dieted like a maniac, went on a binge now and then, and did penance for it with sorrow and fervor at a very expensive spa.

All thanks to Spencer.

Cecily seemed to forget on occasion that Sly wasn't Jared's grandfather. She forgot that Jared's now long-deceased mother had been Spencer's mother's sister, and though his father was still alive and kicking and sometimes worked for Sly, it was Spencer's determination to make Jared a part of things that kept them in cars and not just comfortable but lush housing. It was also true, though, that Jared had worked for Sly since he'd finished the Harvard education that Sly had helped him get. And it was also true that he'd thought he deserved more than he got at times. And now Spencer was making him nervous as hell.

Cecily had forgotten their conversation for the moment. As she gazed over his shoulder, she drew her hands down over the satin nightgown she was wearing, trying to see whether there might be a bit of a bulge. "Jared, why wouldn't someone want to have an affair with me?"

He sighed, feeling a sudden surge of affection for her. "I didn't say *someone,* Cecily. I said *David* wouldn't have an affair with you. I don't know whether he'd want to or not. I just know he *wouldn't.* You're married to me. Things like that matter to David."

"Well, Spencer was married to Danny!" Cecily said, almost belligerently.

"Yeah, and he wouldn't have slept with Spencer, either," Jared said. He'd picked up the paper again and was studying the article once more.

"I just can't believe she was running around a stupid cemetery. At night!" Cecily shuddered. "Gruesome. And it was Spencer. It had to have been. She's not going to let this go."

"Damn it, Cecily, quit worrying about Spencer."

"Someone has to worry about her!"

"I can take care of business—and Spencer—myself, Cecily."

It wasn't true, Cecily thought. No one could take care of Spencer. Not when she was determined on a course of action. Cecily staightened the half-knotted tie around his neck. Jared could be such a fool at times. She wondered now if she didn't love him the same way she loved William and Ashley. As if he were a child. He looked the part of an entrepreneur just fine, she thought with a certain satisfaction. He had all his hair, without a wisp of gray setting in. He had a home gym and stayed in shape. And though he played Mr. Executive at the office, he would be a liar if he said that he didn't like the actual work itself. The happiest any of those three fools—Sly, Spencer and Jared—seemed to be was when they were in the midst of a cloud of sawdust, restoring some old place by hand, or poring over old books and records, trying to discover just when and where some fabulous architectural piece had been made. It was good for Jared, though. Kept him fit.

"Don't look at me like that!" he snapped suddenly. "I *can* deal with Spencer. She's my cousin."

"Your blood," Cecily agreed with a smile. She made a face at him. "Don't forget. She's always been my best friend. Auntie Spence to the kids."

"Cecily, drop it."

He was irritated. She kind of liked him irritated. Kept things lively.

"Jared—"

She broke off because the phone started ringing. He stared at her for a minute. The machine clicked on.

"Jared, pick up. It's your father. I know you haven't left the house yet. Have you seen the newspaper?"

Jared picked up the receiver with a sigh. "Yeah, Dad. I've seen it. Spencer is trying to find out who killed Danny. It's not a big surprise, really, do you think?" he asked wearily.

"Don't be flippant with me, boy."

"Dad, just leave Spencer alone, all right?"

"You keep an eye on things!"

"Yeah, Dad."

"And bring the kids for supper soon. I miss them."

"All right, Dad. Maybe we can do some fishing from your dock."

"Right. You keep an eye on things, now!"

Jared hung up thoughtfully. He was getting one hell of a headache. Between his wife and his father...

You'd think one of *them* had knocked off poor Danny.

He turned around. Cecily was staring at him. She looked good this morning. She wore her hair short and very blond. Her eyes were her best feature. They were huge and amber. Not brown. Real amber. They were glittering now.

"You handled him well," she said.

He grinned. "You're getting turned on because I handled my father well?" he queried dubiously.

She shrugged. "Maybe." She came close and kissed him, teasing his earlobe with the tip of her tongue, licking down the side of his face with a hot rush of breath. "You can bet Spencer's going to be in to work late today."

"Umm." He backed away long enough to meet her eyes. "So that's it! You're thinking about Spencer maybe taking up with David again."

"I am not!"

"Yes, you are. You're thinking about David Delgado. Maybe about trying to have an affair. Maybe not an affair. Just one afternoon with a muscle-bound refugee who always turned you on."

"Jared, you're being disgusting."

"You'd love it if I were a hell of a lot more disgusting," he said lightly. When she started to protest, he said, "Hey, Cecily, this is me, remember? And I don't care. I don't give a damn about your fantasies because they just make it all the better for me." Her eyes were still on his, still amber and just a little glazed. He reached for her hand to lead her from the sitting room to the bedroom. It was up-to-the-minute plush. The peach carpet was soft on the toes, and the bed was big, silk covered and strewn with pillows.

But Cecily balked, moving close to him again. "Uh-uh. Here."

"Marie could come in."

"Then we'd shock the pants right off of her."

"You are an exhibitionist."

She was tugging at his belt. He started to help her. "No, no, not all the way off. You can't be *that* late. Let's just be hard and fast and deep and dirty."

He dragged his fingers through her perfect blond hair. The harder and faster the better. He dragged up her satin gown, throwing toast and coffee from the table so he could lower her onto it, and onto his own engorged sex at the same time. Her hands slid beneath his waistband, cradling his buttocks, drawing him tightly to her.

"I bet you'd like it if Marie walked in," he told her.

"Maybe."

"I bet you'd like it even better if David Delgado came in right now."

He got his answer. She came the instant the words were out of his mouth, and she held on to him, limp, as he finished himself.

A few minutes later he slipped on his jacket. Cecily was sitting at the table again, reading the paper and ignoring the toast and coffee on the floor.

And they were supposed to have such a great marriage, he thought irritatedly.

"Be careful with Spencer!" she warned as he was about to leave.

He sighed. "You know, Cecily, she *is* my cousin. I've known her all my life, and I know how to be careful with her. And you know something else? I really love her. In all the right ways, Cecily. Platonic ways."

She stared at him with surprise for a moment, then nodded and smiled. "Yeah, I understand."

He kissed her forehead and started out.

Maybe his marriage wasn't so bad after all.

* * *

In a penthouse on South Beach, someone else was reading the morning paper.

Ricky Garcia stared at the front page, rubbed his cheek and swore in his native Spanish. *¡Cono!* The damned fool woman!

He set the paper down, stood up and stretched, staring out the picture windows that gave him a bird's-eye view of so much that was beautiful about his adopted home. The bay shimmered beneath the rising sun, stretching out in colors that were at once both vivid and tranquil, hypnotic to behold. Soft puffs of clouds moved very slowly across the horizon. Boats lined the docks below him like a flock of birds, while others moved across the deep blue and green waters, stirring the imagination. He loved sailing. Loved the breeze. Loved salt air on his face...

He'd come here with nothing. Nothing. Just the shirt on his back, and that had been ripped. And he'd looked at everything there was to be had here. But not by petty thievery. No, the price to be paid for what you could gain by such a silly crime was too high.

Ricky had known from the beginning that he needed to play on people's desires, on their fantasies, their needs. He'd started with the girls. All they had known was how to stand on the streets. He'd known how to make them look good standing there. He'd added class to the action. Then, with a little bit of capital, he'd gotten into bookmaking and gambling. He didn't like drugs; he wouldn't dream of taking them himself. But drugs were a part of his world, the underworld, and there was money to be made from them. They were also a damned good way to keep firm control of the people working beneath him.

One way...

Another was that he wasn't the least bit averse to violence. Nowadays his underlings usually took care of such matters for him. Yet everyone knew that if something needed to be taken care of, Ricky could take care of it himself without blinking an eye. If he had to. It was a good thing. It was important. He kept his people and his world under control.

And now... this.

David Delgado and a woman in the cemetery. Delia being brought in for questioning. The whole thing would be ripped open again. They would be hounding him again, the cops. Day and night, day and night.

He turned away from his sweeping windows with their million-dollar view and walked across the room to a black lacquered desk, opening the top drawer. He rifled through the papers there until he came to a picture.

Danny Huntington at a policemen's benefit ball. With his wife. Spencer. In heels she was at least five feet ten or eleven. Her hair was swept up; her neck was long. She wore a shoulderless cocktail dress with a flared skirt in royal blue. Even in the picture, it caught the color of her eyes. She was flawless. Regal.

Spencer Huntington.

He slammed the drawer shut, swearing in Spanish again.

Maybe he would just have to have a little chat with Spencer Huntington.

Someone needed to tell her to keep her nose out of other people's business. And maybe he was just the man for the job.

6

David helped himself to coffee just after Spencer opened the door. He knew his way to the kitchen and walked past her to reach it. He knew where the mugs were kept, as well, and didn't mind helping himself. She followed him in, watching, waiting, while he took a first sip.

"Decent?" she inquired after a moment.

He didn't actually answer her question. "I can cook a little, but I've never managed to make coffee come out right."

"American or Cuban?"

"Either." Even while he responded to her question, his eyes were moving critically up and down the length of her. "Trey Delia asked his attorney to reach me," he said. "We'll be going right into the jail. Who knows who we'll meet up with. A few drunk drivers, perhaps a couple of vagrants—and some murderers, rapists and thieves. Not to mention Delia himself, and we're not quite sure what he is at all. Is that all you've got to wear?"

Spencer looked at her clothing. She was wearing a black rayon business suit with a tailored peach blouse. She stared at David.

"Spencer..." He paused, then set his mug down with a bang. "That—that creation hugs every inch of you." She was staring at him now.

"It's just a business suit."

"It's too erotic for the jail."

"Erotic?"

"It fits like a a second skin and ends above the knee. How about jeans and a sweatshirt?"

"I'd die of the heat before anyone could do me in."

"Yes, but you'd go quickly, without being tortured."

Spencer let out a cry of frustration but whirled, left the kitchen and headed for the stairs. When she reached the top, she realized that David had followed her. He was standing in the marble entryway at the foot of the stairs, observing the living room.

He'd been in her house often enough, she thought. Danny had insisted on it, though she'd managed to have something to do most of those times.

She couldn't help wondering what he saw when he looked at the place now. Did it look cold to him? she wondered. Was he looking around and judging the way rich girls grew up?

His eyes touched hers suddenly, and he scowled. "Spencer, I haven't got all day."

"You should. Aren't you supposed to be following me? Sly's orders?"

"I don't take orders."

"Not even from Sly?"

"Not even from Sly."

"Good, then you can quit following me!"

"I agreed to accept the job he offered me. I took a check from him. Like I told you, Spencer, if you've got a problem with Sly, take it up with him."

"I intend to."

"And if you want to talk to Trey Delia, get your butt in gear."

She gritted her teeth, staring at him, dying to tell him what he could do with himself. But she had a chance to talk to Trey Delia, and she wasn't going to blow it by getting into an argument with David.

"I'll be two seconds," she said icily.

She came down a bit more than two seconds later in jeans and a short-sleeved cotton blouse. He didn't look much happier.

"Don't you own any loose clothing?"

"These are not too tight!" she said indignantly.

He sighed with exasperation. "All right. I guess you'll do."

Despite having spent virtually her entire life in the area, Spencer had always managed to avoid the Dade County Jail.

She was glad she had.

There was something spooky about a facility that housed so many of the down-and-out, the pathetic—and the vicious. As they reached the perimeter, Spencer saw her first inmates. They were behind an electrified fence in an exercise yard. She felt the eyes of some of them on her. David had been right. They assessed her, assigned her a money value, just about counted the change in her handbag. Maybe they did more. Stripped her, raped her and cut her to ribbons—throat first.

When she and David entered the building, a scent hung in the air, a miasma of unwashed bodies, urine and hopelessness.

She felt the clammy air moving around her while David showed his identification to a guard, who arranged to have Trey Delia brought to a private interview room to see them.

A man passed by, handcuffed, between two guards. He was in a gray Armani suit. He noticed her with David but was intent on hollering belligerently at his guards. "You gotta get me out of here, quick! Do you know who I am?

Hey, you think you're going to put me in here with the human refuse? Get me out of here before something happens to me. I'll sue the shit out of you assholes if you don't get me out of here!''

The guards ignored him and kept walking, their prisoner between them. "Drunk driver," the desk officer told David with a shrug. "The guy's an attorney himself. He knows the rules. He probably will get himself off—and because of him an eight-year-old girl is in the hospital right now, fighting for her life! But you know the story. Here's Caplan," he said, indicating another uniformed guard. "He'll take you to meet with Delia," he said. "You think Armani Joe there was howling, you should have heard the uproar when we had Delia in a communal cell."

David arched a brow. "Thanks for your help," he told the man and took Spencer's arm firmly as they followed Caplan down a corridor to one of the small rooms where prisoners usually met with their families and attorneys.

Caplan pushed open a door. "Hey, Delia! Your visitors are here."

Spencer stared at the man standing behind the room's one piece of furniture, a plain wooden desk. She'd never seen anyone quite like him.

He was of mixed heritage, and his appearance gave evidence of every one of them. His skin wasn't black, or even brown, but coffee-colored. His eyes were a strange, almost glowing yellow green. He wore Rastafarian dreadlocks, something that looked like an old seventies Nehru jacket and faded denim jeans. Crosses in gold and silver and wood hung around his neck, along with what looked like a few chicken's feet. When he smiled at her, his teeth were capped with gold. "Hey, mon! Boss!" he said to David. "You brought the lady along. I'm glad. I wanted to talk to her."

The door started to close behind Spencer and David. "I'll be right outside," the guard said. "Knock when you're ready to leave."

Spencer had thought she wanted the truth about Danny more than anything in the world. Now she wasn't so sure. She had told herself that she wasn't going to cling to David in the effort, but something like primal fear was gripping her now that she was shut in this tiny room with a man who was suspected of doing who knew what with human body parts. She hesitated, but David didn't seem to notice. He had his hands on her shoulders, watching Delia.

And Delia was staring straight at Spencer.

The world seemed to dim for a minute. She heard two sets of footsteps somewhere outside, in a hallway that led past the holding cells. One set was heavy; the other was clicking. One set belonged to a man, the other to a woman. She could dimly hear their speech, hear the man's deeper voice, the woman's soft but crisp one. Spencer realized that the woman was an attorney, and that she was arguing with the man. She must have been young and attractive, because Spencer could hear catcalls and whistles, too.

"Cut it out, fellows, cut it out!" the woman called. Laughter—and a few foul suggestions—followed. Spencer gritted her teeth. From the sound of her voice, the woman was probably young, younger than Spencer. Making her way in this rugged, ragged, filthy world. She seemed to know her way around it. Cecily would have called her a woman with balls. Spencer decided that she needed to work on acquiring a few herself.

Delia was grinning. The sounds from the corridor faded away.

"So you are Spencer," Delia said, drawing out the two syllables of her name. He had a light but masculine voice, almost melodic. Despite her fear and Delia's strange appearance, she could feel the hypnotic appeal of the man. He was fastidious, she noticed. Even here, his nails were clean and long, and his face seemed scrubbed. He looked a hell of a lot better than the man in the Armani suit.

But the way he said her name...

"I would offer you something...café con leche?... tea?...but alas, look where we meet. I would have liked to meet you at my home. Not yours, eh? You would have been looking at your security system, thinking about buying a big dog, no?" He laughed softly. Then he looked from Spencer to David. "I'm glad that you came."

David shrugged. "You always agreed to see me when I asked."

Delia nodded. "Honor among thieves! Well, you see, they do not understand me." He looked at Spencer again. "I knew your husband well, Mrs. Huntington. He was constantly on my back. He did not quite understand, either. But I liked him. I didn't mind the investigation. He asked questions that mattered. I think that I will now be locked away for some time, and I understand it was your fault."

Spencer gasped. David's hands tightened on her shoulders.

"Listen, Delia," David began. "I don't know what you heard, but—"

Delia's laughter, surprisingly light and amused, interrupted him. "I do not blame Spencer Huntington. She is looking for answers, and you have not found them. She is the one who listens to the truth, because she is the one who wants to hear it. I want you both to know this—I didn't kill Danny Huntington. There are things which your very white world calls crimes of which I *am* guilty, but I did not kill your husband. I have sought the spirit and the strength and soul of life. I have crushed human bone for meal, and I have drunk blood for the giving of life, but I did not kill this man. When I am locked away, they will try to make it seem that I was guilty, and they will pat Spencer on the head and try to assure her that her husband's murderer has been put away. I repeat, I am innocent of his blood, and I bear you no malice, Spencer." His smile deepened, with a slightly wicked curl. He glanced at David, his eyes still sparkling. "I am not angry with you, either, Delgado. Maybe you will speak well for me when I come to trial."

"Doubtful," David said matter-of-factly. "But I bear *you* no malice, either, Delia."

"Goodbye, Spencer," Delia said.

Spencer was surprised when she extended her hand to the man, still caught by the curious, green-gold light in his eyes. He was crazy, she thought. But not stupid. He calculated his every word; he was, in a way, extremely sane.

"Thank you for seeing me."

He smiled again. "I have long wanted to see you. Danny Huntington, he always wanted to go home to his Spencer. I pray for his soul. And for you."

David tapped on the door and called to the guard; in moments the door was open and they were out in the corridor again. In a few minutes they had left the jail behind, and Spencer was back in the passenger seat of David's Mustang. She refused to let David see her fingers shaking, so she kept them tightly laced in her lap. She stared straight ahead.

"Well?" David said, and she felt him watching her.

"Well what?"

"Did you believe him?"

She hesitated. She didn't want David laughing at her for being gullible or falling prey to a strange man's stranger magnetism. But then she blurted out the truth. "Yes."

To her surprise, David shrugged, eyes on the road as he guided the wheel. "Yeah, I believe him, too. He really did like Danny. He loved to get into long theological arguments with him. Danny was one well-educated cop, and along the way Delia managed to get himself into a few good schools, as well." He glanced at her. "What now? You want to go home? You want to go to work? You want to get something to eat?"

"I want to take a shower," she said, and shivered despite herself.

But he didn't laugh; he didn't even crack a smile. He didn't give her any speeches about some women being cut out for the realities of life, but not pampered little rich girls like her.

"Yeah, I kind of know how you feel. That place can really get to you."

Spencer tightened her lips, staring at the road. David would know. From both sides. He'd been behind bars once. Her mother had him put there.

She winced and said nothing, but she felt as tight as a bowstring. He didn't speak, either; they both knew they were thinking of the same occasion.

You can't go back and undo the past! she wanted to shout. It was something she knew far too well. They both knew it. There was nothing she could say about what had happened all those years ago. Nothing he could say, either.

She sat tensely and stared straight ahead. She simply wouldn't think about it.

It wasn't far from the downtown area to Spencer's house in the Grove. She left the car quickly and stood staring at David when he got out, too. "I'm all right," she said. "You don't—"

"We have to talk, Spencer," he said flatly.

Right, she reminded herself. Sly had hired him. David had taken Sly's money. He was on the job.

"Suit yourself, but I'm taking that shower," she said angrily, and turned and walked toward the house.

He was behind her as she twisted the key in the lock, and he caught the door when she would have let it fly in his face. She ignored him and started for the stairway.

"Spencer, you've got to realize that you can't run around doing stupid things like you did last night!" he yelled after her.

She paused, her hand on the railing, looking at him. "Stupid things? At least I got Delia arrested! That was more than the rest of you incredibly intelligent people managed to do in over a year."

She didn't want to hear his answer; she continued up the stairs.

He didn't intend to let her have the last word. She was sure he'd never been up these stairs before, but he followed her, right to her bathroom door.

"Spencer, you might have gotten yourself killed in that graveyard."

"But I didn't. I had the great and noble David Delgado there to save me, thanks to my grandfather's money."

"Spencer—"

"Do you mind?" she cried out furiously, stepping into the bathroom and slamming the door.

She heard him swearing, then sitting down on the foot of her bed to wait.

She turned on the water. Hard. Steaming. She stepped out of her jeans and shirt and underwear and tossed them on the floor. She stared at them for a moment, then picked up the lot and crammed them into the small trash basket in the bathroom, knowing that she would never wear any of them again. If David *had* said it, he would have been right. She wasn't cut out for such things. Such places. Her heart went out to the street people, but she hated the dope dealers and the brutal criminals who were trying to tear down the city she had loved all her life. She would do anything she could to set Danny to rest, but she didn't have to like doing it. She admired the young attorney who had dealt with the leering prisoners with such a cool demeanor. She applauded her. But she wasn't like her.

She stood beneath the streaming water, and she let it run and run and run.

She winced when she heard his fist slam against the bathroom door. It wasn't locked; but he didn't open it.

"Spencer! You can't get rid of me that way!" she heard David shouting.

She wrenched the water off in a fury, grabbed an oversize towel and wrapped it around her, then slammed open the bathroom door, totally unsure as to exactly why she was so angry.

He'd moved away from the door and was by the foot of the bed again. He'd worn jeans, and a tailored blue cotton shirt, open at the neck. She knew he was agitated, because she could see a telltale pulse ticking away at his throat. His eyes glittered, still appearing black as coal rather than blue. She stood in the doorway, the towel wrapped around her, still dripping. "Talk, talk, talk! What is it you want to talk about? You were the one who threw me bodily out of your office! Now you want to talk. Why? Am I suddenly making the lot of you—you and all of Danny's cop buddies—look like fools?"

"One more time, Spencer, try to get this. You almost got yourself killed!"

She walked toward him, eyes narrowed, a finger pointed straight at his nose. "Cut the macho crap, David! Danny was a guy, a tough guy, a carry-a-gun guy. And now he's dead. So—"

"All the more reason for you to get out of this and stay the hell out of it! Danny knew what he was up against. He joined the force and he took his chances. What is it with you, Spencer? You won't be happy unless you wind up dead, too?"

She shoved his chest, intending to walk around him to her closet. "Fuck you, David," she told him succinctly.

She started by him but felt his hand grip her shoulder, pulling her back with angry force. "No! Fuck you, Spencer!" he snapped in return.

And it was then that she lost her towel.

She'd never believed in people just falling into other people's arms. There was some kind of conscious thought involved in every deed performed by man. And it wasn't that she didn't know what she was doing. She did.

For a long moment they were dead silent. She felt the blood race to her cheeks and considered grabbing the wayward towel so she could hide behind it once again. But she felt the heat of David's gaze on her, and it was almost as if she was hypnotized, just as she'd been with Delia. It was as if David were touching her. Her breath seemed caught in her chest. There was something incredibly hot and erotic in that alone; if he touched her, she would melt.

He touched her. He was still angry, explosively so. She wondered if he knew exactly what he was doing.

He did. He knew, all right. Somewhere, distantly, in the back of his mind, David knew this was about one of the most stupid things he'd ever done. But he would be damned if he could stop it. He was suddenly staring at her and she was stark naked. And she was the same wild-haired, high-handed, blue-eyed, perfect little blonde he'd been asinine enough to fall in love with all those years ago. It didn't matter now. Touching her did.

And so he reached out, curled his fingers around her perfect nape, felt the silky softness of that perfect Anglo hair tangle around his fingers. He pulled her close. And he kissed her.

There could be no half measures with Spencer.

Danny Huntington's wife.

Widow.

For a few seconds those thoughts careened through his mind. Then they faded. Maybe his anger had brought him to this; maybe he'd been mad for over a decade. And maybe this would have happened no matter what. A force was there, an energy, a burning frustration, something that had to be appeased. He could strangle her or make love to her. Of course, she could pull away at any minute, shove a knee up into all that energy and frustrated heat....

But she didn't. She didn't really move at first; she was still while his lips moved passionately over hers, while his tongue forced its way between them, tasting and savoring her. Then suddenly he heard a little sound from her, a whimper. And then her fingers were moving into his hair, and all that nakedness was pressing against him while her lips moved hungrily against his own.

It was all over for Spencer Anne Montgomery. Screw everything that had ever come between them. Including Danny.

He didn't think he'd ever been so painfully hard in his life. He wasn't even really aware of where he was, of exactly what he was doing, what steps he was taking. She had always been tall, slim, light. In seconds he had her on the bed and his fly was open, his lips on hers again. His weight was wedged between her thighs.

Her mouth was sweet with the hickory taste of coffee and a touch of mint. He stroked it hard with his tongue, reaching down with his hand to find the warm center of her. His palm brushed over a soft field of pubic hair. He didn't have to see it to know it was blond. His fingers sought her. Found her hot, damp. Touched, stroked, deeper. All the while his lips were on hers, sounds catching in her throat, in his mouth. It was strange. He'd wanted her so badly, needed her so badly, that he hadn't even allowed himself to think about it. But beyond the fevered force of pure, gut-wrenching desire, instinct had stepped in. This had to be good for her. She wasn't forgetting this one.

He suddenly shoved himself against her body. There was only so much you could forget. And so much you had no choice but to remember, even after more than a decade. She had been worth remembering. She had perfect breasts, full, firm, with large pink nipples, hard now. He laved one. Tasted it, teased it with his tongue. Kept his rhythmic touch moving within her. Sucked on her nipple. Heard her crying out, felt her fingers tearing into his hair.

He moved lower, lifting her hips. His tongue replaced his fingers. She was gasping, crying out words that were incomprehensible, or which he chose to ignore. She tensed against him, straining, then ceased to fight him. He felt the sudden surge of her body, the slight easing of those fingers in his hair. She came with a wicked shudder, and he rose over her then, blanketing her with his body, driving into her with all the wild, hard desire that touching Spencer had always evoked. Eliciting it all over again in Spencer with the sheer force of his passion, the near desperate desire that washed over him.

Then it was quick. Her fingers digging into his shoulders, her body moving with his. The world seemed all but wiped out except for the need for surcease, and for Spencer. Slick now, still so damned slim, soft, almost angelic, except for the way she moved.

He seemed to erupt rather than climax. Maybe that was what happened when someone stayed in your dreams all your life. The whole damned world seemed to blacken briefly. Consciousness returning, he admitted to himself that it was the best sex he'd ever had. Moments later, while his heart was still pounding and he was gasping for breath, satisfaction was making him feel warmer and more content than he could remember being in a decade.

Sex was sex, he argued with himself. He'd had some damned good sex over the years since he'd parted ways with Spencer Anne Montgomery. Even in a world where everyone was being careful, he'd had some damned good sex.

But nothing like Spencer. Because he'd never gotten over her. Never would. And now he was entangling himself like a foolish fly caught in a web all over again, just because of some idiotic loyalty to Sly and his obsession with her. And any idea of careful sex, responsible sex, had flown out of his head, along with any sensible questions, like, Just what in God's name are you doing here, Delgado?

How quick the deed, how painful the repercussions.

It wasn't as if she shoved him aside or anything so obvious. But she went from lying next to him, gasping for breath, her heart pounding, perfect one-hundred-percent-Anglo flesh sheened and damp and still touching his, to turning away. Suddenly she was sitting on the side of the bed, her slim back to him, and shaking slightly. He couldn't see her face, but he knew that silent tears were running down her cheeks.

He was lying in Danny's bed; his head was on Danny's pillow. In Danny's room. Danny's house.

He almost screamed aloud. But he didn't.

Instead he rose from the bed and fixed his clothing. She didn't move; she wasn't even shaking anymore; she was just sitting there. He wished he could say something, but he didn't know what. He felt guilty enough himself.

But she was crying. Because she'd slept with him. No, they hadn't slept, they hadn't even dozed. She'd fallen into bed with him. His fault. He'd followed her up here. Her fault. She hadn't thrown him out fast enough. Oh, bull, it was his fault.

And now she was crying, hiding it from him, but crying anyway. Was she crying because he wasn't Danny and she wished he was?

Or because he wasn't Danny and she had been glad of it? As her shoulders rose and fell, his temper snapped. "Quit it, Spencer."

"Quit what?"

"Crying."

"I'm not crying."

"You didn't do anything terrible."

"I didn't say I did."

So she thought he was the bad guy here, huh? "I didn't do anything terrible either, Spencer. Danny is dead. You didn't betray him, and neither did I. We're all grown-up now, and you've been alone a long time. People have needs."

"Would you stop!" she exploded suddenly, rising and staring at him. She was still naked. Still Spencer.

Still perfect.

All that blond hair still wild, those beautiful blue eyes huge. Body a little flushed, flesh a rosy hue, breasts swollen, nipples still hard . . .

And cheeks dampened with her tears.

She felt his eyes then and realized that he was dressed while she wasn't. She strode across the room for the fallen towel, wiping the tears from her cheeks before she reached for the towel, and wrapped it around herself. "I want you out of here—now. I'm not blaming you for anything—"

"You sure as hell better not!" he snapped, grabbing her arm and forcing her to face him.

"David, I'm asking you to get out of here."

"Spencer, it's a damned good thing I've got an ego or you'd make me feel like a two-bit whore myself. What is this, the same old story with you year after year? You want something you're not supposed to want, something from the wrong side of the tracks, so you think you can just take it and then throw it away? You need a little dirt in your pristine life and I'm it? You can't admit it, though—"

"Stop it! I was your best friend's wife!" she cried.

She was hurting, and he knew that, but he couldn't seem to stop himself.

"Just what the hell do you want, Spencer?" he suddenly snapped out. "A little erotic interlude? How do you like it? Quick, out of sight, as down and dirty as you can get in ten minutes?"

She inhaled sharply. He knew she was raising a hand to slap him, and he could have stopped her, but he didn't. Maybe he was as bad as she was, because he wanted to feel the sting of her hand on his cheek, wanted to take that with him when he turned away.

What was wrong with him? Maybe he was angry because she had been able to give only so much, and if he was going to have any of her, he wanted it all.

He'd never had it all. He hadn't had it ten years ago, and he couldn't have it now.

He felt the sting of her hand fading from his cheek. Her eyes were glazed now, holding just a bit of wariness of what he might do in response.

"I'll be downstairs, Spencer."

She paled and shook her head, moistening her lips. "I want you to leave."

"So you can wallow in self-pity? Sorry. Sly *has* paid me, after all."

"And you always give people their money's worth!" she exclaimed angrily.

"Yeah. Yeah, I do."

"I could call the police."

"Call them. If you get one of my old buddies, be sure to say hello for me."

He managed to turn away then, and he finally left her bedroom. And all the while he was damning himself for ever having entered it in the first place.

7

When Spencer got downstairs, he was still there. Sitting in the living room, thumbing through the newspaper.

She ignored him, walked into the kitchen and swallowed two glasses of water.

She had some Valium in the cupboard that she'd been given when Danny died. She toyed with the idea of taking a few. That wouldn't make David go away, nor could it really do anything to stop the emotions ripping into her heart. She decided to pass.

She strode into the living room. She'd dressed defensively in a sleeveless silk suit with a high mandarin collar, stockings and the highest heels she owned. She'd twisted her hair up, as well, determined not to let him look down at her. "Perhaps *you've* been paid to sit around all day," she told David as coolly as she could manage, "but *I've* got to go to work."

He stared at her long and hard, nothing in his bronzed features giving away any thoughts or feelings. Even so, she felt there was a certain contempt in his expression. She'd felt it before when she had been younger. And maybe she deserved it.

She didn't want to think about that. She was going to pretend it had never happened. And no matter what, she was never going to let him know that she still couldn't stop shaking, that she hated him, hated herself....

And that she couldn't stop wanting him all over again. In Danny's house. In Danny's bed.

"I'll drive you," he said, his tone flat, without a spark of emotion. As if he had already forgotten what had happened. As if it hadn't meant a thing to him.

Well, maybe it hadn't. What did she really know about his life anymore? She and Reva had more or less cut their ties after high school. She'd seen David as infrequently as possible since her marriage to Danny. And David did have a life of his own. He'd been living it just fine without her. Sex still seemed as natural to him as breathing. He was too good at it not to have been enjoying it all these years.

A flush crept up to her face. They were living in the nineties. What the hell was the matter with her? She hadn't even thought about safety. She'd just wanted to feel him as fast as possible. Have him. A burning shame invaded her. No one should just fall into bed so irresponsibly.

But she had. And then she'd wanted to ignore it. Now she couldn't seem to get it out of her mind for an instant, but there was David, cool as ice, staring at her with that strange glitter—mockery? contempt?—in his eyes.

"I want to take my car. I don't suppose I can stop you from following me, but at least it will get you out of my house."

"Don't you mean Danny's house?" he asked softly.

She had no answer for that. She spun quickly and started for the front door, heels clicking on the marble floor of the foyer. But before she could escape, the doorbell rang. She flinched at the sound, instantly tensing.

David did more, drawing his gun from his shoulder holster and stepping past her, looking through the peephole. He frowned, instantly sheathing the gun and opening the door. "Fried! What are you doing here?"

Spencer could see Danny's last partner standing awkwardly on the front porch in a wilting brown tweed jacket. He seemed surprised to find David there, then stared at Spencer a little sheepishly. "I just came to see Spencer for a minute." He straightened, as if inwardly yelling at himself for wavering in his purpose so quickly. "Actually, Delgado, I'm glad you're here. I wanted to try to talk a little bit of sense into her."

David arched a brow, pushed the door open farther and crossed his arms over his chest. He looked from Jerry Fried to Spencer. "Be my guest. This ought to be good."

"Come in, Jerry," Spencer said wearily.

He stepped inside and looked around, and Spencer wondered if he liked the old house, with its warmth and elegance, or if he simply resented the fact that Danny had lived here. The two men hadn't gotten on particularly well, but a lot of that might have been Danny's fault. David had been his partner before Jerry, and in Danny's eyes, no one could have lived up to David. Danny had thought that Jerry was nice enough, a good fellow. Just not as sharp as David.

"Want some coffee, Jerry?" Spencer asked politely.

"Are you kidding? It's hotter than a mother out there! Oh, sorry, Spencer."

"Cold drink? Soda, ice tea?"

Jerry shook his head. Then he plunged in. "Spencer, I've just gotta tell you, you're hurting us all."

She frowned. "I'm hurting you . . . all?"

"Come on, Spencer, you lived with a cop long enough. You were his wife. You know we're doing everything we can. We practically camped out on Delia's door. We followed up on every single thing Danny was working on when he died. We haven't given up. We're going to get the killer. You just have to give us half a chance.''

"But I'm not interfering with anything you're doing!" Spencer protested.

He shrugged sheepishly. "Spencer, come on, you were prowling around a graveyard at night, for chrissake!"

"I had a hunch."

"A hunch, huh?"

"Jerry, I shouldn't have been there, all right? But my hunch was on the money, and you do have Delia in jail."

"Yeah, and we're glad about that, Spencer. It's just that you gotta believe we're going to go after Danny's killer with both barrels blazing. Tell her, Delgado, please!"

David, arms crossed over his chest as he watched the exchange between them, shrugged. "Spencer, it's true and you know it. Cops look out for their own. Hell, they all know they could be next!"

She lifted her hands in surrender. "Jerry, I won't snoop around in any more cemeteries. I promise."

He turned, ready to leave. Then he turned back to her. "Spencer, if you know something you're not sharing with us, you need to come clean. Do you hear what I'm saying?"

"I—I don't know anything," she said stiffly.

David was staring at her again.

"See you, then, Spencer. You take care. And I swear, I'll keep you up-to-date on anything I learn," Jerry said.

"Thanks," Spencer said.

David gave her a hard look, then followed Jerry Fried to his unmarked car.

"What was that all about?" David asked.

Jerry slid into the driver's seat, shaking his head. "I don't know. It just seems like she must know something she's not saying. She's got to have a connection we don't. Something." He stared at David. "Christ, we've got to get a break here somewhere! We've got nothing, David. No prints, no murder weapon. No witnesses. Nothing. And he dies—a cop, for God's sake—without giving us a clue, just whispering his wife's name." He shook his head. "Hell, I'd pull out my own teeth to solve this thing. Just to get the lieutenant—*and* Ms. Spencer Montgomery Huntington—off my ass! Sorry, Delgado. I know he was your friend. And he was a good guy. A good partner. But damn it, I think even Danny knew stuff he wasn't sharing with me, and that sure pisses me the hell off now!"

David shrugged noncommittally. "Danny was a good cop."

"Yeah," Jerry muttered. "You working for her now?"

David shook his head.

"For old man Montgomery?"

"I'm working on this one for Danny, and for myself. See you around, Fried."

"Yeah, see you around."

As Fried started to drive away, Spencer was already getting into her little Mazda. David strode to his Mustang, settling in just as she whirred the Mazda to life.

"Bitch!" he said softly, burning rubber to get out of her driveway quickly enough to fall in line right behind her. She wasn't going to shake him. Not unless he decided to let her.

He followed right on her bumper, almost as close as if the two cars were attached, watching for any sneaky moves. But it seemed that she really was going to work.

He picked up his car phone and punched in Sly's private office number. Sly picked up right away.

"Spencer's pulling into the parking lot now. I'll be at my office for a while."

"Fine. Thanks," Sly said.

"Call me when she's going to be on her own."

"I'll do that," Sly agreed. "You think you're going to be able to keep a tail on her all the time?"

David opened his mouth to reply. Spencer sure as hell wasn't going to be happy having him around. It didn't matter. He would be out on the street. She couldn't stop him.

"Yeah, Sly. I'll keep on her. She's yours during the day, and I'll handle her coming and going. Be careful. I think that things may be starting to break now. If you can watch her during the day, I can use the time to see a few old friends—and enemies."

"I'll keep an eye on her," Sly promised, then hung up.

Sly was as good as his word, though the weekend promised to be rough. But Sly had told David that he and a dozen stonemasons would be with her most of the time—neither Saturday nor Sunday had been planned as a day of rest.

David followed her to church and home again on Sunday, keeping a fair distance from her. She wasn't aware that she was still being followed, or if she was, she gave no indication of it.

Late Sunday afternoon, she sat out by her pool. Then she swam, and he felt both the hunger and the pain she had reawakened in him stirring again as he watched her. He swore at himself, mocked himself, but he kept watching her. As the sky darkened, she sat on the edge of a lounge chair and pressed her temples between her fingers. She was crying again, he thought. Well, Danny was dead, and maybe he was a poor substitute. Or maybe she wasn't ready to forgive herself for wanting a substitute. He didn't know which. But he couldn't say he didn't care. Because he did.

The weekdays went a little better, but his nerves were definitely on edge by the time Friday arrived. Nothing had happened. Juan, another of David's employees, had kept him up on Ricky Garcia's movements. Ricky had kept a very low profile recently, probably because the police were breathing so closely down his neck.

David had used his police connections to make sure that the alarm company went out to Spencer's house, supposedly on a routine check, to do a thorough evaluation of the system. Each night he checked the doors himself, then called the company and made sure that Spencer's system was being monitored.

He'd been sure that something would happen quickly. As a result, he'd been so tense that the week had gone excruciatingly slowly.

If he'd only kept his damned distance from Spencer...

But he hadn't.

On Friday he followed her in to work at a discreet distance. He still didn't know whether she was aware that he was following her constantly or not. It didn't matter.

David stayed on Main while she turned into the parking lot for Montgomery Enterprises. His office wasn't far down the street. He pulled in. Reva was at the front desk. She gave him a curious look when he walked in.

"How are things going?"

She shrugged. "Marty is working on that insurance fraud thing. He called in to say we're right on track with it. Juan has been down in Little Havana, seeing what he can find out about everything Ricky Garcia is into. Someone called with a divorce case."

"You turned it down."

"Yes, big brother, I turned it down. God forbid, we don't want to do anything that actually makes us a whole bunch of money here!"

He shrugged and walked into his office, pulling out his files on Danny's case. Reva followed him.

"Coffee?"

"I've had some."

"Lunch? I can microwave some of Tia Anna's black beans and rice."

He shook his head again. "I'm not hungry."

"Spencer Montgomery has quite an effect on your appetite, big brother. Has anything happened since you took her to see that guy in jail?"

He folded his fingers together, looked at his sister and he shook his head. "I did pay him a second visit."

"And?"

He shook his head unhappily. "I just can't believe Delia killed Danny. I do believe he's completely out of his head, and I'm certain he's murdered some of his followers. But I don't think he killed Danny."

"You're putting all your time into this one case."

"Hey! I'm the boss."

"You refused to accept a salary from Sly Montgomery, didn't you?" Reva asked.

David stared at her. "Yeah. Yeah, I refused to accept his money. Reva..."

"I know, David. He put us both through school. I didn't think you'd accept anything from him."

"I've been on this thing forever anyway."

Reva stood, ready to leave his office. "David?"

"Yeah?"

"Just watch out around Spencer, huh? She's caused enough heartache in your life already."

"Reva, I've hardly been stumbling through life doing nothing."

"No, you haven't. You've done well, done just about everything you wanted to do. But you've been doing it alone."

"Reva, my Friday nights tend to be just fine."

"Yeah, I know. An Anglo one week, a Hispanic the next. A model, a woman judge, a bartender, an attorney. No one could ever accuse you of having any prejudices. But where's your home, David? Where are those Saturday afternoons you should be spending with your son at Little League? It's as if you gave up all those things when you gave up Spencer Montgomery. I just don't want to see you tangled up like that again, David. Time has passed, but we haven't changed what we are, and the Montgomerys sure as hell haven't changed what they are!"

He found himself bolting to his feet. "Sly is the second most decent human being I know, Reva. Second only to Michael MacCloud. And how you can forget that—"

"I haven't!" Reva told him earnestly. "Honestly, you know I love Sly! I just love you more, David."

He sat, staring at her. "I get to go to Little League with my nephew, Reva."

"I want you to be happy."

"I'm as happy as a damned lark," he told her.

Reva stared at him. "Have it your way," she said, turning to leave. "But bear in mind, when you wind up ready to beat your head against the wall again, I won't hesitate to say I told you so! And if her folks get in on it, don't expect me to bail you out of jail again!"

She left. What an exit line.

* * *

It wasn't that Spencer had really done anything so horrible. Except that...

Cuban males were known for being jealous. Possessive. And he had been in love with Spencer.

All the kids knew they were an item. A hot item. He felt as if he were living just for the moments when he could see her. Not that he didn't keep up with the other things that were important. He owed it to Sly and the memory of Michael MacCloud, to get good grades. Michael had passed away the year before, after having spent the last fifteen years of his life trying to make America the land of promise for his grandchildren. David had to watch after his little sister. He was all Reva had left, and he was determined that the courts weren't going to put her in a home somewhere. Plus he was a Big Brother to an orphaned kid who had made it over from Cuba on a raft.

He'd started junior college, too, while he waited for Spencer to graduate. Their relationship had grown from that day at Sly's. Movies every Friday. The beach on weekends. Picnics with the others. He'd almost begun to believe that all men *had* been created equal in America. He'd been to Spencer's house for dinner, and her parents had been cordial enough, though once he'd heard her mother refer to him as "that refugee Spencer brought home." He hadn't let that bother him. He knew that Sly liked him, believed in him. And anyway, only Spencer really mattered; she was the one he was in love with.

And for over a year the love between them was deep and passionate.

They had some tempestuous times, of course, Spencer taunting him about looking at Terry-Sue, him ready to chew her out over a boy she might have teased in the hallway. But the fights just made their time alone more important, all of it stolen time, illicit time. Time they had to create. Once it was a tourist hotel on North Miami Beach. Once it was the beach itself, when the sun was setting and the tide was ebbing and the world looked glorious in shades of russet and crimson and gold.

When Michael died, David had only survived because he had Spencer at his side. He'd thought he needed to get away from her, from everyone, to be alone. But it turned out that he'd needed Spencer more than ever that night, and he'd made love to her more passionately than ever before, almost furiously. She'd understood his love for Michael, though she hadn't really understood what it meant to be alone in the world. He'd been an infant when his mother died, a child when he'd left the only home he'd ever known, waving a gun and escaping with his sister. He'd been only eight when Michael MacCloud had gently broken the news that his father had died in the Cuban prison where he'd spent his last months writing pamphlets on liberty. And now Michael was gone, as well. David was alone. Alone with a sister to protect. True, he had cousins and aunts and uncles who meant well, but they weren't *close*. They didn't count. He had to make a living. He had to keep Reva with him; he couldn't let the two of them be separated.

He knew about hard work. He'd been working as long as he could remember. And he loved Spencer, needed Spencer, but she had never once known what it was like to be adrift and afraid in the world. Spencer was cherished by her parents, adored by Sly, protected by all of them. Money and security wrapped her from head to toe.

Perhaps he had built his first wall against her when Michael had been laid to rest. Maybe he had even begun building the wall that night when he had held her so heatedly.

But the breakup came when her parents brought down a houseguest from Rhode Island. Bradford Damon.

He was Spencer's age. Anglo. Rich as Croesus. He'd spent his life learning to sail—with golf as an extra on the side. His grades weren't stupendous, but he'd won entry into an Ivy League school following his father's large donation to the university.

At first he and Spencer had joked about Bradford. She'd moaned about having to entertain him, and she'd apologized profusely each time she had to break a date with David to see that Bradford made his way around all right.

He'd had a job at the school then, pulling scenery for the theater department. After work one Friday, he'd gone to her house at nine to pick her up. In no uncertain terms, Spencer's mother had turned him away from the door. "She will not be home tonight. She's gone to the dance at the club with Brad, and they will not be back until well past midnight. It's a private affair this evening, David. I'll thank you not to go there and cause trouble."

He hadn't caused any trouble yet that he knew about. But he did go over to the club, staying on the fringes of the party, watching from the park that flanked the club. Spencer was indeed there with Bradford Damon. And Bradford wasn't really such a sorry specimen. He was tall, lean, blond, lanky. He wore an expensive suit very well.

It seemed as if he was dancing right on top of Spencer, and he laughed a hell of a lot. Worse, Spencer laughed, too.

He kissed Spencer, and it sure as hell looked as if Spencer kissed him back.

That was enough. David left the party, but he walked the streets half the night.

After midnight, he went to Spencer's house. He stood beneath her window, gathering a few pebbles to throw at it to get her attention. He froze when he heard laughter. Spencer's. A man's.

He threw a pebble at her window. Hard. A second later she looked down. She was pale, her hair a golden cloud around her face. She was wearing a robe, but one that seemed to emphasize the roundness of her breasts and the curve of her hips. She stared at him with shock. "David!"

Then he heard the sirens. He was still staring at her when the police came to arrest him.

If she protested, he never knew anything about it. The next thing he did know, he was behind bars. Being taunted by nasty-looking men of all colors, men with no front teeth and needle marks down their arms.

Sly got him out.

And the next day Spencer appeared at his house, pushing his door open to rush in. "David! David, I'm so sorry!"

"Go to hell, Spencer."

She stood dead still, staring at him. "David, I didn't have anything to do with what happened. I didn't even know until this morning!"

"Yeah. Right." He was ready to kill her. He wanted to wind his hands around her perfect throat and throttle her. "You were kind of busy last night, weren't you? Just how is Bradford Damon, Spencer? Are blond boys different?"

She inhaled in a rush and started to slap him. But caught her hand and sighed, suddenly very, very tired. "Go home, Spencer."

Her blue eyes sparkled feverishly, her perfect white teeth clenched. "Damn you. You have no right—"

"I haven't got many rights, Spencer, but one of them is to have a girl who won't cheat on me."

"I didn't cheat on you."

"I saw you with him, Spencer."

Her cheeks colored, and she didn't deny anything. Maybe that was what hurt the most.

"¡Puta!" he said softly. Whore. Rich whore, but whore nevertheless.

"Cubano! Refugee!" she lashed out.

He reached for her suddenly and drew her into his arms. Then he kissed her. Deeply, hungrily. Jealously.

Maybe she thought then that things were going to be all right, that she could play with her parents' choice and have him, too. But he was incensed. He was never quite sure he could call what he did to her that day making love, but he'd never known a greater anguish. The whole time he touched her, he wondered just what Bradford Damon had done with her. She cried out at one point, but she clung to him and never protested. Yet at the end, he was not appeased. The anguish, the restlessness, grew. He stood up and walked away, looking out the window in the small room in the very small house that Michael Mac-Cloud had managed to buy for them.

"I'm sure my parents never meant what happened, David."

"What about you, Spencer? Did *you* mean it?"

"I don't know what you mean."

"I'm not sure I do, either." He walked around her like a caged cat. "All I know is that you're a little lackey to your folks, and they're just a pair of rich bigots."

She gasped, quickly rising, and grabbing her strewn clothing. She dressed quickly, angrily, lashing out at him.

"How dare you? How dare you say such things about my parents? It's not a crime to be born with money."

"Well, even if it isn't illegal, it *is* immoral to lie and cheat and hurt others just because you were born with more than they have."

"I told you, they didn't mean—"

"And what about you, Spencer? Did you *mean* to sleep with their little houseguest?"

Again she didn't deny the charge. She stood up and walked over to him and slapped him hard.

He stared at her, afraid to move. He wanted to hold her, because he was afraid that if he didn't, he would never see her again, but he was shaking with rage and misery and humiliation. "I guess we've both been screwed real good, honey, haven't we?" he asked her softly.

She gasped. "You bastard!" she hissed.

Finally he simply lifted her out of his way and left the house. His own house. He left her standing there.

That afternoon he learned she'd left the state.

Numbed, he went about doing the same thing himself. He methodically saw to his sister's college arrangements and made sure that his aunt would help Reva move into a dorm. And when he was assured that his sister would be all right, he made his final move to make certain he couldn't possibly spend his time trying to find Spencer, beating his head against a wall, trying to make things right.

He signed up for the United States Army.

His intercom was buzzing. He started, then pushed the button.

Reva spoke to him. "Pick up line one, David. It's Sly, and he sounds upset.

He picked up the receiver. "Yeah, Sly?"

"She's gone, David. She's out of here."

"All right, I'll—"

"No, no, you don't understand! She isn't just headed out to lunch or to get her hair cut, or even to take the afternoon off!"

"Sly, you've got to tell me what you're talking about."

"She's gone to the airport! Her flight leaves in less than an hour."

"What?"

"She bought a ticket for home. Newport via Boston."

David's fingers tightened around the receiver. "Then she'll be with her folks," he said lightly. "She'll be fine."

"You can't be sure! You know Spencer. She didn't run home to see them. She ran out to avoid being here for the weekend!"

"Sly, I'll follow her to the airport, but she'll be okay in Rhode Island," he said. But his argument was weak, and he knew it. He already knew he was on his way to follow her.

"I don't know!" Sly exclaimed. "Damn, boy, I just don't want her alone. I don't like to ask this of you, but David . . . please, follow her."

David winced, his fingers gripping the receiver so tightly that they went white.

Sly spoke again. "For the love of God, David, I'm begging you. I've just got this feeling. . . . Follow her, please?"

He couldn't talk for at least thirty seconds. Then he let out a pent-up breath. "Yeah, Sly. Yeah. I'll follow her."

He hung up the phone and stared at it for a moment.

Damn her! She'd gone and done it again.

8

The Huntington house was quiet. The nondescript man in the blue sedan had been watching it since nine this morning, parked down the street in front of a neighboring house. The man knew he wouldn't be disturbing the occupants of the home; he had been watching the neighborhood on and off for a long time. These people were like clockwork. He kissed her goodbye at eight and left in a maroon Volvo. She left with the kid at eight-thirty.

She didn't come home on Fridays until eight-thirty, and she did so in tight, shiny workout clothes. Fridays were gym days. He didn't get home until almost nine—he took the kid to Grandma's each Friday without fail.

The man in the blue suit knew almost as much about them as he knew about the comings and goings of Spencer Anne Montgomery Huntington.

Spencer Huntington was neither punctual nor predictable. Sometimes she worked at the office; sometimes she worked on-site. But she usually came home somewhere around five o'clock. She knew the traffic started to get really bad after that, and she liked to come in, then go out after seven if she had shopping or the like. She hadn't had much of a social life in the past few months. She liked to swim at night or in the early evening. She had at least a dozen swimsuits, and he liked every one of them. Especially the blue bikini. She wore it a lot on Fridays.

She dove; she swam. She lay on a big float and spent time just staring at the sky. He could just see her between the slats of the wooden fence that surrounded the pool behind her house. He made a point of leaving the car to watch her when he knew she was swimming. There was dense foliage all around—one of the things he really loved about the Grove. It was easy to keep an eye on her without being seen.

She was a lot to look at. So beautiful, so sad. Lonely? Missing Mr. Huntington? Officer Huntington?

The man in the blue suit would have dearly loved to make up that loss to her!

Of course, a monkey wrench had recently been thrown into things. David Delgado, honor-cop-commando-turned-P.I., was in on it now. And eventually he would notice the strange cars that were regularly parked in the area. He would hear the snap of twigs in the bushes surrounding the huge lots. Twice now he'd had to leave because of Delgado.

Eventually Delgado would discover him, no matter how careful he was. *If* Delgado continued to keep his eye on the woman. Things had been still. Dead still. Delgado might decide that someone was being paranoid about Mrs. Huntington and give up the assignment. Or he might not. That remained to be seen. If Delgado did come any closer, then something would have to be done.

When Spencer didn't show up at five, the man wasn't too worried. He was supposed to be keeping an eye on her all night, but even Spencer Huntington could get caught in traffic now and then.

Five-thirty rolled around, then five forty-five.

He picked up his car phone and dialed in. "Someone tell the boss that our blond bombshell hasn't come home yet."

"All right. Sit tight. We'll get back to you."

He sat tight. And waited.

The phone rang once. He was still holding it. "Yeah."

"Bring it on in. She's leaving town for the weekend."

"Coming in."

He hung up and revved his engine. Pity. He liked to watch the wife come home in her workout clothes. She wore them exceptionally well.

And Fridays were blue-bikini day for Spencer. He was going to miss that, too.

What a bum way to start the weekend.

It didn't occur to Spencer until she was settled in the first-class section of an Airbus 300 on her way to Newport via Boston that this was very much like something she had done once before. Newport was a place to run away to. She'd grown up in Miami, but her folks had always kept the Newport house as a getaway. And she'd used it for exactly that, so long ago.

So long ago—and yet when she closed her eyes, she could remember the occasion all too clearly. She could remember the awful things she had said. The awful things David had said. She would never forget the look on his face. She would never stop wondering how anyone could be so passionately angry and coldly determined all at once.

So she had run away. From his anger, and from her anger against him and against her parents. Leaving had seemed the only thing to do.

She hadn't consciously made a decision to run away this time. It was just that the office had suddenly seemed so dreary. There were no new projects, and all the old ones were running smoothly. She'd barely closed her door before Audrey was knocking cheerfully on it, entering with a sheaf of files.

"Spencer, Mr. Matson just went over and saw his fireplace all cleaned up and restored, and roses are on the way. The architect is spending the afternoon at the Hillborn house with a carpenter and an electrician, and they'll both get back to you by next Wednesday. Your realtor called, and she's very excited. She wants you to see a house that just went up for sale in Coral Gables, part of the Colonial Village, on the golf course—but no one can see it until a week from today, because the owner wants to get his mother settled elsewhere first. She says you mustn't miss it! Now, that's it for business." She plopped on the corner of Spencer's desk, wriggling her backside and getting comfortable. "This is the first chance I've had alone with you since that cemetery thing. What really happened out there? Tell me. After all, I *am* the one who got you thinking!"

Spencer sat in her comfortable swivel chair behind her beautiful golden oak desk and tried not to smile at Audrey, but her lips were pursed and for the first time in a long time, she felt like laughing. Audrey was the epitome of the word "cute." She was about five foot three, just a little bit round, with a short pixieish haircut. She smiled quickly and often; she could handle the most irate client with a wave of her hand and one of those smiles. "Cute," however didn't hide her intelligence, and Spencer was well aware that the wheels in her mind were constantly turning. She'd talked more about Danny's death with Audrey than she had with anyone else, including her family.

"Cut and dried, pretty much just what you saw in the papers," Spencer told her, riffling through the files. She frowned. She needed to be busy today, and there wasn't anything here that couldn't wait.

"Spencer!" Audrey said. "This isn't fair! Last Friday Sly was with you all day. Then you worked on-site all weekend. This week you've been in meetings every day. I had a dentist's appointment yesterday. This is my first real chance to pry into your life!"

Spencer looked up, laughing. "I'm sorry, Audrey! It's not as if my life is worth prying into."

"At the moment it is," Audrey said simply. "Spencer, think back while it's still fresh in your memory!"

Too many things remained fresh in her memory.

"Weren't you terrified when those men arrived? Weren't you terrified *before* that, being all alone in a pitch-dark cemetery? I'd expect hands to be coming out of the ground. Moldy hands, grasping hands! I'd imagine *Night of the Living Dead,* I'd—"

"I admit, I had a few bad moments," Spencer said, but she smiled wistfully. "Danny's buried there."

"I know. But then . . . ?"

Spencer shrugged. It seemed so long ago now.

"The grave robbers got wind of me, I started running—and a hand *did* come out of a grave."

"I would have died!"

"No, you wouldn't!" Spencer told her wryly. "You'd have smacked the hand."

Audrey grinned.

"Honest to God, that's about it. You know the rest. It was David Delgado. He phoned the police—"

"He phoned the police from a grave?" Audrey queried dubiously.

"Cellular phone. He's one man who's always prepared," she said lightly. Always. Except for what happened the next day. He hadn't been prepared at all.

Neither had she.

"So are you still seeing him?"

"Seeing him?"

"Delgado. Mr. Sex. Mr. Macho," Audrey said. "Dark, masculine. Tall. Handsome. Great voice. All the right things."

"I didn't know you knew him."

"He's been in the office a few times this week. I admit, my heart went flutter-flutter."

"Audrey, your heart goes flutter-flutter every time you pass a construction site."

"Same difference," Audrey assured her with a smile. "Are you seeing him?"

"No."

"But you did."

"Years ago. Before time began."

"Umm. Well, all I know is that you did come in very late last Friday. So just what were you doing then?"

Meeting an old lover in my dead husband's bed, Spencer thought. Just what you're waiting to hear....

Never.

"Audrey, you know where I went. I went to the jail and saw Delia." She shrugged.

Audrey nodded, suddenly serious again. "You seemed very nervous when you came in later, you know. Was he as frightening as he seems?"

"In a way. But I don't think he killed Danny, so I guess it was a dead end, as far as finding out anything about what really happened back then. Of course, in my mind, it doesn't hurt that Delia is in jail anyway. The police don't seem to appreciate it very much, but..."

She shrugged, losing her concentration. She didn't think she could bear to sit there any longer, answering questions.

The week had been rough. Now it was worse. She knew David was following her. Watching her all the time. Keeping his distance from her. Well, she couldn't blame him for that, after the way she'd acted. The problem was, she didn't want to see him, and yet she did. She just didn't want to admit it.

"That's it, honestly," she told Audrey. "You were right on the money about the route Delia's followers were taking."

"It was obvious," Audrey said modestly.

Spencer smiled slowly. "Well, it wasn't obvious to the boys at the station, and though they're glad to have Delia, they're a little embarrassed."

Audrey smiled, then started for the door, as if sensing that Spencer needed a little privacy. "Any other brainstorms, I'll let you know," Audrey promised.

"Thanks!" Spencer told her. She picked up the files on her desk and started to flip through them. Then she set them down and rose from her desk, prowling around her office. There was a 1930s photograph on the wall of one of the hotels they were restoring on the Beach. She loved the hotel. But she couldn't start working on it yet; the building inspectors needed to make sure it could be salvaged. Sly had insisted on it. Ever since that stupid beam had fallen the other day, he had become an incredible dictator. They'd always been careful. Now they were being almost ridiculous.

She could do paperwork. Correspondence. She could answer the stack of invitations in her in box.

She just didn't want to.

Maybe she should just go away for the weekend, she decided later that afternoon. Up to Newport. It wasn't likely that David would follow her; there would be no reason for him to. Danny had been killed down here; she couldn't cause much trouble in Newport.

And David hated her parents.

She hit her intercom. "Audrey, see if you can get me on a plane to Rhode Island, will you?"

"Going up to see your folks?" Audrey sounded surprised.

Well, Spencer did love her parents, but there were so many other emotions mixed in with that love. "Getting away to breathe a bit," she said.

"You haven't been back that long."

"I'm not going away for that long."

"I—" Audrey began, then cut herself off abruptly.

Spencer wondered whether Audrey had been about to ask if her leaving had something to do with David Delgado and then thought better of it.

Audrey was the most efficient person Spencer had ever known. Spencer had barely completed riffling through her files again when Audrey had stepped in to tell her she was booked out on a 6:35 p.m. flight.

Great. She could leave right from the office. She kept a bag in the office with a few bare essentials for unplanned overnight trips when she wound up looking at properties up the coast. She could just drive straight to the airport. David could follow her if he wanted, but he would just wind up at the airport. And he wanted nothing to do with Newport.

Jared stuck his head in, tapping on the door. "Hey, cuz."

"Hey," she said, waiting.

"Oh, no. What are you up to now?"

"Nothing at all, I promise."

"Audrey's out there with your overnight bag. Just promise, no more graveyards."

She nodded, grinning. "No more graveyards."

He smiled, but then his handsome features sobered. "Spencer, this is serious. You've got to be careful."

"I will be."

"Then tell me, what are you up to now?"

"Nothing! Honestly. In fact, I'm going up to the folks' place for the weekend."

"Yeah?" He arched a brow.

She nodded.

"Sly know?"

"I just decided."

"How come?"

"I don't know. I just need to get away."

"It may be a good idea, but...Newport? A weekend in the Bahamas might be nice."

"I don't think I'm ready for—for a weekend in the Bahamas."

"Yeah," he said wryly. "You're still into suffering! Parents can make you suffer all right!"

"Jared!" she protested. But was he right?

"Just kidding. Well, all right, I'm not really kidding, but you know what I mean. Personally, I think a weekend in the Bahamas would be good for you. But then again, your mom and dad will be glad to see you. But you know, Cecily and I miss having you around, too. The kids are nuts about you, Spencer. And we haven't seen a whole lot of you since..." His voice trailed off, and he shrugged. "Since Danny died."

"Yeah, I know. I'll make it up to them."

"That's not what I mean. You don't need to make anything up to anyone, we just...miss you. Dad asks about you all the time. He wants the kids to come over and do some fishing sometime soon. Can I count you in?''

She wanted to tell him that she wasn't fit company for anyone, but then she decided that maybe it was time for her to make an effort, to start becoming fit company again. "Yeah, sure."

"By the way, how's David?"

"What?" Absurd. Her heart was pounding furiously at the mere question, as if she was guilty of something.

"David Delgado. Cecily puts his name on just about every invitation she sends out. Reva's kids play ball at the same park as mine, but we don't seem to catch David too often. Remember what a tough kid he was?"

Was he taunting her? Or just being nostalgic? Spencer wasn't sure.

"He seems to be . . . fine," she said.

"It's nice to have him around again. Seems like old times. Except that now—"

Now Danny was gone. The words were left unsaid between them.

"Well, I haven't really seen him. Sly has him around, so it seems."

He shrugged. "Well, I'll let you go. Give my aunt and uncle a kiss for me. Wait, give my aunt a kiss and my uncle a handshake. I'll be holding the fort—along with Grandfather Atlas in there—till you get back."

"Thanks. Tell Cecily I'm sorry. I'll be better company when I get back. Promise."

He gave her a thumbs-up sign and left her office. She glanced at her watch. She was going to have to hurry to make the airport.

But she couldn't leave without telling Sly what she was up to. She walked into his office. He was on the phone, so she sat on the edge of his desk to wait. He flashed her

a smile and she smiled back. Sly didn't look a day ove
sixty, and a debonair sixty, at that. She slid off his desl
and kissed his cheek. He slipped his hand over the re
ceiver. "What's that for?" he asked.

She could hear someone still talking on the other end
"I'm out of here. Off for the weekend. I'm restless an
my projects are in limbo. I'd have you feed my cat, ex
cept that I haven't got one."

He looked alarmed. Old for minute. "Where are yo
going?"

"Newport."

"You want to go to Newport *now?*" he demanded.

"Sly, I know you've got David following me, and i
isn't necessary—"

"It was necessary in that graveyard."

"I'm going to be with Mom and Dad. What coul
happen—except that I could expire from being suffo
cated with affection, or drown in mineral water!"

She strode for the door, waving to him. "Love you
I'm going to miss my plane."

"What plane—" he began, but she closed the door a
if she hadn't heard him. She was, after all, a big girl. Wel
over the age of twenty-one.

It wasn't until the plane was taking off that she bega
to ask herself just why the hell she was going to New
port. She loved her parents, but spending any amount o
time with them could be torture.

Her mother had come along a bit in the past few years
And after all, she couldn't help her upbringing. Sh
Montgomery had worked for the fortune he ha
amassed, the fortune that had sent her father to the bes
schools—and put him in a position to meet her mother.

Her mother's family had had money for so long that no one was quite sure anymore where it had come from, other than land speculation. Her mother was a member of the Daughters of the American Revolution, and a proud one, at that. She still considered the Irish who had come to Boston a hundred years ago to be newcomers.

And the Spanish-speaking Latin Americans in South Florida remained "aliens" to her, even those who had been born in America.

Spencer sighed, sitting back. The flight attendant came by, offering champagne before takeoff. Spencer smiled and accepted a glass. It was good, but she needed to go slow. She was going to rent a car in Boston for the trip out to Newport.

She closed her eyes and felt a wave of heat sweeping over her. She couldn't seem to stop torturing herself.

She'd made love with David Delgado. Just thinking about it made her palms damp, her breathing ragged. She could remember each little intimate detail with shocking clarity. She could even remember the musky scent of him, the feel of him. And there was nothing in the world like it. Nothing so fast, so hot, so passionate. So intense. So damned alive and vital. In that way, things had changed so little between them that it was terrifying. Even after that last time, the day after he had been arrested...

She would never forget what had happened. The nightmare of it. Her mother had promised to square things with David when Spencer had agreed to go to the dance with Brad.

Damn, but she'd hated Brad. Right from the start. He was above everyone in creation, an ace polo player, golfer, yachtsman—according to him. His father was a newspaper mogul, and his mother was a member of the D.A.R. he had already been given the deeds to three of the family homes. His future was assured, whether he cared to work or not.

Her folks had pleaded with her to be nice to him—she hadn't realized that they had been certain she would fall for the "right" type of boy if she was just exposed to him for a while. At the dance, for the first time, he'd shown a little humility, admitting that he bragged so much because he was afraid of not being able to live up to all that was expected of him.

She'd never meant to kiss him. And it had been such a pathetic kiss, too, lacking everything David's lips had ever offered. Brad's kiss had almost made her ill, especially when she compared it to the absolute passion that resulted from David's touch.

When she got home, her mother didn't say a word about David. Apparently, he hadn't even come by after he got off work, and he had promised he would.

In retrospect, she realized that she should have known what was going on. Her mother had been especially down on anyone with the least hint of Hispanic blood ever since the Mariel boat lift. There had been such a hue and cry over it, some people shouting about human rights and others absolutely furious because Castro had managed to empty his prisons into South Florida. The old-time Hispanics were often as angry as the Anglo population. Crime had soared afterward. Spencer had tried very hard to explain to her mother that she couldn't blame all Cubans for the actions of the criminal few. Even her father had read the papers and been able to see reason. But not her mother. She should have realized that her mother would have done just about anything to destroy her relationship with David.

But she'd been young. Naive. And hurt that David hadn't come by.

So she'd had hot chocolate with Brad and played a game of Monopoly. He'd been decent that night, and she'd wound up laughing.

Then she'd heard a commotion below and looked out just in time to see David being dragged away by the police. And no protests on her part had meant anything.

Not to her parents. But David should have known.

Then she'd found out that David had been watching her at the dance, deciding without giving her a chance to explain what had happened. She could remember how furious she had been when she found out. She could also remember the way he had held her, the way he had behaved, the rock-hard fury that had been both terrifying and exciting....

Until the end. Until he had called her a whore and all but thrown her out of the way, then walked out. Out of his own house—and her life.

Poor Reva. She had come home just as David slammed out. And Spencer had been so upset that she called David every single derogatory name she could call to mind. Refugee. Spic. Greaser. Reva had been ashen faced, and Spencer had been sorry. So sorry. But she hadn't been able to say so, because her heart had been breaking.

So she'd run away.... To Newport, she thought wryly.

Wonderful, she considered a little hysterically. It seemed like every time she had sex with David Delgado she could only stand herself if she ran away afterward. Every time...

No! There could be no more times! Because this time it had been in Danny's bed, reminding her that she had married Danny knowing she would never want him the way she had wanted David. The way she still wanted him. Oh, God, she had to stop. She'd loved Danny. Maybe it had been different from the way she'd felt for David, but

Danny had never known how she had felt. She had been a good wife to him, and their life had been good....

Just different.

Life was just so damned strange. She'd run away all those years ago because she'd been so sure she was right. He hadn't given her a chance to explain. Maybe she didn't have a good explanation for the kiss, but he should at least have listened to her. Instead, he'd actually accused her of worse, of making love to Brad.

David had meant everything in the world to her. She'd learned to see through his eyes, to think through his mind. She'd even acquired a taste for Cuban coffee and *arroz con pollo*.

She'd thought he would follow her. That he would beg her forgiveness.

But he hadn't followed her. And after a while she had realized just what he must have felt like, being dragged out of her yard and thrown into jail. He wasn't coming for her. She'd humiliated him, and he hated her. He'd preferred to join the army. Boot camp had looked better than meeting up with her again anytime soon.

Danny had shown up in Rhode Island that summer. A friend. Just there to be with her. They'd never discussed David. And they hadn't gotten involved then, either. They'd both been taught that college was essential, so they'd gone their separate ways. Then Spencer spent time touring Europe with some friends from her graduating class. After that, she'd gone home and started working for Sly. She'd been home for a few years, working, beaching it, spending a few nights at the clubs, when she had run into Danny again and realized just how much he loved her. She realized, too, that he was right for her. Life should have been perfect for them.

Then David had become his partner....

Her head hurt. She'd drunk the champagne too quickly. She pressed her thumb and forefinger to her temple, trying to ease the pain away.

Someone slid into the seat beside her, and she sighed. She had hoped to have her side of the aisle to herself for the trip.

Selfish! she taunted herself. You can't hog a whole plane just because you're having personal problems.

She opened her eyes, determined to be remote but polite to her seatmate.

But when she opened her eyes, her hello froze on her lips and she just stared.

It was impossible.

David was sitting next to her. Watching her. Waiting for her reaction.

She groaned and closed her eyes again. When she reopened them, he hadn't gone away. This time, it seemed, he was willing to follow her.

After all, Sly had paid him.

"You charged my grandfather for first class?" she demanded, outraged.

"Damn right," he told her with a grim smile.

The stewardess offered him champagne, along with a dazzling smile. He accepted the drink, returning the smile. His deep blue eyes flashed, and a single, small dimple showed in his left cheek. Spencer ached inside to see it. She wanted to hit him. She wanted to scream. She wanted to run away.

Damn it, she had *tried* to run away!

But though she needed it desperately, that luxury was being denied her.

She'd met up with the demon of her past once again, and it seemed they were plunging into hell together.

"I'm going to my mother's house, you know."

"So I was told."

"I doubt you'll be welcome. My parents aren't exactly your biggest fans. Not that they ever were."

He arched a brow. "How perceptive. Although it took you long enough to notice."

"You don't have any right to judge them."

"Whatever gave them the right to judge me?"

She ignored his question and said, "They won't let you stay, you know. You're not the kind of person they like to see me hanging around with."

"You're all grown-up now, Spencer. Don't you choose your own friends yet?" he queried.

"What makes you think I'd ever consider you a friend?"

"All right. Then I'm the enemy you like to fuck once a decade."

She gritted her teeth hard, felt her body tightening.

"Don't you ever go away?" she demanded.

"Yeah, Spencer, I do go away," he said softly. He was staring straight ahead, features tense. "I went to the army once. Saw the Middle East. Ended up in Europe. I went away, and I stayed away. And even when I came back and joined my best friend on the police force, I did my best to keep out of your life. I think I did a damn good job of it, but then, the scars I carried all those years might have made it a little easier. Then Danny died—and you decided to play Miss Marple. So, yes, I will go away. But not until this is over."

"And when will that be?" Spencer asked on a soft breath.

"I guess when Danny's killer is caught."

"That could be a long time. No one has managed to turn up anything yet."

"But that's changing now, Sherlock. Remember, you've already landed Delia in jail."

"Which someone might have the grace to be happy about."

"Lots of people are happy about it. And lots of people know you're suddenly determined to delve into their lives because of Danny. Maybe you're the catalyst we need to stir things up, Spencer. But if that's true, it means you're in danger."

"So you're going to follow me. Even to my parents' home. Because of Sly."

"You're perceptive tonight."

She started to rise, but his hand pressed hers down on the armrest. "Spencer, this is an airplane. You can't run away from me here."

"Are you sure you have a first-class ticket?"

"It's the damnedest thing. They'll sell a first-class ticket to anyone. Even an alien."

She turned her back on him, slamming a hand against the small pillow she had been given. "Pity," she said succinctly.

She could almost feel him stiffening. His pulse would be ticking in his throat. Only his tension would give any indication of his anger as his eyes darkened to near black.

"¡Arpis!" he said softly.

She clenched her teeth and leaned her head back, closing her eyes. Once, a long time ago, she'd learned a lot about his world. She'd studied Castro and Cuba, and she'd made a point of learning about his father. She'd learned to like Cuban food, and she'd learned a lot of Cuban words.

That one, loosely translated, meant bitch.

You don't understand! she wanted to cry out. But she didn't understand herself, so there was nothing to say.

The past had never really ended for them. And Danny still came between them, almost as if he had a seat right there between them.

She could feel the heat emanating from David. Could smell his scent. Without meaning to, she remembered when he had touched her, how he had made her forget the world.

How much she had once loved him. How passionately. Even now, he could make her forget....

Forget Danny.

She had to find his killer. She had to. If she didn't, she would never feel that Danny had forgiven her.

God! If she could only get away.

But David was right. They were in an airplane, thirty thousand feet above the ground.

There was nowhere for her to go.

9

To Spencer's amazement, she managed to sleep through most of the flight. Thank God for champagne.

She also managed to miss dinner. By the time they landed, she was starving. She exited with David right behind her, making no attempt to help her with her overnight bag or jacket. He followed her step for step, and he was right behind her when they reached the car rental desk.

"Do I have to rent my own to follow you? Or are you going to let me share yours? Either way, Sly gets the bill."

She cast him an irritated glance and signed the agreement.

"Will there be any other drivers?" the pretty young agent asked.

"No," Spencer said.

"Yes," David told her, opening his wallet and setting his license next to Spencer's.

Her head was really beginning to pound, and her stomach was growling. She had to get out of there.

"Two drivers, then?" the clerk said.

"Whatever," Spencer said, trying to keep her voice level and noting that the woman gave David a glance sympathizing with him for having such a nasty traveling companion. She also noticed that David flashed a handsome smile in return.

Spencer started out to the courtesy shuttle. David fe
in behind her, looking around.

"You've never been to Boston before?" she asked hin

He shook his head. "New York, Chicago, Londoi
Madrid, Paris, Rome—but never Boston."

The shuttle dropped them off in a few minutes an
Spencer found herself reaching across another counte
for the keys. David followed her to the car, automat
cally approaching the driver's side and reaching for th
keys.

"Excuse me, I'm letting you share my car. I'm not le
ting you drive."

"Spencer, do we have to argue over every—"

"No! It's my car."

"It's a rental car!"

"It's *my* rental car. And we're in a town I know an
you don't. Plus you know nothing about Boston driv
ers. The only thing a New York cabbie fears is a Bosto
driver."

"I'm sure they'd be thrilled to hear your low opinio
of them."

"I didn't say they were bad drivers, just aggressive."

"Yeah? Well I can be pretty damned aggressive, too
Now give me the keys."

She could see that it would be pointless to keep argu
ing, so she dropped the keys in front of him. She walke
around to the passenger side and slammed her way i
while he bent to retrieve the keys.

He took the driver's seat, then switched on the igni
tion.

The traffic around Logan airport could be a killer, es
pecially on a Friday night. David managed to thread hi
way through it as if he'd lived in the area for the past fift
years.

"Straight to Newport?"

"Yes!" she snapped, then hesitated. "No," she amended. She was starving.

"Hungry?" he taunted. "Ah, yes. You did miss that great steak on the plane. I imagine you know all the posh places in town. I won't mind if you take me to one."

"I do know some incredible places," she said sweetly.

She gave him the directions to Boston's Hard Rock Cafe, and when they got there, she leaped out of the car while he was still staring at the door. The valet came around to take the car, and David climbed out, casting her an evil glare as the sound of the music blasted him.

She saw the look he gave her and hurried in. The music was exceptionally loud, and there was a long line. But, as luck would have it, they were a party of two, and those waiting were all groups of four or more. They were seated immediately, the perky hostess assuring them in a loud shout that they were incredibly fortunate.

Spencer wondered what she was doing. She had a splitting headache. The Hard Rock could be fun. She loved to walk around and study the rock memorabilia.

But not when her head was splitting. Like now. She'd brought David here because she knew he was tired and aggravated, as well, and probably wishing that no matter what he owed Sly, he hadn't agreed to watch over her. Unfortunately, she was going to be as sorry as he was.

But above all, she was starving. She ordered coffee and a grilled chicken salad. He ordered coffee—obviously, one of them *had* eaten on the plane.

The music did seem painfully loud. And the Friday-night date crowd was out. Execs in suits, sweet young things in very short skirts. David didn't even try to talk. He sat back, sipping coffee, idly observing the action.

She hadn't wanted to talk, but because he wasn'
making conversation, she suddenly found herself askin,
a question.

"Your usual Friday night?"

He shrugged. She realized suddenly that she didn'
know anything about his life. When Danny had beer
alive, even when she'd been avoiding David, she'd beer
dying to know what was going on in his life. But Danny
had tried not to talk about David, and she had neve
dared to ask. She was irritated to realize just how hun
gry she was for the details of his life, and how jealous she
still could become where he was concerned. Absurd
Surely she hadn't imagined that he'd spent his life alone'
Not a man like David.

She should just shut up. But she couldn't. "What do
you do these days?" she asked him. "When you're no
following someone like a bloodhound."

He shrugged. "It depends."

"On what?"

"Who I'm with."

She sipped her coffee, trying not to blink. He leaned
toward her suddenly to be sure she could hear him over
the music.

"Why don't you just come right out and ask me about
my sex life, Spencer?"

She managed not to exhibit a single spark of reaction.
"I do have the right to be just a bit concerned."

"Oh?"

She felt her cheeks reddening despite her best effort to
stay cool. "We weren't exactly careful when we..." Oh,
come on, Spencer! she silently taunted herself. She was
a big girl now. But she couldn't seem to find quite the way
to describe what they had done. "Made love" sounded
nice, but somehow it didn't quite fit the bill. Cruder

words might fit, but she didn't feel like spitting them out, either. Or maybe she did.

In the end, no words came at all.

He stared at her for a long moment without replying, but he didn't need to hear more, and finally he said, "You don't need to worry about disease, Spencer. You done yet?"

"What?"

"Are you done with your dinner? I've got a headache, and I'm tired of shouting."

"Well you could have woken me so I could have dinner on the plane."

"With the mood you were in? I don't think so, Mrs. Huntington. And you could have chosen another place to eat this particular evening."

She arched a brow. "You don't love rock 'n' roll anymore?"

"Sure I do. Just not tonight. Can we get the check and go?"

The check had come already. Spencer had slipped it beneath her plate. Now she pulled it out to read it.

"Give me the damned check."

"Why?"

"Because I'm a chauvinist or whatever else you want to call me. Just give me the damned thing!"

Surprising herself, she did. They exited the restaurant in silence. By the time the valet brought the car, it was nearly midnight.

"You know, I am the one who knows the way," Spencer said.

"Get in the car, Spencer. Please!" The last was added as she glared at him. She climbed in.

The Friday-night traffic was thin. Spencer sat tensely for the first part of the drive; then her eyes began to close. Finally she leaned her head back and dozed.

The next thing she knew, she was being shaken awake. She opened her eyes to find herself lying on David's lap. She was comfortable there. A fleeting heartbeat of nostalgia assailed her. Yes, she was comfortable with the scent of him, the feel of him, the texture of his trousers. The hardness of him.

She sat up quickly, blinking.

They were at the gate to her parents' home, not far from the mansions that were open to the public, the Breakers, Rosewood and the others. She supposed that her parents' home might well rank among the most beautiful in the area. It had been built in 1900 and enhanced ever since. It was absurdly large for two people, but until the snows fell each year, her parents lived here alone, except for their staff.

"This it?" David asked.

She nodded. "How did you know?" She was still half-asleep. Disoriented.

"Sly gave me the address. Not that you can really find an address around here. I asked at the gas station down the street for the Montgomery house."

"Oh."

"How do you get in—without getting arrested?"

She flipped her straying hair from her face and pointed to a call box. "Hit the button."

"It's pretty late."

"My mom is a night owl."

He didn't comment but hit the button. Spencer had to lean over him to talk.

"Yes?" a cautious, masculine voice said.

"Henri, it's Spencer. Can you open the gates, please?"

"Yes, Mrs. Huntington. Right away."

David looked questioningly at her. "Henri?"

"The butler."

"And he's a night owl, too?"

"Probably not. But he's very well paid." The gates slid open. "Let's go," Spencer said.

They drove along a winding lane. The house sat on an acre, with ten thousand square feet of living space. There were massive Greek columns in the front, and a huge bricked drive. David stopped in front of the columns. "We may need a few hundred more people to keep an eye on you in this place."

She cast him a malicious glare. "Right. The butler might attack me."

"Could be. I don't know the butler. What do you think?"

"I think Sly is wasting his money."

David ignored that. "What do I do with the car?"

"Leave it. The chauffeur will take care of it in the morning."

The foyer was several hundred feet square, David thought, entering. The chandelier above his head was probably worth enough to feed half the homeless in Dade County for a year. To the left stretched a huge ballroom, to his right, a library larger than several of the public libraries he had been in.

Dead center was a marble and wrought-iron stairway that curved elegantly to a balconied second story. They were barely through the front door before Spencer's mother, in a flowing negligee and matching robe, made her appearance, her husband, in a velvet smoking jacket, following right behind. David felt as if he had stepped into a prime-time soap opera.

"Spencer!" Mary Louise Montgomery threw her arms around her daughter, delighted to greet her. Then she looked over Spencer's shoulder and saw him standing there in the foyer, waiting.

"David!" she gasped, and her tone was quite different, though she struggled valiantly to retain some semblance of a smile.

He'd seen Spencer's parent's at Danny's funeral, of course. They had all been polite and cordial to one another—what else could people do when they were burying a guy like Danny? And when they had to consider Spencer's grief.

But now...

Mary Louise kept struggling with her composure, pulling away from her daughter to look at him. "Spencer, you've—you've brought David with you."

"Not on purpose, Mrs. Montgomery," David said, stepping in with their overnight bags. "I'm on guard duty," he said flatly.

"What's he talking about?" Joe Montgomery demanded, stepping forward. He pulled Spencer from his wife's hold, giving her a long hug but staring at David over her shoulder.

"Nothing, Dad."

Spencer swung around and stared hard at David. He shrugged, his look clearly telling her that he'd assumed she would rather have her parents know that Sly considered her to be in danger, rather than let them think she had brought him along for a fun weekend.

"David, what's going on, please?" Joe asked in a low voice.

David shrugged again, a little sorry for his rashness. He didn't particularly like or respect Joe Montgomery, but there was a lot of Sly in the man, especially the way he looked, tall, dignified, lean. David didn't think it was so much Joe who held the grudge against him. Spencer's mother had simply decided that David wasn't right for Spencer, and Joe had just gone along with what she thought was best for their only child.

"Nothing much, really. Sly is a little concerned because a few things seem to be heating up in the investigation into Danny's death. He asked me to keep an eye on Spencer."

"Even here?" Spencer's mother demanded a little indignantly.

"Sly is a cautious man."

"You know," Spencer cut in, "it's really very late. I'm absolutely certain there's a guest room available for David, and I'm exhausted. We can talk all this out in the morning. I'm going to bed."

She walked to the door, taking her small case from David's hands. "Thanks," she said briskly, and started for the marble stairs.

She could feel three pairs of eyes boring into her. No, four. Henri had appeared silently, magically—in a robe not much less elegant than her father's—to see to David's comfort. She gave him a wave. "Hi, Henri!"

"Welcome back, Mrs. Huntington."

"Thanks."

Spencer kept on walking. Let them stand there staring all night.

But that wasn't what happened.

"Join me for a brandy, David?" she heard her father ask. "Henri can take your things, and I'll show you the guest room when we go up."

"I . . . sure," David replied.

"Perhaps I should have something," Mary Louise began.

"No, perhaps you should go on up. I'll be along soon," Joe countered.

Spencer, past the landing, turned back, unable to resist looking over the balcony to the scene below.

Her mother was stunned, but her father looked very determined. Mary Louise allowed a hand to flutter to her throat, and her voice was totally disapproving. "Well, I suppose..."

Spencer sympathized with her mother. She was dying to know what the two men were going to say to one another. She was almost ready to go running downstairs, demanding admittance to their private meeting.

Unfortunately, she was certain she would be just as firmly rebuffed as her mother had been. And she *was* tired. Exhausted. If she didn't lie down soon, she would fall down. She was dead tired.

Dead...

What an awful word to use. She shivered fiercely and hurried along the hallway to her room.

It was always ready for her. It had hardly changed from when she'd been a little girl and had come here for the summers. It fit her much better now, for it had never been much of a little girl's room. The draperies were a golden damask, and the canopy over the cherrywood bed was the same, as was the comforter. The floors were hardwood, covered by a plush Persian carpet. The wrought-iron radiators that remained despite the conversion to forced-hot-water heat were painted a soft beige. The walls were paneled to a point, then the sunburst wallpaper rose to the moldings that rimmed the ceiling. It was a handsome room, an attractive room, done many years ago by a talented interior designer. Spencer didn't dislike it. But she felt there was little or nothing of herself here. The only thing she really liked was the bathroom, with its old fixtures and huge claw-footed tub. And she liked the balcony as well; it over-looked the rose gardens and the pool, which was kept heated year-round for those very few occasions when someone might actually go in it.

She dropped her bag at the foot of her bed and walked out of the balcony. She could smell the roses in the garden as she looked out over the pool. The balcony stretched across the rear of the house, but she might have been absolutely alone in the world, the night was so silent. She stepped in, showered quickly and went to bed, certain that she was so exhausted she would fall asleep quickly.

She didn't.

Instead she closed her eyes and remembered the night David had been arrested.

His eyes. She would always remember the way he had looked at her. She had felt chilled straight through the heart. She had tried to run down and find out what was going on, but her father had been on the stairway, catching her. She had fought him wildly, hysterically, and he had sounded as innocent as a man could be. By the time she'd managed to fight her way past him, David and the police car were gone. Her mother had been implacable. Of course she would never have called the police if she had realized it was David, but then, it was important for David to learn that trespassing was illegal, and so was trying to break windows.

It had been the worst night of Spencer's life. No amount of arguing had been able to move her mother. And she had told both her parents that she never wanted to see them again.

That had made it easy to leave the next day when David had walked out on her.

She trembled again just to remember it after so much time, so much life and death, had come between them. He'd been her life, and he'd walked away. She'd defended her parents, but she'd hated them then. It had been years before she'd managed to forgive them; she hadn't even come home from school for holidays at first. In fact, if it hadn't been for Sly, she might never have forgiven them, or herself; she had simply been too hurt that the people she loved could have betrayed her so deeply.

It was so long ago. And she had gotten past it. Married Danny, been happy with Danny. But now...

Now she was struggling again. It was so easy to feel close to David again. To feel as if the memories of their relationship could come rushing in and cause her marriage to fade to the far recesses of her mind. She bit her lip lightly and admitted that she had never fallen out of love with David. That didn't mean that she hadn't loved Danny, because she had. But maybe not as she should have. Still, there were moments when the guilt began to fade, and then she would feel guilty all over again for not feeling guilty enough. But despite the guilt there were moments when she forgot everything and simply wanted David. But they were older now, leading new lives. And she didn't dare feel too deeply until...

Until Danny's memory could rest with his soul. And then, maybe...

Her eyes flew open. She heard something. A creak, a whisper. She stared at the French doors that led to the balcony. Moving across the filmy gauze curtains floating on the breeze, she saw a shadow.

Her heart leaped to her throat. Sly had never convinced her that someone was trying to kill her. But the hadow seemed so menacing, looming in the moonlight, rowing larger as it moved closer to the doors.

She bounded out of bed. Streaked across the room and roze against the wall beside the French doors.

One began to move slowly inward. She should have creamed, but she was afraid to. There was a large Lladro igurine on her dressing table. She snatched up the porelain statue as the shadow moved into the room. She aised her weapon and started to bring it down. The hadow spun. An arm deflected her blow, and a palm lattened over her mouth when a scream at last promised o burst from her throat.

"Spencer, they arrested me for throwing pebbles! hey'll have me on death row for breaking into your edroom."

"David!" she gasped, pulling free from his grasp. 'You son of a bitch! You scared me half to death! Why lidn't you just knock?"

"I didn't want to wake you. I just wanted to make sure ou were all right."

She set the Lladro figurine on the dresser, trembling, er heart beating way too quickly again. He was a lamned good-looking shadow. He'd showered and he vas in jeans and nothing else. She loved the clean scent f his flesh. For a moment she was tempted to throw erself at him, to tell him that she was scared and needed im to stay the night beside her. She wanted to feel the iving warmth of his flesh, wanted to feel hot again, so ungry that the world was forgotten.

What would he say? That they would wake to a firing quad? But that wouldn't really matter to him. He didn't ive a damn what her parents thought; he'd learned the ard way that self-respect was the most important thing.

She closed her eyes, feeling slightly sick, ashamed of herself for how quickly she was able to forget that she had loved Danny. How quickly everything could fade away, the past *and* the future, when she got too close to David. An aching was all that remained, a longing. And then...

The pain was something she would only remember later.

Danny had been one of the world's most wonderful guys. And she had loved him. She had really loved him.

But once she had loved David, too.

And if he touched her again, just touched her...

But he didn't. He turned, heading for the French doors. "Amazingly," he said, an ironic tone in his voice, "I'm just the next room over. They seem to trust me as a watchdog. If the littlest thing happens, scream. I'll leave my door open."

"Nothing is going to happen here," she said.

"Why not?"

"Has anything happened since the incident in the cemetery? And if I was in danger then, it was my own fault. As you and a number of others have been so willing to point out."

"Spencer, be a good kid and behave, huh?"

"Nothing is going to happen. Not here. We're a million miles from home."

"Yeah, well, I hope so." He hesitated. "Maybe you should move up here for a while—"

"And maybe not!" she said indignantly.

"You were quick to run away."

"I didn't run away."

"Yes, you did. You've always run, and run fast. But this time it might not be such a bad idea."

"David, I came for the weekend. That's all."

He shrugged. "Well, it's late. We can argue it out to-morrow."

He started to walk away, but she called him back. "David!"

"Yeah?"

"What did my father want?"

"A private conversation with me."

She set her jaw and repeated evenly, "What did my father want?"

David hesitated for a second. "He apologized. He said he was sorry for having me arrested all those years ago."

The breeze rustled; the gauze curtains rose and fell.

"And what did you tell him?"

"That it was a long time ago. And it didn't matter anymore. Good night, Spencer."

He paused, watching her for a moment. Then he disappeared and she lay there awake, thinking of him.

Sleeping in the next room.

So very close.

She dozed, and she remembered. . . .

She awoke with a start, sat up, shivered. Groaned. Tried to sleep again.

It was a long night.

When she woke the next morning she found the rest of the household already up, having breakfast on the porch. The day was cool, but the sun was strong; it was a perfect morning to sit outside and feel the breeze and the touch of heat. David had a cup of coffee in hand. He wasn't exactly sitting at the table with her parents like a long-lost friend, but at least he was there, drinking coffee as he looked out over the expansive lawn.

"Spencer, dear!" her mother said. "You look awake and refreshed. I'd thought that perhaps since you were here, you'd come with me to a luncheon at Daisy Eaton's house this afternoon.''

"Sorry, Mom, I want to see the beach and the mansions today. Get a few ideas for some projects."

"Spencer, you don't even need to work," her mother said unhappily. "And Daisy Eaton's house is far nicer than any of those gaudy public mansions. If only Danny had lived, you might have been pregnant by now, and he could have given up his foolish notions of crime fighting. You two—"

"Mary Louise!" Joe said sharply.

Spencer would have protested herself, but her mother's words had created the most awful pain in her heart, as if someone were twisting a wire coat hanger into her flesh.

She glanced at her father, a little surprised. He was leaning toward her mother, staring at her firmly. "Spencer and Danny had the right to choose their own way of life, just as you are free to pursue your desires. Reminding Spencer that her husband was murdered does not seem constructive to me in any way."

Mary Louise gasped, staring at her husband. Hurt filled her eyes; she was about to burst into tears.

Spencer thought of all the times her mother had manipulated her life, and for a moment she sat very still. She'd always forgiven Mary Louise. She'd never wanted to hurt her. But her father was right. Mary Louise could see only one road—and it was time she acknowledged some others.

Spencer stood up. She felt her parents watching her and David staring at her curiously. "I've got to go," she said softly, and turned to leave them. She was striding to the garage when she realized David was barely two steps behind her.

She spun to face him. "What? No applause?" she demanded bitterly. "I think that was just about as good as a slap in the face, don't you?"

"Spencer..."

She didn't want to hear any more. She opened the garage and saw the rental car sitting there, keys in the ignition. She strode over to the driver's seat and slid in, slamming the door behind her.

He crawled in on the passenger side.

She eased out of the driveway, staring ahead, completely miserable. She owed Danny so much, and she was failing him. And just what the hell was she doing now?

David was silent beside her.

"Say something!" she demanded.

He was silent for another moment; then he said softly, "I can't pretend that I've respected your mother in the past."

"You hated her."

"I didn't care much for her. But I'm sorry for her now, and maybe I've finally seen something myself. She can't help being what she is, Spencer. You grew up with a broader vision. You were sent to a preppy school, but it was bordered by a neighborhood filled with ghetto kids. You watched the refugees pour in your whole life. You saw what you had and what others didn't. Your mother never had that experience. She grew up rich. She was surrounded by wealth and only wealth. She couldn't accept what she didn't know, and she still can't accept things that scare her. But she can change, Spencer. Anyone can change. And she loves you."

She turned to stare at him, incredulous.

"The light, Spencer!"

She stared at the red light ahead of them, just at the bottom of a sharp incline. She slammed on the brakes.

Nothing happened.

"Spencer! Hit the brake!"

"I *am* hitting it. There *are* no brakes!"

They were going very fast, the incline giving the car added momentum. At the bottom of the hill the cross traffic moved by lazily. Beyond the light was a white fence. Beyond the fence, a strip of rock and straggly grass and flowers. Below the rock—far below—lay the jagged shores of the Atlantic Ocean.

They careened down the slope. Spencer cried out, slamming her foot again and again on the brake. David threw his body across the car, half atop her, half beside her. His foot came down on hers.

No amount of force was going to help.

The car picked up more speed, and she stared in horror at the intersection.

The light turned green. The cross traffic stopped. All that loomed ahead of them was the little white picket fence. The ragged strip of land.

The water and the rocks . . .

They flew into the intersection.

And then a void of sky and ocean seemed to stretch out endlessly before them.

10

David swung the wheel hard to the right. They took the turn, along with half the white picket fence. They careened into the traffic. Thank God there wasn't much of it. Horns blew as the car tilted, sliding along on two wheels, fighting to right itself.

The road still led slightly downhill. Enough to keep the car's forward motion going. Terrified, watching cars and people seem to rush toward her, Spencer forced a hand up. She slammed it hard on the horn.

The cars coming toward them jerked to either side of the road. Wheels screeched against pavement. Other horns began to sound. Up ahead, there was a curve, and after it, an embankment of thick brush.

"I'm going for it," David said tensely.

A no formed on her lips but got no further. He was right. There would be another turn, another picket fence. Then a flight into nothing, a crash down to ocean and rock.

Or there would be a car, a bus, a motorcycle. Something with which to collide. Others who could be killed.

She kept silent, her throat frozen. They spun sharply around the next curve, and then he straightened the wheel, sending them tearing into the brush. Spencer screamed as she heard the foliage rip and tear around them, battering the automobile. Glass shattered and spilled over them like prisms of deadly rain. Spencer instinctively closed her eyes. The shattered glass missed her face, falling instead upon her hands.

Amazingly, the car came to a halt.

Spencer just sat there, afraid to open her eyes. She felt a weight against her. Something warm. David. Was he dead?

She dared to open her eyes just as he was carefully shifting away from her. Glass fell between them.

"You all right?" he asked softly.

She stared, then forced herself to nod. There was glass in his hair. She reached out. He caught her hand. "Careful. Stay where you are. I'll come around."

He forced open his door. They were smack in the middle of a clump of bushes. A tree branch had broken through the passenger side of the windshield. David had missed being clubbed by about three inches.

He jerked on her door, swore, slammed his body against it and pulled on it again.

Spencer heard sirens and closed her eyes momentarily. She hated the sound of sirens. It always made her flinch. Even when she knew they were coming for her. And even when, by the grace of God, she and David were still okay.

He got the door open. Reached for her. His features were tense, handsome, matter-of-fact. "Nothing broken? You're certain? Neck trauma, back—"

"I'm all right." She managed to say it without a tremor in her voice. She took his hands.

"Careful. Slow. Watch the glass," he told her.

Motorists had stopped. Pedestrians who'd been strolling along the beach walk were hurrying across the road.

A police car got there first, swerving onto the curve beyond the car. The officer looked as if he couldn't be more than twenty, but he moved like lightning, reaching them, asking them if they were all right.

"Jesus, it's a miracle that you're okay!" he told them, scratching his head, staring at the vehicle. "What the hell happened?"

"The brakes went." Spencer said.

"Rental car?" the officer asked.

She nodded.

"We picked it up last night in Boston," David said. By then an emergency vehicle had arrived. A female paramedic with short curly dark hair and a gamine's easy smile took hold of Spencer, telling her that they had a special vacuum with them to sweep the glass particles out of people's hair.

Spencer found herself being led away to have her head vacuumed while David continued to talk with the officer. She watched while he drew out his license and the rental agreement, then realized there was a jagged tear in his shirt. His dark head glinted when the glass particles were touched by the sun.

"How's that? All right now?" the young paramedic asked. She looked at Spencer. "I think you should both come into the emergency room just to be safe."

"I'm all right. Honestly."

"You're going to be sore from head to toe. In an accident like this one, you instinctively tense up for impact. A hot bath helps. And keep moving, okay? It helps to work the soreness out."

Spencer nodded absently, still watching David. He seemed very insistent about something, and the cop was scratching his head again. At last the cop nodded, and David walked back to Spencer.

More police cars arrived. An older man in plain clothes came over to talk to Spencer, and the gamine paramedic melted away.

"You were the driver, miss?"

Spencer nodded.

"And you say your brakes just went?"

"That's right. They just went."

"No matter what, the driver is responsible for the vehicle. You'll be ticketed for a moving violation. You're incredibly lucky, young woman."

"You're going to ticket me?" Spencer said incredulously. "We only picked up the car last night! Ticket the rental agency! They gave me the car," she went on indignantly.

"Sergeant, wait!" someone called. Another young officer who had been talking to David came hurrying over. "Sergeant, this is Spencer Montgomery Huntington."

The older man's eyes narrowed. "You're a Montgomery?"

"Yes," she replied dryly, glacing over his shoulder to where David stood.

"We'll see what we can do," the man said gruffly, walking away. The younger officer gave her a broad smile. "I'd be delighted to be of service, Mrs. Huntington."

"Thank you," she murmured. They'd been just about to hang her, but David had seen to it that they knew who she was. The Montgomery name had done the rest.

A tow truck arrived. David was occupied with the wrecker and the cops for a few minutes longer; then he strolled over to her.

"Think you need to go to the hospital?" he asked her. She shook her head firmly. "What about you?"

He smiled slowly. "Not on your life. Come on. The officer over there has offered us a lift back to your parents' place. I *would* like a shower and fresh clothing."

The young officer with the great smile ushered them both into the back of his vehicle. "They wanted to give me a ticket," Spencer said wryly to David. "We almost died, and I was going to get a ticket."

"It's the way the law works."

"But then you told them I was a Montgomery."

David hesitated a minute. He shook his head. "I didn't tell them you were a Montgomery. I told them you were a police widow. Someone knew the name—apparently you've contributed heavily to help police widows who aren't Montgomerys, and to help their children."

Spencer felt her cheeks redden. She looked at her lap, staring at her fingers. There was a small cut on her ring finger, right by the plain gold band she had always wanted and Danny had given her.

"Danny and I didn't have kids. Lots of guys who are killed do. Their mothers struggle to cope with their pain and raise the kids alone. They deserve some kind of a break."

"You don't have to explain it to me. I was a cop." He paused, then took a new tack. "Maybe now you'll have the sense to admit that your life is in danger."

"What?"

"Spencer, we were nearly killed—"

"The brakes failed! We're not in Miami, we're in Rhode Island! Come on, David!"

He nodded, waiting for the echo of her words to die away. Then he looked at her sternly. "Ricky Garcia is a millionaire. Trey Delia can command a fleet of cultists across the country. And Gene Vichy is basking away in a truckload of his wife's money. You don't think that any one of them could have extended a hand to Rhode Island?''

Spencer stared straight ahead. "That's absurd. I don't know anything."

"But as you keep pointing out, you did manage to get Trey Delia arrested," he told her curtly. "Maybe Garcia thinks he's next."

"But as *you've* pointed out, Ricky Garcia is extremely rich and powerful. If he really wanted me dead, wouldn't I *be* dead?"

"Is he going to walk up to you in the street and shoot you, bang bang, you're dead? No, he's much more subtle than that. Automobile-accident subtle!"

"Then he'd get me at home."

"It would look far less suspicious if you were to perish in Rhode Island."

"You're exasperating," Spencer told him.

"Spencer..."

She suddenly elbowed him in the arm, unaware when he winced. "That's the house ahead. Warn him to pull in."

David gritted his teeth and angled forward, pointing to the drive. The man nodded, smiling again. When he paused by the gate, Spencer got out to hit the call box for entry, then waved them past, deciding to walk up the driveway and maybe shake off a little more glass. And maybe think a bit about David's words. By the time she got to the house, both men were out of the car waiting for her. The officer was staring at the house with undisguised curiosity.

"Can I offer you a soft drink or a cup of coffee?" Spencer suggested, heading for the steps.

"No, thanks, I'm on patrol," he said. "But I'd sure love to take a rain check for another time."

"Freely given," Spencer assured him, shaking his hand.

He tipped his head to David. "I'll keep in touch, Mr. Delgado."

"Thanks," David said.

"What's he keeping in touch about?"

"He's going to keep me posted on the brakes."

"Meaning?"

"They'll be trying to find out just how and when they were tampered with."

"What makes you think they were tampered with? They might just have been faulty," Spencer said.

"Yeah, they might have been," he said. "Just like I could fly—with a little bit of fairy dust. Let's go in."

His hand at the small of her back, he propelled her up the front steps. Henri was standing at the front door, a questioning look in his eyes.

"We had a little accident with the rental car, Henri," Spencer said smoothly.

"Can I get you anything? Do anything?" Henri asked. "Your parents have already gone out to your mother's luncheon. They're not due to return until late this afternoon."

"Good," Spencer said softly beneath her breath. David heard her, and arched a brow her way. She ignored him and started for the stairs.

"I'm just fine, Henri," she said.

"I'd like a great big snifter of brandy," David said pleasantly.

"I shall bring it right up, sir," Henri assured him.

David shrugged to Spencer as he passed her on the stairs. "Something to get all the creaks out," he informed her, then hurried to his door.

In the shower, Spencer stood beneath the hot spray for long minutes, hoping that any remaining glass was being rinsed away. She washed her hair very carefully, keeping the water steaming hot all the while.

David had to be wrong. It was just a mechanical problem.

The only time she had really been in danger was when she had put herself into the very path of it—at the cemetery. Admittedly, that had been foolish. But Sly must be getting paranoid to think that a falling beam in a tumbledown house was anything but an accident. And brakes did fail; accidents did happen. She had been arguing with David at the time; maybe she had unwittingly done something wrong.

You're reaching there, Spencer, she told herself.

But she still couldn't believe that she was in danger, especially not here.

She stepped from the shower and pulled on a fluffy terry robe. She took a brush to her hair, staring at her pale reflection in the mirror. She set the brush down firmly and walked out to the balcony. She moved to stand in front of the open doors that led into David's room. She could hear him singing something from the bathroom. An old Beatles tune. He had a decent voice.

She gingerly entered the guest room, something stirring deep inside her, something warning her that she was making a mistake, that if she had ever walked into danger, that time was now.

She walked in anyway. She tried to conjure up Danny's face. She tried to tell herself that she had just come in to talk. She and David were older and wiser now. Mature enough to know that their differences and a dozen other barriers stood between them like a high brick wall.

She almost turned around.

Then his voice lashed out at her suddenly.

"Who's there?"

Well, what kind of P.I. would he be if he didn't hear footsteps padding into his room? she mocked herself.

"It's Spencer," she said. Well, she'd come this far. She strode on in to lean against the doorframe to the bathroom.

The guest bath had been extensively remodeled. A huge Jacuzzi with marble steps and gold-trimmed porcelain faucets sat along the far wall. David was deeply ensconced in the tub, the water whirling. He was sitting up just straight enough to roll the liquid amber of his brandy in a big snifter. He cast a glance her way, one that told her beyond a doubt that she was interrupting a moment of privacy.

"If all else fails, I think you'll be able to join a rock band," she told him.

"Thanks, I'll keep that in mind," he told her. "What do you want, Spencer?"

"David, you and Sly have to be reasonable. He only got scared to begin with because a beam fell. A beam!" She forgot for a moment just how funny it made her feel inside merely to walk into a room and find him naked...wet.... She walked across to the tub and sat on the edge of the marble step. "David, I don't have a death wish. I really do want to keep on living. I just can't believe that what happened here today has anything to do with Danny's death. Danny was a cop. Cops make enemies—"

"And sometimes their widows like to stir up trouble."

She sighed. "David..."

"What are you doing in here?" he demanded suddenly, irritably. "I was enjoying a hot bath and a peaceful brandy. Would you please be so good as to get out?

What would your mother say if she were to come home and find you with a naked Latino refugee?''

Spencer felt her whole body go stiff with anger. But it didn't seem to matter to David. His eyes were narrowed on her. The pulse at his throat was ticking.

"Weren't you the one defending my mother this morning?" she asked him coolly.

"This is her house," he pointed out. "Not that I think she ever believed that you slept with me way back then. She would have passed out cold to think that a Latino refugee had touched your lily-white flesh."

"Go to hell!" she told him, rising. On second thought, she snatched the snifter from him. "And if you're going to talk that way about my mother, you can get your lips off her brandy."

"And her daughter?" he inquired politely.

She spun around. He caught the hem of her robe, giving her a firm jerk. She lost her balance on the marble steps and let out a frightened yelp before falling into the Jacuzzi. Her robe was immediately soaked as she found herself seated on his lap, her legs dangling just outside the tub. She realized with a gasp that he was as hard as steel, and there was a metallic glint in his eyes as they bored into hers. "Let's see how you turn this into my fault, Spencer. *You* come cruising into *my* bath. In a towel, no less."

"A robe."

"A towel with sleeves."

"David—"

"Did you come because you wanted something, Spencer? One would think so. But then again, you can't admit that you might actually want something as basic as sex, not when you've only been a widow for just over a

year. I mean, it happened once. But then you just about
rolled over and died yourself. Now you want it again.''

"David, just let me up!" she began.

But he didn't. The brandy glass was plucked from her
fingers. She didn't have time to wonder where it went,
because he kissed her. Her eyes closed as she felt his lips,
hot, wet and slick, on her own. Felt the steam from the
Jacuzzi whirling around them, felt the simmering movement of the water washing over her, around them.

Her towel with sleeves bubbled up.

His mouth seemed to devour hers. His hand had
slipped beneath her, rounded the curve of her buttocks.
She felt his touch, bold, determined, never giving quar-
ter. Seeking. Finding. Giving.

The steam seemed to enter her flesh. It spiraled between her legs, where he found and teased, stroked and
tested, the tiny bud of her greatest sensuality. Her head
fell back, she could scarcely breathe. The pleasure built
in her unbearably. A whimper formed in her throat, but
his lips were on hers again, catching the sounds that
might have escaped. She squirmed against him, desperate to be free, desperate to have more. Her climax burst
violently through her, convulsing the length of her. She
felt him withdraw his touch, then felt herself moved,
manipulated, brought down atop him, slowly impaled as
he stared silently into her eyes.

As he drove into her, she was still bathed in the sweet
aftermath, her face flushed and sheened, her flesh hot,
then chilled, until it began to grow hot very quickly once
again. She didn't want to feel his eyes, so she lowered her
head, burying her face against his shoulder, feeling again
the swift building of sensation, his hands on her, on her
shoulders, her buttocks, moving her until she caught the
rhythm and the hunger again. His hands pressed down on

her shoulders, crushing her onto him. A harsh cry rang
from his lips as his body went rigid before seeming to ex
plode. She fell against him, amazed at the ripples tha
swept her as the force of his climax swept into her
bringing on her own.

She fell against him, her heart pounding fiercely. Sh
heard the rasping of his breath, the continual whir and
bubble of the water.

Then remorse struck her again. Pain. Confusion. Wha
was she doing? Thank God they weren't in Danny's bec
this time. This was her mother's house, and she wasn'
afraid of her mother. She didn't mind standing up to her
and she wasn't in the least afraid of pointing out to her
that she was a *wee* bit bigoted. It was just that some
thing felt dishonest. She didn't feel guilty about her parents, but she did feel guilty about Danny, and she fel
guilty because ...

Because there had been times, even when Danny was
alive, when she had remembered being with his best
friend. And now Danny was dead, and she *was* with his
best friend, needing him, hating him, wanting him, re-
senting him.

A psychiatrist could have a field day with her, she
thought.

She wasn't cheating. She was a widow, she told herself. Danny shouldn't be dead, but he was. It was like a
cry of anguish in her heart. Maybe if it wasn't David ...

If it wasn't David she wouldn't be wanting this way,
aching this way, needing this way. Remembering. The
hostility wouldn't be there to create the fire; her hunger
would never be the same. She had loved David once.
Then he had hated her, and she had hated him. Now they
and the world had changed, but not really.

He groaned suddenly, lifting her cleanly from him, staring into her eyes. He got to his knees, setting her atop the edge of the tub, touching her face. She hadn't even known she'd been crying until he wiped a tear from beneath her eye, his expression suddenly very cold, very grim. Then he swore softly. He spoke in Spanish, but she'd lived in Dade County long enough to learn some of the language. It wasn't complimentary.

He stood, drawing her up with him. Her soaked robe fell into the swirling waters, but he went for it quickly, pressing it to her chest as he stepped out of the Jacuzzi, picked her up bodily by the shoulders and carried her to the open doors, through which a cool breeze wafted. It didn't seem to have a cooling effect on his temper, though. When he spoke again, his voice wasn't soft anymore. It was harsh and guttural.

"Spencer, if and when you're ready to make love without crying about it afterward, you let me know. But until then, keep your clothes on and stay out of my bathroom, will you? You came in here because you wanted to, but you always have to pretend you're not a part of what happens between us. What you do, Spencer, you do because you want to. Now you damned well better learn to live with it!"

To her amazement, he set her down on the balcony, where she clutched her soaked robe to her chest and stared as he turned on a dime and left her here, disappearing into the bathroom. Leaving her there, a cool breeze blowing over her nakedness.

11

Spencer realized after a moment that her butt was facing the pool. Her bare butt.

She spun around, praying there were no gardeners on duty and that Henri wasn't checking out the patio. The lush trees surrounding the property bowed and dipped in the breeze. The crystal clear water of the pool rippled in the lazily fading sunlight. There was no one in sight.

Spencer fled into her room, closing the doors to the balcony behind her. She dropped the soaking robe into the tub and grabbed a dry towel. Then she dropped that, as well, and leaped into the shower, not moving as she let a cascade of water plummet over her. Cool water. Water to soothe her wounded soul.

When she finished showering, she shrugged into jeans and a big fluffy sweater. Restless, she combed through her wet hair, played with her makeup, then stepped out on the balcony again.

She could hear him—still swearing in Spanish. He couldn't still be going on about her, could he?

She took a step toward his room. Well, she wasn't in a towel and he wasn't in the bathroom. He was standing in front of the antique dresser mirror, staring at his back.

"Is there a problem?" she inquired lightly.

The swearing stopped. He spun around. He was dressed in jeans, as well, his feet and chest still bare.

He stared at her. "Yeah, there's a problem. Come in here."

"Come in here?" she said, repeating his tone.

"Come in here, please," he said.

She walked in, and he turned around. For the first time she noticed a thin ribbon of blood running down his back. "You're hurt!" she said.

"I know that. There's a sliver of metal caught there. I didn't even notice it until my back started rubbing against the tub. You can be a hazard."

She froze. "You mean that—" she began, than broke off. Of course that was what he meant.

"You're a big boy!" she reminded him softly. "I didn't exactly force you at gunpoint."

"No, Spencer, you just like to seduce a man—then slam him on the head for being seduced."

"I repeat, you're a big boy. And one who had better be careful," she warned. "If you want my help."

"Just get in here and see what you can do."

"Come in and sit on the commode. The light is better there."

A moment later he was seated and she was dabbing at his back with a peroxide-soaked piece of gauze while she tried to get a good grasp on the sliver that had pierced his flesh.

"Ouch!" he persisted. "Quit digging."

"I have to dig."

"Do it more carefully."

"If you'd quit bleeding, it wouldn't be so slippery."

"I'm *so* sorry!"

"If you'd sit still . . ."

She got the piece of metal. Got a good grip. Just as it came free, there was a thunderous pounding on the hallway door, and then it burst open. "David, Spencer, oh, dear Lord, where are you?"

Joe Montgomery, perfect silver hair mussed and blue eyes wild, appeared in the bathroom doorway. He looked as if he was about to encompass Spencer in a protective hug, but then he saw the blood on David's back.

"Oh, my God, you *are* injured!" he gasped.

"It's just a scratch, sir," David said.

Her dad was bad enough, Spencer thought. But, inevitably, her mother, crying her name hysterically, came running up behind her father and stared at them both. She saw the blood, moaned and wavered on her feet.

"Mother, David's tough—" Spencer began.

"She's going to pass out," Joe said matter-of-factly. And he turned smoothly, catching Mary Louise as she slipped into a dead faint. He carried her over to the bed and set her gently on it.

"I'll get some smelling salts," Spencer volunteered, running to her mother's room, returning quickly to snap open the vial beneath Mary Louise's nose.

Her mother came around slowly, gave her a wan smile, then reached for her, crying softly. "Oh, Spencer, we were stopped by the road by a nice officer and he said there'd been an accident, that the car was destroyed, and you—you—"

"Mother, I'm fine," Spencer said firmly, patting her hand. Guilt assailed her, a new form of it. Mary Louise, for all her strange ways, loved her. Completely. "Mom, honest, I don't have a scratch on me. And David... well, it's just a scratch, but I need to put a bandage over it before he drips blood all over your Oriental carpet."

"Spencer, how you can joke...!" Mary Louise began reproachfully, struggling to sit up. She looked at her husband. "Joe, they're really all right?"

"They look pretty good to me," Joe Montgomery said, eyeing his daughter. Spencer saw a slight smile playing at the corners of his lips.

For a moment she wondered what would have happened if her parents had returned thirty minutes earlier. Instead of finding a medical interlude in the guest bath, they would have discovered something quite different.

"Are you all right, Mrs. Montgomery?" David asked.

Mary Louise looked at him and nodded. "Yes, thank you. I'm fine. I apologize for being such a—a sissy."

David shrugged. "We had three-hundred-pound guys on the force who passed out when they were supposed to give blood. Some people just can't deal with the sight of it, so you don't need to worry about being a sissy. Spencer," he said, looking from Mary Louise to her. "Think we can finish up?"

Spencer had gone still, amazed that David could speak so kindly to her mother.

"Spencer?"

She nodded and followed him into the bathroom to finish patching him up. Her parents were still sitting on the bed when they came out of the bathroom.

Spencer's father cleared his throat. "Think you two would like dinner soon? If you're up to it, of course. Mary Louise and I would like to take you to one of our favorite spots." David started to say something, but Joe raised a hand. "A casual place. So casual, in fact, that you bring your own wine. It's lobster served on wooden tables, all you can eat, and the best in New England."

David glanced over at Spencer, an eyebrow raised. She shrugged imperceptibly.

"Yeah. Sounds nice. Thanks," David said.

"Now I'm going to call my lawyer," Joe said.

"About what?" Spencer asked.

"That rental car company."

"The police will be questioning the people there. And also your chauffeur, and anyone else who works around the grounds," David said.

"Anyone who works for me?" Joe demanded, startled.

"I don't think it's necessary—" Spencer began flatly.

"Maybe someone saw something, knows something," David suggested.

"Do you mean to suggest that what happened today might not have been an accident?" Joe demanded.

Spencer's mother gasped. Her hand flew to her chest. She looked as if she was about to pass out again.

"No!" Spencer said emphatically, staring hard at David. "You know the cops. Well, of course, you don't know cops like I know cops," she said, trying to keep things light. "They feel compelled to question everyone. Besides, the officer who gave us a ride home was crazy about the house. He probably just wants a chance to see more of it."

"Spencer! You didn't ask him in?"

"Of course I asked him in, Mother. But he was still on duty and couldn't take the time."

Mary Louise stood up, followed more slowly by Joe. "Dinner, then," she said firmly. "I never did like that chauffeur," she said reproachfully to her husband. She looked at Spencer and David. "He has a drinking problem."

"Had a drinking problem. He's a fully recovering alcoholic," Joe said.

"Can there be such a thing?" Mary Louise demanded.

"Yes!" Joe said firmly. "We will get to the bottom of this!" he assured Spencer and David.

"Yes, we will," David agreed.

Joe and Mary Louise left the room. David turned to see that Spencer had gone out the back way, just as she had come in.

He headed to the phone and dialed the police station. They'd already started checking the brake system of the totaled automobile. "It's going to be hard to prove anything," the sergeant in charge told David. "There was a tiny hole in the hydraulic line. Could have just happened. Could have been purposely punctured. To tell you the truth, if you weren't involved, we would just assume it was mechanical failure and nothing more. But the rental agency is emphatic about the care they give their cars. Still, a leak like that would be almost invisible."

"How did so much fluid leak out so fast without being seen?"

"It could have been leaking from Boston to Newport. We've had a brief conversation with the Montgomery chauffeur, and he swears he didn't touch the car other than to pull it into the garage. And he says the Montgomery property is well protected. We'll be talking to other people, of course. Let me know if you need anything more."

David thanked him, hung up, then dialed Sly. He told him about both the accident and the police report.

"What do you think?" Sly demanded.

"I don't know what to think anymore."

"You thought I was a paranoid old fool, just like Spencer did."

"I've never thought of you as a fool, Sly," David told him wryly.

"Hmm. You returning Sunday?"

"That's what the tickets say."

"Keep me informed."

"Yep."

As David started to hang up he heard a click on the phone and hesitated.

Someone in the house had been listening in.

Jared and Cecily Monteith had brought the children to his father's house to spend Saturday afternoon.

It wasn't the kind of quiet day Cecily particularly enjoyed. She couldn't help it, she was a people person. She liked parties on boats, luncheons and cocktails and the clubs on South Beach. She liked fund-raisers and benefits, the ballet, a good show brought down from New York.

But her father-in-law's place wasn't bad. It was right on the water, with a long dock that stretched into the bay. She could walk out on it with the children, and they could watch the pleasure craft in the bay. And they didn't come that often. She liked her father-in-law well enough; she would have liked him better if he'd had a little more gumption, but then, she would have liked Jared a little better that way, too.

Jon Monteith had worked for Sly before he'd had heart attacks two years in a row, forcing him to semi-retire. But that had been a few years ago now, and Jon was healing nicely. He talked about coming back into the office soon. He golfed with Sly at least once every two weeks and spent a lot of time puttering around his small garden. And, like Cecily, he enjoyed the dock; he kept a small boat just so he could motor around a little bit now and then. His passion in life was his grandchildren. Cecily had to admit that he was good to the kids, seven-year-old William and five-year-old Ashley. She had beautiful children, if she did say so herself. And she was glad. They both had tawny blond hair and her wide amber eyes. And Jared, whatever his faults, was a good father, and she had a very good housekeeper, so she wasn't overly burdened with their occasional tantrums.

That evening, Jon barbecued platefuls of ribs, chicken, burgers and dogs.

He boiled a few hot dogs as well, since Ashley didn't like the barbecue "black stuff" on hers. Cecily had brought the kids in from the dock, and they were all lounging around by the pool, waiting for Jon to finish up.

Cecily was stretched out, thinking of her most recent dilemma. She had loved the sun all her life. She knew she looked better with a tan. Everyone looked better with a tan. Even those damned little cellulite cells that attached themselves to her thighs no matter how often she worked out looked so much better tan.

But she wasn't a kid anymore. Tanning caused wrinkles, no matter how much she doused herself in lotions and creams. She should cover up. She'd allowed herself her hour of sun with two tons of sun block.

She was only vaguely aware when the phone started ringing.

"I'll get it, Dad," Jared offered.

Cecily wished she could change places with Jared at times. He didn't care if he burned or not. Men were supposed to show a bit of weathering. It gave them character. Women just looked like worn-out luggage.

"Sit tight, son," Jon said cheerfully. "Last hamburger is off. I'll grab it."

Even Jon! Her father-in-law, for all his health problems, was a handsome man. Like Jared. Still tall and lean. He even had thick hair. White, but thick. He was in the water all the time, in the sun all the time. On the damned golf course all the time. It didn't seem to hurt him any. Jared's mother had died years ago at a comparatively young age, and these days there were a score of older women after Jon.

Younger ones, too, Cecily thought resentfully.

Jon had gone into the house. He suddenly appeared at the door to the patio, his arms hanging limply at his sides. He stared from Jared to Cecily.

"There's been an accident."

Jared leaped up, staring at his father. Cecily, startled, not quite grasping the tension in her father-in-law's voice, got to her feet more slowly.

"What happened?" she demanded.

"Damn it, Dad, what happened?" Jared echoed.

"There was an accident in Rhode Island. Spencer's rental car lost its brakes."

"And ... ?" Jared nearly shouted.

"Delgado was with her."

"In the car?"

"Yes. Between them, they steered the car into a clump of bushes."

"Are they all right?" Cecily whispered. Suddenly she heard a whimpering and then a soft cry. Ashley was at her side, slipping her small hand into her mother's. She'd been listening. She'd sensed the tension, as children were so prone to do.

"Is Aunt Spencer hurt?"

Cecily couldn't answer. She simply stared at Jon.

"They're fine. That was Sly. He said they're both fine."

Cecily stared at Jared, closing her eyes, feeling weak.
Then she knelt by her sniffling daughter. "Yes, she's fine.
She's just fine. Didn't you just hear Grandpa? She had a
little car trouble, but she's all right now."

Her daughter was still sobbing, huddled against her.
"Don't let Aunt Spencer be dead, Mommy. Please, don't
let Aunt Spencer be dead like Uncle Danny."

Cecily's heart seemed to catch in her throat.

She drew Ashley even closer to her and stared at Jared
over her daughter's head.

There were some things Spencer wanted to attend to
herself. David was occupied, she was certain.

And here on the grounds of her parents' home, she had
to be safe.

She left the house, walking determinedly to the garage. Her feet crunched on the gravel drive. She knocked
loudly on the side door that led to the chauffeur's apartment.

There was no answer. "Hello? Mr. Murphy?" she
called. Still no answer. She pushed the door open.

Murphy was about sixty. Balding. A little plump, with
a drooping white mustache.

He was seated in an old recliner, looking as if he had
just lost the entire world. There was a bottle of Jack
Daniel's at his side. It was brand-new, unopened.

"Mr. Murphy?" Spencer said.

He stared at her with watery eyes. He lifted a hand,
and it fell back to the arm of the chair. "Mrs. Huntington. I'm glad to see you alive, that I am. Pray God that
you can believe that, at least!"

"Thank you. Of course I believe it," she said awkwardly. "I just came to ask you—"

"You came to ask me, the police came to ask me. Your father came to fire me."

Spencer gasped. "But—"

He stood up, coming toward her. She'd never realized he was such a big man before. She almost backed away, but she didn't, and he stopped right before her, shaking his head sadly. "I'd not harm a hair on your head. You're a fine lady, and I'd swear it on my dyin' bed to my maker. I moved the car into the garage, and that was it, ma'am."

Spencer stared at him, wishing with all her heart that she could figure out who was telling the truth and who wasn't. But Murphy wasn't lying. She was sure of it.

"Mr. Murphy, you're not fired."

"Ah, now, Mrs. Huntington—"

"Give me the Jack Daniel's. It's a big man who can lick a drinking problem. Stay big. Give me the bottle. And I'll tell my father you can either keep working for him or come south and work for me."

Murphy didn't believe her at first. Then he started to smile. He handed her the Jack Daniel's. Tears started running down his red cheeks. "Bless you, Mrs. Huntington."

"Nonsense! It's my fault Dad was angry with you."

"But—"

"I'll take care of it," Spencer said. She turned and headed to the house.

David, on his way to see the chauffeur, hesitated and stepped inside the door when he saw Spencer. She didn't see him as she strode into her father's elegant study.

"Murphy is innocent," she said flatly.

"Now, Spencer, you don't understand these—"

"I'm over thirty, Dad. I've got a very decent grasp of right and wrong these days. I'm asking you to give the man his job back."

Joe was silent for a long time. "Fine."

"I'll talk with Mother, convince her."

"No, you won't, young lady. I listen to her advice, I always have. But I make my own decisions."

David knew he shouldn't have been eavesdropping, but it was part of a P.I.'s job. And he was damned glad he *had* been listening.

He left the house, closing the door softly behind him. He still wanted to talk to the chauffeur.

To Spencer's vast relief, their dinner out seemed to be all right. Mary Louise was a little uncertain, but Joe carried the conversation. He talked about growing up in the thirties, and how the Indian villages had extended eastward to places that were now giant shopping malls. "Funny to think that this was once a nothing little town. You should hear Sly talk about the gondolas that used to come in from Tahiti Beach to the Biltmore."

"I've heard him," Spencer and David said in unison, and even Mary Louise smiled.

The lobster was great, and David had brought the wine. Her mother sipped it very carefully at first, but she seemed pleased to discover that David knew wines. Spencer hadn't felt quite so relaxed in months.

No, since Danny had been alive.

Everything went well until some friends of her parents came by. The Greshiams were among the most elite people in Newport. She sponsored countless charities; he sat on countless boards. Their oldest son was a senator, their second son was a biochemist changing the world, and their daughter was a lawyer, about to become a senator.

Mary Louise seemed dismayed to have been caught by such a pair and stumbled over the introductions. "You do remember my daughter, Spencer, and..."

After the "and," Mary Louise went blank. Dead blank.

"Mr. David Delgado. A friend of Spencer's late husband," David supplied.

"Oh, yes!" Mrs. Greshiam said, silver head twisting, and matching silver eyes falling on Spencer. "My dear, we are so sorry about the tragedy."

"Thank you," Spencer said. She looked at her mother. "David is a friend of *mine,* Mrs. Greshiam," she found herself emphasizing.

"Yes, yes, of course, dear," her mother said awkwardly. She looked relieved when the Greshiams moved on.

Mary Louise, Joe and David ordered coffee. Spencer decided on espresso. David watched her curiously, one brow half-raised. She wanted to tell him that people everywhere ordered espresso, that she wasn't trying to make any statements about his background because espresso and Cuban coffee could be so similar. He seemed amused. She found herself growing annoyed.

This was ridiculous. She wanted to leap up and tell him that this was America; she could order anything she wanted any time she wanted. And he didn't have a damned thing to do with it.

Except that he did. She had learned to like espresso during her senior year of high school, when she had first tasted his.

He was still watching her. She looked at him questioningly, and he shrugged, then turned to answer some question her father had just asked him.

By the time they headed back to the Montgomery mansion, David and Spencer's parents seemed to be getting along just fine.

Once in the house, Spencer deserted them all quickly, saying she was tired. She could hear David downstairs. He was socializing with both her parents tonight. She dressed in footed flannel pajamas, and crawled into bed. She dozed off, then awoke with a start, realizing that a shadow was standing just outside her balcony door. She pushed herself up to a sitting position.

"Good night, Spencer," he said.

"Did you enjoy the evening?"

"Compared to the car accident?"

"Did you?"

"It wasn't bad. Let me see—you did introduce me as your friend. Much better than saying that I'm the enemy you sleep with *twice* a decade—or once a week."

Spencer threw a pillow his way. She heard the throaty sound of his laughter as he disappeared along the balcony.

The breeze blew in, lifting the curtains. Spencer lay back, almost smiling.

But when she fell asleep, she dreamed of being in the car again. Racing down the hill, desperate to stop, unable to. The sea and sky stretched before her, and she was plummeting forward at breakneck speed. Sheer rock cliffs scraped by her, rose before her.

She flew from the cliff into a void, into nothingness. But she knew that the sharp rocks were below, waiting. She could hear the slash of the cold ocean against them....

Suddenly the car was gone, along with the rocks and the ocean.

Danny was there. Dripping wet, covered in seaweed. He was walking toward her. Smiling, easy. Gentle. Just like Danny. "Spencer, it's all right. You always did like him best. It doesn't matter."

Then she awoke, shivering in the night. She lay awake for hours, afraid to go back to sleep. Afraid to ride in that car again.

So afraid that Danny would come back. Not a mean Danny or a vengeful Danny.

A kind Danny.

The one who had loved her. Who had always been such a good friend.

Who had always trusted her.

She wished she had the nerve to walk into the next room for comfort. To cry over her dreams. To make them go away. To make her feel better. To make her understand...

She had to find some kind of peace and understanding, and she had to do it herself. Not even David could help her.

And still she wished fervently that she could go to him. Just lie beside him. Feel his gentle touch on her skin, in her soul.

But she couldn't go to him.

Not now.

Maybe not ever.

12

When Spencer arrived at her office on Monday morning, she found Audrey at her desk. The other woman inclined her head toward Spencer's office to warn her that it was occupied. Surprised, Spencer walked in to find Cecily in her office, staring at the pictures on the wall.

"Hey, Spence!" Cecily said, hurrying over to give her a fierce hug. "What a weekend, huh?" She drew away, staring at Spencer carefully. "You're definitely okay, hmm?"

Spencer gave her a hug back. "Definitely."

Cecily never wore something as Miami simple as cut-offs with a T-shirt or tank top. She loved to shop, she had an eye for clothing, and she wore it beautifully. This morning she was in a navy-style outfit. The top was sleeveless, and the pants had slightly belled legs, and everything was trimmed in gold that seemed to highlight her perfect hair—her roots never did seem to grow back in. She was extremely attractive and, Spencer had to admit, always an asset at any company social function. They'd been friends all through school. Spencer had been in Cecily's wedding party, and Cecily had been in Spencer's. They were still relatively good friends, even if things had changed after high school. In high school, their conversations had tended to be high-pitched and excited. Later they were often edged with a slightly bitter twist as the years passed and dreams turned out to be not quite what they had once seemed.

"How did you hear about the accident?" Spencer asked, drawing away and moving behind her desk. She indicated the chair in front of it.

Cecily laughed. "How did I hear? In this family? Are you kidding? Sly called Jared's dad right away. Then your mother was on the phone to Jared's father a few minutes later. Spencer, come on, we're talking family here. If you sneeze in Rhode Island, we hear about it."

Spencer nodded in reflective agreement. "Right. So what did you hear?"

"Your mother thinks you should stay in Rhode Island. You were nearly killed there, of course, but you know mother logic, right? Anyway, she told my father-in-law that she would sit on you—*sit on you!*—to make sure you were safe if you would just stay. Then she thought about flying down here."

Spencer groaned, leaning her head on the desk. "She *did* sit on me. All Sunday. Okay, not literally. But she wasn't more than a few feet away at any time during the day."

"Interesting," Cecily said, devilishly arching an eyebrow. "How did she get on with David?"

"All right."

"How are *you* getting on with David?"

"Sly hired him to watch me. That's the only reason he's hanging around with me."

"So where is he now?"

Spencer shrugged. David's recent behavior was a bit of a mystery to her. He'd been within shouting distance all day Sunday—not a difficult feat, since Mary Louise had kept her home with a poolside barbecue. David had been remarkably quiet, his eyes hidden all day behind dark glasses. He'd been quiet on the plane trip home, too, then followed her home. He'd seen her into the house, inspected every inch of it, then left—after yelling at her to set the alarm.

This morning, when she'd left her house, she'd discovered a handsome young man in his early twenties lounging alongside a dusty black old-model BMW. He'd been a good six feet tall and built like a boxer, but he'd had a youthful, friendly smile when he introduced himself as Jimmy Larimore, an employee of David's just looking out for her.

He'd followed her in to work and parked beside her. He hadn't come in, just pulled out a newspaper and started reading, waving as she walked into the office.

"Spencer?"

"I guess he's watching someone else for the moment," Spencer told her.

"So what about the weekend?" Cecily probed.

"What about it?"

Cecily let out a sigh of disgust. "Spencer, I want the juicy details, and you just aren't giving me any."

"None to give," Spencer lied.

Cecily smiled and shook her head. "I don't believe you. In high school you two were hotter than the sidewalk in August."

"Cecily, in case you haven't noticed, we graduated from high school over ten years ago now."

She moaned. "I've noticed! Believe me, I've noticed! Crow's-feet! Can you imagine me with crow's-feet? Of course, when they really set in, I won't let them stay long. If surgery can fix it, I'm all for surgery."

"Cecily, you look great. You don't need surgery on anything."

"Yes, I do," the other woman said with a sigh. "Now you, dear girl, are still in great shape. But that's because you've got a P.B.B."

"A what?"

"A pre-baby body," Cecily explained. "Having one of those little buggers can do you right in!"

A swift pang, as sharp as a knife, ripped into Spencer's heart and cut off her breath. She wanted to strike Cecil, but then Cecily had never known just how badly she and Danny had wanted children.

She couldn't know that Danny had died on the day they had been planning to chase after parenthood with their very best efforts.

"Children are worth whatever toll they take on your body," she told Cecily softly. "I envy you yours with all my heart."

"Oh, Spencer, they *are* wonderful. Of course they are. I sound terribly selfish, don't I? I have two beautiful children, and you haven't even got Danny anymore. I'm sorry, Spencer, honestly. It's just that aging can get so confusing, you know. When we were first married, I always knew that Jared was crazy about me. And I was crazy about Jared. Now I'm out at a party with him and I see his eye wandering to some twenty-year-old in a short skirt, and I want to scratch his eyes out. Not that I don't have a few fantasies of my own."

Spencer couldn't help but smile. Cecily had a certain honesty that could be both amusing and sad.

"Cecily, you two have lots of money, two great kids, and you're still just as pretty as a set of Barbie and Ken dolls. Relax."

"Okay. So tell me about your weekend with David. Let me live vicariously through you!"

"Cecily, it wasn't exciting almost being dashed onto the rocks!"

"Not that part, the rest of it."

Spencer groaned, leaning back in her chair. "Cecily..."

"All right, all right, so you're not going to tell me anything. Spencer, you were more fun in high school. But that's all right. Listen, make sure you keep a week from Friday free. My father-in-law wants to have a family barbecue. Jared, me, the kids, you and Sly. And whatever bodyguard you're dragging around at the time. Okay?"

"I'll be there," Spencer assured her.

Cecily got up to leave, but she paused in Spencer's doorway. "You've got to use that pre-baby body before you lose it, you know."

"I'll keep that in mind. Thanks."

"I guess I'll give my honey a kiss and get on going. Big day. PTA meeting."

Spencer grinned as Cecily left.

Audrey stuck her head in almost immediately. "Want to tell me about your weekend?" she asked hopefully.

Spencer grinned, shaking her head. Audrey hesitated for a minute. "You know, Spencer, it *is* all right for you to have a life."

"I *do* have a life."

"A *sex* life."

"Audrey..."

"Yeah, yeah, I know. All right, down to business. You've got a lunch meeting at Christy's with Sly and a few of the board members from Anderson, Tyrell and Cummings. They want to talk about an old Deco hotel they've just purchased on South Beach. Your realtor called to remind you about the house on the golf course.

And Sly is demanding to see you the second you walk in—you're late.''

"I'm on my way into his office right now," Spencer promised and headed out.

David walked into downtown police headquarters. He strode into homicide and sat down on Jerry Fried's desk. Fried looked up at him with a pained expression and groaned. "Let's switch things around here, Delgado. What news have you got on Danny's death?"

"Just an interesting twist. I was with Danny's widow in Newport, Rhode Island, this weekend. Guess what happened?"

Jerry stared at him. "I haven't got a clue, Delgado. What happened?"

"We had an accident. A bad accident. The car Spencer rented nearly went off a cliff."

"But it didn't."

"It came close enough."

Jerry pointed a finger at him. "Then maybe, if you've got any influence with Danny's widow, you should convince her to get off the case. Pack her off to Siberia, talk her into knitting sweaters or selling daisies. Keep her out of the police station and out of things that don't concern her."

"Her husband's death concerns her."

"Solving his murder is not her business."

"Are you threatening Spencer in any way?"

"Of course not!" Fried said indignantly. "Jesus, Delgado, has being off the force driven you crazy or something? Have you forgotten how to read the street? You know she's in danger if whoever killed Danny thinks she has something on him."

"Or her."

"Don't play word games with me, Delgado." Fried ared at his desk for a minute, then looked up. "Damn . I wasn't with Danny that long. He kept things from e. You know more about what he was up to than I do!"

David was still, staring at the man. He slid off the desk. Where's the lieutenant?"

Fried inclined his head toward Oppenheim's office. avid went on in to find Oppenheim on the phone. He :sitated when he saw David. "Call you back," he said, d hung up. "David, David, are you going to become a gular feature in here on Monday mornings now? If so, u ought to rejoin the damned force, get paid for com- g in."

"No, thanks."

"You don't just come to say hi 'cause you miss me."

"Spencer Huntington was nearly killed in an accident is weekend."

"Where?"

"Rhode Island."

"Rhode Island?" Oppenheim said incredulously. He aned forward, shaking his head. "David, I'm working one of the biggest cities in what is considered to be one f the most dangerous counties in the country. And I'm ipposed to have some control over what happens in *hode Island?*"

David placed his hands on Oppenheim's desk and aned forward. "I'm doing all right, Lieutenant, but I'm ill a small operation. You guys owe me. I've always iven you anything I had that you needed. I want help on is one."

"David, I'm doing what I can. But you know I don't ave the manpower to—"

"Find some!" David said, and added, "please."

Oppenheim exhaled loudly.

"You'd be helping to catch a cop killer. Damn
Lieutenant, you know I'm a good investigator. I've c
tivated some good snitches, and I can get in places wh
no other cop ever could. Something's getting close no
Something has heated up since Spencer pulled her stu
in the graveyard, and I need departmental help on this
believe that Danny's widow is in danger. Someone
afraid she's going to find out something. I can't do t
investigating I need to if I don't get help from you
protect her."

"I'll do what I can. I'll let you know what I come
with."

David nodded and turned to walk out of the offic
"Hey, Lieutenant?"

"Yeah?"

"Get to the gym or lay off the German sausage. Yo
middle's been growing."

"Thanks. Thanks a hell of a lot for noticing. Now g
the hell out of here."

"I'm on my way."

"By the way, just what are you up to?"

"I think I may go hang out under a bridge and eat sta
doughnuts with a few homeless fellows downtown."

"Hey, sounds great."

"Yes. It's a great way to spend the afternoon."

It was a hell of a day. He spent hours under a bridge
Overtown among the homeless and several toughe
looking individuals—probably the usual murdere
rapists and thieves, he thought wryly, sunk down again
his little square of concrete as he watched the down-an
out and dangerous around him.

He half closed his lids while a couple of guys ran out
and water-sprayed the windows of a Mercedes, hoping
for a buck for having cleaned them.

The pale woman inside the car paid up.

Later the same pair started on the windshield of a kelly
green Jag. This time the woman inside started screaming
hysterically. Deciding to see what was going on, David
ambled forward. "Hey, you two, no trouble here."

The men, one black, one white, spun around and
stared at him. He must have looked pretty big in the
oversize army jacket her wore. The two took off. "Lady,
this isn't a great area for you to be driving around—" he
began.

"What the hell are you doing out here on the streets?
Get a job!" she shouted at him.

So much for being a good Samaritan, he thought
grimly.

By afternoon there wasn't a drop of cloud cover in the
sky. The sun was merciless; the humidity was worse.
Danny's snitch had yet to make an appearance.

Just when he was about to give up and stroll the mile
back to Bayside—where he'd felt safe leaving his car—he
saw a skinny little black kid Danny had worked with on
occasion. The kid saw him, too, and started to run.

David caught up with him two blocks down, right in
the heart of the riot zone. He didn't dare think of what
was going to happen to a a Hispanic caught running
down a black boy here if he didn't have a good explanation.

"Spike, stop! What do you want to do? Get me
killed?" he called, coming to a halt. He waited. His
words had paid off. The boy stopped, his back stiff.
"Keep away from me, man," the boy said. But he turned
around.

"I need to see Willie," David said.

"You need to be careful, bro', that's what you need!"
Spike told him. He was an incredibly handsome ki
Lithe, ebony black. At fourteen he was nearly six feet ta
David had still been Danny's partner when they first m
up with Spike. He had been picked up for a minor i
fraction and was about to be booked when Danny, ev
the crusader, stepped right into the fray. Naturally D
vid joined him. Spike was the oldest of six children wi
different fathers and a hardworking mother who couldr
quite keep track of all the kids. Or pay for them. Sl
lived in a three-room apartment right next to a crac
house. But so far not a single one of the kids had go
bad, and Danny had been convinced that an arrest migl
turn Spike the wrong way.

Between them, David and Danny had gotten Spike of
And he'd stayed clean—and made a fair amount c
money from keeping his ear to the ground and lettin
Danny know what he heard. David still checked on hi
now and then. He'd just started at Miami Edison. Tl
kid was bright—he was in honors courses and carrying
3.8 average. He was also bright enough to keep up h
tough-guy image on the street.

Spike headed toward him, wagging a finger his wa
"Keep to the streets, Delgado. I'll get word out to Wi
lie. But listen up, man. Listen up good. There's word or
that Ricky Garcia is on the warpath 'cause the cops ai
bearing down on him and his operations again. They sa
he knows you're involved with all the misfortune comir
his way. So keep your eyes sharp, huh? And keep coo
Willie'll find you."

Spike ran on. It wouldn't be good for him to be see
talking with David too long. David let him go. Still a li

tle winded, he started jogging down Biscayne Boulevard toward Bayside.

Hell of a day.

And a hell of a week stretched out before him.

Jimmy Larimore followed Spencer home. She'd had her mind on one of her projects when she left work and had forgotten her handsome young watchdog.

She only realized he had followed her when she went upstairs and moved to close the drapes before slipping out of her clothing. She stopped when she saw him across the street, leaning against his car. He waved to her, and she waved back.

She called out for pizza that night. She ordered two small with the works, and when they came, she walked one across the street to him. He grinned and thanked her.

"You can come in, you know," she told him.

He grinned again. "It's a great night. It's actually cooling off a bit. I'm fine."

She left him with his pizza.

When she was about to go to bed, she pulled the drapes and looked outside one more time, expecting to see that Jimmy was still there.

He wasn't.

David Delgado was sitting in his car across the street. There was a man in the passenger seat, and David didn't see her watching him because he was talking with the man.

Spencer slowly closed the drapes.

Ten minutes after she crawled into bed, the phone started ringing. The sound was so loud she nearly jumped out of her skin.

"'Night, Spencer," a male voice said softly when she picked up.

"David?"

"Yeah. I'm still outside your window. Were you spying on me?"

"Spying on you while you were spying on me."

"Something like that."

"Where are you now?"

"Still here. Cellular phone, remember?"

"Oh, yeah..."

"Go to sleep, Spence."

"What about you?"

"I'll be here for a while."

"Enjoying the cool night air, right?"

"Is that what Jimmy told you?"

"Yes, actually."

"Were you trying to seduce poor Jimmy?"

"David, take a hike, huh?" she said sweetly, and hung up, carefully refraining from slamming the receiver down.

The phone rang again almost instantly. Spencer picked it up quickly. "What now?" she demanded.

Silence greeted her demand for several seconds. Then a throat was cleared and a man said, "Mrs. Huntington?"

"Yes?" she said carefully, slowly.

"My name is Vichy. Gene Vichy. Mrs. Huntington, the police are breathing down my neck."

She held still for a moment. "Perhaps they should be," she said at last.

"Your grandfather and I are members of the same yacht club, Mrs. Huntington. I thought that perhaps we could have a conversation there. We would meet by chance, of course."

She moistened her lips. "Why?"

"Because I want to convince you of my innocence, of course. And perhaps..."

"Perhaps?"

"Perhaps I know some things that might interest you." The deep, husky sound of his laughter chilled her. "I'll be there next Monday afternoon, just after lunchtime. Don't tell anyone, or I won't show. And make sure you're alone. If you're interested, of course."

"Why Monday?"

"Good night, Mrs. Huntington."

"Wait—"

The line went dead.

The week crawled by, even though Spencer was busy. She was constantly on edge, waiting for something to happen.

She never had anything resembling a real conversation with David. Jimmy Larimore waved to her each night when she closed the curtains, and then David relieved Jimmy sometime during the night. He called Spencer every night at eleven, like clockwork, though.

He always sounded tense as he asked brusquely if she was all right. She barely had time to answer before he hung up.

The hell with him. If he'd given her half a chance, she might have mentioned her meeting with Gene Vichy. Of course, Vichy had told her not to say anything, but how would he know?

David might show up anyway. He and his crew might follow her even more closely than they had been. He'd already added a third man; she had seen him a few times in front of the neighbors' house.

But the bottom line was that she would get Sly to take her to lunch at the yacht club, and then she could make some excuse to sneak away and find out what Gene Vichy knew. Or didn't know. And she would be safe, because there were always other people around at the club.

Apparently his wife hadn't been safe from him, though.

He'd never been proven guilty. The police had never managed to gather enough evidence for the D.A.'s office to indict him. Maybe he *was* innocent.

And maybe he had killed Danny, she reminded herself.

When Friday morning arrived she was delighted to look up from some building plans to find that Audrey had let her realtor, Sandy Gomez, into her office. Spencer greeted her with pleasure, asked Audrey for coffee and sat back while Sandy described her latest find.

"Spencer, you're going to kiss me when you see this place!" She waved a hand in the air. "All right, no kiss needed, dinner will do. It's perfect for you. It hasn't been touched. They haven't even had a cleaning crew in yet. The original owner from 1925 is just moving out. She's going into one of those Sun City places now. Spencer, you should see it! Tiles imported from Malaga. Architecture to die for. You may want it as a re-do for the company, or you may want it for *you*."

"I'm sold, I'm sold. *When* do I get to see it?"

Sandy, a tiny, dark-haired whirlwind of energy, smiled broadly and dangled a set of keys before Spencer's nose. "Any time you want, *chica*, any time you want! I'm so certain you're going to buy this house, you keep the keys and just call me with your offer so I can write up the contract."

Sandy was barely out the door before Spencer buzzed Sly to tell him that she was going to take off to see the house. He sounded as if he was in a bit of panic. "You're going to go now?"

"Yes, why?"

"Because—because . . ."

It wasn't like Sly to be at a loss for words.

"Ah!" Spencer said softly. "I think I've got this. David and his goon squad don't keep watch on me while I'm actually at work."

"Not all the time," Sly admitted. "I'm here," he said quietly after a minute. "Jared is here. And Audrey may be tougher than any of us," he said, trying to add a note of levity.

"Jared can come with me. He'll need to assess the place if Montgomery Enterprise is going to pick it up as an investment property."

Sly hesitated for a second. "Fine. I'll call your cousin."

"I can call him myself, Sly. Honest. I can handle it."

"You let me know when you're back in the office."

"Yes, sir," she murmured, then hung up and buzzed Jared. He heard the excitement in her voice and promised to shelve his other work so he could accompany her to see the property.

Spencer drove, noting that the house was only about a block and a half away from Sly's home. Maybe the house would be more than just an investment—it might be a good place to live. It wasn't that she had fallen out of love with her own place, or that she wanted to forget Danny, ever. But maybe she did need to begin again. And Sly *was* getting older. He was in perfect shape, his wits were sharper than ever, and he certainly wouldn't want her taking care of him, but if she was to move just down the street from him . . .

"Looks good from here," Jared said as she turned into the circular drive and stopped.

It did. More than anything, the old grande dame needed a good coat of paint. The codes in Coral Gables were strict; houses could only be painted certain colors. But it was impossible to tell what color this place had originally been painted. Something pink? Or peach? Mold had encroached over the face, vines had climbed to the arched balconies and wrought-iron railings, and they'd practically obliterated the four Grecian columns that stood sentinel over the massive front porch.

"Got the key?" Jared asked her.

She dug into her purse for the set of keys Sandy had given her, then passed them over to Jared.

They walked along a broken-tiled path to the front door. Amazingly, a little angel fountain in the courtyard was working, and the sound of the running water was pleasant and light. Jared turned the key in the lock and they stepped into the foyer. It was slightly dusty, but it was beautiful. A dome rose high above their heads, a curving staircase led to the second floor landing, and dual arches led in opposite directions, one toward the huge living room, the other toward the kitchen.

In silent agreement they moved into the living room.

It was one of the largest Spencer had ever seen, more of a ballroom than a simple living room. Arches at the rear led to a screened porch, and the beams high above still held traces of meticulous stenciling. A pair of French doors led out to a patio and an old, cracked and empty pool.

"Major restoration," Jared warned.

"But that's what we do," Spencer said. "And look at this living room!" She moved more deeply into the room and turned around. The ceiling was two stories high, and a landing on the second floor looked down on the room, just like a minstrels' gallery. She could even imagine a trio of musicians set up there for a party on a cool night. The French doors could be thrown open to the rolling greens of the golf course and the redone patio and pool.

"Jared! It's sensational!" she gasped.

"Spencer, you must be the only woman I know who can stand in the midst of spiderwebs and mud and call something sensational."

She made a face at him. "You know what this place could look like."

"And you know that you can triple its value if you haggle down the price just a shade," he commented.

She shrugged, unwilling as yet to admit that she might want the house for herself. "I'd love to get closer to the stencils," she said.

"Shall we go up?" Jared asked. He sounded bored. He'd seen enough to judge its worth. He wasn't hands on. He liked the deal-making part of the business, the buying and selling and hiring. Spencer liked the work itself. From this point on he was merely humoring her. They both knew that the house was a steal, and that its restoration would be a real feather in the Montgomery Enterprises cap.

They started up the stairs. "We owe Sandy a good dinner for this one."

"Sandy makes lots of money off us," Jared said dryly.

"But she also works very hard and is good at what she does," Spencer commented with a slight frown furrowing her brow. His mood was definitely on the sour side today. He wasn't usually so down on people.

When they got to the landing Spencer gave a little cry of delight. A hallway led to one side, and the door to the master suite was perhaps twenty-five feet in front of her. To her left the balcony stretched out, ever larger than it had appeared from below. And the living room, with its beautifully stenciled beams and arches and French doors, was an incredible sight.

Spencer walked to the balcony, Jared close behind her.

"The railing is low," he commented.

"It's perspective. From below, it looks tall," Spencer told him, sliding her hands over the old wooden railing. She noticed that the rungs were rotting in places. "It's such a shame this place was let go for so long."

"This railing could break through in a dozen places," Jared agreed, coming to stand next to her. He gripped the rail, as well, looking over.

A trickle of unease swept through Spencer as she watched her cousin. "Jared, you shouldn't lean over like that. You know this place is in bad condition."

"Strange, Spencer, that they would have made this so short. Even for perspective. Imagine someone with small children. A little seven- or eight-year-old having a fight with his brother, the nine- or ten-year-old. They come out on this balcony, squabbling, horsing around. Sam makes a jab for Harvey. Harvey moves. Sam goes sailing on by. Over the railing. Splat. It really is a long way down from here."

He shivered suddenly. It looked as if he was about to topple over at any second.

"Jared!"

"Spencer, you should look straight down. God, it's chilling. Come over here. Look."

He looked at her, stretching out an arm toward her. His eyes seemed strangely glazed. She was suddenly frightened of him, no matter how much she reminded herself that he was her cousin.

Her blood.

A curious smile curved his mouth. "Spencer..."

He was reaching for her, determined. She started to
ack away. Too late.

His fingers caught hold of her wrist.

She stared at him. Into his eyes, ready to tense. To
ght. He was over six feet. Tall, strong. In good shape.

"Jared," she began softly.

"Spencer." His voice seemed like a hiss from far away.
Chills exploded along her spine.

"Spencer!"

This time her name was called out sharply in a deep
trong, masculine voice. Called out from below.

Jared instantly released her hand and stepped back.
pencer inhaled deeply. Her cousin seemed to give him-
:lf a shake.

"Spencer!" came the sharp sound of her name again.

From a distance she peered carefully over the rail. Her
eart was still pounding. Even before she saw his tense,
pturned face and the thick thatch of dark hair falling
ver his forehead, she had known who she would see.

David.

Thank God.

He'd been so far away, and now he'd finally come
lose.

Just in the nick of time.

13

"It's David," Jared said. "Hey, Delgado! Can yo
imagine growing up in a place like this?" he called dow:

Spencer had already turned. Already started dow
stairs. She collided with David halfway down. He caug
her by her shoulders, steadying her.

Strange, when he held her like this, looking into h
eyes for the source of her panic, she felt foolish. Jare
couldn't have meant to push her over the railing any mo
than he had meant to topple over it himself.

"We would have destroyed it," Jared continued, fal
ing in behind Spencer. He was smiling, greeting Dav
with a handshake. He looked as innocent of any poss
ble evildoing as a Dalmation puppy.

"Well, I definitely can't imagine me growing up here,
David agreed. He gave Spencer another curious look ar
started up the steps again, heading for the balcony th
had seemed so beautiful to her when she had first a
rived.

"Don't go too close to the railing!" she warned.

"It's all right—David is steady on his feet," Jared sai
Spencer felt everything inside her tense up as Jared joine
David at the railing and pointed out something below th
David bent to see. As far as Spencer was concerned, bo
men were in precarious positions.

"Would you two quit acting like adolescents and get away from that railing!" she demanded irritably.

Both men turned and stared at her with surprise. "I was just trying to show him the way the support beams were cut," Jared said.

Spencer didn't say anything. Instead she went to inspect the bedrooms, trying to keep the house uppermost in her mind. She couldn't quite do it. Inside, something was screaming that her cousin, a man who had been her friend all her life, might have been about to kill her just a few minutes ago. But no man could attempt murder and then appear so completely innocent of any wrongdoing right afterward. Could he? She had overreacted. He had encouraged David forward in the same way, and nothing had happened. Jared couldn't have meant to kill her.

But she was still afraid.

There were five bedrooms on the second floor. The master suite was large, with a beautiful sitting room that looked over the golf course and pool. The baths weren't small, but they weren't particularly generous, either. Most of the grande dames built in the twenties had many of the same characteristics; the downstairs entertaining areas were beautiful and lushly proportioned, while less attention had been given to some of the details that were so important today, such as big bathrooms and large closets. But everything here was wonderfully workable. The master suite was definitely large enough for her to enlarge the bathroom and add a much larger closet at the other end of the bedroom.

David and Jared stepped into the room behind her. Jared leaned against a wall, watching her with what looked like affectionate amusement. "What are you still looking around for? You know you're going to buy the place." He looked at David. "And she doesn't like the balcony railing, so it's the first thing she'll change."

Spencer crossed her arms over her chest. "Whether I like it or not, it has to come down. But first we have to rewire the electricity and redo all the plumbing, even some of the lathing, I imagine. And all that will be well before I decide on what kind of railing I'm going to use."

"*She's* going to use?" David said. "Don't you get any say in this?" he asked Jared.

Jared smiled again, watching Spencer. "Usually, of course, I would. And Sly would give his opinion, too. But this isn't going to be a corporate acquisition, is it Spence? She's buying this one herself."

David looked incredulously at Spencer. "Really?"

"Possibly," she said defensively.

David looked around the room. "Lot of work."

Spencer sighed, repeating herself. "It's what we do," she reminded him.

"How did you happen to be here?" Jared asked him frowning. "I mean, I know Sly has you watching Spence but she was with me."

David hesitated just briefly.

Did Sly mistrust Jared for some reason? Spencer wondered.

But then David answered quickly. "Reva is having party tonight. My nephew's tenth birthday. She hasn't seen much of Spencer in years, and she was hoping that maybe she wouldn't mind coming by with me. Of course I know she'd be pleased if you and Cecily could come along, too. With your own kids."

Spencer and Jared both stared at him.

"How about it, Spence?" David asked softly.

"I..."

"I think Cecily would love it, and I know the kids would," Jared said. "What time do you want us there?"

"She planned it for seven-thirty. It's a half Cuban, half American household, so that means thirty minutes late is about average," he said. "Spencer?"

"I—sure," she said, just a little uncomfortably. Did Reva really want them at her party? Or had David said that because he didn't want Jared to know that he was in some way suspicious of him? "But I need to go back to the office first. I want to let Sandy know I definitely want the house."

"You think you're really going to move into this place?" David asked her.

"It's…possible. It's just down the street from Sly's," she said. "And it's not a bad idea to be close to him now."

David nodded, watching her.

"And she loves the house," Jared said, his hands on Spencer's shoulders. She felt her body go tense as he touched her. "You okay?" he asked, frowning.

"Fine. Let's go."

They went down the stairs. There was a lot of the place that she hadn't seen yet, but it didn't matter. She wanted the house. And she also wanted to lock herself in her office, where she could be alone. She couldn't believe she was suspicious of Jared; she had to be mistaken. And she didn't want David noticing that anything was wrong.

Spencer hurried out to her car. Jared swept in beside her. David followed in his car.

Jared talked all through the drive. He'd seen more of the house than she had realized. He had suggestions for turning closets into more spacious baths, and making closets out of the some of the smaller rooms. They were good suggestions, things Montgomery Enterprises would

definitely have done with the house. Things she might d
herself.

"I'll get an architect out on Monday and close the dea
as soon as possible," Spencer told him.

"*Are* you keeping it for yourself?"

"You don't mind?" she asked him.

"Spencer, I need another house like I need a hole in th
head. I have over five thousand square feet and big-tim
taxes now. And Cecily is big on contemporary pleasures
you know that. I think the house is great for you. Eve
if it's not business, I want to help you in any way I can.'

He couldn't have meant her harm. Couldn't hav
meant to send her flying over the railing.

When they reached the freestanding Montgomery En
terprises office on Main, David pulled into the small lo
beside Spencer.

"I just need to see Sly for a minute," he said, joinin
them as they walked inside. Spencer left him with Jare
in the entryway and hurried past Audrey, shutting th
door to her office and leaning against it. She stared at he
hands. They were shaking.

What if Jared *had* been trying to kill her?

But why would he want to?

She sat behind her desk, then leaned her head on it
Why did *anyone* kill? She'd heard so much from the po
lice about motive. There was almost always a motive fo
murder. She'd heard it so many times because of Danny
Every time the police questioned her they had apolo
gized and told her how often the wife was the one with
motive when her husband was killed. But Danny's deat
was different. She had no motive, and plenty of othe
people did. Someone might have wanted revenge, lik
Ricky Garcia. And Trey Delia could hardly be consid
ered sane. Almost anyone Danny was investigating migh

have been afraid of something he knew. Someone might have hated him simply for his love of justice.

And Jared? Why would her cousin hate her?

Even as her thoughts flew, she heard a tapping on her door.

"Spencer?" It was David, and he had already opened the door.

"Spencer, Mr. Delgado isn't big on being announced!" Audrey called from behind him, her annoyance clear. "I'd call security, except that as I understand it, he *is* security."

Spencer stood and stared at the pair of them.

"I need to talk to you," David said.

"He won't go away," Audrey told her.

Spencer lifted an arm in invitation. "Come in, David."

David gave Audrey a firm glare. She lifted her shoulders and turned up her nose. Spencer smiled at her and shrugged, and Audrey shook her head and left the office. Spencer walked behind her desk, indicating that he could take a chair.

"Taking chances with your life, aren't you, Delgado? I might have been wearing nothing but a towel."

"The risk didn't seem too great," he said, glancing over the pictures on her walls, then taking the chair in front of her desk. He leaned forward. "All right. Let's have it. What happened?"

She shook her head. "I don't know what you're talking about."

"Something happened. You looked at me as if I were Christ and it was the Second Coming when I walked into that house."

She shook her head. "Nothing happened. That rail ing just gave me a moment's unease. I asked you not t go near it, remember?"

He folded his hands in his lap, staring at her. Weigh ing her words. Disbelieving her. Maybe thinking that h wasn't going to get the truth right now no matter what.

"What did you think of the house?" she asked him.

"It was great," he said coolly.

"You don't have to be sarcastic."

He lifted his hands, baffled. "I thought it was a grea house. You do need a new railing, but that balcony has fantastic view. I could see a small sofa of some kind—'

"A Victorian?" Spencer suggested.

"Yeah, something like that, maybe a few bookcases It would be a great place to sit. You can see out to th back from there, as well as the whole living room. It wa a great house. Not for everyone. For a lot of people i would just be too much. But for you, it's definitel right."

Spencer smiled suddenly. "Hmm. I think that's th first approval I've gotten from you on anything."

He stood up. "You've gotten approval from me on lot of things, Spencer. I've got to go now, though. I have few things to do. I just came by to see if I can pick you uf at your place around seven."

"You don't have to. I can drive—but then, you'd b following me anyway, right?"

"Right."

She shrugged. "Pick me up at seven."

He left her. She wasn't alone, though. When she lef the office, Jimmy Larimore was waiting. "Hi, Spencer How was your day?"

"Pretty good."

He followed her to the house and parked in front. After she parked her car she went over to talk to him. "Jimmy, am I under some kind of a twenty-four-hour watch now?"

He shrugged. "Pretty much. You might want to take it up with David."

"I might do just that. Thanks, Jimmy." She started toward the house, then came back. "So are you off tonight? Do you get to go out and do something fun?"

"I'll be at the party," he said with a frown. "Reva always asks everyone from the office to her parties."

"Oh," she said softly.

He grinned. "I will get to go home for a shower, though, once David shows up."

"Glad to hear it."

Spencer went in and took a shower herself. She dressed in jeans, a mauve cotton blouse and sneakers. David showed up at exactly seven, in jeans and a blue polo shirt. He waited for her on the porch.

When she was seated in his car, she found herself studying his terse profile. "If I didn't know better, I'd think you were afraid of me."

He glanced her way. "I *am* afraid of you, Spencer. Terrified."

She looked straight ahead again. "Sorry. I didn't know that sex once or twice a decade was so wretched."

"It's damned good sex, Spencer," he said lightly. He was watching the road as they drove along the tree- and brush-shaded street. The foliage was beautiful, having grown back thickly after Hurricane Andrew. Bougainvillea sprouted along fences in all kinds of colors, purples, oranges, reds. "I just prefer mine with a partner who doesn't cry afterward. And I'm not a kid anymore, Spencer. Not ready to forget the bitter facts of life just to hop into the sack. There are things I'm definitely no looking for. Crying is not what I want."

"Well, you're not always exactly what I want!" sh lashed out, hurt, humiliated. Embarrassed. Wishin she'd never spoken. "You're not—"

"No, I'm not Danny!" he said angrily. She saw hi knuckles tightening around the steering wheel.

"That's not what I meant."

"What *did* you mean, then?"

She shook her head vehemently. "I can't explain. I— it's hard. Life's hard. Getting on with life is hard." Oh God, what was she saying? Even in the silence of he mind, her thoughts seemed terrible. How could she eve explain her feelings to anyone? She had loved Danny. Bu she had once loved David more, and she could love hir that way again. It wasn't fair to Danny. And yet . . .

"What are you trying to say, Spencer?"

She sighed, suddenly very tired. "I really don't know I just . . . How far does Reva live?" she asked miserabl after a moment.

"Just around the next bend."

Spencer didn't think she'd ever been quite so happy t get anywhere before. Reva came out of the house smil ing. Maybe she really had wanted to invite Spencer an Jared and Cecily tonight.

"Hey! Thanks for coming!" Reva told her, giving he a warm hug.

"Thanks for the invitation. Wow. Something smell wonderful!" Spencer said. It did, too. The cooking aro mas were scrumptious.

"The family, you know. Dad's side. Grandpa Mi chael's haggis was still sheep stomach, no matter wha you called it!" she said, laughing.

"I never did have to try it," Spencer admitted.

"He was always kind to guests. Come on, come on. The family is anxious to see you, David. Spencer, you haven't really met my kids. They were at Danny's funeral, but..." She trailed off, looking as if she wanted to slap herself.

"I think I remember them. You have a very handsome little boy, right? He looks a lot like your brother, actually."

Reva winced. "Don't tell my husband. He thinks Damien is the spitting image of himself. But please, come on in."

She caught Spencer's hand and led her into the house.

It was a big, sprawling ranch, with a living room that opened into a big family room that opened out to a big pool-patio area. There were about ten kids playing out back already, while the grown-ups were in clusters around a cherrywood bar, the patio tables and the outdoor lounge chairs. Reva drew Spencer along to greet her husband, George. Reva had barely put the two of them together before someone called out to her for help finding something in the kitchen.

"Excuse me, Spencer. I'll be right back. I leave you in good hands, I promise."

Spencer remembered George from the funeral. He was of medium height, with sandy hair, pleasant freckles and expressive green eyes. He gripped her hand warmly. "We're delighted that you could come. I don't know if you remember me—"

"I do," Spencer assured him with a smile.

"I'd have to remember you," George told her. "I heard all about you from Reva."

Spencer felt her cheeks growing warm. No doubt he'd heard about the last time she had really seen Reva until recently—that awful day when she and David had parted.

"Oh," Spencer said.

"She told me you were the first person in the United States to make her feel as if she really was their equal, as if she could make a home here. She told me that your grandfather put her and David through school, but she only survived it because of you."

"I beg your pardon?" Spencer said.

George grinned. "She said that you accepted her and became her friend. And because you did, everyone else did. I think she's missed you a lot."

"I—I've missed her, too," Spencer said. She realized suddenly how much she meant it. She shrugged awkwardly. "It's hard sometimes. You know how life can be. Work. Schedules. In your case, children and their schedules."

"Yes, I know. It can be hard. But I do hope we get to see more of you now that you know the way to the house."

"Thanks. I hope so, too."

"Spencer? Spencer!"

She turned around.

Small, round, like an enegetic little dark-haired apple, Tia Anna stood behind her, arms outstretched. Spencer hadn't seen her in over ten years. She was David's and Reva's father's sister. Next to Michael MacCloud, she had been their closest relation while they were growing up. She had nursed broken bones, measles and mumps—and wounded egos, as well.

Now she came forward and crushed Spencer to her ample bosom. *"¡Povrecita!"* she crooned, holding her. Poor little one. *"¿Como está?"* Anna demanded.

"Good," Spencer told her. "I'm doing fine."

"You're thin. I'll put meat on your bones. You come out to the pool and sit down, I'll make you a plate. Along with that wayward nephew of mine. He eats standing up half the time. Go on now, go out and sit with him.''

Reva had disappeared and George had been taken over by another guest. David was standing by the pool, watching the kids as they horsed around. Spencer walked out, smiling to people she didn't know, who smiled in return, and reaching the empty white, wrought-iron table Anna had indicated. She pulled out a chair.

A second later Anna appeared, a plate piled with enough food to feed half a football team in each hand. "There!" she said, setting one down in front of Spencer. "My *arroz con pollo,* Natalia's palomino steak, Reva's black beans and rice, fried plaintains, *ensalada,* good Cuban bread and George's fried sausages. You eat now." She raised her voice. "David, come over here with Spencer. Sit, eat, enjoy."

David turned, looking a bit surprised to see his aunt staring at him like a determined bulldog.

"I've made you a plate," she told David. She winked at Spencer. "You diet on Monday, eh?"

Spencer laughed. "I'll have to, after this!"

David came over, taking a chair. He had barely taken his seat before another aunt came over to embrace him, followed a moment later by the ten-year-old birthday boy, Damien. He was fresh out of the pool, a tall, lean boy with large, very dark blue and expressive eyes. He tried to wipe his palms before shaking hands with Spencer, and she smiled, taking his damp hand and wishing him a happy birthday.

"Thank you for coming. It's very nice to have you here," he said politely. Then he hesitated, and she realized that he had the natural curiosity of any bright child. "Tia Anna told me that you've been grieving a long time and that we must try to make you have a nice evening. I hope you've been doing well since your husband died. We were all very sorry. I don't know if you remember, but Mom and Dad brought us to the funeral home."

"Yes, I remember," Spencer told him. "It was very nice of you to help me say goodbye to Danny. And please don't worry. Time passes. We still miss people, but we learn to go on. And I know I'll have a very nice evening."

"Danny was Tio David's best friend. Mom said he was one of the best people she'd ever met in her whole life. She said he might have changed the world, and he would have started right here in Florida."

Spencer nodded, liking this child very much. He was so grave and polite, intelligent, and so sensitive for his age. He reminded her of someone else.

David.

When she had first met him, he had been so solemn and serious. A little overwhelmed by the world Danny had suddenly dragged him into. David had been very mature for his age. A little boy who had been forced to grow up too fast. Somber, but also street smart and intelligent. And because of his own emotional upheaval, so empathetic regarding the fears and uncertainties of others.

"Danny would have run for public office in time," she told Damien. "And he might have changed things. He really was a very good person."

"You must miss him very much."

She felt David's eyes on her. She kept her own on Damien. "We all do. Sometimes I can be selfish, and I forget that other people miss him, too. But, hey, it's your birthday. Danny loved parties, and he wanted people to have fun at them. I wasn't quite sure what you'd like, so

I brought a Toytown gift certificate. You can choose your own present.''

"You didn't need to bring anything," Damien said, and she thought that he was about the most perfectly behaved child she had ever seen. But then his blue eyes lit up with the true sparkle of a little devil. "But I'm awfully glad you did! Thanks, Mrs. Huntington."

"You're welcome."

"And you're dripping all over our food, which is getting cold. Go have fun while you're young and still can!" David told him sternly.

The boy grinned, hugged his uncle, soaking him, and ran off to the pool. David watched him go with obvious affection and pride.

Then he glanced at her, arching a skeptical brow. "How did you manage a gift with so little time?"

She shrugged. "I may not have children, but I have friends with kids who keep Toytown certificates around for emergencies at all times."

"Hmm, pretty clever."

"It helps in a pinch. Did Reva really want us here, or did Sly send you after me?"

"Reva really did want you here. Sly buzzed me, too, though. He doesn't like having you out of his sight if you're not being trailed. Why do you ask?" His eyes narrowed suspiciously.

"I was just wondering," she lied innocently. Then she smiled and sought a way to change the subject. "No kids of your own, huh?" she heard herself ask softly.

"I haven't been married yet, Mrs. Huntington."

"It's not exactly a must anymore these days."

"It is for me. I see enough kids on the streets who don't have fathers or mothers. Well, I'll be damned!" he said suddenly.

Spencer swung around, startled. Jared and Cecily ha arrived with their kids. Ashley suddenly saw Spence There was a strained look on her pretty little face, and sh let out a cry and came catapulting toward her aun Spencer caught her, lifting her up on her lap. "Hey, li tle one! What's all this?"

Ashley didn't answer, only hugged Spencer fiercely Spencer shrugged her confusion to David.

A second later, having finished greeting their host an hostess, Jared and Cecily came to join David and Spen cer at their patio table. "Ooh, look at all this food, wi you?" Cecily said with a sigh. "I can just see the pound adding up. Oh, well, never mind, tomorrow is alway another day—to diet." Jared pulled out a chair for he and she slipped into it. He sat across from her. Willia came up quickly, ignoring his little sister, to plant a quic kiss on Spencer's cheek. "Hi, Aunt Spencer."

"Hi, sweetie, how's it going? Do you have a swim suit? You can join the boys in the pool."

He nodded, but looked at the group in the pool wit trepidation.

"Come on. I'll introduce you around," David tol him. "Excuse me."

He left the table hand in hand with William. Spence watched the introductions. Once again she felt as if sh had been transported back a million years. Damie greeted William politely, clearly determined to make hi just another one of the guys.

She cradled Ashley's soft head, still all but glued to he shoulder, and arched a brow questioningly at Cecily "What's the matter with little bit here?"

Cecily sighed. "She's been worried sick about you eve since she heard us talking about your car accident. Ash ley, honey, look at Aunt Spencer. She's fine, see?"

Ashley nodded, but didn't pull away from Spencer.

"Spence, I'm sorry, you can't even eat with her on you ke that," Jared said, looking up momentarily as David ame back to the table, taking a seat.

"It's all right," Spencer said. "I can manage a plain-in or two."

The plaintains *were* delicious. Sweet. But it wasn't any reat hardship for Spencer not to eat, because she sud-enly felt ill.

Was it having Jared so close to her again?

Was she afraid of her cousin?

What was going on today? she wanted to shout.

"It was nice of you to come and bring the children," avid said to Cecily and Jared.

"Hey, it's kind of like old home week, huh?" Cecily aid. Even as she spoke, Reva, looking a little frazzled, ulled up a chair alongside them. As she did, they all urst into laughter.

"Was it something I said?" Reva asked.

Cecily shook her head. "I just said it's like old home eek. I can't remember the last time we were all together ke this. Of course, we're missing a few."

"Terry-Sue," Jared said with a wistful sigh.

Cecily kicked him. "I do see her now and then. Those aagnificent boobs of hers hang nearly down to her knees ow."

"Oh, tacky, tacky, my love!" Jared teased.

"We were together the most, though," Reva said. The five of us and—" She broke off with another of 1ose looks as if she wanted to kick herself.

"The five of us . . . and Danny," Spencer said evenly. Reva, it doesn't hurt to talk about him anymore. It ac-1ally feels good."

Reva flushed. "I still can't believe it, I guess," she said softly. "Hey, I hear you found a great house."

"Great if you're Spencer!" Cecily said with a shudder. "She has this thing for places that reek of rot. Give me modern plumbing, a Jacuzzi, an intercom and all the modern conveniences anytime."

"Cecily, you *can* mix the modern with the old," Spencer said. It was an endless argument between them.

"Actually, I hear you have a great house now," Reva said. She reached out and smoothed Ashley's soft hair. The little girl looked up and smiled. "Hi, Ashley. I'm Reva. Come see me?"

Ashley hesitated a second, then slipped over to Reva's lap.

"Come see it," Spencer invited. "It is a nice house. It's—"

"Free from ghosts!" Jared said with a snort.

Spencer stared at him, startled.

"Sorry," Jared murmured.

"The new one is close to Sly," Spencer said determinedly.

Reva leaned her head against Ashley's, rocking her gently. "And free from ghosts," she said very softly, agreeing with Jared. "I think it's good for you to take on a new place." She sat up, talking to Ashley. "I have a little girl for you to meet. She's just a bit older than you are. Her name is Diana. Want to come meet her?"

Ashley nodded shyly.

"I'll be back in a minute," Reva said.

While Reva was gone, Jimmy Larimore made an appearance and sat with them. Two other men from David's office came by, as well, talked for a while, then moved on to join the rest of the party.

The conversation at the table turned to golf, then the past and the ways the city had changed. Cecily and Jared filled their plates; Spencer played with her food. She glanced at Jared now and then, and each time he offered her an encouraging smile.

She couldn't eat.

"Spencer, I am so jealous!" Cecily wailed. "How can you just let that delicious stuff sit there?"

It had seemed earlier as if everyone was talking at once. Now all three of them were just staring at her. "It's so rich, I guess. I haven't had anything Cuban in a while."

David's eyes were really on her then, as if to say, *Oh, yes, sweetheart, you sure have!*

She stared at her plate, and he seemed to take pity on her for some reason. He rose, taking it away, bringing a beer for Jared and a white wine for Cecily. Spencer, nervous, wound up, asked for the same.

The aunts, the other children, slowly went home. Spencer met Reva's daughter, Diana, the spitting image of her mother, a little eight-year-old porcelain doll with sweet manners and a soft voice. Ashley had been instantly enthralled with her.

By midnight everyone else had gone. Cecily kept saying that she needed to get her kids into bed, and each time Jared told her that it looked like their kids were doing just fine.

Something was happening at the table. Maybe they were all just caught in the grip of nostalgia. The laughter would no sooner die away than someone else would say, "Remember when we all ..."

They were good memories. And Danny was part of most of them. His name came up again and again. She had lied when she said that talking about him didn't hurt, but she hadn't lied when she said that it felt good. It was a combination of both, yet more good than bad. She wanted to laugh and cry all at the same time. She realized, being here, talking, that she needed to reconcile her feelings over everything that had happened.

David had made it easier to forget Danny. He had made her feel all the old emotions for him again. Just like talking about Danny, in a way that hurt, and in a way it felt good, too. Maybe she could learn to let go. If only Danny's killer were caught.

If only she could quit being afraid.

She drank too much wine, feeling David watching her until finally it was time to go.

When she stood, she felt the effects of the wine, but she forced herself to remain steady. She was definitely glad she wasn't driving, though.

Ashley hung on to Spencer again when they were leaving, starting to cry.

"She's overtired," Cecily said.

"Don't die, Auntie Spencer," Ashley said.

Spencer felt a chill shoot along her spine. Ashley said the words as if she had some kind of premonition. It was unsettling. Spencer gave herself a mental shake. Danny had died while he had been young and healthy. And then Ashley heard that Spencer had been in danger. That was all there was to it.

Unless Ashley's father was trying to kill his own cousin, but... *why?*

"I'm not going to die, sweetheart." The chill seemed to deepen. What guarantee did she have to say that to a child? "Ashley, I promise to do my very best not to die," she said instead.

"Cross your heart?"

Spencer solemnly performed the motion. "Cross my heart."

The goodbyes stretched. Jared, Cecily and their children managed to leave first.

"Thanks again for coming," Reva told Spencer as George walked with David toward the car.

"Thanks again for having me," Spencer said. She suddenly felt awkward standing there. Spencer had been glad to hear from George that Reva hadn't held anything against her over the years, but still . . . "Reva—"

Reva spoke suddenly, in a rush, as if determined to say something before the men noticed they hadn't come along to the car. "I'd like to say that I'm dying to see more of you, Spencer. That I've missed having you in my life. And that's true. But not with David. I don't want to see you with David."

"Reva!"

"I don't like to see him in pain, Spencer. And he is in pain every time you're around."

Stunned, Spencer could think of nothing to say. She started to turn away, but Reva suddenly cried out, giving her a fierce hug. "I'm sorry. Honestly, I'm sorry."

"Hey, it's late! Get a move on!" David called, effectively ending their conversation.

Reva released Spencer, who felt as if she was sleepwalking the rest of the way over to the car. David was waiting by the passenger seat, holding the door open. Spencer slid inside.

She leaned her head back while they drove, eyes closed, suddenly very weary and very sad. What had happened to the years? How could the old hurts come back to haunt them all so fiercely?

They didn't talk until they reached her house. David pulled onto the embankment in front of the tiled path to Spencer's front door.

"So, are you glad you came?" he asked her.

"Yes, but I..."

"But you've lost your taste for Cuban food."

She smiled, shaking her head. "My nerves are just o edge, I guess. Everything was wonderful. I just wis sometimes that..."

"That what?"

"That we could go forward. Sometimes the past seem like a ball and chain." She shrugged. "Never mind."

"The wine talking?" he teased.

"Maybe."

"Let's get you inside."

She got out of the car and walked to her door, turnin the key in the lock.

"Don't forget the alarm, Spencer," he told her.

She paused. "Do you really just sit out there in you car all night?"

He shrugged. "Sometimes. Sometimes Jimmy is here or Juan. You met him tonight—he comes by."

"Is he the fellow in the blue sedan?" Spencer asked.

David frowned immediately. "Blue sedan?"

She nodded. "I'm not sure what it is. It's deep blue— dust-covered. Maybe middle to late eighties."

"You mean your neighbor's car?" he said, his frow deepening.

She shook her head. "You mean the cute yuppies dow the street? Are you kidding? She has a Mercedes, and h drives a Volvo."

Even as she spoke the words, David turned, and Spen cer felt a trickle of unease shiver along her spine. He ha heard something. Maybe she had heard it, too. Just whisper of sound, leaves rustling in the breeze, excep that there wasn't a breeze.

"Get in the house!" he told her.

"David, I want—"

"Spencer, for God's sake, get in the house. And if I'm not back in twenty minutes, call the police."

He opened the door and thrust her inside. "Keep it dark, and switch on the alarm. Now!"

He pulled the door closed with more force than necessary.

She stared at it for a few seconds, trembling. She could hear David moving away, into the front yard. She headed into the living room, almost turning on the overhead light, then remembering that he had said not to. She started to draw back the drapes on the front windows, but then she hesitated, turning around.

She could see through into the family room, and through the family room to the etched glass doors that led to the pool.

It looked as if something was moving back there. Trees? Shadows in the night?

She stared to walk through the house, silently, slowly, determined to see whether something was out there or not.

She stepped under one of the archways, her eyes beginning to adjust to the darkness, allowing her to see the pool, illuminated by soft night-lights.

Someone was back there, hunched against a bush on the far side of the pool.

Someone waiting.

She had to warn David.

She whirled around, ready to run screaming out the front door.

But she never made it. She seemed to run right up against a brick wall. A hand clamped down hard over her mouth, and her scream was a silent one that raged in her heart alone.

14

"I told you to set the alarm!" David grated in a whisper, his hand easing from her mouth, his hold relaxing. He was staring over her shoulder, into the back.

The terror ebbed from her slowly.

"Damn you! You scared me half to death!" she seethed.

His eyes briefly met hers. "Maybe that will teach you to set the alarm!" he told her. He continued to stand dead still, staring into the yard. She turned to stand beside him in the darkness, looking outside, too.

The shadow in the bushes straightened slightly. Because of the glow of the lights surrounding the pool, the intruder had the sense to stay in the bushes and virtually out of sight.

"How can I get behind him?" David asked in a low voice.

"The cabana bath is just down the hall," Spencer said. "You can get out that way without being seen."

He slipped away down the hall.

The yard grew brighter as a cloud moved away from in front of the moon. The shadow became more distinct. Definitely a man. And holding something glistening.

A gun.

Spencer tore down the hall after David. She caught up with him just as he was about to open the cabana bath door.

"David!" she whispered fiercely. "Wait! He's got a gun."

He turned to her in exasperation. "Spencer, so do I."

"Call the police. Let them handle it."

"Spencer, I was a cop. I know what I'm doing. And if we wait, we may lose our chance to get our hands on him and find out what's going on. Please, Spencer, this once, do as I ask. Stay here quietly out of harm's way and let me slip around behind this guy and nab him!"

She stepped back, biting her lower lip.

He managed to open the door without a single creak. "Lock it behind me. Please, Spencer. Do as I say."

Then he was gone, and Spencer prayed that she could close the door as quietly as he had opened it. She didn't know if she succeeded or not.

She hurried down the darkened hallway to watch out the back as David slipped through the bushes around the back side of the pool, coming up right behind the shadow.

A cloud drifted over the moon. Except for the pool lights, the yard was suddenly pitched into darkness. Spencer clenched her teeth tightly together, praying. The seconds seemed to tick by with ungodly slowness.

Then she heard the sharp report of a single shot, and a strangled cry sounded in the night.

"Damn you, David!" she mouthed in passionate silence. She could see nothing; she knew nothing.

Then she fell back. Two shadows had risen into the light. But they were no longer shadows; they were distinct physical forms. David had his weapon trained on a middle-aged, middle-size man with a squarish face, small eyes, a poorly fitting dark suit and a blackened eye. David indicated that she should open the French doors and let them into the house.

Fingers trembling, heart thundering, she did so. He urged the man forward into the house.

"Hit the lights, Spencer."

She did, and David got his first good look at his prisoner. "Harris!" he exclaimed.

"Delgado?" the man said, his voice carrying both hope and trepidation.

"What in God's name were you doing out there?"

"Should we call the cops?" Spencer asked anxiously.

David looked at her, frustrated. "He *is* a cop," he told her.

"Oh!" She stared at the man David had called Harris. "So what were you doing in my backyard?"

"Trying to watch over you," Harris said sheepishly. "Lieutenant Oppenheim *is* trying, David."

"Oppenheim sent you out here?"

Harris shrugged. "Hell, I've got the whole neighborhood, but I'm supposed to be keeping an especially close eye on Mrs. Huntington and her place, especially when she's out of it and you and your men are tailing her."

"Do you drive a blue sedan?" Spencer asked.

Harris shook his head. "An unmarked beige Plymouth."

"Where's your car?" David asked.

Spencer put up a hand. "Wait. Don't say anything— until I get back." She started for the kitchen.

"Spencer, what are you doing?" David demanded.

"Since Mr. Harris is a cop, I think the least we can do is to try to keep his eye from swelling any more. I'm getting ice. And I mean it, don't say a word!"

Of course they didn't listen to her. When Spencer returned with an ice bag, the men were deep in conversation. "Last time I try to be a humanitarian!" she warned Harris, seating him on the daybed next to the fireplace in the family room.

He glanced at her apologetically. "Sorry. I'll repeat everything. I was in your yard, Mrs. Huntington, because I followed someone else into it."

Spencer glanced at David, then back to Harris. "Who?"

Harris shrugged unhappily. "I'm sorry, Mrs. Huntington. I lost him. I usually ride with a partner, but we were really short tonight. Carla called in sick, so I was on my own. I drove by, and I thought I saw someone hopping over the back fence. I didn't want him to run when he saw the car, so I parked down the street and leaped the fence myself. I heard movement in the back, so I came around and saw someone at the French door right there. Then something spooked whoever it was. The clouds moved, I blinked, and he was gone. So I watched and waited and then…" He paused, shaking his head. "And then David jumped me, and you know the rest."

Spencer glanced at David. "Should we call in to police headquarters or something? Couldn't someone come out and check for fingerprints?"

Harris shook his head, looked at David. "Won't do any good. He was wearing gloves."

David frowned. "It was dark and you were at a distance. How do you know that?"

"He was dressed in black, head to toe. Must have worn a ski mask, even. I'm telling you, David, I would have seen a reflection of the moonlight on his flesh—if there had been any flesh to reflect anything."

"You keep saying he," Spencer noted. "It was defi
nitely a man?"

"Sure," Harris began, then frowned. "At least,
thought it was a man. I still think it was a man, but..."
He sighed. "Like I said, he—or she—was wearing a sk
mask and dark clothing. All I can really say with an
certainty is that the figure was covered from head to to
and wearing gloves. You're not going to get any prints."

"Not fingerprints. But maybe there's a shoe print o
something out there. You never know what the lab guy
might find. I'm going to go ahead and call this in."

Harris sighed.

Spencer soon knew why.

She was grateful to the police; she knew they wer
overworked and underpaid, and that most of them wer
dedicated, loyal, diligent—and laid their lives on the lin
daily.

But the night stretched on very tediously.

She answered questions, but with David and Harri
there, she was spared the bulk of them. Her house wa
gone over and over; fingerprints were lifted from the
doors, and the yard was combed for footprints.

Most of what they found belonged to David and Har
ris, but a smiling young technician told Spencer that he
might have one good heel mark, and who knew, it jus
might help.

Still, they had come home late, and by the time the
scene the crime team finished up, it was past four o'clock.

Spencer had acquired an acute headache. Some of it
came from drinking too much wine, some from being up
for so many hours. She had taken some aspirin when
she'd made coffee for the police, but all it had done was
make her stomach queasy.

She was getting an ulcer, she told herself mournfully. She was too young for all this stress. Or too old for it anymore.

She wasn't sure which.

But finally she was standing behind David at the door as the last police car drove away. He would be next, she supposed. "I know," she said, exhausted. "Turn on the alarm. I promise. I won't forget it again."

He shook his head, staring out. Amazingly, a tiny shaft of pink light was just beginning to show up in the east.

"I'll take care of it. I'm going to sit up tonight on the daybed."

"David, you don't have to do that. You must be ready to keel over yourself. Get someone else."

"Spencer, go to bed."

"David, I can't just let you sit up. I do have a guest room. I can—"

"Spencer, damn it," he said, running his fingers raggedly through his hair. "Go to bed! I'll be fine."

"But you would be more comfortable—"

"The last thing I want is to be comfortable right now," he said irritably.

"Fine! Suffer!" she told him, and started for the stairs. At that moment she felt as if she would melt like the wicked witch in *The Wizard of Oz* if she couldn't just lie down and close her eyes. "Go right ahead and suffer!" she repeated when she reached the landing.

David watched her go, frowning slightly. He winced when he heard her door close sharply.

"I've been suffering since you walked into my office, Spencer," he said softly. "Since you walked back into my life." He headed to the family room and stretched out on the daybed, staring at the patio.

Harris! Who would have thought?

David was glad that Oppenheim had taken him ser
ously and was doing his best to look after Spencer. As th
weeks passed, David had become more and more co
vinced that she was in danger, that the ''accidents'' tha
befell her weren't accidental. David wondered why O
penheim hadn't told him he'd assigned guards to Sper
cer, but he thought he knew. Oppenheim hadn't wante
to promise manpower he might not have.

Harris had seen someone come into the yard. And the
had a heel print. Of course, it might belong to one of th
garbagemen, or a meter reader. Still, it might be a legit
imate clue.

At the moment there was powder all over Spencer'
immaculate house. She would have it cleaned up b
morning, he was certain.

Who the hell had been in the yard? And why? Mayb
just a sneak thief. David loved the Grove, just as Spen
cer did, but the area was far from crime free. Breakin
and entering was a fairly common crime, unfortunately
Maybe someone had just been looking for a new TV o
stereo.

No. He knew in his bones that someone had wante
something in this house. Or some*one.*

Spencer.

Her car had been here; someone might have though
she was at home. Alone. Sleeping soundly upstairs. It wa
easy to discover a person's habits. He knew that wel
enough.

The pool glistened in the moonlight. He closed his eye
to shut out the sight. He'd sometimes come here wit
Danny in the afternoon. Danny had loved the water
Loved the sun. They'd sat and drunk beer and talke
about the latest Dolphins game and the Florida Pan

hers. Mostly, they had talked about the Marlins. Danny ad loved baseball most.

He closed his eyes, suddenly remembering with pain-ul clarity the day Danny had been attacked.

If only he had said something helpful! Given him a lue to his attacker instead of whispering Spencer's name. pencer...

David rose restlessly. "Damn you, Danny!" he said oftly to the moonlight. "I'm doing my best. Honest to jod, I'm doing my best. If you could just have given me nore to go on, just a little more.... What is it that I can't quite see? I'd do anything, old buddy. Anything. I love er, too...."

He clamped down hard on his jaw. Yeah, well, that vas it. He loved her. Always had, always would.

The sun was rising, and he knew that nothing else was ;oing to happen that night; he had just been too un-nerved to leave her.

He started to lie down on the daybed, but hesitated and hen found himself silently climbing the stairs. He paused igain, then carefully opened her door.

She was out for the count, sleeping in a big old T-shirt. One of Danny's.

Her hair was spread out like spun gold on the pillow. Her features, even in sleep, remained tense, as if she was lreaming, troublesome dreams. He wanted to walk into he room, touch her softly, smooth away the tension in er face.

He almost did it.

Then he saw the picture on the bedside. Her and)anny. Not a wedding picture. A vacation shot. Her and)anny together in a petting zoo, laughing because a goat vas trying to eat Danny's collar while someone else took he shot.

David closed her door softly and started down the stairs. He sat wearily at the foot of them.

He'd thought that maybe...maybe she was getting over Danny. Over the guilt. That maybe she'd even come close to admitting to herself that...

Old emotions might fade, but they never died. And the emotions between them had burned so brightly!

The picture had probably been there for a long time. She probably slept in Danny's shirts out of habit.

He just wished...

He wished it had been his shirt.

He needed to get up, to at least stretch out on the sofa. But he couldn't seem to move; he was too damned tired. He leaned his head against the wall at the foot of the stairs.

And that was where Spencer found him when she finally awoke, sometime the following afternoon.

Spencer knew she was overly tired, and that her nerves were just about raw. Maybe that was what caused the trouble that day. Or maybe it wasn't her fault at all—David woke up growling like a bear.

When she came down the stairs behind him and tapped him on the shoulder, she thought she had seldom—under any circumstances—come closer to death. He spun on her like a commando, ready to kill.

"Spencer!" He dragged his fingers through his hair. "Damn it, why did you sneak up on me like that?"

"I didn't sneak up on you. I just walked down the stairs."

He backed away from her, teeth clamped together, rubbing the back of his neck.

"I did tell you to go home," she reminded him.

"Yeah, and I told Sly that I'd keep you alive."

"I would have remembered the alarm."

His look assured her that he doubted her capabilities. he decided to put a little more distance between them nd edged against the railing to make it down the last few airs.

"I'll make coffee," she murmured. "You're welcome take a shower," she said uncomfortably. "I'm sure I've ot something up there that would fit you if you want a lean shirt. I—"

"You still have all Danny's clothes?" he asked her.

"I just haven't had a chance to get rid of his things," he said defensively.

"It's been more than a year," David said. "There are ts of organizations that would make good use of his ings. Let them, Spencer. It would have mattered to im."

She stared at him stonily. "Thank you. I'll keep your dvice in mind. And if it makes you uncomfortable to ear something that was Danny's, I think there's a Dol-hins shirt up in the closet that's actually yours. He must ave borrowed it from you at some point." She turned nd walked into the kitchen.

She spilled the coffee as she tried to make it, but fi-ally she got the pot brewing. She wandered out to the ack, looking into the yard. It was absolutely beautiful, eaceful and serene. Lush foliage and crystalline water nat danced in the light of the sun. It was going to be an-ther really hot day. Ninety in the shade, as the old-imers like to say. She could already see the heat dancing the air above the brick patio. She would miss this house she did sell it. The back was completely enclosed by a vooden fence. Of course, Harris and someone else had umped it last night, but most of the time it seemed like a very private Eden. She and Danny had spent lots of time together there.

Was she trying to leave the ghosts behind, as Jared had suggested?

Maybe. But she had a feeling that Danny was a ghost who would follow her all her life. She needed to learn to live with him. He was a good ghost. And that was why it hurt so badly sometimes to have him with her. Maybe she could come to terms with that...

She spun around suddenly. David was standing behind her, drinking coffee from a mug. He was wearing the Dolphins T-shirt. He was freshly bathed and shaved, his dark, wet hair slicked back.

"Jimmy's on his way," he told her. "I've got to go on for a while. What are your plans for the day?"

He asked the question like a dictator snapping out demands. She folded her arms over her chest. "You know, this is getting just a little bit ridiculous."

"Spencer, don't argue with me. I'm not in the mood for it."

"And I'm not in the mood to have a dictator run my life! This is crazy—"

She broke off. It *was* crazy. She didn't know what was happening anymore. But one thing was true. She had been afraid of Jared.

But he wasn't the one who'd jumped her fence last night. He had been in a car at the time, with his wife and children.

"What?" he demanded, cocking his head as he watched her.

She shook her head. "Nothing."

"Spencer..."

"Jimmy's going to be here, right? If I make any sudden, wild plans, I'm sure he'll let you know."

"Don't try getting on an airplane again or anything, Spencer. I'll drag you right off it."

"David..."

"Damn it, Spencer, I can't have you working against me all the damned time!" With that he spun around and walked to the front door.

A moment later he was gone.

Oppenheim was off, sitting in his backyard in South Miami, watching one of his grandkids play in the wading pool.

He groaned when David approached him.

"I know, I know. I've read Harris's full report," he said.

"So you know someone was trying to break in."

"David, I love Coconut Grove. It's one of my favorite areas of the city. I even love it on Friday and Saturday nights, when it's wall-to-wall people, outside cafés filled, rickshaws going, music seeping out from the clubs, traffic jammed. But, David, it's a high-crime area, too. You know damned well just how many robberies there are in the Grove."

"This is different, and you know it."

"David, face the truth! A concerned grandparent hires you because a beam fell in a dilapidated old house! Spencer Huntington sticks her nose in where she shouldn't and ends up in danger in a graveyard. There's a problem with a rental car—in Rhode Island, no less!—and then a robbery attempt. And you're on my back again!"

"I'm not on your back. You did have Harris there."

"Then what more do you want from me? I'm doing my best."

"I just came to make sure you knew that I was righ
that Spencer is in danger."

Oppenheim sighed. "Oh, sweet Jesus."

"Are you keeping someone on it?"

"As much as I can."

"Thanks," David said. He started to walk away, wav
ing to the three-year-old splashing in the pool.

"David!"

"What?"

"You'd better keep your people close to her for the res
of the weekend. Saturday nights are hardest for me. Yo
know this city—weekends can be murder."

No pun intended, David thought.

"Yeah, thanks, we'll stick to her through the week
end. I want to get down to the lab, though."

"It was a heel print from a Frye boot," Oppenhein
said. "No fingerprints. None that helped. We lifte
yours, but don't worry, you're not a suspect."

"Thanks," David said dryly. He decided to stop by th
lab anyway.

Downtown, he found Hank Jenkins on night duty
David had gotten lucky since Hank had been the one t
receive the samples the night before.

"Frye boot, a size nine, for whatever good that will d
you," Hank told him. He shrugged. "Good boot, no
cheap, but there are probably hundreds of thousands i
existence. Nine is a bit small, though. And the depth o
the print would indicate that your perp is small, on
hundred and twenty to one hundred and fifty pounds
maybe. Might even have been a woman."

"A woman?" David asked, surprised.

"There *are* female thieves."

"This isn't an ordinary thief," David said. Then h
thanked Hank and left, glancing at his watch. The day

was gone. Entirely. And half the night, too. It was already after nine. He was still tired. He was too old to sleep on steps.

He drove to Spencer's house, the restless feeling that he couldn't leave her alone stronger than ever.

When he rounded the corner, he saw a beige Plymouth sedan parked just across the street.

Harris was sitting in it. He lifted a coffee cup to David, who waved in return.

Jimmy's car was in Spencer's driveway, but Jimmy wasn't in it. He was probably inside, David thought sourly.

He was.

When David rang the bell, Jimmy answered. He was in cutoffs and a T-shirt—Danny's old clothing. At least he had the grace to look a little abashed as David stared at him.

"Mrs. Huntington sent out for pizza. Harris was outside, so I figured it was all right to come in. I've been alert, though. You know I'm good."

David nodded. Jimmy was going to start stuttering any minute.

"It's been so damned hot...she spent the day out by the pool, reading. I did some swimming, too. She said to live in for a while, so I did."

David was still staring at him.

"I swear to you, I didn't let my guard down for a single second, David."

"It's okay, Jimmy," David said at last, though it wasn't exactly the right way to guard a client. He sighed. "It's okay because Harris is out here. But if he'd left—"

"I would have known. He said he'd call in if he had to go out on a call."

"Oh."

"Well," Jimmy said awkwardly, "if you're here, guess I'll take off." He looked at his feet. He was bare foot. "I'll just get my shoes and take off."

David nodded again. He waited while Jimmy went out back, said good-night to Spencer and came out—shoe in hand.

"Good night. Do I take the morning again?"

"Yeah."

"See you around eight?"

"That will be fine."

Jimmy left. David set the alarm and walked throug the house. Lots of good the alarm was going to do for th moment, with Spencer outside, caught in the soft glare o the pool lights and stretched out on one of the lounges.

He didn't think her bikini had been designed with th absolute intent to seduce. It wasn't a thong bikini; in fact it wasn't especially bare at all, not compared to a lot o what you saw on the Florida beaches.

It was just the way Spencer wore the damned thing. I was downright erotic.

Her knees were up, a copy of *Architectural Diges* leaning on them as she studied it. A slim, frosty glass o something sat by her side on a little wrought-iron patio table. Her hair was wet and slicked back, her face makeup free. She looked somehow very young, very in nocent.

Yeah, right.

Was this a setup? Apparently not. She looked up an groaned at the sight of him.

"What if I were to buy a very large Doberman?" she asked him. "Would you just go home then? We can shop the kennels tomorrow."

He walked over to her, picked up her glass and swallowed some of its contents. Ice tea. He'd hoped for something stronger.

He sat in the lounge opposite her, folded his hands and watched her. "Nice outfit. Seducing poor Jimmy, eh?"

She kept her eyes on his. "You'll notice that there is something called a pool behind me. And I'm wearing a bathing suit. Something people wear in pools."

"Quite a suit." He nodded.

"Perfectly decent."

"Well, I suppose it's better than a towel—or nothing," he said agreeably.

"So let me get this straight. You really are accusing me of trying to seduce your employee?" she inquired. Her tone was light. Amused.

Furious.

He shrugged. "You are good at seduction. I know that firsthand."

"Now just why would I want to seduce Jimmy?" she asked him. "After all, you were the first one to notice that I wasn't incredibly happy after stumbling into bed with you."

"After stumbling into bed with me...hmm. Interesting." He leaned forward. "Maybe that's the problem, Spencer. It's me. Maybe you wouldn't be half so miserable if you 'stumbled into bed' with half a football team."

She sat up, setting her magazine aside. "You're an idiot, David. A complete idiot!"

She stood up and walked away, executing a perfect dive into the deep end of the pool, then swimming to the opposite end, as far from him as she could get.

He watched her for a minute. God, he *was* an idiot.

He stood up. Ripped the Dolphins shirt over his head
Kicked off his shoes, jerked off his socks. Hobbled h
way out of his jeans and briefs.

Spencer was at the far end, staring, ocean blue ey
narrowed sharply on him.

"What the hell are you doing?" she demanded.

"Swimming," he told her briefly.

He cut into the water after her. He thought she woul
dive away beneath the surface, try to elude him.

She didn't. She remained leaning against the edg
watching him tensely as he broke the surface.

He meant to say something. Anything. He didn't. In
stead he reached out for her, pulling her to him, the
backing her against the cool cobalt tiles that rimmed th
edge of the pool. His mouth crushed down on hers whil
he slipped his hand beneath the bikini bottom, sliding
down over her hips and buttocks, then discarding
completely.

He moulded the curves of her backside with his palm
then brought his hand in front, rubbing his knuckle
against her even as he all but devoured her mouth, forc
ing entry with his tongue, so damned hungry that he wa
determined to force the fire that filled him to leap to he
as well. A sound escaped her, but barely. She was stiff
but just briefly. Then her fingers were on his cheek, hi
shoulders. Running down the length of his back. Nail
just brushing his buttocks.

He caught her hand. Curled the fingers around hi
thrusting sex. Groaned against her mouth.

Her lips broke free of his. "We shouldn't be doin
this," she told him, her voice rasping.

"I know."

They shouldn't be doing this. But he would shoo
himself if they didn't. She stroked him, and then her fin

ers dipped lower, cradled his balls. He groaned again.
he bikini bra had a hook in front, and he popped it
pen, then leaned forward and caught a taut pink nipple
etween his teeth.

"David... This is crazy," she gasped.

"Yeah. It's one of the definitions of insanity, you
now," he told her.

She shook her head, blue eyes on him, confused.

He smiled. "This is crazier than you think. Going in
ircles. Doing the same thing over and over again and
xpecting a different outcome. We'll make love. You'll
ry. I'll go away furious with myself. Right?"

"Then don't—"

"No." He pressed a finger to her lips. "Just call me
ucking insane," he told her.

He lifted her suddenly, setting her on the tile edge of
he pool. Then he parted her thighs and buried his face
etween them. She cried out, trembling. Seconds later,
he cried out again, and he caught her hips, dragging her
nto the water, on top of him, slowly, impaling her as he
owered her. She seemed to close around his shaft like
lowing lava. He held her against the side of the pool,
huddering with the force of his desire as he slammed into
er, his arms around her, holding her.

This seemed like the only true drive in life. But it was
little like dying, as well. Finally his force was spent. The
unger exploded, shattered. Exploded from his body,
wept into hers. She was limp, arms around him, hold-
ng him.

He didn't move. For the longest time, he simply didn't
nove.

Hell and damnation. He couldn't believe what he'd
een tonight. He'd been all but glued to the narrow slit in

the fence, but, *cono,* what a night. And it was eve
sweeter because he'd eluded the cop sitting out front.

He leaned closer for a better look. His knees trem
bling, and his blood racing, he eased one foot back.

David shifted at last. She was shivering. The night a
was cool, the water a shade warmer. But the intense hea
of the day was gone. Chills were setting into her.

Either that or she was sobbing again.

"Don't cry!" he told her. "Damn you, don't sta
crying again!"

"I'm not crying," she grated out.

He started to set her down so he could look in her eyes

Then they both heard it. A snap in the foliage beyon
the fence.

"Son of a bitch!" David swore. He was out of the wa
ter in a flash, wrenching on his jeans in one fluid mo
tion. He didn't try for his shirt or shoes, but leaped fo
the fence, half jumping, half crawling up it.

He leaped down the other side as a car engine revvec
from the other side of the block.

He tore through the brush tripping over a sprinkler i
the yard behind Spencer's.

Some bright dog finally started to bark.

He hit the street just as a car went flying along it.

A blue sedan.

15

Spencer dispensed with the idea of trying to find the pieces of her suit quickly, leaped from the pool and dived for her beach robe. As she huddled into it, she felt absolutely ill. Violated.

Someone had been out there. Watching them.

She nearly screamed when David suddenly—and all but silently—vaulted over the fence into the yard. She stared at him, pale and stricken, but he ignored her, walking to the open French doors. "Get in and lock up," he told her.

"Should I set the alarm?"

"I'll do it from the front. What the hell happened to Harris?" he demanded.

He was talking more to himself than to her, Spencer realized.

She locked up the back and followed him to the front door. He was looking out into the night in disgust.

"Gone. He was supposed to call in if he was going to leave the house. Damn him! We could have had our man!"

"Did you see—"

"I saw a blue sedan. Speeding away. There isn't a prayer of catching it now. I've got to call in and report our peeping Tom. And find out about Harris. You can call it a night, if you want."

He was almost casual. Very matter-of-fact. Ignoring what had just happened.

Spencer felt as if she were a vivid crimson hue from her hair roots to her toenails. "You can't call it in. What are you going to say?"

"I'm going to say someone was in the bushes, staring in through the fence!" he told her.

"They'll ask questions."

He set his hands on his hips. "Don't worry. I won't report just what Danny's widow, Saint Spencer, was doing."

"Fuck you, David."

He arched a brow. "Again? Twice in one night? This could become habit-forming."

She spun around, starting for the stairs. She was going to start crying again, but he would never understand why. Not when she couldn't articulate her feelings, even to herself. Not when they were so confused. If only he wouldn't mock her.

But maybe he had to. She had hurt him badly once. And David was a careful man. He wasn't going to leave himself vulnerable a second time. Not with her.

She started up the stairs, turning back at the landing. "You sure as hell can't blame tonight on me!" she told him.

"I don't know. I think maybe bikinis fall into the same category as towels, robes and nakedness."

"David, you are a—"

"Spencer, I'm not blaming anything on you, all right? Any time, any thing, I take full responsibility for what I do, okay?"

She turned without answering and walked to her room, where she paced the floor. She could hear him on the phone. He seemed to be talking forever.

He was probably on with Oppenheim. Robbery and homicide were handled by different divisions, but in situations like this, where the two cases ran together, the different units worked together well. More men would probably come out and look for more clues. Which would be fine—as long as they didn't question her.

She hesitated, then went to the linen closet and found an extra pillow. After slipping it into a pillowcase and taking the matching sheets, she went to the top of the stairs. She couldn't hear him talking anymore.

"David?"

He came to stand at the foot of the steps and she threw the bedding down to him. "The daybed is much more comfortable than the stairs," she told him.

He caught the pillow, but the sheets ended up draped over the banister.

"Thanks," he told her.

Spencer nodded coolly, then turned and went to her bedroom.

Lying down on her bed, she stared at the picture of her and Danny together at the amusement park. Fingers trembling, tears stinging her eyes, she turned the picture facedown. She was going to start flat-out crying again. But tonight it was different, she realized.

She wasn't crying for Danny anymore. Tonight she was crying for herself.

David made up the daybed, then walked around the house, checking windows, doors, bolts, locks and the alarm. Finally he stretched out to rest. The daybed actually *was* fairly comfortable.

You know, he told himself, if you're going to keep starting things with Spencer, it's too bad you don't do it

at bedtime. Sleeping might be a hell of a lot more com
fortable that way.

No. He didn't want to wind up in Danny's bed with
Danny's widow again. He would just have her in the poo
instead, he mocked himself.

And *he* had been ready to admonish poor Jimmy fo
the way he had been behaving!

He tossed and turned in bed, the sheets twisting around
him. When he got his hands on Harris, he was going to
twist his neck, he thought angrily.

What the hell was going on here? Last night it had been
someone small in Frye boots, tonight a voyeur in a blue
sedan. The same person? Two different people?

And *why?*

The doorbell was ringing. David rose, blinking in the
sunlight, and went to answer the summons, certain it was
Jimmy, come to take his turn on watch. He stumbled to
the door and looked through the peephole.

Sly was standing on the walk.

Sly, in a white-and-gold shirt and beige shorts, standing ramrod straight, as always, but just a little bit thin
now for his height. David stepped back, turned off the
alarm and opened the door.

"Mornin'," Sly said. "Everything all right?"

"Ah...yeah." David wasn't ready to tell Sly too much
yet.

"Coffee ready?" Sly asked.

"Spencer's not up yet," David began, but Spencer *was*
up. She was coming down the stairway in bare feet and a
sundress, blond hair pulled into a ponytail at the back of
her head.

"Sly!"

"I've come to take you to breakfast," her grandfather
ld her. "Both of you."

"Sorry, Sly, I can't go. I've got a little bit of catching
 to do this morning," David said.

Sly gave David the once-over. "You do look like pure
ll, boy."

"Thanks," David acknowledged dryly.

"Spencer, I won't take no from you," Sly said.

"I have no intention of refusing you," Spencer said.
You can come to church with me after." She glanced at
r watch. "Or first. I'll just get some shoes and a purse.
ou can let David out for me, right? Unless he wants to
ake some coffee for you?"

"Are you kidding?" Sly said. "I've had his coffee!"

"Jimmy should be here any second, right?" Spencer
id, staring at David. "Maybe he'd like to come to
eakfast with us, too, Sly." Watching David, Spencer
ivered. Why on earth had she baited him that way?

Then David looked over at Sly. "That's Jimmy pull-
g up outside right now. He'll be taking the day shift.
nd I'm sure he'd enjoy breakfast." He shifted his at-
ntion to Spencer, his eyes suddenly cold. "He seems to
ijoy everything Spencer has to offer."

David turned and disappeared into the family room,
turning a moment later with his shirt and shoes in his
ands. He didn't even bother to put them on. He just told
ly goodbye and walked out.

Spencer felt ill again, worse than she had felt yet.
Iaybe she *was* getting an ulcer. Her emotions had been
awing away at her insides for a long time now, but she
used so much of her pain herself. She wondered if there
as a way to tell David that she was finally coming to
rms with herself over Danny's death.

She wondered if there was a way to tell David an
thing.

David went home to shower and shave, then drove
his office. He began going through his files while he b
the play button on the phone answering machine. Th
first three messages were inquiries about his services. H
would have Reva get back to them on Monday.

The fourth call had come from the police lab dow
town. The cops had combed the bushes and the groun
outside Spencer's fence again. This time they'd foun
only one fairly mangled print, but the lab had identifie
it as a size-twelve Rockport men's loafer.

The fifth call caused him to stop dead still. It had con
from one of the officers who'd been investigating th
accident in Rhode Island.

"We're not sure if this is anything or not yet, Mr. De
gado, but the rental agency called us about somethir
rather strange. The mechanic who'd worked on the ca
Mrs. Huntington rented disappeared a few days after th
accident. Of course, the agency blamed it on us, sayin
we'd destroyed his confidence with our questions or som
crap like that. But when we tried to check him out fu
ther, we couldn't come up with anything on him. All th
information he'd given on his application was false. W
checked his social security number and discovered it be
longs to someone who's been dead for nearly twent
years. Anyway, we got one of his fingerprints off a to
he used, and you'll never guess…he was an ex-con. He'
escaped from prison, where he was serving ten to twelv
on an armed robbery conviction. And guess who he'd la
been working for? A man I'm sure you know. Rick
Garcia. That's all we've got so far, but if I can be of an
more help, give me a call. The number here is—"

David was already dialing as he listened.

Spencer spent the entire day with Sly. And Jimmy.

It was surprisingly nice, relaxing. Over breakfast she toyed with the idea of mentioning that she wanted to go to the yacht club for lunch on Monday, but she was afraid that Sly would just turn around and tell David, ruining her chance to meet with Vichy. As far as she knew, David still felt she was safe when she was at work, so he wouldn't be watching her tomorrow, leaving her free to inveigle Sly into taking her to the club.

After church and breakfast, they went by the house Spencer had told Sandy she planned to buy, since she still had the keys. As far as she was concerned, it was already her house.

"Are you buying this place just because it's close to me?" Sly asked.

"You know me better than that," she said.

"Are you?"

She shrugged. "It *is* a bonus that you're just down the street."

"What are you going to do with your place?"

"Sell it, I guess. I don't need two houses. And it's going to cost a fortune to fix this place up."

Sly looked around slowly, staring up the stairs to the balcony. Spencer shivered, remembering how frightened she had been when she stood there with Jared.

It must have been her imagination! With everything else going on, she was crazy to be frightened of her cousin.

"What's wrong, Spencer?" Sly asked, sensing her changed mood.

"Nothing."

"You look scared."

"Nothing's scaring *me. You're* the fussbudget."

"A man gets no respect once he gets old."

"No whining. You're younger than guys who could be your grandsons. Age is just a state of mind, remember?"

"I remember, but my kidneys don't always. And let me warn you, young lady, youth is no guarantee of safety!"

"Ah, but I have a grandfather to set guards on me day and night."

"Come on, it's not that bad."

She remembered how frightened she had been with Jared the other day and realized that she was actually grateful to be guarded day and night. She just wasn't sure she was grateful that the guard was so often David.

"Let me show you the rest of the house." She looked around him to Jimmy. "Want to see the rest?" she asked.

"Sure," he said politely.

She smiled, starting through the living room. Jimmy was absolutely unimpressed with the house. All he could see was the decay. He was being polite.

He was being a marvelous watchdog.

She decided to cook that night. Roast leg of lamb, new potatoes, asparagus, salad with her own raspberry vinaigrette.

She didn't know if she was calm because she was hoping David would appear, or glad and relaxed because he didn't. In any case, Jimmy and Sly were both very complimentary about the meal.

Sly left about nine, and Jimmy told her that he was going to keep vigil in front of the house.

At eleven she gave up waiting for David and went to bed, where she lay awake, praying for her inner tension to unwind. She couldn't go on living like this. Something had to break—fast.

Sometime after twelve she fell asleep.

Sometime after two she woke up again.

She looked out the window. David was standing vigil now, leaning against his car.

Half of her wanted to go down and insist he come inside. The other half of her wanted him to go away. Far, far away.

She lay down. She had to stay away from him, she thought, the tension within her knotting even more tightly. She closed her eyes and tried to sleep. Pounded her pillow. Rose, paced. Lay down and pounded her pillow again.

It was another long night. When morning came she felt like hell. Not even coffee tasted good.

David parked in front of the club.

Sly had called him about an hour ago to let him know where they were going. The club was always busy, and at first, David hadn't felt any concern. Then, for no reason, trepidation had started to set in, and he realized he hadn't had lunch here in a long time, so why not now?

He was walking past the large outdoor pool that overlooked the rows of docks and sleek, expensive pleasure craft when he heard someone call his name. He paused, turning toward the pool. Cecily Monteith was there, stretched out on one of the lounges, dark glasses over her eyes, her mostly exposed body shiny with oil. "You really are right on my cousin-in-law's trail like a bloodhound, aren't you? I haven't seen you here in years."

"I haven't been here in years."

She shrugged, looking around. "I always love coming here. Especially in summer. There's a day-care kind of thing, you know. They teach the kids how to sail."

"That's nice. Did you come with Spencer and Sly?"

Cecily shook her head, smiling. "I'm not into the business thing. I just like the sun. Want a drink?"

"Thanks anyway, but I think I'll go see what Sly and Spencer are up to."

"Lunch, a boring business lunch." Cecily made a face, then smiled, very much the flirt. She could be bluntly, blatantly honest, sometimes funny, sometimes sweet. And, when she wanted, damned catty.

She hadn't changed much since high school, he thought wryly. Maybe none of them had, not inside, where it counted.

"Sit down for a minute," she invited. "I'm worried about Spencer."

"Why?"

"Come on, sit a minute!"

He sat down. A poolside waitress in short shorts came by. He ordered a beer.

"Why are you worried about Spencer? Sly thinks she's in danger, but I thought pretty much everyone else was of the opinion that he was being paranoid."

"Oh, I don't know about that. Anyway, it's not her safety I'm worried about. I mean, she's got you, David the wonder boy, protecting her, right?"

"Cecily..."

"Oh, don't be such a stick-in-the mud. I'm teasing."

His beer came, and as he sipped it he realized that Cecily loved the idea that she was sitting half-naked with a man other than her husband. She was still an attractive woman. It was a pity she felt so insecure. "So, you were saying...?" he said, trying to get her back on track.

"Well, I think Spencer's . . . sick. *You know.*"

"*No,* I don't know. What are you talking about?"

Cecily sighed. "Maybe I've made a mistake."

"Maybe you have."

She sighed again. "I probably shouldn't be talking to you. . . ."

"Cecily, you're obviously trying to tell me something, whether you should be talking to me or not, so spit it out now or I'll throttle you."

"Ooh, I love it when you talk tough!" she teased.

"Cecily . . ."

"Oh, all right!" She paused for a moment, savoring her power, then went on. "Well, she didn't eat any of that Cuban food the other night. And Sly was clucking like an old hen today because she hadn't touched her breakfast yesterday."

"Cecily, just what are you getting at?"

She leaned forward. "I'm wondering who she's seeing, that's all. I'm telling you, wonder boy, I'd be willing to bet that my saintly cousin-in-law is in a very delicate position. *Pregnant,* David. And I'm just wondering who the daddy might be, since Danny has been dead too long for a posthumous baby, don't you think?"

He would have loved to slap her. Instead he slammed his beer glass down and stood. "Cecily, maybe you should discuss this with Spencer herself, since you seem to be so curious. Personally, I think she might consider it none of your business."

"Let's just hope she doesn't think it's none of yours," Cecily said sweetly.

"Thanks for the beer," he told her curtly, then threw his jacket over his shoulder and headed inside.

16

Getting Sly to take her to the club had been easy. Leaving him for long enough to have her meeting with Gene Vichy was not.

She finally escaped when they ordered coffee, telling him that she was going to the ladies' room and then had a few quick calls to make. From that point on, though, it was a piece of cake. Vichy found her.

"Mrs. Huntington."

He was all in white, silver hair neatly brushed back, his appearance dapper. He'd been wearing dark glasses, but he removed them as he stood and offered her the chair opposite him.

She sat down, assessing him. He was a striking man, with an extremely handsome face. Very sensual lips, bright eyes. At any age, she thought, he had been a lady killer.

Perhaps literally.

"Can I get you coffee? Or something a bit stronger?"

"I'm having a coffee with my grandfather. Just say what you've got to say, Mr. Vichy."

"My, my, you're a feisty little thing. Stronger than your husband, Mrs. Huntington."

"If you've got something to tell me—"

"I wanted to tell you that I did not kill your husband," he said, leaning back. "I did not kill my wife, an

did not kill your husband. It's very strange. I am suspected of killing my wife with a blow to the head and of
shooting your husband. It's almost like a game of Clue.
My wife in the bedroom with a blunt object. Your husband on the street with a gun. But things don't happen
like that in real life, Mrs. Huntington. I asked to meet
you because I hoped you would find me sincere when we
spoke. I'm growing very tired of this constant police harassment, and you are a big reason for it. I hoped to
convince you to ask the police to leave me alone. Then,
of course, if that doesn't work, I want you to know that
I'll sue you."

"You'll sue me!" Spencer said, astounded.

"Indeed."

She rose, looking at him incredulously. "Mr. Vichy, let
me assure you, you don't have a snowball's chance in hell
of winning a case against me! I'm not guilty of anything
in regard to you, so you can just take your threats
and—"

"He threatened you?" The words sounded more like
growl than a human voice. She was trembling inside as
she spun around.

Damn it! David!

"No," Spencer began.

Vichy was on his feet, staring at David, and looking
decidedly pale. "Delgado, if you even come near me, I'll
sue you for assault and battery."

"Touch her, call her, say her name again, asshole, and
you'll be too damned dead to sue anyone for anything!"
David snapped.

"David!" Spencer said firmly.

Vichy smiled. "Police harassment."

"I'm not a cop anymore. You won't be able to (anything to the force because of me, Vichy. And yc know what? Eventually, they *will* fry your butt!"

"Mr. Delgado, alas! Birth will tell. Your kind shou not be allowed in this club."

"Mr. Vichy, your kind shouldn't be allowed anywhe on the streets, and I assure you, I will be doing my be to see that you're kept off them! Come on, Spencer."

"David—"

What in God's name was wrong with him? His finge were wrapped around her upper arm as if they we bands of steel, and he was walking so fast that it was ha to keep up, especially since she was wearing heels.

Was he angry because she hadn't told him about th meeting? But how could he know it had been planned She might simply have run into Vichy here. Suddenly sl realized that he was heading toward the boats.

"David, Sly is in—"

"Sly is on his way back to work," David said briefl "You're coming with me."

"Wait a minute!"

"No!"

She didn't balk until they reached the *Reckless Lady* Sly's sleek yacht. Thirty feet, she slept six comfortabl with every amenity known to man.

David knew the yacht well enough. Sly had owned for at least fifteen years.

"Hop on," David told her.

"No. I've had it. I have absolutely had it with th' whole thing. I would rather be shot—"

"I'll shoot you myself if you don't get on!" he ir formed her.

He leaped over to the bow and extended a hand tc ward her. It was her chance to escape, but she was afrai he would tackle her if she tried to make it back to the club.

"I'm not dressed for this. Walking around on board a boat in heels—"

"You've got plenty of clothing stored on the *Lady*. And more shoes than Imelda Marcos."

"The hell I do!"

"Come on." He reached for her hand again, caught it, and brought her aboard. Then he released the tie lines and left her standing on the bow while he went to the stern and started the motor.

She made her way precariously from the bow to the stern in his wake. By the time she got there, he had backed the vessel from her berth and headed her out to the bay.

"Where are we going?" She had to shout to be heard over the roar of the motor.

"Out!"

"Out where? And why?"

"I'll know when I get there, and I'll tell you why then."

She climbed carefully down the ladder to the cabin below. She came to the galley first, and dining area and chart desk. Two small sleeping cabins came next, one on either side of the narrow aisleway, while the master cabin was beneath the bow. He'd been right about one thing; he did keep sneakers and some casual clothing here. She changed into white cutoffs, sneakers and a sleeveless tailored shirt.

When she went topside again, the vessel was moving quickly, slicing cleanly through the water. Spencer sat on one of the seats in the stern, still completely baffled. He wouldn't be this keyed up over an accidental meeting with Gene Vichy, so he must have known that she'd planned it. But if he had known *that,* why hadn't he stopped it?

He faced the onrushing wind, not even looking at h
Finally, when they were just off Bear Cut, he cut
throttle.

The heat was intense; it was another of those summ
days when the air seemed to dance and sizzle. The s
beat down on the water, giving it the appearance o
field of diamonds. The waves were light, and the ya
rocked slightly.

David dropped the anchor, then stood, looking off
the little island of shrub and sand in the distance.

"David, tell me what the hell is going on—right now
or I swear I'll take my chances swimming back."

He spun to face her. "All right. Why didn't you
me?"

This *was* over Vichy.

"I—there was nothing to tell. He called me, but—"

"What are you talking about?" he demanded.

"What are *you* talking about?" she asked carefully

"*Who* called you?"

"What are you talking about?" she repeated, ignc
ing his question.

"The circle game again, pure insanity," he sai
throwing up his arms. He was wearing a lightweight su
but since coming aboard, he'd doffed his jacket. Now
jerked at his tie, loosening it, then ripped it from arou
his neck and undid the top buttons of his tailored shi
"Who called you, Spencer? Vichy?"

"I—" She wanted to lie, but she felt his eyes on h
and knew it was time for the truth. "Yes, Vichy calle
Friday. He said he'd be at the club today and wanted
talk to me. It didn't seem like a bad idea to hear what
had to say."

"Jesus Christ, Spencer, you should be smarter tha
that! If you really want to get to the truth of things, we'

t to play together. How in goddamned hell can I fight
r you when you're always against me?''

She leaped up. ''Maybe, just maybe, he would have
id something to me that he wouldn't say to you. Some-
ing that would help!''

He sat suddenly, running his fingers through his hair,
s head down. Then he raised his head and stared at her.
All right, Spencer. Please, from this point on, let's
ake it a team effort.''

''Are you going to treat me like a part of your team?''

''Spencer, I don't want to see you killed. I owe that
uch to Danny.''

''Right,'' she said evenly.

''Let's play twenty questions,'' he said.

''All right,'' Spencer said, confused and wary. ''You
ll me what—''

''No, no. I get to start. *You* tell *me*, Spencer. Just ex-
tly what relationships have you formed since Danny
ed? Is there someone out there who you're not telling
e about?''

''What?'' she asked incredulously.

''Who have you been sleeping with?''

She stared at him, astounded, then rose, feeling as if an
-cold wall had formed around her.

''How dare you?'' she said quietly, her temper sim-
ering beneath the tight lid she was trying desperately to
ep on it. ''You have no right—''

''I've got to know, Spencer! Is there someone in your
st who could—''

''You're accusing me of having had an affair with
meone? Someone who might have killed Danny? Who
ight be trying to kill me now?''

''No,'' he said softly.

''Then what?''

"Spencer, answer the question, please."

"It's none of your business."

"The hell it isn't!" he raged.

She backed away from him. She hadn't seen him li[ke] this since...

Since the day she'd walked out of his life. Years ago

"Damn you, David," she grated. "I don't know wh[at] this is about, but there's no one else in my life. There w[as] Danny. But he's dead. And now there's... Oh, you know[.] Satisfied? Do I need to swear on a Bible?"

"Damn you, Spencer!" he said softly, turning awa[y] from her for a moment, eyes brooding as he stared acro[ss] the water. Then he looked at her and spoke, his voice lo[w,] deep. Passionate. "All right, I'll get to the point. Tru[st] me, I have no intention of making demands, of intrud[-]ing in your life. But I am telling you one thing. Don't yo[u] dare get an abortion."

"What?" Spencer breathed.

"Cecily told me. That you were pregnant."

Thank God there was a seat immediately behind he[r] because she fell into it, amazed. "What?" she repeated[.]

"Cecily told me—"

"But—" Spencer began.

Then she broke off. And watching her, David realize[d] that Cecily had probably been right. But Spencer hadn[']t been keeping anything from him; she had just now rea[l]ized the possibility herself.

She shook her head. "Don't be absurd. Cecily couldn[']t possibly know such a thing. We're barely talking thre[e] weeks. I—"

"Maybe you should check, then."

"You don't know—"

"For God's sake, I have a sister. I have eyes. I watch television. Buy one of those tests with the plus and minus signs or the blue lines or whatever it is."

"Oh, my God! Plus and minus signs, blue lines!" she exploded.

Then he was suddenly worried, because she started to laugh, tears streaming down her cheeks. She buried her face in her hands for a moment, then looked up at him and started to laugh again.

"Spencer..." He took a step toward her, gripping her shoulders. "Spencer, stop it!"

"You don't know!" she whispered. "You don't know!"

She wrenched away from him, leaped to the deck, then lunged into the water.

What in God's name...!

He kicked off his shoes and socks and plunged in after her.

The water felt good. He followed her ashore to a stretch of sand that was totally private on a Monday afternoon. She was sitting half in and half out of the water, knees up, arms wrapped around them, head down on her arms. Her wet shirt and shorts clung to her, and a strand of seaweed hung from her hair.

He sat down beside her. "Spencer, please..."

Forcefully, he lifted her chin. The misery in her eyes was so stark that he was taken aback, seeming to tighten against the pain that knifed into his heart. She didn't want anything to do with him, and she didn't want to be pregnant. Not with his child.

He released her chin, stared at his soaked suit pants, his bare heels digging into the wet sand. A fiddler crab was running past.

"I told you, I don't intend to intrude in your life," h
began.

"It's not that!" The words were spoken in barely
whisper. He glanced over to see that she was staring at th
water, tears forming in her crystal blue eyes. "You don'
understand." She paused, moistening her lips.

"Spencer, what—"

"I don't know whether Cecily is right or not," sh
said. She was lying. He could tell. She knew, or at leas
she suspected. "But I..."

"What?"

"I wouldn't get—an abortion."

He felt dizzy. Thank God. Thank God for every littl
favor...

She stared at him. "Danny...Danny came out that da
to—to tell you he was coming home. We..."

"You were trying to make a baby," David said, lool
ing out over the water himself.

She winced. "Damn it!" she said, suddenly fierc
"You knew!"

"He was my best friend, Spencer. Yes, I knew you tw
were trying to plan a family." He hesitated. "And I di
find you naked except for a black tie that day."

"It's just not fair," she whispered. "He wanted a bab
so badly, and now—it's like God is laughing at us. *I*
me."

Suddenly irritated, David stood, then reached dow
and caught her by the shoulders, drawing her to her fee
"Danny is dead. I'm sorry. You're sorry. We both love
him, and neither of us would ever have wanted anythin
to happen to him. Damn it, Spencer, if you loved him s
much, remember what he was like! He would hav
wanted you to be happy."

She jerked her shoulders free, stepping back. She didn't want to hear this. Not from him. And certainly not now. "I'd like to go home," she told him.

"Fine." He pointed to the boat. "Sorry. There's no choice but to go back the way we came."

She nodded and kept staring at him. Under other circumstances he might have smiled. He'd never seen Spencer Anne Montogmery—Huntington—look so lost in her life.

She walked into the water and started swimming. Once again he followed behind her, climbing up the stern ladder first when they reached the boat, then extending a hand to help her up. She hesitated for a second.

"Dammit, Spencer."

She grasped his hand, a flash of anger in her eyes, and disappeared into the cabin as soon as she was aboard.

Spencer showered and changed. He stayed in his salty, stained trousers and bare feet.

Just before they made it to the club, she appeared on deck. Her makeup was gone, her face fresh scrubbed, and she was still pale. But her eyes were clear.

She helped him tie up the yacht, but when he would have leaped off, leaving her alone, she called his name. "David."

"What?" he asked warily.

"I'm sorry. I don't even know if this is happening yet, but I didn't mean to be so hateful. I just need some time. I suppose I need to find out if it's true, as well."

He nodded, leaped to the dock, then reached for her. She stepped out alongside him, wearing a soft, sleeveless yellow knit dress and sandals. She walked ahead of him to the parking lot, then paused.

"Sly is gone, remember? My car," he whispered against her ear.

Her shoulders squared, but she followed him without a word. He opened the passenger door, seated her, then settled into the driver's seat.

"Home?" he asked her.

"Yes, please. Wait, no. I've got to go to the office for my car."

At least she seemed to be coming back to the land of the living, he thought, driving through Coconut Grove to her office. Traffic was already growing heavy. There were a number of private shools along the winding roads that hugged the bay, and every day at about this time, things started to clog up with school buses and parents out to pick up their kids.

His heart suddenly seemed to quicken. Kids... The world was full of them. He liked them. He'd always liked them. Their enthusiasm, their trust. Their belief in miracles and in magic. He'd always wanted them, too. He wanted to share his father's dream of freedom with them. The dream of success in America that Michael Mac Cloud had given his grandchildren. He wanted them to feel the sun, to learn to sail, to grow in this melting-pot community where all things were possible.

And, once upon a time, he'd even dared to want children with Spencer.

He was glad his hands were on the wheel. Otherwise they would have been trembling, and he didn't want her to see just how shaken he was.

He reached the offices of Montgomery Enterprises and let her out by the door. "I'll see you at the house," he told her.

She nodded and tried to close the car door, but he held it open. "Spencer?"

"Yes?"

"You're still in danger. You know that. I have to keep
promise to Sly, whether you want to see me or not."

"I'm not arguing," she told him, then closed the door
d disappeared into the office.

He stared after her a moment, then dialed Jimmy on
e cellular phone. "Can you make it here quickly? I
nt a tail on her at all times now."

"Sure. I'll just drive right over the school buses,"
mmy said cheerfully. David started to reply, then real-
d that Jimmy was already on his way. He smiled and
cked off.

There was a lot he had to do, he thought as he drove
ay. For one thing, he had to spend some time with Mr.
ne Vichy. Plus he needed to find Willie, get back to the
wport police and check in with his contacts on the
ami force.

Today, they could all wait.

Spencer saw Jimmy when she left her office. She waved
him, trying hard to look calm, though she felt any-
ing but.

As she drove home, she wondered how Cecily had re-
ized what was going on before she did herself. Any-
ay, Cecily could be wrong, damn it. Cecily and her
xation with pre-baby bodies!

True, she hadn't been feeling quite right. Not bad, re-
y, just not great. But that didn't mean anything.

It was just that she was usually as regular as clock-
ork. So regular that she didn't even think about it. Of
urse, she was under a lot of stress. . . .

She reached her house and got out of her car mechan-
lly, then headed for the door as Jimmy pulled up bend her car.

She was trying to find the right key on her ring wh
she looked up.

David was there, standing on the front porch, waiti
for her. He took the keys from her fingers.

"David," she whispered uneasily. "I need a little bit
time to think—"

"So do I," he said flatly. "But I want to know wh
I'm thinking about."

"What do you mean?"

"I mean that it's time to find out if we've got a plus
a minus sign."

"But I don't have—"

He held up a small bag from the drugstore. "But I d
Moment of truth, Spencer. Then I'll leave you alone ar
give you time. I swear it."

She felt as if the blood had drained from her face, h
whole body. The possibility of a plus sign . . .

She almost started laughing, but she didn't dare, b
cause she would have laughed until she cried again.

He'd changed cars. He was certain Delgado had see
the blue sedan, so now he was using a ten-year-old blac
Mercedes coupe.

Didn't matter. He couldn't park on her block an
longer. He didn't even dare get too close to the house, be
that was all right. He'd dressed as a meter reader th
morning and combed his way through the nearby back
yards, ripping up enough foliage to get a good, straig
line of vision from the street where he was parked alon
side the Huntington house to the cars parked in the fron
Now he could tell who was coming and going, and whe

He picked up his car phone. "Mrs. Huntington
home. Delgado got here first and waited for her at th
door. Larimore came up behind them, but he's gone now

think Delgado and Mrs. Huntington are in for the
ght."

"What makes you think that?"

He snickered. "Just a hunch."

There was a moment's silence while a conversation
ent on at the other end of the line. Then, "Stay with
em," followed by a click, then static.

He continued to stare at the house, wondering if he
ould risk a walk through the foliage to the fence again.
o, they wouldn't be out by the pool again. They'd
nown he'd been watching. Delgado had almost caught
m.

He wondered what the boss would decide to do about
e woman. If the boss decided to whack her...

What a waste. He sure as hell hoped he'd get a chance
ith her first.

He got out of the car, unable to sit any longer, his
nagination on fire. He wasn't supposed to be taking
sks, but he was in a new car. The cops weren't around;
e one P.I. had already taken off. And Delgado would
:...involved.

He walked forward another step, finding a knoll, try-
g to peer over the fence.

A branch crackled behind him, and he spun around.
oo late.

Something smashed into his face with the power of a
eel battering ram. Dimly, just before the blackness de-
ended, he heard the cracking sound as his nose broke.

17

"This is insane. I don't owe you anything, and I do[n't] have to agree to anything."

"Humor me."

"Why?"

"Because I'm trying to keep you alive."

"Well, I can't very well humor you. The directions sa[y] that you're supposed to test in the morning."

They were standing in Spencer's kitchen. With a grea[t] deal of marked aggravation she'd taken the bag fro[m] him, the box from the bag and the instructions from th[e] box. Then she'd poured herself a glass of wine, whic[h] he'd snatched away. Next she had gone for a diet sod[a.] He hadn't liked that, either.

"May I have water?"

"I don't know. Is there lead in the pipes?"

"Oh, will you stop?"

"No."

"We don't even know whether—"

"So take the test." At that point he took the instru[c]tions from her.

"Spencer...look. It doesn't matter if you test fir[st] thing in the morning if it's after the first few days."

She snatched the paper back. "It hasn't been lon[g] enough."

"You're lying."

"I don't believe this!"

She grabbed the box and started out of the kitchen toward the stairs.

He was right behind her.

She swung on him. "What do you think you're doing?"

"I don't trust you."

"You are not following me any farther. I draw the line at that. So help me God, David, I mean it."

His knuckles whitened around the banister. "Swear to God you'll be honest."

She hesitated.

"Spencer?"

She exhaled. "Yes."

He walked away, and she started up the stairs. She could hear his footsteps as he paced the living room.

The test took less than a minute to perform, but you weren't supposed to check the results for at least three minutes, so Spencer set the little white stick on the back of the commode and stared at her pale reflection.

She was amazed to realize that she was feeling a flicker of excitement. If only the circumstances had been different....

She closed her eyes. She didn't know how she felt. Her emotions were in a tremendous uproar. It had hurt so badly at first to think how hard she had tried with Danny. This possibility had seemed too ironic, the most incredible joke. And now...

She was afraid, and she wasn't even sure why. Perhaps because the love she and David had felt for each other had been so intense that it had all but self-destructed. Back then, there had simply been too much against them.

And now, dead or alive, there was Danny, standing between them.

She didn't even know what David really wanted. He had promised to stay out of her life. He wanted her to have the child, but...

Did he think they could make it? That they could put the past behind them and create a new world for the future?

How long had it been? Ninety seconds...

She started to splash cold water on her face.

Then she heard a fierce pounding on her front door and David shouting her name. "Spencer!"

Even knowing that he had to hurry, David had locked the door behind him when he'd gone walking around her fence, certain that he'd seen a form in the bushes.

Sneaking up on the bastard had been easy.

He hadn't meant to break the guy's nose; he had just turned at the right minute for his face to connect with David's fist.

The son of a bitch was heavy, David thought as he dragged the man around to the front of the house. He was out cold, dead weight. Of corse, he knew that dead weight could turn lively quick enough, and as he stood on the porch, waiting for Spencer to come open the door, he tied the bastard's wrists behind his back with his own necktie.

The door opened at last. Spencer stared from him to the man with the bloody face. She gasped with horror, then stared at David again.

"Our peeping Tom," he told her. "Or *Tomas*. He definitely Hispanic."

"I'll call the police," Spencer breathed.

"No! Wait!"

"Why?" she asked incredulously. "David—"

"Get me some cold water, maybe a towel with a few ice cubes."

"Oh, God, what did you do to him?"

"His nose is broken, Spencer." He sighed. She was still staring with horror. "Spencer, I didn't mean to break it, but bear in mind that this guy would probably be willing to snuff one of us without blinking. I want to talk to him."

"David, I don't want him in here."

"Spencer, I'm coming as far as the foyer. Please, get me some ice, huh?"

She turned unhappily and headed for the kitchen as David propped the unconscious man against the wall. When Spencer returned with crushed ice in a towel, he pressed it firmly to the guy's face.

The man groaned. A second later he tried to sit straighter and his eyes flew open. He saw David, then Spencer, and groaned again.

"Who are you?" David demanded. "And what the hell were you doing back there spying on us?"

"*¡Batardo!*" the man murmured, groaning again. He tried to raise his hands to his injured nose and discovered that he couldn't.

"Mrs. Huntington wants to call the police," David said calmly.

"*Bueno.*"

"I told her no," David continued lightly. "Because I want to find out why you were back there before I do anything. Nose hurt?"

The man stiffened against the wall. He was about five-ten, dark haired, dark eyed, sallow complected. He sucked in his cheeks as he looked at David.

"What you going to arrest me for, eh? Being a vagrant? Trespassing? *¡Cono!* How long do you think I'm going to stay in jail?"

"That's why I'm not in any hurry to call the police. I can do what I want to scum bags like you now that I'm not on the force. So, I'll ask you again, what were you doing here?"

The man sputtered something in Spanish.

Some very eloquent cursing, Spencer thought. She'd heard something very like it quite recently. From David.

"Last time. What are you up to?"

The man didn't answer. David swung his arm back as if to strike.

The man screamed, trying—and failing—again to raise his hands to protect his injured nose. "Wait!"

"Go on."

"I talk to you, I'm dead."

"Who are you working for?"

"You don't understand. I talk to you, I'm dead."

David sat back, thoughtfully watching the man. "You can call the police now," he told Spencer.

"But I thought you wanted to know—"

"I do know. He's working for Ricky Garcia. Call the police, Spencer. And the paramedics. His nose needs some attention."

It barely took a minute for a police car to reach her house. And this time she didn't even have to talk. She simply stood beside David while he explained that he had seen the man watching the house and gone after him. David was certain he was the same man who had been watching the place all along.

When the man had been taken away, a young uniformed cop stood on the porch talking to David. "You know, sir, we don't have much to hold him on."

"He won't be in a hurry to go. And if you need something, you can try holding him for questioning on the murder of Danny Huntington."

"You think this guy—"

"No. But I think the fact that he's watching Spencer's house has something to do with the murder. Call Oppenheim. He'll think of something. And if the guy somehow gets out on the streets again, let me know."

"You got it. Mr. Delgado, Mrs. Huntington, good night."

"Good night. Thank you," Spencer said quietly, her mind turning a million different ways.

The cops left with the man, whose name had been revealed as Hernando Blanco, secured in the back of the police car.

"They were fast," Spencer commented, closing the door. "But how can you be so certain that he was working for Ricky Garcia?"

"Because *he* was so certain he'd be dead if he gave anything away." He hesitated. "And there's more."

"What?"

"A guy who was once connected with Ricky worked on that rental car we nearly got killed in in Rhode Island. He disappeared right after the accident, but the cops up there got one of his fingerprints and pulled his records."

"But that—"

"Is one hell of a coincidence," David said.

"So you think Ricky Garcia killed Danny?"

"Or had him killed."

Spencer moistened her lips, feeling almost guilty with relief. She prayed it had been Ricky Garcia, because that would mean Jared was innocent.

Not that she'd ever really believed Jared was involved in Danny's murder. But he *had* frightened her half to

death in that old house. And yet, at first, she had almost
thought he was getting ready to jump himself....

"Why would he be after me?"

"Because you're stirring things up. Like you keep telling me, Spencer, Trey Delia is in prison because of you.
Maybe Ricky just doesn't want to be next."

"So what happens now?"

"I talk to Ricky again," David said softly. "Go
through the files. Again." He hesitated. "Did Danny
keep any files here?"

"I turned his papers over to Oppenheim right after the
attack."

"Were there any papers that weren't in those folders?
Papers that might have been private?"

"Maybe," she said slowly. "Some of his things—
newspaper clippings, notes, old stuff, are still up in the
office."

"That's where I'll start, then," he said softly. He
paused, staring at her. "Well?"

"Well what?"

"The test."

"The test!" she gasped, then turned, heading for the
stairs.

He passed her halfway up.

"Damn you, David! This isn't fair. So help me, I'm
warning you..."

But he was ahead of her. He burst into the bathroom
and found the little white stick on the back of the commode. He picked it up, turning his back to her.

"David, this is absolutely—"

She broke off. He had turned to her, blue eyes incredibly dark, lips white, features drawn and taut.

"What?"

"A bright blue plus sign," he said softly.

A blue plus sign . . .

She could still remember that day over a year ago when he had taken a different test. When she'd gotten a little blue line to say that yes, the time was right. She could remember Danny's face, clearer in her memory than it had been for a long, long time.

I'm blue, Danny, blue . . . .

And then he had gone out to meet David, and her whole world had changed.

The world began to spin and, with amazing speed, it turned from blue to black.

Ricky Garcia loved South Beach. There was no place quite like it in the world.

Cafés opened their doors to let in the welcome breezes of the night. The ocean whispered in the background, waves shifting, surf endlessly rolling.

Then there was the sea of humanity. Shifting, changing, as endless as the flow of the ocean. People walked by alone, in twos and threes, in groups. Short-haired, long-haired. Hispanics, Anglos, Germans, Canadians, tourists, natives. In leather and in lace. They walked beneath the Deco lights, dressed in mauve and pink and turquoise. They listened to the beat of the music from the clubs, a beat that washed over the sidewalks, sizzling by day, alive with the pulse of drums by night. And the women . . . So many women . . .

Young women, old women. Blondes, brunettes, redheads. Beautiful, tall, sleek black women, Haitians, Brazilians, Hondurans. Pale white Northerners. Women in tight pants, women in short shirts. Women on the arms of their lovers, women on the make, crawling the night . . .

Ricky enjoyed them all. He liked the night. Liked the beat. Liked the café con leche served at every café. He

often sat at a table alone, secure in the knowledge that h
two burly bodyguards were just a few feet away.

Sometimes the police came to harass him, but not too
often. They had come after Danny Huntington had died
They had started coming again when his widow had re
turned to Coconut Grove.

Two of them had come tonight—early—and take
seats near him.

They had ruined his view.

But the police didn't have anything on him, so they ha
left; they'd had no choice. He had good lawyers, and h
wasn't afraid to take the police to court.

Now his night was disturbed again. As he lit a thi
cigarillo, one of his men came by and whispered in hi
ear, "Hernando is in Dade County Jail."

His match flared. Died. "Hernando is a fool," he sai
"Fools are better off dead." He flicked a minute particl
of lint from the sleeve of his gray silk shirt. "Hernand
was worse than a fool, I think. He was not right up here."
He pointed to his head. "Not where it counts for a man."

The man bowed his head and backed away, everythin
completely understood.

It was time to take matters into his own hands, Rick
decided. Soon. But for the moment...

He saw a girl, generous curves contained within black
velvet stretch pants. She had wavy, jet black hair, smooth
bronze skin. She giggled a little annoyingly. It didn'
matter. He would not be with her long.

She walked down the street. He lifted a hand. His ma
would go after the girl. Invite her to the penthouse. En
tice her with promises and money. And she would come

Ricky had never been wrong about a woman.

He hadn't been wrong about Spencer Huntington, ei
ther. Something would have to be done. Now.

And he was going to have to do it himself.

Cecily stepped out of the shower. She'd gotten too much sun today. Oh, God, when was she going to learn? Her looks just weren't going to last forever.

She reached for her lotion, then stepped out of the bathroom to glance at the bedroom television. Jared was there, stretched out on the bed, flicking the channels on the remote control.

"You're home!" she said, surprised.

"I am."

She perched on the edge of the bed, staring at him. "Did you fix things?"

"No."

"Damn it, Jared. She was out of the office most of the day!"

He rolled over and stared at her. He looked tired. Worn. Still handsome, though. "Cecily, she came back after lunch, rushing around like a tornado of energy. She swept through the place at a thousand miles an hour. She was into files, into the computer, into everything. If I had been fixing anything, I would have been in big-time trouble today."

"It has to be fixed!" Cecily said. "Jared, our lives depend on it!"

"But Spencer's life—"

"The hell with precious little Spencer and her life! You've got to think about us now, Jared. Think about the children. Look, I think I caused some trouble for Spence today. Enough to keep her a little off kilter for a while, anyway. Jared, you must—*you must!*—take care of things!"

He groaned and turned his face into the pillow. "I will, Cecily," he said hollowly. "I will."

He sounded exhausted. Like a man who had absolutely reached his limit.

"Jared, things will be all right afterward. I swear, we make everything all right... after."

She moved closer to him, and he laid his head on he lap. She rubbed his temples soothingly.

"It's funny, isn't it?" Jared said. "So damned funny But I do love you, Cecily."

She frowned. "It's not all that funny."

"Maybe it's habit."

"You want to hear something really funny?" she queried.

"What?"

"I guess I love you, too."

He started to smile, then he reached up and pulled he face down for a kiss.

He was going to be all right. Yes, he was going to be a right, and it—life—would be all right, as well. Just a soon as this business with Spencer was finished.

When Spencer opened her eyes, she discovered that sh was lying on her own bed. She still felt light-headed.

David was sitting on the side of the bed. Not touchin her, just watching her.

"You okay?" he asked her.

She nodded. "Just not prepared..."

"Yeah, well, I can see that. I'm really batting a thou sand here, huh? Let's see, sex with me and you cry you eyes out. A pregnancy and you pass out cold. Spencer, you're not careful, you'll be letting all this go straight my head."

"David..."

He stood up. "I know. I said I'd leave you alone. I ju wanted to make sure you were all right. I'm leaving now.

She struggled to sit up. "You don't understand."

"No, Spencer, my problem is that I *do* understand. I'm ot Danny. I can't be Danny. And this isn't Danny's hild. It's yours, and it's mine, and that's enough. I can't elp but be glad. I want children, Spencer."

"But under the circumstances—"

"I don't give a damn about the circumstances, Spen- er," he said softly then started out of the room.

"David!" He paused in the doorway, but he didn't ok at her. "You don't understand. I—I want this aby."

His body seemed to quicken. He was afraid to go close o her again. Afraid to push.

He stayed in the doorway. "If it helps any, Spencer, I ant you to know this," he said. He had to pause. Had regain his breath and force himself to speak steadily. I love you. I loved you all those years ago, I never opped loving you, and I love you now. Keep that in ind, will you, when you're thinking?"

He left the room, closing the door behind him. He was aking.

He started down the stairs. Carefully. Walked into the tchen, picked up Spencer's wine and downed it in a gle gulp.

Spencer was going to have a child. His child. He was ing to be a father. She could still change her mind, he minded himself. But she wouldn't. Spencer adored ildren, and they adored her. She and Danny had been ving...

He winced and walked to the family room to stare at e pool. He could almost hear Danny's voice again, nny's laughter.

For a moment he felt a shaft of the misery Spen
must be feeling at the irony of it all. She was pregnan
last—but with *his* child.

He closed his eyes, torn.

Then he was suddenly at peace. He had told her
truth that afternoon. He loved her. He always had. /
he had loved Danny, too. No one had been a be
friend. And no one had known Danny better.

Danny Huntington would never begrudge them a 1
ment's happiness.

"Come to terms with it!" he told himself softly
loud.

All right. He loved Spencer. It didn't matter wha
had ever tried to tell himself. She was going to have
baby and, come hell or high water, he was going to m
her his at last.

All he had to do was keep her alive. . . .

18

eave it to David, Spencer thought. First he'd dragged
r out on that boat, then forced her into taking a preg-
ncy test, finally ground out something about having
ved her all his life—and then walked out on her again.
But not completely. David still owed Sly, and he wasn't
ing to quit protecting her.

When she went downstairs that night, David didn't
n mention the test, or anything remotely personal. He
st wanted to see all of Danny's remaining papers. She
ok him into the office, where she had done a quick job
stuffing Danny's personal papers, notes and clippings
o file cabinets. Despite appearances, Danny had been
ganized. He had always told her that there was a
thod to his madness, and it was true; he'd always been
le to find what he was looking for right away.

'There's really nothing here,'' she told David.

'There must be. Someone is trying to break in here for
eason.''

'The guy downstairs was just watching the house—''

'But Harris stopped an intruder.''

'Breaking and entering in any big city.'' She hesi-
ed. ''Besides, I thought someone was supposedly try-
to kill me?''

'Yeah, someone *is* out to hurt you, Spencer. But I
ik that someone wants into the house, too.''

"The house sat empty for months while I was awa after Danny died. Why didn't they break in then?"

"Because until you started stirring things up agai scaring someone, they didn't see any need." He too several of the files and tucked them under his arm. ' think I'll start with these."

He walked out of the room and started toward th door. She followed him. "You're leaving?"

"Spencer, my clothes are crusted with salt, and I' tired. And I told you that I'd leave you alone. Besides, be truthful, at the moment I need to get away from yo too."

And that was it. He left. Juan was outside, on watc The next morning, Tuesday, Jimmy followed her work.

She wanted time; she had told him that, and she meant it. One minute she still felt an almost hysteri sense of irony, as if she had betrayed Danny a thousa times over in her heart and in reality. The next minute s would manage to get a grip on sanity. There was som thing she was reaching for, something she had to kno something she had to understand. And if she could j touch it, she would be all right....

Each time her careening thoughts and emotions f lowed that swing of the pendulum, she wanted Dav She wanted to shake him, to ask him if he'd meant w he'd said about loving her. There *was* something th between them. There always had been, a link that n ther time nor distance had erased, and which had ploded anew when circumstances brought them toget again.

She couldn't do any work to speak of on Tues morning. But later she was forced into thinking when got a call from Sandy about a problem with the p

ase of her new home. She had used a check from her
sonal account for the down payment, and, for some
son she couldn't even begin to guess, that check had
unced.

'I can't understand it,'' she told Sandy, frowning. She
itched on her computer and drew up the account rec-
ls. According to the screen, the money was there.

'The seller is getting antsy on this one,'' Sandy said
happily. ''Maybe someone transferred those funds
mewhere else? Or perhaps you could write a check on
other account?''

'Yes, I'll do that. Swing by. I'll have another check for
u in a matter of minutes.''

She hung up. There would be no problem borrowing
oney from one of Sly's accounts, but she certainly
uldn't do it without asking him. She hurried from her
ice to his, unaware that Audrey was staring at her as
e hurried by.

''Sly, there's something wrong with one of the money
irket accounts. My records don't coincide with the
nk's, and I have to straighten it out. Until I do, I need
oan. A big loan.''

Sly arched a brow and sat back at his desk. ''You can
e anything you want, you know that, Spencer.'' He
wned. ''You don't mean that money is missing from
: trust fund Danny set up, do you?''

''No, I've never touched that.''

''Why not? He left it for you.''

''But I didn't need it, Sly. And somehow, I feel that it's
od money. I guess I never intended to keep it. I haven't
ided exactly what to do with it, but I'm leaning to-
rd splitting it between a children's hospital and the
nd for the children of slain officers.''

Sly nodded. ''It's a lot of money, Spencer.''

"I've never needed as much money as people seem to think," she remarked lightly.

Sly smiled. "What was David's big beef yesterday" he asked her, catching her off guard.

"I..." she began, then stopped. She wasn't ready get into this with anyone. Not even Sly.

Maybe especially Sly. Although she almost smi imagining her mother's expression if she were to call w the truth. "I know how you felt about my marrying D vid way back when, Mom, but don't worry. I'm not ing to marry him—in fact, he hasn't even suggested I'm just going to have his illegitimate child."

Ah, yes, that would go over very well....

She would tell a lie at the moment. A very white lie. ran into Gene Vichy at the club."

"Ran into him?"

"All right, he'd called and asked to see me."

"I see," Sly told her.

"That's all? You're not going to say anything about being an idiot?"

"Do I need to?" he asked.

"All right, no, but it wasn't dangerous. Really. He j told me that he was innocent."

"Spencer, are you expecting someone to call you a confess?" he asked.

"You never know," she said stubbornly. "Someth just might slip out somewhere."

"I hear David caught a peeping Tom in your yard man who worked for Ricky Garcia."

"So David thinks."

"I imagine he's right." He hesitated for a minute. just talked to him a few minutes ago. The man was fou hanged in his cell this morning. The other three guys there didn't see a thing."

She felt sick. Absolutely sick. "I have to go," she
hispered to Sly.

Moments later she passed Audrey again, slipping in-
de her office, and closed the door, then leaned against
, resting her cheek against the cool wood.

A peculiar sensation crept along her spine. She spun.
Jared was there.

"Jared!"

"I have to—I have to talk to you, Spencer."

She sat down uneasily, indicating one of the chairs in
ont of her desk.

He sat. He looked gray.

"I took the money, Spencer."

"What?"

"I ran up some gambling debts. You were away. I
uldn't tell Sly—I'm not his precious granddaughter."
r a moment, he sounded very bitter. "God, Spencer,
n sorry. I've spent the time since trying to replace every
t cent I took, but I was bleeding it back in through the
mpany account and I ran out of time."

She felt cold, numb. As if huge waves of ice water were
shing through her. She tried to form words, but she
uldn't, so she just sat there.

Finally her voice began to work. "Did you plan to push
off the balcony of the house when we went to see it?"

"What?" he demanded.

"You heard me. Did you try to kill me, Jared?"

"God, no, Spence!" He leaned forward, pressing his
ıples with his palms. "God, no! I swear it! Is that what
ı thought? Sweet Jesus, for a moment there I did think
ıut jumping, but I wouldn't hurt *you*, Spencer, not for
world."

She sat back, desperate to believe him. "Why didn'
you just come to me when you were in trouble?" sh
asked hoarsely.

He lifted his hands, shook his head. "Spencer, yo
were practically bleeding yourself when it happened
Danny had just died. You didn't really hear anythin
anyone said to you. Then you were gone. And I couldn
just take the money from one of Sly's accounts. He ma
be old, but he's got an eagle eye." He stood up, lookin
worn-out and old.

And Sly thought I looked like hell! Spencer thought

"I didn't tell Cecily at first, and we nearly split up—sl
thought I was having an affair."

"Were you doing that as well?"

"Briefly," he admitted uncomfortably. "It was how
got started gambling. I confessed to Cecily—about t
gambling—because I didn't want my marriage to fa
apart." He sat down again. "You know, the years go b
some of the excitement goes... sometimes you're loo
ing for other things, or trying to get the excitement bac
But I do love my wife. You know Cecily, though. If I
fallen into disgrace, she wouldn't have been too willi
to come along with me. At first I went to my father, b
he's retired. He couldn't cover what I owed. I real
thought I could get it all back into your account befo
you found out, but then you decided to buy that damn
house.... If you'd waited even a few more days, ever
thing would have been okay."

She sat there, staring numbly at him. He got up an
went around to her side of the desk, then went down
one knee next to her, taking both her hands. "Spenc
I'm sorry. I swear to you, I'm sorry. And I still can't l
lieve you thought I would hurt you."

She believed him. She didn't know if it was only because she wanted to, but she believed him. She exhaled slowly.

"How did you make the money back?"

"It took a while, but I sold my investment acreage up in Jupiter. I got lucky. I more than tripled my investment." He sighed, looking down. "And I went into the kids' college funds, but I'll make that up, too." He stood. "Are you going to tell Sly?"

She shook her head.

He smiled a little bitterly. "Are you going to wait until the company's yours and then fire my ass?"

She had to smile at that. "I could wait a long time. Sly may be in his nineties, but his grandfather lived to be a hundred and thirteen, so he tells me. By the time Sly is gone, we could both be old and senile. I'd probably have forgotten what you did."

"Thanks, Spence," he said softly. He headed for the door, then looked at her.

"Spencer, I swear I've worked hard for this business. I've done well with our investments, I know the architectural history almost as well as you do, and I've always put my heart and soul into the operation of Montgomery Enterprises. For all my sins, I never wanted to be the cousin hanging on to your shirttails."

"I know that, Jared."

He nodded and started to speak again, but he couldn't seem to find words.

"Two things, Jared. If you're ever in trouble again, be honest with me, damn it."

"Yeah," he said huskily. "What's number two?"

"Go away and don't talk to me about this anymore. And don't go looking over any more railings, scaring me half to death."

He grinned. ''I think you hit three and four, as well.'' He swallowed painfully. ''Thanks, Spence.''

''Number five, Jared. Quit saying that.''

He nodded and left. After the door closed behind him, Spencer looked down. Her fingers were trembling. Had he been telling her the truth? The *complete* truth?

It had to be the truth. It would be too painful if it was anything else.

David sat at his desk, yawning. He sipped his coffee, blinked hard and looked at the papers spread before him.

Danny's personal files were a mess.

He'd kept dozens of newspaper clippings, some of them bits about mysterious deaths, some of them articles on the grave robberies attributed to Trey Delia and his followers. At least Trey Delia was still in prison.

Perhaps he was still ruling his empire from behind bars? Not perhaps—certainly. But that didn't mean he had killed Danny, or that he wanted to kill Spencer.

David started sorting through the papers again. He came across a magazine article on a witchcraft case during Louis XIV's reign. Even the Sun King's mistress had been involved, playing with different potions. Some of her ''aphrodisiacs'' had turned out to be poisonous. The woman had gotten away with her crimes, though she had lost the king's affections. Dozens of others had burned.

David set it aside, then picked it up again and read it more closely, looking to see if the witches had raided cemeteries and used human body parts. Nothing on it. He set the article down again.

More clippings, these on Ricky Garcia's alleged crimes.

Then still more clippings, this time on the death of Gene Vichy's very rich socialite wife. She'd been found slumped against the coral rock fireplace in her elegant bedroom. Despite all the masterpieces in the exquisite house on Bayshore Drive, only her diamonds had been taken. And not a fingerprint—other than those that should have been there—had been found. She'd been bludgeoned with a statuette from the mantel, but the killer had apparently worn gloves. Only the maid's prints and Mrs. Vichy's prints had been on the statuette. Gene Vichy's had been absent. And no one had ever suggested that the maid had killed her mistress, or that Vickie Vichy had conked herself on the head.

He set the pages down and rubbed his eyes, then clicked the intercom. "Reva, would you mind getting me some coffee?"

His sister's soft chuckle sounded as if she was right next to him. "*Café cubano,* brother? Something to keep you up?"

"Anything with lots of caffeine."

"Coming right up."

"Thanks."

He clicked off and studied the clippings again, then ripped through his files on the case.

Vichy had killed his wife. David was certain of that. But it had been a damned near perfect crime. Vichy had been at the yacht club at the time of death the coroner set. Dozens of witnesses had seen him there.

But David didn't care where Vichy had been. He had ordered the crime and paid for it. Unfortunately, he'd done such a careful job of planning it that no one—not the police, the D.A.'s office, or the private investigators Vickie's family had hired—had been able to prove it. The day he was attacked, Danny had been coming to see Dad to talk about Vichy and see what they could come up with together.

David was rubbing the back of his neck as Reva cam
in with his coffee. "You look like death warmed over,"
she told him, perching on the edge of his desk.

He took the coffee from her, a small cup of rich, thick
syrupy Cuban coffee. It could warm the blood. Maybe i
didn't even go into the stomach. Maybe it shot caffein
straight into the veins.

Whatever. It tasted damned good right now. He swal
lowed it down in one quick gulp.

"You know," Reva told him, "you keep thinking yo
can solve this overnight, but you need to be realisti
Look at all the time that's gone by since Danny died
You've got to face up to the fact that his death may neve
be solved."

"It has to be."

"Why?"

"Because Spencer won't be safe until it is."

Reva hesitated. "Spencer won't be safe, or the two c
you won't be able to get on with your lives?"

He looked at her. He started to deny her words, the
shrugged. "Both," he told her.

Reva turned to leave his office. "David?"

"Yeah?"

"A long time ago, I said some not-too-nice thing
about Spencer."

"Yeah, so?"

"I take them back, that's all."

She walked out of the office. David smiled and turne
to his work, but the words seemed to run before his eye
Suddenly he picked up his phone and punched in Op
penheim's number. He had to wait several minutes to g
the lieutenant.

"What now, Delgado? When men quit my team, the
usually leave me alone!"

"Do me a favor. Get Vickie Vichy exhumed."

"*What?*"

"Do it, Lieutenant, please. Somehow."

"For what? She died because her head was smashed in by a blunt instrument. The weapon was found right by her body, covered with blood and brains, for Christ's sake! We hardly even needed the autopsy."

"But they weren't looking for poisoning. Maybe something very obscure."

Oppenheim was silent. "If we don't find something, Gene Vichy will probably sue the whole damned city."

"I've been going through Danny's personal papers," David said. "And I've got a hunch. I think he was on to something."

"Vichy paid a killer. We all know that. We just can't prove it."

"But I think he did that because she wasn't dying fast enough his way and he didn't dare hurry the process along. Lieutenant, please."

"I'll think about it, David."

"Think fast, will you?"

A click was his reply. He had just barely replaced the receiver before Reva buzzed him.

"Willie the Snitch on line two," she said tensely, well aware that David had been trying to find the man.

"Yeah, Willie! Where the hell have you been?" David demanded. There was silence. For a sinking moment, David thought Willie had hung up on him. "Willie, damn, you there? I hung around under that damn bridge for hours looking for you, so you'd better be there!"

"Why'd you do that?" Willie asked, perplexed.

"Why? I need information."

He could almost see Willie shrugging. ''From what hear, you're tight with Huntington's widow. She know how to get me.''

''What?'' David said. His head was suddenly pound ing.

''Yeah,'' Willie said huskily. ''Danny and I were close He must have made sure she knew how to get me. Mayb she helped him sometimes, I don't know.''

''She contacted you recently?''

''Sure,'' he said proudly. ''How do you think she knev to go to that cemetery?''

David groaned inwardly, glad Spencer wasn't ther right now. He wanted to shake her. But shaking would b bad for her. For her and the baby.

Off the subject! he warned himself.

''Why are you calling me now, Willie?''

''Why were *you* trying to get *me?*''

''You first.''

''I need money,'' Willie admitted. ''And I've got som information.''

''All right.''

''When do I get paid?''

''You know I'll pay you.''

''Mrs. Huntington pays better.''

''Yeah? Well I'll break your teeth if you don't answe up and accept my meager wage scale,'' David warne him.

Willie thought that over; then he sighed. ''You're pe suasive, Delgado. What I know is this—Ricky Garcia ha had a man watching the Huntington house ever sinc Spencer Huntington moved back into it.''

David clenched his teeth. ''I know that, Willie. Th man is dead.''

''You killed him?''

"No. He died in jail."

"How?"

"Hanged himself."

"Yeah, well, maybe." For a moment Willie sounded
worried. "But what you should know is that Ricky wants
you dead. He's mentioned it a few times, and you know
how that works."

"I can take care of myself. What else?"

"Well, sources say he just wants to talk to Danny's
widow. That he has information he'll give to her but not
to any cops."

"I'm not a cop anymore."

"Doesn't matter. You still smell like pork to Ricky."

"That everything?"

"Yeah. You keep an eye on her, huh?"

"Yeah."

"I mean a good eye. All the time."

"All right. Willie—" David began, but the line went
suddenly dead. He stared at the receiver.

A good eye. All the time.

Even with Jimmy on the job, he suddenly felt uneasy.
He stood up, knocking half the papers off the desk, and
left his office quickly, telling Reva on the way, "I'm going over to Montgomery Enterprises. I'm not sure how
long I'll be. If you need me and I'm not there, try the car
phone or Spencer's number."

He was out of the office and in his car in a matter of
moments.

He hit the school traffic. By the time he reached
Montgomery Enterprises, neither Spencer's car, nor
Jimmy's, was in the lot.

He leaped out of his car quickly and rushed inside. He
stopped in front of Audrey's desk.

"Where's Spencer?"

"Really, Mr. Delgado, doesn't Mrs. Huntington serve *some* privacy? Anyway, one of your watchdog already on the case," Audrey told him, then frowned. something wrong? Perhaps I can find her for you if yo explain to me what's happening."

Sly was standing by his office door. He had heard whole exchange and didn't seem to need explanatio "She went home to meet with her realtor. She had change a few of her financing plans."

"Thanks," David said, starting out again.

"David!"

David turned at Sly's concerned call.

"*Is* anything wrong?" Sly asked.

David grinned. "Nope. Just thought I'd get back the job myself and give Jimmy a break."

As he started out, Jared emerged from his offi "Something wrong, David?" he asked.

"Nope," David replied lightly, offering a smile an dismissive wave. He never quit walking, his pace beco ing quicker with each stride.

David didn't believe in hunches. But he'd been a c for a long time. He *did* believe in gut instinct. And ri now his gut instinct was somehow urging him on.

He swore at the traffic all the way to Spencer's hou

As he drove up to her place, his heart began to pou deafeningly in his ears, and his palms began to sweat. jerked the wheel, screeching his way onto the embar ment in front of her house, drawing his gun.

And then he started to pray.

19

Being at the office just hadn't felt right. Not after Jared's confession. All she could think about was Danny's office back at the house.

David had thought the files there were important, but he hadn't taken all of them. Maybe she could put something together from what was left.

She reported to Sly and Audrey, then walked out to the parking lot. Jimmy was waiting. "Hey, Jimmy. Back to the house."

"Okay."

She hesitated. "Don't you get just about bored silly watching me all the time?"

He grinned. "Naw. I've had much worse cases."

"Oh, yeah?"

"I've had to watch some really ugly women."

"Oh," Spencer said.

"It was just a joke," Jimmy assured her.

"Okay, then. Home, James."

She drew out into traffic. A school bus was in front of her, but it didn't matter. She was in a fifteen-mile-an-hour zone, and she wasn't in any kind of hurry.

The school bus started forward and Spencer followed. Then another bus drew up behind her. She was sandwiched between the two, with Jimmy stuck somewhere behind her.

The traffic began to inch forward once more and sⁱ
inched ahead with it.

Finally she was able to turn off onto her own quⁱ
street. She drew into her driveway, frowning as she g
out and noted that Jimmy hadn't caught up with her.

A new-model black Mercedes drove up behind he
blocking her in.

Spencer looked around. The neighborhood was ﹔
lent. Dead silent. There were no gardeners around. ℕ
children playing outside. Her neighbors were still
work.

She stared at the Mercedes, then started backing ⁴
ward her house. Her keys were in her hand, but s
would never make it to the door and open the lock
time.

Two men got out of the Mercedes and began walkⁱ
quickly toward her. Spencer started to scream, th
turned and ran, determined to make it through the do
or wake the dead, one or the other.

She wasn't exactly tackled. Each man simply caug
one of her arms. She struggled but found herself turⁿ
around anyway, facing a third man.

Slim, well-dressed. He was decent enough looking, ᵇ
somehow slimy.

"Don't be afraid. I've only come to talk with yᵒ
Mrs. Huntington," the slim man said. "I am Ricaⁱ
Garcia, and I know that you have heard of me. You v
get in the car now."

Spencer inhaled. "No!" she said succinctly. She v
shaking like a windblown leaf, terrified, and her knﹾ
were threatening to buckle.

But she wasn't going anywhere with him. If he v
going to kill her, he was going to have to do it right he

she was going to claw the skin off of someone and
e the cops something to work with.

Mrs. Huntington, I only want to talk. I want to help
, and then I want to be left alone to pursue my busi-
s.''

'Your business is murder.''

'Sometimes men need to die,'' he said regretfully.
ut not your husband.''

'Where's Jimmy?'' she demanded.

'The young man who was following you? He met with
accident.''

he swallowed hard, tears stinging her eyes. ''If you've
t him—''

'A *minor* accident, Mrs. Huntington. His wheel blew
. His car has merely run off the side of the road. He
. be fine. Now, I have offered you good faith. You will
ase come along with me.''

'I will not—'' she began. She stopped when Garcia
ved closer.

Ie was exquisitely dressed in a beige silk suit, and his
ce was as soft as the fabric when he said, ''I said
ase.'' Then he drew a large revolver from a shoulder
ster beneath his jacket and brought it to her temple,
icating that his men should step away.

'*¡Madre de dios!* You *will* come with me!''

The other men hurried to the car, one opening the
ver's door, the second opening a back door. Garcia
ed her to follow them.

Just as she was about to be forced into the car, she
rd a screeching sound. David's car careened onto the
bankment in front of her house, and he leaped from
. vehicle, both hands on the gun he was leveling at
ky Garcia.

'Let her go!'' he shouted.

Garcia paused, then said something in Spanish softly. Both his men aimed guns at David.

"I'll kill you, Delgado," Ricky Garcia said in glish, just as softly. "Alfonso will put a bullet thro your head. Louis will tear open your heart. Now, get of my way."

"Let her go!" David repeated furiously.

"You'll die!"

"Then I'll fucking die, Garcia, but so will you. know me. I can pull this trigger while those asshole yours are still thinking. I'll hit you right between the before you can twitch, and you damned well know I do it."

"You'll still die."

"And I won't give a damn! Let her go! Do it!"

Spencer barely dared to breathe, crushed aga Ricky's side, feeling the metal of his gun against temple. She was going to fall any second, she thou; whether she was shot or not.

Garcia's hold on her suddenly eased, and he shoved forward, right into David's arms. She was trembling hard that she could barely walk but she forced hersel dredge up some strength, knowing she couldn't falter

David shoved her behind him, his gun still trained Ricky.

"You got something to say, Garcia, say it now!" vid demanded.

"All right, I'll say what I know!" Garcia spat out. smiled, looking at Spencer. "I didn't kill your husba Mrs. Huntington. But my life has been hell ever since died! Ever since you came back to town. So, yes, I h watched you. Carefully. Your husband was a smart c But not smart enough. You are not looking close enou

home. You want to know who killed Danny? Start
king around you. ¿Comprende, eh, Delgado?''

Ricky turned then and slipped into his car. The other
n kept their guns trained on David, who kept his on
m, as they got into the black Mercedes.

The car's souped-up motor was gunned. It spat and
red, and the Mercedes shot out of the driveway.

'You all right?'' David asked her huskily.

Spencer nodded. Good God, he was always coming to
rescue. She gasped, ''I'm all right, but Jimmy...!
rcia said he was alive, but there was an accident—''

'Let's get in the house,'' David told her.

She tried the front door, her fingers shaking. He
rted to take the keys, but she managed to make the
ht one work, and they went inside.

David headed straight for the phone. Spencer watched
he dialed.

''Who are you—''

''Jimmy's car. No answer. Shit!'' Then there was a
unding on the door.

''Spencer. Oh, Jesus Christ. *Spencer!*''

She had opened the door by then. Jimmy, a bruise on
e cheek, streaks of sweat sliding down his face, stood
the porch. panting.

''I ran,'' he told her. ''Oh, God, I ran—''

''It's all right,'' David said, stepping past her.

''How the hell did you know to come?'' Jimmy de-
anded, staring incredulously at David. ''I couldn't call
u. The phone was smashed. The whole damned side of
e car was smashed. If I'd had a passenger...''

''I'll call the cops,'' Spencer said. ''They can look for
rcia.''

''It was Ricky Garcia?'' Jimmy asked, still breathless.
Oh, God—''

"He's gone now," David said.

"Oh, God!" Jimmy repeated.

"It's all right!" Spencer told him. "You did y
best."

"Not good enough."

"Jimmy," she murmured, "I'll call the cops. So
poor fellow on the beat will go crazy when he finds y
car and no driver in it."

"I'll take care of it," David said. He took the recei
from Spencer's hand. "They're getting very accuston
to crazy calls coming from me."

"I'll, uh, get Jimmy some water," she said.

Later David started prowling through the files aga
and Spencer did the same, but they didn't speak muc.

Jimmy had gone with the cops to see that his car w
towed and to describe the accident. David had alrea
given an account of their run-in with Ricky Garcia.

Jerry Fried had come out on the call, reminding Sp
cer of a very tired, sad Eeyore from *Winnie the Pooh*
he listened and wrote in his notebook. "I may be able
have him arrested for assault, but he's got sharp la
yers. I won't be able to keep him very long."

"I know. Just do your best."

"I'm still homicide, you know. This isn't really
beat."

"This *is* homicide! It's about the death of Dar
Huntington."

"By the book, Delgado, it was an assault."

David snapped. "It was attempted kidnapping as we
Fried, do what you can. Just remember, it was yo
partner who got killed that morning."

Iow the light was fading, and Spencer and David were
ie. She was already cramped from sitting on the floor,
it was the best way to spread things out.

'What's this?'' David asked her suddenly.

pencer looked up. "What?''

There's some scribbling on this clipping—it's from
Living section of the paper, on a benefit perform-
e by the ballet. Vickie Vichy was in attendance. But
ny wrote something here. I can't quite make it out,
the main number for Montgomery Enterprises is
tten next to it.''

pencer rose and stared at the clipping, intrigued, filled
h hope. Then she sighed, disappointed. "It just says,
idrey.' My secretary. He must have been calling me.
: number is where I work, and Audrey is how you get
"

'Oh.'' David set the paper down and stretched, eas-
the cricks in his neck. Then he leaned forward, rub-
g his eyes. "Back to the drawing board,'' he
rmured.

'David?''

'Yeah?''

'I—I was terrified when Ricky Garcia had that gun to
head today. But more than that, I'd never felt more
pless.''

Ie looked down for a moment, then met her eyes.
)encer, I swear, I'll never let you be alone like that for
much as a minute again.''

'David! No one can promise that. If you tried, it
uldn't be fair. I—I want you to teach me how to
ot.''

'Spencer, you've never held a gun. They can be dan-
ous when you don't know—''

"That's the point. I want to know. David, I need t
Please."

He stood up. He wasn't getting anywhere with the f
"All right. Let's go. You got a weapon?"

"Danny's Glock. I think I was supposed to have
turned it, but I left town."

"Get it."

He thought about bringing her down to the police
get range. Despite regulations, he could probably slip
in. He decided against it and took her to a gun club
west on Eighth Street.

She listened. She did well. But he wasn't happy ab
the situation.

"This child could be born with hearing problems,"
joked, trying to dissuade her.

She didn't miss a beat, just aimed and fired. "Bu
least it might have a chance to actually *be* born this wa

"Ricky Garcia told you to look closer to home,"
said suddenly. "Who close to you might have been
volved with Danny's death?"

This time, her aim was off. Way off.

"Spencer?"

She shook her head. "Ricky Garcia is a murderer a
a thief. Why would I believe anything he has to say?"

"I don't know," David said smoothly. "So why
you?"

"I don't!" she exclaimed.

He took the police Glock from her, checked the saf
and steered her from the target area. "Enough for
night. It's late."

As he drove to her house, something kept playing
his mind. He couldn't quite touch it. Maybe that w

ood. It kept him from brooding about his relationship
ith Spencer.

He went into the house with her and locked the door.
Maybe you should stay away from work this week."

"I can't stay away all week. I've got meetings. Sly
eeds me."

"Sly needs you safe and alive."

"But, David, if I completely stop my life, whoever
lled David has won."

He was quiet.

"David, I was good with that gun. I'll keep it with me
all times."

He sighed. "I drive you. Everywhere you go."

She nodded.

"Good night, Spencer," he said, and headed to the
ybed in the family room.

She followed him. "There *is* a guest bedroom," she
id softly.

"I like it down here. Good night, Spencer," he re-
ated firmly.

She turned around and left him.

The week was long and tedious. Spencer insisted on
ing to work, and wherever she went, David went, too.
 spent most of Wednesday baby-sitting her out on
uth Beach, standing back and listening while she ex-
ined to a group of suited gentlemen what could and
ildn't be salvaged in their hotel, and just what it would
t them. They looked grim at first, until she told them
 research had shown that the entry hall floor tiles had
n imported from a castle in Spain—they were worth
urge portion of the price the men had paid for the ho-
just in themselves. By the time she was done, the men
 e not only happy with the money they had already

spent, they even seemed happy with the money they in
tended to hand over to Montgomery Enterprises.

Sly was quiet until the end of Spencer's speech. The
he leaned against a wall near David. "You're worth you
weight in gold," Sly told him. "I wish you'd let me pa
you. No client should demand this much time."

David shrugged. "Danny was my best friend."

"And what about Spencer?"

"Spencer is a friend, too."

Sly snorted, straightening as he saw that the men we
about to leave. "Marry her. Get it over with."

"Can't. Not yet."

"Why?"

"Because she won't marry *me*."

"Make her. Damn it, force her to be happy if nothin
else will work!"

David grinned. "Sly, give me a chance. Let me catch
killer first. Danny isn't really buried yet. Not for eith
of us."

Sly seemed to accept that. He joined the group, wi
David behind him.

The whole group had a late lunch at a café on t
beach, watching the roller skaters drifting by, along wi
muscled beach bums, half-naked beauties, a few less th
perfect bodies and a few senior citizens out enjoying t
sun. Spencer was in the midst of the executives, and S
was quietly watching her like a hawk. David thought
was safe to put in a call to Oppenheim.

The lieutenant seemed resigned to hearing from hi
"Well, we arrested Ricky, but he didn't stay long."

"Figures. What about exhuming Vickie Vichy?"

"I'm working on it. I'll let you know."

"Thanks."

He returned to the lunch. They talked through the
cocktail hour, and it was getting late when they left the
lunch, Sly, Spencer and David driving across the cause-
way together, all three fairly quiet.

"Did your cousin finish paying that money back?" Sly
asked Spencer suddenly from the back seat.

Startled, Spencer met his eyes in the rearview mirror.
"He, uh—"

"Did he or didn't he?" Sly asked impatiently.

"Yes. How did you know?"

"What did he know?" David demanded.

"Oh, Jared just took out a little unauthorized loan,"
she said lightly. "I guess he thought I didn't know about
it. I thought it was something he and Spencer should set-
tle themselves."

"And it *is* settled!" Spencer said firmly. She spun
around, frowning. "Sly, you don't intend to fire him, do
you?"

"I would have if he hadn't confessed to you. Despite
her mother and his father and the whole damned bloody
family!"

"But—"

Sly shrugged. "But he confessed. And I let everyone
make one mistake. It's been my way my whole life. One
mistake, and a chance to fix it."

"It's fixed," Spencer said uncomfortably, meeting
David's eyes in the mirror. They were cobalt, narrowed.
Furious.

And that damned pulse was ticking away in his throat
again.

They took Sly home first. Then David took her home,
walking into her house in ominous silence.

Then he exploded. "Spencer, goddamn it, how many
times do I have to tell you! I cannot win this thing with

you constantly playing against me. Why the hell di‹
you tell me about Jared?''

''There was nothing to tell,'' she said, moving into
kitchen.

''Then there was Willie!'' he snapped.

''Willie?''

''Yeah—like you just happened to be in the gr›
yard! You were fooling around with a snitch who c‹
have gotten you into real trouble, who almost did get
killed. And you didn't come clean—''

''You didn't ask about Willie!''

''I damned well *did* ask about the source of your
formation!'' he told her.

Then he went still suddenly.

''What?'' she murmured.

''I want to know what Jared was up to,'' he said fla›

''He borrowed money.''

''A lot of it?''

''Yes.''

''Without asking?''

''But he put it back. David, you can't believe ›
Jared killed Danny! They were friends, too. Rela›
Jared's kids called him Uncle Danny!''

''Some men, Spencer, would kill their own mother›

''Not Jared,'' she insisted.

''When did he borrow this money?''

''About eight months ago.''

David exhaled slowly, shaking his head. ''Then...'›

''Then what?''

''Then you're *probably* right. Whatever is going ›
must have started before David was killed. I'm going ›
to the office. Good night.''

Spencer watched him start up the stairs. What ›
wanted to go through the files, too? she thought. She

ost shouted the words at him. But she didn't. Instead
he bit her lip and went to make herself a cup of tea. Fi-
ally she gave up and went to bed.

Thursday morning Cecily came by. She breezed into
pencer's office with a huge smile.

"Don't forget, my father-in-law is having a barbecue
morrow night."

"Right," Spencer said, staring at her.

"What's wrong?" Cecily asked defensively. The her
ice fell to a hush. "If you're mad at me over the money
ared borrowed—"

"I'm not mad at you over the money, Cecily. I'm fu-
ous because you had no right to step into my life the
ay you did and give David hints about—about a con-
tion you think I might be in!"

"I didn't give him a hint," Cecily said, pouting. "I
id it straight out, plain and simple!"

"Cecily..."

"Spencer, I was right, wasn't I? Trust me, I can tell
ings like that. I've been there!"

"Cecily, what would make you tell David?" Spencer
manded.

"I..." Cecily sighed and plopped down into a chair.
thought that if you were either fighting with David or
oling around with him more, you wouldn't be so prone
notice what was going on with the accounts."

"Cecily!"

"Oh, Spencer, it was stupid. But we were all in a panic,
red, Jon, me... Don't you understand, Spencer? Jared
our cousin, not *Sly's* blood relation."

Spencer sighed deeply. "All right, Cecily."

"You won't hurt Jon's feelings and skip tomorrow, will
u? It's right after work."

"I'll be there."

"Thanks, Spencer. And . . . thanks for being so under
standing about everything. He's not always perfect, bu
Jared isn't bad."

"It's over, Cecily."

Cecily stood, started toward the door, then paused
"Well?" she said.

"Well, what?"

"Was I right?"

"Go away, Cecily."

Audrey stepped in. "Excuse me, Spencer. Sandy is o
line three."

"Thanks."

Cecily waved. "I know I'm right," she said, grinning
and disappeared.

Spencer worked late that night, trying to catch up c
some research. She had managed to forget her own li
for a while until she looked up to find David in h
doorway, staring at her.

"Don't you think you ought to quit working so har
Give the baby a rest, for God's sake."

She felt her cheeks redden. "Would you please spea
a little more softly?"

He lifted his hands. "Why? There's not a soul left
the office."

"Oh!" She glanced at her watch. It was almost eig
o'clock.

"You really should feed that child, you know."

She had to smile. "Does that mean you're starving?

"Sure as hell does."

"The Taurus? It's close, great seafood, and it's quick

He nodded. Spencer set her work aside and stood, then
grabbed her purse and found her keys so she could lock
the offices. "Sly didn't say good-night."

'Yes he did. Your nose was too deep in a book."

They left in his car and drove straight to the restaurant.

It had been a long day. Too damned long, what with
the bedlam Spencer Huntington and Delgado were creating. If he had just been left alone to take care of things in
the first place...

The phone rang. He picked up the receiver; the voice
on the other end was already speaking.

'There's going to be a barbecue tomorrow night at Jon
Monteith's house. I'll be there. Make sure you are, too.
And whatever you come up with, make sure it's not too
messy, for Christ's sake. There are going to be little kids
there. Make it look like an accident. You can do that."

'I'm getting sick and tired—"

He broke off at the strangely evil sound of husky
laughter. "Do it. Because if you go down, you'll go down
too!"

The line went dead.

New Rosh

...in pocket. Spencer ... her work clothes and slipped ...
... had put a coat around her. Keys so she could lock...
...he car keys. Silly, didn't they good-night.

Yes, it did. Your mom was too clever a cook
..., and Joe ... and drove straight to the restau-

20

...hand her. I don't care how long, what with
...cream, cheese, Italian ices and Danish to
...

"They make the best fish oreganato in the wo
here," Spencer murmured, looking over her menu.
smiled at the waitress waiting by her side. "I'll have w
wine and the snapper oreganato."

"*I'll* have white wine and the snapper oreganat
David interceded. "*She'll* have a coffee—no, coffee
caffeine, right? She'll have a ginger ale and the fish."

"David—" Spencer began.

"Don't drink, Spencer." He hesitated. "Please."

"I forgot, all right?"

He eased back in his chair, watching her. "Shoul
you have gone to a doctor by now?"

She smiled ruefully, leaning forward slightly. "Da
I spent lots of time with doctors. Danny and I were
a couple of babes in the woods, in a way. We were so s
that something was wrong. I'm not trying to be ne
tive, or pretend that I'm not pregnant, but I don't w
to get excited or plan for...for a child until I'm
tain."

"But you took the test."

"I know. But they usually tell women not to test
early. Most miscarriages occur almost immediate
which is one of the reasons women are supposedly j
late sometimes. It's important to see a doctor early,
not this early."

He was quiet, watching her. "So, in other words, you
y get excited—eventually."

"Of course."

"Even if it's my child, not Danny's?"

Spencer hesitated, then spoke evenly and softly. "I
uld love to have had a child with Danny. He was a
nderful man, and there should have been something
of him in this world."

His fingers curled over hers. "Spencer, there will al-
ys be something left of Danny in this world as long as
re in it. We'll never forget him, any of us who knew
1. And we'll never forget his dreams."

She nodded, pulling her hand away as the waitress
ught their drinks.

The woman winked at Spencer. "You know, I can slip
a wine, honey."

Spencer laughed, shaking her head. "No, it's all right.
anks."

"Let's go to the salad bar," David said. "Vegetables
good for both of you."

"What are you, the Galloping Gourmet or the stork?"
ncer demanded.

"A little bit of both."

Somehow they managed not to talk about either
nny, the case or their own curiously twisting relation-
p. David talked about his sister. Spencer described her
ns for the old house on the golf course.

When they got to her house, David told Spencer good-
ht and walked to the family room.

She hesitated, watching him. The room was dark; his
iouette was just caught by the pool lights. His shoul-
s looked so broad, his hair very dark, his stance very
ight.

She was making a mistake, she told herself.... Ah, the mistake had already been made.

She walked up behind him.

He knew she was there. "What is it, Spencer?"

"I don't want to sleep alone," she said softly.

He turned to her. She couldn't quite see his feature the shadows of the room. "Spencer, you don't s alone," he said softly. "Danny is still in that bed you."

"There is another room. With a real bed," she s When he was silent, she exploded. "Damn it, David, not going to beg you! I'll be there. You can do what want!"

She turned and left, hurrying up the still-darke stairs to the second floor. She bypassed her room headed for the guest room at the rear of the house, k ing off her shoes as she walked to the bed, shedding clothing. She showered, dried, slipped beneath the she

Waited . . .

He didn't come.

She felt like an idiot. But a tired idiot. Eventually dozed.

She was asleep. Well, he was a fool. He'd figured out a long time ago.

He hesitated, then walked into the room anyway. In shadows, he could see her clothing strewn across floor.

He shed his jacket and shirt, letting them fall on to her things. He took off his shoes and let them clunk the floor. She didn't move. He lost his trousers briefs, and sat on the edge of the bed, shedding his so

Damn it. She was still sleeping like a little princess.

hat thought gave him pause. He smiled slightly,
ed beneath the sheets, leaned over and kissed her.

was hardly a sweet, fairy-tale kiss, but it did the
. He tasted her lips, coerced them open. Plundered
sweetness of her mouth with his tongue. She mur-
ed deep in her throat, her hands moving to his
lders.

e was still groggy, but awakening quickly. He used
weight of his body to part her thighs and hiked him-
just slightly above her. It was a tantalizing position.
was hard already, his sex just brushing the portal of
. Her flesh was hot and silky, her thighs hugging his.
er eyes opened fully. "David?"

Who else would I be? Or do I feel like a damned
t?"

e arched against him, angered by his mockery. But
t his hand gently against her cheek and spoke softly.
encer, you invited me here. I just want to make
ned sure you don't start crying on me later."

e hesitated, staring at him. Then she promised, "I
't start crying."

e kissed her lips again as his arms went around her,
sing her against him. He lifted her buttocks while he
deeply into her, and she locked her legs around his
, her body arched to meet his.

was the best damned sex....

e brought them both to a writhing precipice, then
ed them satisfaction as he withdrew from her tight
. He found her breasts with his palms, his fingers, his
ue, his teeth.

er lips slid along his naked flesh. Bathed his shoul-
, ran down his spine. Teased over his belly. Her
th enveloped him. His fingers dug into her hair, a cry
ght explosively in his throat.

Then he was inside her again. Frantic, fevered. Mee ing the sky blue of her eyes. Touching the slick beauty her secret flesh, her breasts...

Capturing her lips again. Playing with her tongu Feeling the shudders that swept her.

Exploding in climax, his body expelling his seed, st feeling the warmth and vibrance of her as he came insi her, pulse after pulse....

Minutes ticked by. He was afraid he was hurting he He rolled from her, withdrawing his spent sex, and la his head on the pillow by hers.

Her eyes were open, and he touched her cheeks.

"I'm not crying."

He smiled slowly. "It's a start."

She smiled back and curled against him.

Spencer was amazed to realize first how late she slept, and then that David was gone.

She was even more surprised to discover that he h not only left the bed, he had left the house.

She was glad she had showered and dressed befe ambling downstairs. Not that Jimmy was in her hou but he was right out on the porch, reading a detect novel. When she found him, Spencer stared at the t with amusement. *"Inspector Tyre and the Murder in Attic?"* she asked.

He shrugged. "It's not half-bad."

She smiled. "It's just that in your line of work... Ne mind. Where's David?"

"He said he had to go into the office for a while. I don't worry. Juan and I are both here. See—he's out the car. Someone would have to be really good to get both at once," he assured her.

'I'll bet. Well, come in if you want. I'll have coffee
ly in a few minutes.''

Ie refused. He was being more than usually careful.
he day seemed to pass very quickly. David called at
n to tell her that he had found something curious in
ny's files. "And guess what?"

'What?"

'Oppenheim has arranged the exhumation order on
kie Vichy.''

'Oh?''

'I may be called in to the lab later today.''

'Don't forget, I've got a family thing tonight.''

'I won't. I'll try to be there. Jimmy and Juan will keep
ch outside. And Oppenheim is trying to keep the po-
close by, too. He's already apologized for having to
Harris in the other night.''

'Well, you know where I'll be.''

'Still not crying?'' he asked softly.

he hesitated. "Still not crying.''

'I'll see you later. I promise I'll show up before it gets
late.'' He hung up, then looked down at his files. He
ked up the phone again. "Reva, I need some records.
ything and everything you can get. If you get me a
h date and a place, I can call in a few favors.''

'On who?''

houghtfully, David gave her the name.

'And cross-check all this with Gene Vichy,'' he said.

on was glad to see Spencer, and he pulled her aside
nediately. "Spencer,'' he whispered. "Honey, we're
t so grateful to you....''

'Uncle Jon, I've asked Jared to forget it, and I want
t to do the same.''

'But if Sly knew—''

"Sly does know."

"Dear God."

"Uncle Jon, people make mistakes. Sly knows tha

Jon exhaled, then smiled. "Spencer, even when
were little, all the kids used to say that you were real cl
They were right, honey."

"Uncle Jon, please..."

"Right. Want to help me with the burgers? You can
me how things are going. We were all horrified to h
about the accident in Rhode Island. What have
found out? Have the police done much yet? How ab
David?"

Spencer stood beside her uncle at the barbecue, try
to bring him up to date. Then the kids arrived, and A
ley seemed almost shy, hugging her, smiling, hugging
again. She didn't leave Spencer's side until Cecily t
the children into the house to change into their sw
suits.

Sly, Jared and Jimmy were in the living room, wat
ing sports on television. Jimmy and Juan had dra
straws, and Juan had gotten stuck with the first sh
watching the front of the house for uninvited guests.

The doorbell rang. "I'd better get that. Excuse m
Jon said. Through the open back doors, Spencer co
see him answering the door. She was expecting Da
and she was surprised to see Audrey, instead.

She started into the house, but Audrey was alre
hurrying toward her. On her way, she paused, scoop
Ashley up when the little girl rushed over to say hello.
set Ashley down by the pool and kept walking tow
Spencer, who was alone in the yard, waiting for her.

Audrey was smiling, a sheaf of papers in her ha
"I'm sorry to interrupt, Spencer, but I know how m

house you're buying means to you. And Sandy
ed, and—"

he broke off, lifting the papers slightly. Spencer stared
er, astounded.

lidden underneath the papers, Audrey was carrying
in. A gun leveled straight at Spencer.

.udrey's tone of voice didn't even change as she kept
ing. "We have to talk. Not here. Follow the path
in to the dock. Now."

Audrey, I will not—"

Spencer, I can blow you away right here. But I'd kill
kid first. You know I don't bluff, Spencer. Let's go."

You won't shoot me—"

Sweetie, I didn't have the slightest problem in the
ld shooting Danny. I won't bat an eye if I have to
ot you, too. Now move. Unless you want Ashley to
as well. And I'll do it, Spencer. Don't even question
Vhat do I have to lose? They can only electrocute you
e, no matter how many people you kill. What I don't
e is time. Move!"

Why?" Spencer demanded.

Start walking and I'll tell you."

Audrey, if I'm found shot to death—"

Oh, you won't be." Her eyes glittered, and her mouth
ied up in a small smile. "You're going to drown. Ac-
ints will happen...."

Right after five, Oppenheim called David and sug-
ted he come down to the coroner's office.

David did, watching with Oppenheim as the Dade
unty coroner cut into the body of a young man who'd
n found in a river. He turned away, waiting for Cyril
gess, the coroner on the Vichy case, to finish up so he
ld talk with them about Vickie.

A little while later, Burgess, portly and balding with incredibly shiny head, came toward them grimly. shook hands with both of them. "Seems you gentlen were right. She *was* being poisoned. A little one day little the next. Nothing that would show up in a sim blood or urine test. But nothing accidental, either. It I to have been done by someone close to her. Proba someone who lived with her."

"Her husband?" Oppenheim said.

"Good guess," Burgess responded.

"Put out an all-points bulletin for Gene Vichy," (penheim told the uniformed officer who had accomp nied them. The man quickly left to do as he'd be bidden.

"You were right," Oppenheim told David ruefu "But what I still don't get is why he killed Danny."

"Danny knew."

"But he didn't tell any of us. And he didn't ident Vichy when he was dying."

"No, he just kept saying Spencer's name." Da paused, realization flooding his mind. "As if he w warning her..."

A clerk with big horn-rim glasses came up to the "One of you Mr. Delgado?"

"Me," David said.

"Your secretary is on the phone, sir. This way, pleas David answered the phone. "Reva?"

"David, you're not going to believe this. You w right! Audrey is not what she appears to be. Audr Betancourt was last known as Audrey Highland. Befc that, she was Audrey Grant. She went to school as A drey Ennis, which was a name she adopted from her fc ter family when she was taken away from her father. S

born as Audrey *Vichy*. I still don't believe this. She's
e Vichy's *daughter!*"

Reva, you're a gem. I'm going straight to Jon Mon-
1's house to find Spencer. I'll keep you posted."

Ie said a hurried goodbye to Oppenheim and went out
is car. Rush hour. The expressways were going to be

.

inally David broke free of the last of the heavy traf-
Just as he did, his car phone started to ring.

"Yeah?"

"David, it's Reva."

"Yeah?"

"I called over to Jon Monteith's to ask Jimmy if ev-
thing was all right. He said it was, but then the line
it dead. David I think something's wrong."

"Shit."

"I'm trying hard to get this," Spencer said, striding
wn the slope of her uncle's lawn, her heart sinking as
: realized she would soon be out of view of the house.
/hy would you kill Danny? What did he ever do to
1?"

"What did he do? He wanted to send me to the elec-
: chair!" Audrey exclaimed.

"For what?" Spencer spun around. "Faulty memos?"

"Keep walking, Spencer."

She had come to the dock. It was surrounded by heavy
iage, and mangroves grew into the brackish water,
idowing everything.

"Audrey, this is insane."

"Well, they say I'm not quite normal."

Spencer was halfway along the dock when she tur[n]
"Audrey, I'm a good swimmer. Everyone knows th[at]
wouldn't go for a walk with you and just drown."

"I'll be half-dead myself, hysterical. Ready to weep[
the rest of my life over how you tried to save me be[fore]
you died."

"Audrey, shoot me. I won't drown for you."

"Yes, you will."

"Audrey, why? *Why* did you kill Danny?"

"I had to kill Danny because I love my father, Sp[en]
cer. I loved him when I was little, but they took me aw[ay]
I found him again as soon as I grew up. But neither o[f]
had anything—I was a secretary. Then Dad met Vic[kie.]
The old crone, the bat." Audrey shuddered. "She [was]
hideous. I cringed every time I knew he was going to[
with her."

"Your dad met Vickie? Vickie Vichy?" Spencer sa[id]
suddenly feeling weak.

"She wasn't Vichy then. He had to marry her. For [the]
money. Then she died. I did that, too. Dad tried to p[oi]
son her, but she wouldn't die. And he was worried. Ev[ery]
time Danny talked to him, he knew Danny was gett[ing]
close to the truth and that Danny would find a way [to]
make them exhume the old bitch. Danny came to see [me]
one day, talking about how people could be poison[ed]
slowly, with such small amounts that they might not [be]
detected. He talked about all the murders through[out]
history that had been committed that way. He *had* to [die.]
He knew too much. I'd managed to get the job with y[ou]
by then, and that helped. I knew Danny's habits. and [an]
awful lot about you. I made most of your appoi[nt]
ments. It wasn't hard to get to either one of you whe[n I]
needed to. Once Danny was dead, I thought that was [it.]
Dad and I would be okay. But then, when you came ba[ck]

own and started getting so nosy, we were in trouble
in. I needed to get into your house, because we were
ain Danny must have left some papers behind, some
e to what he'd suspected. Then all of a sudden David
gado got involved . . . plus I had to sneak around that
id thug Ricky Garcia hired." She started to laugh.
u thought it was Jared! What a laugh! I can't tell you
I enjoyed watching you become more and more
icious of him!"

pencer wondered if help might eventually come if she
ld just keep Audrey talking. She had to try.

t might mean her life.

That beam that fell and made Sly think someone was
ng to kill me, was that you?"

"A fine piece of work. Except you didn't die."

"The car accident in Rhode Island?"

"Assassins work for pay."

"But he had worked for Ricky Garcia."

"A job's a job. Money is what matters. Dad has lots
t now."

"No wonder Ricky Garcia was in such a state."

"He's scum. I'm a class act, Spencer. Just like you. Let
see, what else? I did try to break into your house, but
t bumbling detective stopped me. Really, though, ev-
thing was easy once Dad got his hands on Icky Vick-
money."

'Great father. He let his little girl do all the killing for
1."

Audrey quit smiling. The look she gave Spencer was
rely vicious. "You wouldn't understand. We have a
ationship, my father and I. You just don't know, you
n't see how close we are to one another. He loves me.
has always loved me."

Audrey had changed, subtly. As if she was trying
convince Spencer—and herself—of her words. "Don
you dare talk about my father! You just don't unde
stand a man like him, you don't understand—us!"

"Oh, my God!" Spencer breathed, realizing as s
looked at Audrey, as she listened to her, that she was d
scribing much more than a customary father-daught
relationship. She thought about Vichy, the suave, arr
gant man she had met at the club. A man who seemed
think anything he did for his own gratification and m
terial reward was all right.

"Spencer, don't give me that look!" Audrey co
manded. "You don't understand—"

"I suppose not," Spencer said, "but I think I'm b
ginning to. I'm imagining how it all began. He abus
you, probably from the time you were very young."

"He never abused me—"

"Rape is abuse, Audrey."

Bingo. Oh, God, that was it! He'd raped her, h
turned her into his little puppet. His own daughter.

"Bitch. I didn't actually want to kill you, Spencer
thought I liked you. But I was wrong. You think y
know everything. You're just like the others. Judgme
tal. Well, you're all wrong. I love my father, and my
ther loves me. You deserve to die."

Spencer saw movement over Audrey's should
Someone was coming through the bushes.

"Audrey," she said, hoping to keep the other wom
from hearing help approach.

But her ploy didn't work.

Audrey swung around. Still Spencer felt hope rising
her heart. Jerry Fried was there. Danny's old partner.

"Jerry!" Spencer said, hope and relief evident in I
voice.

ut Audrey started to laugh, watching her. "Oh,
icer, for such a smart little cookie you can be so
ined dumb! Why do you think Danny never trusted
d? Danny was no idiot. His partner was on the take.
I now poor Jerry just has to keep on taking and tak-
He's really not happy about it, Spencer, but guess
t? He's the one who actually gets to drown you."

ooking at Jerry as he walked down the dock, Spen-
realized that Audrey was telling the truth. Jerry Fried
n't happy about it, but he was coming to kill her.

he spun around and starting running toward the end
he dock.

'Son of a bitch!'' Audrey cried.

he fired her gun. The shot whizzed past Spencer's
d. Spencer didn't know how deep the water was here,
she had to chance a dive. She plunged into the ocean,
nming hard, down, down....

hand snagged her foot and she was twisted around.
beneath the depths, she saw Jerry Fried's face. She
d to shoot upward, but she was dragged ever down-
d....

)avid burst into the house. "Where's Spencer?" he
ianded.

veryone was watching the game, but when they heard
fear in David's voice, Sly leaped up and Jimmy spun
und. Jon Monteith was calm at first. "She's just out-
, turning the burgers, chatting with Audrey."

\udrey... David's blood ran cold.

hen Ashley ran in screaming.

pencer twisted, pulled and writhed for all she was
rth. She broke the surface and gasped in a breath just
^ried's hand found her again. This time he grabbed the

top of her head to push her under. He was being carefu
He didn't want any bruises to show.

Audrey was in the water, too, yelling at Fried. "G
damn it, kill her! Get it over with!" Audrey rage
"Someone will be here any second!"

Spencer broke free again and surfaced, breathir
deeply. She started to stroke away.

Once again a hand found her, this time clutching h
shoulder. She went down. Fought her way up.

She gasped for air. Gulped water. Oh, God, she w
losing strength....

He couldn't see them at first. Then something in t
water caught his attention. A head bobbing up.

Spencer's head.

He ran.

Suddenly she was free. Free because Jerry Fried h
been dragged away from her to battle fiercely wi
someone else.

David.

David had Fried's head beneath the surface. He mea
business.

Audrey suddenly leaped atop David with a wild cry.
went under, and Fried came up.

Fried caught hold of Spencer again and again. S
gasped for a deep breath just before he dragged her
neath the surface. Deep in the water, she struggled fu
ously against him. Pelting her fists against Fried ea
time she could, she banged against something hard.
was his gun, encompassed by a shoulder holster. S
caught hold of the weapon and pulled it from the h
ster, but she couldn't shake Fried's grip to manage a
kind of aim. She could no longer bear it, she was go

p for desperately needed air; water would fill her
 The world was beginning to spin. She vaguely
a thud. She was only dimly aware that Audrey went
g by her. She was going to drown.

she didn't drown. She saw a pair of hands set down
ed's shoulders, ripping the man away from her. She
 to the surface and gasped in lungfuls of air. Au-
loated at a distance from her. She realized that Da-
d freed himself from Audrey to wrench Fried away
her. The men were engaged in fierce battle. Fried
g, but David was stronger. It didn't matter. Spen-
dn't want to take any chances. She treaded water
sly, pointing the gun at Fried's head.

t him go! Let him go! I'll shoot, you bastard. You
 Danny as much as she did, and *I* won't hesitate to
u!"

ed looked like a mad man. He turned to David,
g from the water with his weight. Both men went

ncer swam to them in the murky depths and found
 far beneath the surface, locked together.

vid motioned her to go up. Fried turned, ready to
 out and grab her again.

the depths of the water, the shot was not very loud

21

"You didn't have to shoot me," David complain

"I *didn't* shoot you. I shot *him*. The bastard isn't
dead. You were just grazed."

"Yeah? Well, my calf is bleeding like a mother."

"You're acting like a two-year-old."

They were seated together out back, still at Jon's
towels wrapped around then, mugs of hot coffee in
hands. The sirens had ceased shrilling; Jerry Fried
Audrey Vichy, alias Betancourt, had been taken aw

Audrey had been half-drowned, just as she predi

Spencer had shot Jerry through the shoulder
would live, as well.

Cecily had been at the dock when Spencer had cra
out of the water, tears streaming down her cheeks. J
had been there, too, and Uncle Jon and Sly—who
ried Spencer more than anyone, because she was so a
he was about to have a heart attack. But Sly was bui
stern stuff; he quickly regrouped his forces and hu
her, as did the rest of the family.

Her family. The kids, Cecily, Jared, Jon. They
sinners, all of them, one way or another. But they
love her. And it was so incredibly good to know it.

"I'll never quite understand it," Spencer murmu

'It was incredibly simple. Danny suspected Vichy. But couldn't prove he was a murderer, because Vichy n't do the killing himself. Audrey did. And she was s, Spencer. I'm sure the psychologists will have to :k it all out, but apparently he abused her as a child. : couldn't allow herself to hate her own father, so she in love with him instead. And she was willing to do t about anything for him.''

'But Jerry...''

'Jerry took money from Vichy for information on nny. And then he wound up in deeper shit than he ited. Once he was on the take, he had to keep on it or go down big-time himself. I almost feel sorry for him. .n't begin to tell you what cops feel for one of their n who helps kill an officer like Danny.''

'I was shaking when I shot him.''

'You didn't have to do that,'' David said a little in-nantly. "I would have won the fight.''

'I'd already lost Danny. I wasn't taking any more inces. One husband is enough to lose to a bastard like t.''

)avid looked meaningfully at her. "I'm not your hus-id.''

'Not yet.''

'Oh?''

'Well, you *are* going to marry me, right?''

-Ie hesitated. Then he smiled. "Hell, yes! A wife who :sn't even cry after sex anymore. How in God's name .ld I turn down an offer like that?''

'David...'' Spencer warned.

3ut he leaned over and kissed her. "I love you, Spen- . I always have. I always will.''

She leaned against his shoulder. "We've set Danny
rest at last, haven't we?"

He nodded, his chin against the drying softness of I
hair. "He whispered your name when he was dyir
Spencer, because he was so afraid for you. And
wanted me to help you. I'm sorry it took so damr
long."

"But it's over."

"Yes, it's over." He stroked her hair gently. "We
ally should get married pretty soon. Let your mother
over the shock before the baby is born."

Spencer smiled. "Just think. Mrs. D.A.R. is going
have a half-Cuban grandchild." She giggled.

"Don't you be cruel to my mother-in-law."

She started to laugh again. And it felt good. So goc
She set down her coffee, stole his, wrapped her tov
around them both and sat on his lap.

"David, I love you. I was so horrible to you becaus
was afraid I'd still loved you when I was married
Danny. But now I know that I loved you both. Ane
learned tonight that I want to live, and that living mea
loving and everything else that's a part of that. You'
been right all along. Danny would understand th
Danny would *want* that."

His eyes sparkled. Deep. Cobalt blue. When he spol
his voice was husky, deep, rich. "Say that again."

"All of it?"

"Just that you love me."

She smiled. "I love you. Oh, God, David, I love yc
For all of my life."

And she started to kiss him.

She was his, David thought, holding her. And this v
the best damned kiss ever....

* * *

The kiss was still going on when Sly saw them on his
~y outside. He veered quickly, still watching them.
Hot damn, he was good! Old, but good.

He chuckled and walked away quietly, leaving them to
~ir kiss.

New York Times **Bestselling Author**

ELIZABETH LOWELL

Brings you another sweeping saga this January with

GRANITE MAN

He had determination of steel and a heart of stone....

Cash McQueen lived for the land and trusted no one. So when Mariah MacKenzie blew into town asking too many questions and digging around his property, he knew there'd be trouble—for both of them. But Mari was a temptation too powerful to resist, and if she wasn't careful, she just might uncover something too hot for either of them to handle....

"Nobody does romance like Elizabeth Lowell."
—Jayne Ann Krentz

MIRA The brightest star in women's fiction

Award-winning author

BARBARA BRETTON

...res you to take a trip through time this November
...th

Tomorrow & Always

...w fast can an eighteenth-century man torn with duty and
...rtache run? Will he find the freedom and passion he craves in
...ther century? Do the arms of a woman from another time hold
...secret to happiness? And can the power of their love defeat
...mysterious forces that threaten to tear them apart?

...tay tuned.

...l you thought loving a man from the twentieth century
...s tough.

...ach for the brightest star in women's fiction with

MIRA™

MBBTA

Do you adore the romantic style of

HEATHER GRAHAM POZZESSERE

Then order these charming stories by one of
MIRA's most successful authors: